The Heart of a Stranger

The Heart of a Stranger

Kathy Hawkins

Grand Rapids, MI 49501

The Heart of a Stranger

Published in 1996 by Kregel Publications, a division of Kregel, Inc., P. O. Box 2607, Grand Rapids, MI 49501. Kregel Publications provides trusted, biblical publications for Christian growth and service. Your comments and suggestions are valued.

Cover Illustration: Ron Mazellan
Cover Design: Alan G. Hartman
Book Design: Nicholas G. Richardson

Library of Congress Cataloging-in-Publication Data
Hawkins, Kathy.
The heart of a stranger / by Kathy Hawkins.
p. cm.
1. David, King of Israel—Fiction. 2. Bible. O.T.—History of Biblical events—Fiction. 3. Israel—Kings and rulers—Fiction. I. Title.
PS3558.A823165H43 1995 813'.54—dc20 95-52676
CIP

ISBN 0-8254-2867-x (paperback)

1 2 3 4 5 Printing / Year 00 99 98 97 96

Printed in the United States of America

To my mother,
Edith Brent Robbins,
who instilled in me a love
of books in general
and the Book in particular.

My thanks to Sandy Schindler, Ruth Franks, and Brent Hawkins for their help, and especially to Ann Severance and Dennis Hillman for all their patient editorial work. A special "thank you" to Murray Severance for permission to use the pronunciation guides in the list of characters which are found in his book *Pronouncing Bible Names,* published by Holman Bible Publishers. Scripture quotations are from the New King James Version, © 1985 by Thomas Nelson, Inc.

Historical Notes

The Arameans occupied the region from northern and northeastern Palestine to the Euphrates from 1600 to 1200 B.C. English versions have translated the Hebrew *Aram* as "Syria." However, the term "Syria" was not in use until near the end of the Old Testament period, so I have chosen to refer to these peoples as Arameans.

God revealed Himself to the Patriarchs using the personal name represented by the four Hebrew letters YHWH. This personal name was latter considered too holy to pronounce, and when readers came to the word in Scriptures, they substituted the word *Adonai*. The Hebrew word *Adonai* was frequently used by the Israelites as a divine title indicating God's transcendence and power and is commonly translated as "Lord." The Hebrew vowel markings from *Adonai* were placed by later scribes with the tetragrammaton YHWH. Early English translators mistakenly rendered this combination as "Jehovah."

The word *Rab* is a Hebrew word meaning great man, or leader.

Gibborim is a plural Hebrew word meaning "mighty ones," a designation for David's thirty chief warriors (the singular form of the word is *gibbor*). Since the Bible lists more than thirty names, it is assumed that when one warrior died in battle or retired, he was replaced to keep the number at thirty.

I have taken the account of David's reign found in 2 Samuel and 1 Chronicles as chronological. Although there are some problems with this view, particularly regarding the building of David's palace, other explanations raise even more questions.

Josephus (*Antiquities* 7:7) says that Uriah the Hittite was one of Joab's armor-bearers. Scripture is silent on the matter, but if it is true, Uriah was one of Joab's closest companions and his right-hand man in many battles. This relationship makes Joab's subsequent participation in Uriah's death even more reprehensible. A close study of Joab shows him to be one of the most malignant personalities in all of the Bible.

Characters

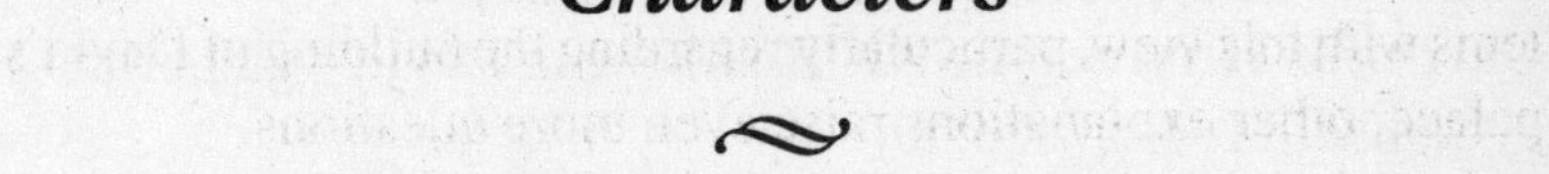

Scripture references mark out historical persons from the Bible. All other characters are fictional.

Ailea (eye LEE uh) young Aramean woman
Nariah (NAHR ih uh) Ailea's mother
Eliada (ih LIGH uh duh) Ailea's father; one of Hadadezer's officers (1 Kings 11:23)
Rezon (REE zahn) Ailea's brother, deserter from Hadadezer's army, leader of a band of desert raiders (1 Kings 11:23–25)
Jonathan, son of Shageh, one of David's gibborim (2 Samuel 23:32–33; 1 Chronicles 11:34)
Shageh (SHAY geh) Jonathan's father, an elder in the village of Ziph located in the hill country of Judah (1 Chronicles 11:34)
Ruth, Jonathan's sister
Ahiam (uh HIGH am) son of Sharar, from the hill country; Jonathan's friend and another one of David's mighty men of valor (2 Samuel 23: 33; 1 Chronicles 11:35)
Judith, wife of Ahiam
Isaac, son of Ahiam and Judith
David, king of Israel (1 Samuel 16–1 Kings 1)

Joab, David's nephew and second-in-command; general over the army (2 Samuel; 1 Kings 1–2; 2 Chronicles 21)

Abishai (uh BISH ay eye) Joab's brother; one of David's generals (2 Samuel 23:18; 1 Chronicles 11:20)

Uriah the Hittite (yoo RIGH uh) one of David's gibborim (2 Samuel 11: 1–27; 23:39)

Hadadezer (had ad EE zur) King of Zobah, one of the Aramean city states (2 Samuel 10:16–19; 1 Chronicles 19:16, 18)

Shobach (SHOH bak) Hadadezer's general (2 Samuel 10:16–18; 1 Chronicles 19:16, 18)

Toi (TOH eye) king of Hamath (an Aramean city state) who became David's vassal (2 Samuel 3:3)

Joram (JOH ruhm) Toi's son who served as an ambassador to Israel (2 Samuel 8:10)

Maacah (MAY uh kuh) daughter of the king of Geshur; one of David's wives; mother of Absalom (2 Samuel 3:3)

Akim (AY kim) servant of Rezon

Haruz (HAY ruhz) young armor-bearer

Habaz (HAY bazh) chief shepherd of Ziph

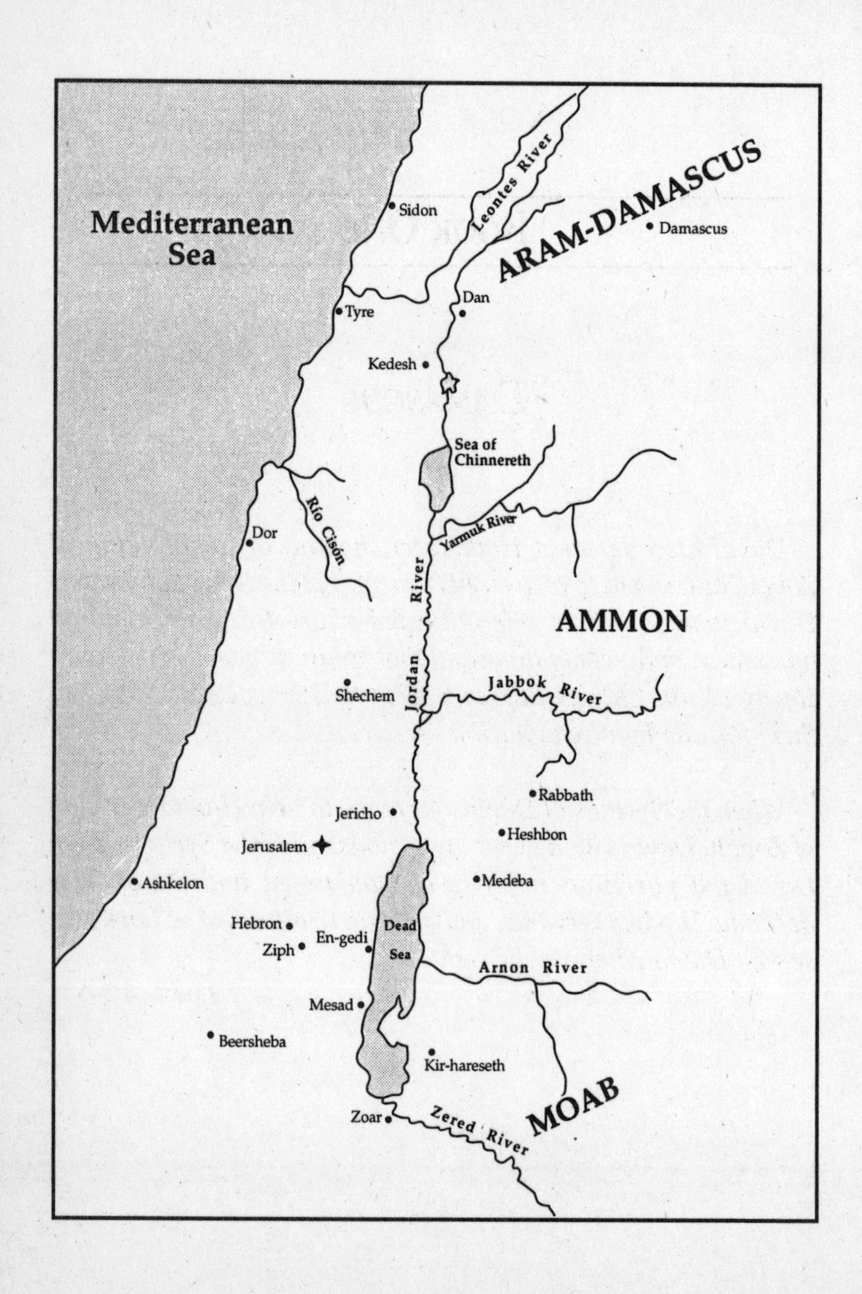

Mediterranean Sea
Leontes River
ARAM-DAMASCUS
Sidon
Damascus
Tyre
Dan
Kedesh
Sea of Chinnereth
Río Cisón
Dor
Yarmuk River
Jordan River
AMMON
Shechem
Jabbok River
Rabbath
Jericho
Heshbon
Jerusalem
Ashkelon
Medeba
Hebron
Ziph
En-gedi
Dead Sea
Arnon River
Mesad
Beersheba
Kir-hareseth
MOAB
Zoar
Zered River

Book One

Damascus

David also defeated Hadadezer the son of Rehob, king of Zobah, as he went to recover his territory at the River Euphrates. David took from him one thousand chariots, seven hundred horsemen, and twenty thousand foot soldiers. Also David hamstrung all the chariot horses, except that he spared enough of them for one hundred chariots.

When the Syrians of Damascus came to help Hadadezer king of Zobah, David killed twenty-two thousand of the Syrians. Then David put garrisons in Syria of Damascus; and the Syrians beccame David's servants, and brought tribute. So the Lord preserved David wherever he went.

2 Samuel 8:3–6

Chapter One

At noontime the Damascus sun smoldered in a white-hot sky, scorching everything in its path. Not even an insect's hum disturbed the heavy stillness.

Ailea climbed up onto the rooftop and looked about cautiously. No one was in sight. Good. She could expect to be alone for at least another hour or so. At this time of day her family and the servants would be seeking whatever relief they could find around the courtyard pool.

Only when the sun sank lower in the sky would the giant cedars and date palms that encircled the spacious stone house provide enough shade to dispel the blistering heat. Then the entire household would gravitate to the roof to relax on the couches and catch any breath of breeze that might be stirring. Reclining in the cool shade of the ancient trees, they would enjoy the evening meal as the last light of evening danced on the edges of the palm fronds. But right now one of those trees would serve a more useful function.

Ailea untied her sandals and removed her outer robe. Clad only in a knee-length linen undertunic, she ran nimbly across the roof, the hot tiles burning underfoot. She shimmied up the ancient date palm that grew on the north side of the house and towered over sixty feet into the air. She hoped no one below would look up to see her doing such an unheard-of thing. For a female of any age to climb a tree was scandalous—but doubly so for one nearly nineteen years old and already a grown woman. But she and her brother, Rezon, had spent many hours as children playing in the leafy fronds of the huge tree, and now her climbing ability was being put to good use.

From her vantage point Ailea could see over the city wall to the confluence of the Abanah and Pharpar Rivers, which made this large city an oasis on the high desert plateau south of the Euphrates. With several trade routes converging on Damascus, caravans entered the main gate in a steady stream. Ailea was proud to be a citizen of this strategic city just as she was proud to be the daughter of Eliada, one of King Hadadezer's generals.

Even now the king's army was gathering out in the desert to the northeast. Her father, commander of the city's troops and mercenaries, would be in charge of thousands in this campaign designed to extend the boundaries of Aram-Zobah, an alliance of city-states that made up Hadadezer's kingdom. Damascus was a vital part of the alliance.

Rezon was accompanying her father into battle. Not quite two years her senior, Rezon had been Ailea's constant companion until three years ago when he joined his father in the military. Ailea missed her brother very much now that he was frequently away fighting. Her brother, who had taught her so many things that most girls didn't know—the game of chess, climbing trees, and the use of bow and arrow and sling—hardly had any time to spare for her anymore. His mind was always on military matters.

Rezon was furious that Hadadezer had drawn troops from Damascus, leaving the city vulnerable. Ailea had listened to the two men discussing the danger of this strategy, but unlike his son, Eliada was the consummate military man. If his superior—in this case it was Shobach, commander-in-chief of Zobah's armies—issued an order, Eliada would obey without question.

Rezon had warned his father that taking troops out of Damascus was a tactical error and made no attempt to hide his disdain for the plan or for Shobach himself. Rezon also believed that Eliada, not Shobach, should have been given the leadership of Hadadezer's army and claimed that Shobach was too arrogant by far. Ailea could barely suppress a smile at these words. In her opinion, it was her older brother who had more than his own share of arrogance.

For the moment Ailea left off her musing and turned her attention to the northeast. Scanning the horizon, she caught a glint of sunlight reflecting off something in the distance. There it was again. Could it be spears? Shields? Maybe the shiny gold helmets worn by Eliada and other officers in Hadadezer's army? She thought the troops were to have been deployed farther north—if it wasn't Zobah's army out there, then whose could it be?

The reflections were coming from the desert—nowhere near the trade routes. Perhaps Toi, the king of Hamath, a minor kingdom northwest of Damascus, had decided to challenge Hadadezer. It was no secret that the two leaders hated each other. But despite his animosity, Toi was no fool. He could not field an army even a quarter of the size of Zobah's.

Could they be troops from Israel? Surely not. King David must know that he, too, was vastly outnumbered by a superior force.

Ailea descended carefully from her vantage point in the palm tree and ran to the other corner of the rooftop where she climbed another tall date palm, but she could make out nothing to the north. In the streets below, however, she saw a number of soldiers who had been left to guard the city, and she felt a renewed sense of security. No one could take Damascus—especially not that low-born king of the Hebrews!

She climbed back down to the roof and donned her robe and sandals, wishing for the thousandth time that she had been born a male. She felt no lack of familial love, and she knew that her mother and father took pride in her beauty, hoping to marry her to a man who would add to their wealth and prestige. But other than a commodity for barter, what good was a daughter? It was Rezon who would inherit the beautiful home she loved; it was her brother who would carry the honor of the family into battle and later into the marketplace.

Men had all the power, she fumed inwardly. They could go wherever they pleased, do whatever they pleased, while women were hidden away at home to cook, bear children, and wait for the return of their men!

Ailea loved her mother dearly. Nariah was kind and beautiful, but she was weak, capable of being reduced to tears by nothing more than a stern look from her husband. And she was a lonely woman, for Eliada's responsibilities with the army kept him away from home for long periods of time.

For that reason Ailea had determined never to marry a military man. No, she would marry an older man who adored her, one whom she could wrap around her smallest finger. If the gods smiled on her, perhaps she could even cajole him into giving her more freedom than most wives even dreamed of. Or better still—and her conscience winced a little at the cold calculation of her thought—perhaps he would leave her a wealthy widow. Only such women had any power at all.

Shrugging aside her dismal mood, Ailea descended the stairs that led to the inner courtyard. Perhaps she could talk Malik into taking her out to the bazaar where she could learn for herself what was happening on the field of battle and whose troops she had sighted from the rooftop.

She found Nariah napping on one of the couches by the pool, her personal servant, Shua, on another couch nearby. Her mother often rested here in the heat of the day for the gurgling of the fountain lulled her to sleep.

Moving quietly to the opposite side of the pool, Ailea removed her sandals once again and dangled her feet in the cool water. She would have enjoyed a refreshing bath, but her splashing would be sure to awaken Nariah.

Restless, Ailea determined to go in search of Malik at once. He would grumble, no doubt. But after twenty years of service to the family, the head steward could be depended upon to do her bidding. She had only to charm him a little before he would consent to take her into the streets of Damascus—a ploy she had used on countless occasions in the past.

Malik believed her to be spoiled, she smiled to herself, but what did it matter? Or that the old servant considered her to be lacking in the feminine graces, that she should be more like her mother? Never! Ailea hoped never to be like her mother whose whole life had been lived in the shadow of her husband, who made herself ill with worry when he was away on a military mission. Ailea would rather be dead than submit herself to such a fate!

Her thoughts shifted again to the army. She could not dismiss the sense of growing uneasiness she felt whenever she thought of her father and brother. Nothing she could do would influence the outcome of this campaign, but—there! She was acting just like her mother, and she gave her head a quick, defiant toss that shook the loose wisps of hair back from her face. Just then she saw Malik enter the courtyard, and she motioned him over with a quick gesture.

"What are you scheming, Cricket?" he asked in a low tone, one brow lifted in a blend of caution and curiosity.

Ailea gave him a wounded look. "I'm not scheming anything, Malik. I merely need to buy some thread in the market, and I want you to take me."

He chuckled softly. "You don't need any thread, Cricket. You wish only to go running about, getting into mischief and asking irritating questions. I call you 'Cricket' not only because of your size, you know. You hop around just as endlessly and make just as much noise."

Ailea knew that Malik was jesting with her for the most part. The loyal retainer still had trouble accepting the fact that she was grown up, even though he knew very well that she had been responsible for the running of the household since her mother's melancholy so frequently incapacitated her. But one thing Eliada had absolutely insisted on was that Malik always accompany her to the marketplace. The last time she had ignored this rule, Eliada had found out and had confined her to her room for a week. Although usually too busy to bother disciplining her, he had a few unbreakable rules, and this was one of them. So Malik knew that Ailea was at his mercy when it came to trips outside the house, and he often used this last bit of authority to get the best of her. But she knew that down deep, Malik was devoted to her as he was to the rest of the family, so she persisted with a little pout. "Please!"

"Come now, you just want to learn news of the battle. Thread, indeed!"

"Well, yes, I just might overhear some news from a trader," she answered, looking off in no particular direction. "You know that Mother and I are worried so about Rezon and Father—just as you are, Malik, aren't you?" Tilting her head upwards and lowering her voice to a conspiratorial whisper, she took a more direct tactic. "Let's do go and talk to some of the soldiers and find out what they've heard."

Malik repressed a laugh at the predictable ploy of his little Cricket and signaled his surrender with a practiced shrug of his rather stooped shoulders. "I suppose I could take you, Cricket—but later, when the sun is not so high." He raised a hand in admonishment. "But you must let me ask the questions. And you must not ask me to take you into the more dangerous sections of the city." He eyed her with a respectful appraisal. "You don't realize the—uh—attention you draw to yourself."

"But I don't try to draw attention to myself!" she argued with a sudden flush of color in her face.

He stroked his graying beard and studied the exceptional features of his master's daughter. "I know, child. I know. But you have grown into a beautiful young woman. You must accept the restrictions that such blessings from the gods bring. Now go and get ready. I will take you in another hour. And, Cricket—don't forget to wear a veil."

Ailea rose and gave the burly servant a hug. "I won't forget, Malik. I promise."

Malik watched the mistress of the house as she left the enclosed courtyard, her hip-length ebony braid swinging behind her. She was small, almost boyish in stature but perfectly formed. And that face—especially the unusual green eyes—he would have to guard her very closely. Malik wished her father would hurry and find a suitable husband for her so that he could be free of the burden of protecting her. But that wasn't likely to happen soon although it was long past time for Ailea to be wed. Eliada had always pleaded that he was much too busy with military affairs to attend to matters of marriage, but Malik suspected that the general was more than a little reluctant to relinquish the beautiful desert flower that had bloomed in his home. With the current skirmish in the desert, he had one more excuse for postponing negotiations. The suitors would have to be patient, Malik thought. As would he.

Besides, her mother did not have the strength to insist on a marriage. If the truth be known, the woman needed to keep her daughter with her, what with Rezon and the master away most of the time. Ailea had taken over most of the responsibility for running the household some time ago, and Malik had to admit that she did it very effectively. She had no concept of her limitations as a woman, however, and Malik felt increasingly ill-suited in his role as head steward and handmaid to the young mistress. Maybe it was time to secure a female servant for Ailea.

Most of the girl's friends were wed by now, some already mothers, Malik fretted. Well, he could only do his best to keep his Cricket out of trouble. "I'm getting too old for this," he muttered to himself. "Just too old."

~ ~ ~

A light westerly breeze had begun to stir in the late afternoon as the old man and his young charge made their way through the crowded bazaar. Here the stench of overheated human bodies, goats, camels, and the aroma of various foods cooked over the braziers of street vendors assailed their nostrils. The bleating of sheep, the haggling of shopkeepers, and the rumbling of wagon wheels combined to make thinking, much less conversation, difficult.

Malik had questioned several of the king's soldiers already with little success. The soldiers guarding the city were not privy to any information about maneuvers against the Hebrews. Furthermore, they were surly, resenting the fact that they had been given the boring duty of patrolling the city instead of the excitement of battle. None of them expected the fighting to reach Damascus, and Ailea had taken this as a good sign.

When they reached the city gate, however, Malik craned his neck, narrowing his gaze to scan the crowd. With an abrupt movement he began shouldering his way through the throng, dragging Ailea by the arm behind him. He came to an abrupt halt, and Ailea stood on tiptoe to peer around his bulk.

A small caravan of three camels and two donkeys had just entered the gate, and the leader was speaking in a loud voice to the sentinels. "I tell you, they are out there! Just five or six miles to the southeast! Their rear guard gave chase to us, but we were already too near the city when they sighted us!"

"Probably a troop from Helam," the tall sentinel told the agitated man.

"No, not soldiers of Aram-Zobah but the army of Israel! I'm telling you, their whole army is out there!"

The wild look of fear in the man's eyes made Ailea pull back against Malik's firm grip. The army of Israel—could that have been the reflections she had seen off in the distance?

"If you did indeed see Hebrew soldiers, it was probably just a scouting party. Now put a bridle on your tongue before you sow panic in the city," the captain of the guard ordered. With that, the soldiers pushed the trembling man toward his camels and mounted the steps that led to the lookout atop the city wall.

Chapter Two

Jonathan, son of Shageh, stirred the dying embers of his campfire, sending sparks spiraling upward into the thick desert darkness. There was only a small sliver of moon this night, but a myriad of stars glittered brightly from horizon to horizon. The fire was for warmth as well as for light since the temperature always dropped quickly after sunset.

Jonathan knew he should be in his small tent, wrapped in his cloak, getting a few hours of sleep, but his thoughts were troubled, and he feared he would face tomorrow unrested. Somehow the thrill that had once preceded the battle no longer came. He had been with David from the early days when David was reduced to being a renegade, chased by King Saul throughout the Judean wilderness. God had chosen David to be king. All the gibborim, David's chosen warriors, believed it. And they had stuck with David through all the hardships and the fighting. Jonathan had done his part as a loyal soldier, but he had seen too much bloodshed, too much death. He would do what had to be done, but unlike others, he no longer relished it.

After this campaign Jonathan planned to spend more time at home in the village of Ziph, located in the hills of southern Judah. It was time he married, had children to pass on his name, and relieved his aging father of some of the burden of village leadership. He would still need to go to Jerusalem often to sit on the war council and train new recruits, but Israel's position would soon be secure enough to allow him to attend to other matters.

Jonathan stood and stretched. He was tall and magnificently muscled, as were most of the gibborim—the thirty mighty men who made up David's war council. These men were all proven in battle to be worthy of their command in Israel's army. Jonathan smiled to himself as he remembered the early days when David had gathered a band of four hundred or so discontented rebels in the mountain stronghold of Adullam.

From the beginning David had shown a particular fondness for Jonathan. Perhaps it was because Jonathan shared the same name as David's best friend, the son of the late King Saul. For whatever reason, David, then in his late twenties, had been kind and very patient with the fourteen-year-old recruit. That had been some fifteen years before.

In those days the men had been poorly equipped and often hungry, but they would have done anything for their leader, the "Sweet Singer of Israel." To this day Jonathan was amazed that a warrior of David's fierceness could possess the heart of a poet, the soul of a holy man. It was still true, although in recent years it seemed that David's spiritual fervor seemed to manifest a certain formality, a matter-of-factness that barely suppressed a discernible restlessness in his manner. Many of those who were closest to the king barely maintained a semblance of religious commitment at all.

Jonathan blamed much of this hardening of heart on Joab, David's nephew and second-in-command. It was Joab to whom Jonathan would report during this campaign although King David was personally leading his army as they camped this night between Hamath and Damascus, ready to bring down Hadadezer's kingdom. Still, Jonathan couldn't help but wish he answered directly to David as he had in the early days when the elite brotherhood of the gibborim had first been formed. Early on, Jonathan had sensed Joab's jealousy as if Jonathan might be Joab's rival for the king's favor. Over the years it was obvious that Joab held no more fondness for Jonathan than did Jonathan for him. The two respected each other as fighting men, and each was assured of the other's loyalty to their master. But Jonathan made a point of never trusting his back to Joab in a battle.

Joab's ruthlessness had tainted them all, Jonathan thought, especially David. Of course at times it was necessary to be coolly detached, even heartless in battle. But Joab had shown an extraordinary penchant for killing from the moment he had slain the first Jebusite on Mount Zion and for that feat earning the leadership of the army. Under him were the Three Mighty Ones, David's generals Jashobeam, Eleazar, and Shammah. Compared to Joab, even that illustrious fighting trio paled in terms of cold-blooded killing power.

Jonathan shuddered as he recalled Joab's calculated assassination of Abner, commander of the army under Saul. Jonathan had been certain at the time that David would order the crime punished. Didn't the king have two men executed for no more than falsely claiming to have slain Saul? But for some reason, David had let Joab off—most likely because Joab was the son of David's half-sister, Zeruiah.

Or perhaps David accepted that Joab had some justification in killing Abner. After all, the man had slain Asahel, Joab's brother. But everyone knew that Abner had borne the young man no ill will. He had pleaded with Asahel to make peace with him, but the younger brother of Joab had pursued the older man, forcing the fight in which he was killed.

One could understand that Joab would want to avenge his brother's blood, however foolishly he had brought about his own death. But instead of an honorable fight, Joab had sought a meeting with Abner, pretending to seek peace, and assassinated the man by sticking a knife in his ribs. It was a cowardly way to kill, Jonathan thought with disgust. David decried the act, but he did nothing to punish his nephew. That episode had also marked the beginning of the obvious distrust and animosity between Jonathan and Joab.

Maybe David's pragmatic side couldn't dismiss the military genius and courage of his nephew. For whatever reason, David had let the crime pass unpunished, and Jonathan's estimation of his hero had been somewhat tarnished ever since.

Jonathan had looked up to all three of David's nephews in those early days—Joab, Asahel, now dead, and Abishai. It had been Jonathan's ambition to become one of David's Mighty Thirty, and he had earned that privilege in battle before his eighteenth summer. And in those days, David had displayed a moral quality that Jonathan had never seen except in his own father, Shageh, the wise Rab of Ziph. Jonathan remembered David's weeping over the burned-out city of Ziklag, humbling himself before the men and accepting full responsibility for the kidnapping of their wives and children, including David's own. Jonathan remembered the determined look on David's face when he returned from prayer and led the men in recovering their loved ones.

He recalled the nights in their wilderness strongholds when David would play for them on his seven-stringed lyre, composing songs of praise to Adonai. Countless times David could have wrested the kingdom from Saul but refused to lift his hand against the Lord's anointed.

Instead, David had insisted that if God wished him to rule Israel, He would see to the matter in a way that would leave no doubt. And that was precisely what had happened. After Saul and his son Jonathan had been killed in battle, David had reigned for more than seven years over his fellow Judahites from the city of Hebron, not many miles from Jonathan's hometown of Ziph. When the great warrior was made king over Israel as well, David moved his capital to the more central location of Jerusalem.

The hair on Jonathan's arms still stood on end when he remembered the day the ark of the covenant was brought into the new capital city with David leading the procession into Jerusalem, singing praises to God, dancing and leaping, flying through the air like one of the Lord's own seraphim! It was the closest Jonathan had ever felt to the presence of God.

The intervening years had brought David undreamed-of glory, and he had generously shared that glory with those who had remained loyal to him in the difficult times. In battle after battle they had won astounding military victories without horses and without chariots but by the courage that came from their faith in God.

And now they were on the brink of another great campaign. Jonathan was not afraid. He had no hesitation about fighting under David's banner nor any doubts about Joab's ability to wrest a victory from the Arameans. But he was battle-weary and burdened by the eroding soul of his monarch and those around him. And what of his own soul? he thought. How much longer before he succumbed to the heartless blood lust of Joab and the others? he wondered as he banked the fire. It was time to get out before he lost his own heart, but more importantly it was to time to get a few short hours of sleep before sunrise. He stooped to enter his tent.

"My lord, what do you require?" The sleepy adolescent voice of Jonathan's armor-bearer reminded him of the lateness of the hour.

"I require nothing but sleep, Isaac, and so do you. You should not have waited up for me," Jonathan said charitably since the lad had long since dozed off.

"It is my pleasure to serve you, my lord."

Jonathan smiled at the fervor of the youngster's voice. The winsome seventeen-year-old was the only son of Ahiam, Jonathan's best friend, also one of the gibborim. It had taken a lot of persuasion before Judith, Ahiam's wife, had consented to allow her son the honor of joining Jonathan as his armor-bearer on this campaign. She thought the boy still too young for warfare; it was still a week before he would turn seventeen, she had complained. In truth, Jonathan reflected with a smile, he himself had been almost three years younger when Ahiam had taken the green recruit under his wing and taught him to be a man of war.

"Why does Isaac have to become a soldier?" Judith had argued. "Why can't my son be a shepherd or a vinedresser like most of the other boys in Hebron?"

"And miss out on all the glory?" Jonathan had teased Judith, who was closer to him than his own sister Ruth.

"Humph! Miss out on all the wounds and pain, you mean! All the time spent away from home and all the good food his mother could be preparing on his own hearth!"

In the end the two men's arguments combined with the boy's pleas had moved Judith to relent, but not before extracting a solemn promise from Jonathan that he would not let Isaac out of his sight.

Lying down near the boy, Jonathan drifted off into a light slumber, troubled first by visions of Shageh pleading with him to spend more time in Ziph and to take a wife and give him grandsons. Then Jonathan's dreams became more violent. A battle was raging around him, and in the fight he lost sight of Isaac. He searched the battlefield frantically, dreading the moment when he would have to acknowledge to Judith that he had failed to keep his promise. On the edge of the fighting he could see a figure fallen face down in the sand. He fought his way to the body, afraid to turn it over and confirm his worst fears.

Jonathan suddenly awoke, startled to find himself in his own field tent with Isaac asleep beside him. A broad band of orange-gold light was spreading across the foothills to the east. It was time to prepare himself to join the battle. This day he would command a regiment of more than a thousand men, the elite troops who would be on the leading edge of the charge against Hadadezer's charioteers.

"All right, lad," he said, giving Isaac a firm shake that brought the young man bolt upright. "Let's get about our business. The sooner done here, the sooner you'll be back at your mother's table for breakfast!"

~ ~ ~

The well-trained force quickly formed into ranks, awaiting the order to march. The rumble of the Aramean chariots could now be heard distinctly from the other side of the low-lying sandy hills. Glancing to the side every now and then, Jonathan saw Isaac gulp as he valiantly strove to swallow his fear. He placed a steadying hand on the young man's shoulder, feeling the quivering bones on the lanky frame. It had been a long time since Jonathan's first battle. He had almost forgotten the feeling of fear, but Isaac's apprehension resurrected a sense of emotion that he had buried long ago

As he inspected his troops, moving man by man down the line, Jonathan saw evidence that the sounds of cavalry and chariots had unnerved them as well, although most were seasoned warriors and better able to hide their anxiety than the lad.

To boost morale, Jonathan began a chant written by David, one that had always summoned courage in himself. As soon as he gave the signal to march, he lifted his voice in cadence.

"Some trust in horses." The answer, in perfect rhythm, came back from his men. "We trust in the name of the Lord our God."

"Some trust in chariots."

"We trust in the name of the Lord our God."

When the troops topped the hill, the superior forces of their enemy came into view. Jonathan shouted above the sound of marching feet, "They will be brought down and fall!" The response was nearly deafening this time as it flew on the wind toward the Arameans.

"We trust in the name of the Lord our God!"

Jonathan gave the command to charge before the sight of Hadadezer's formidable chariot corps cause his men to falter. The Hebrews confidently swarmed down the hill to meet the enemy, knowing that Joab and Abishai were sweeping around with their battalions in a flanking maneuver.

Outrunning even his best men, Jonathan focused on the lead chariot, dodging a javelin and circling low to the right of the horses. Before the driver could turn the chariot, Jonathan pivoted to the left, his shield held away from his body for balance and his bronze-handled iron sword held low on his right. Running at the chariot from the rear, he leaped onto the platform, catching the driver with a quick thrust that pierced the man's leather armor and pushed him down against the bowman who desperately twisted to his right, his legs tangled by the body of the driver. The arrow cocked in the man's bow shot wildly high of Jonathan's head as in one quick motion he withdrew the sword and followed with a shoulder-high swing. For the briefest of moments the men's eyes met, and then Jonathan's closed as he forced his right shoulder forward to follow through the sword's arc with all his strength. It met the narrow gap between the helmet and armor and expertly severed the head from the body which pitched lifelessly onto the ground.

Emboldened by the success of their captain and realizing that the charioteers could not control their teams and hold their shields at the same time, his men pressed the attack. In the first excitement of the battle, Jonathan had forgotten entirely about Isaac who alertly grabbed the reigns of the horses and held them steady while Jonathan surveyed the battlefield. In minutes they had gained control of several of the chariots; the others were retreating. Jonathan barked orders for some of the men to secure the horses and chariots. He briefly considered leaving Isaac with them, but remembered his promise to Judith to keep the boy with him. He motioned Isaac to follow.

The lad held Jonathan's bow and quiver of arrows, as well as his spear, while Jonathan decided to continue the fight with the sword he had taken from a Philistine years before. The chariots regrouped in attack formation and began another charge toward the Hebrew line. This time Jonathan signaled for his men to wait for the chariots which broke formation when they reached the site of the first engagement. In the dust which had just begun to settle from the first attack, the Arameans were soon hedged in by dead horses, bodies, and overturned chariots. Several times Jonathan was saved by Isaac's shouted warnings to watch his back. After one such shout, Jonathan turned in time to see the boy run a man through with Jonathan's spear which Isaac released as the Aramean fell to the ground.

Jonathan placed a foot against the body and extracted the shaft. Isaac's pale face, lathered with sweat and chalky dust, looked as lifeless as the corpses scattered around them. Jonathan recalled how sickened he had felt at his first sight of blood in battle.

"Let's finish this so we can go home," he said, handing the spear back to Isaac. Jonathan, with the sixth sense of a seasoned warrior, had known that the victory was theirs almost from the beginning. But Hadadezer's forces continued to fight bravely as the afternoon advanced. Time and again, his young armor-bearer proved himself a worthy assistant, anticipating his superior's needs without being told.

Jonathan was in a grueling sword fight with a foot soldier when Isaac spotted a large warrior with javelin flanking Jonathan to their right, away from Jonathan's shield. The man took aim at Jonathan. Jonathan had ended the sword play with a slashing cut to the opponent's sword hand and was about to finish the man. Realizing that a shouted warning would come too late, Isaac lunged forward knocking Jonathan to the side.

The javelin penetrated the boy's right shoulder from the rear, passing under the shoulder joint and emerging through the upper arm muscle. A fountain of bright red blood spurted from the wound, but Isaac felt no pain, only a strange sense of detachment as he watched the warm liquid flow down his arm. He struggled to stand up, but the weight of the shaft pulled him off center and then the ground rushed up to meet him.

Jonathan had rolled forward on his shield and quickly regained his balance, bringing his own sword up in time to meet an off-hand thrust by the wounded opponent. Unable to handle his weapon in the left hand, Jonathan quickly parried a second thrust and ended the fight with a backhand swing.

Isaac! Where was Isaac? The boy's name choked in his throat when he saw him, face down with the polished wooden shaft protruding from his back. Just as Jonathan reached Isaac, a soldier wielding a battle-ax swung the weapon over his head and ran at Jonathan.

Jonathan reacted instinctively. He reached down to the fallen armor-bearer and jerked the javelin free. Twisting at the hips, he brought the point around and thrust forward just as the soldier began his downward swing. The bronze spear point met the man's throat just above his armor plate, and Jonathan pushed forward, knocking the man on his back and pinning him to the ground through the neck. The soldier grabbed at the shaft with both hands, but Jonathan leaned on it full weight until the sickening gurgle of blood in his throat stopped, and the man lay silent.

Oblivious to the fighting going on around him, Jonathan gathered up Isaac in his arms. He examined both the entrance and exit wounds which continued to seep blood, too much blood he feared. Jonathan quickly ripped the boy's cloak into swatches of cloth and placed one compress over the back wound. He wrapped another piece around the upper arm and pressed it against the side. Then he wrapped several long strips around the chest and back to hold the bandages in place. Calling for Isaac to be removed to the rear of the battle and tended well, Jonathan turned back to rally his men for another attack.

By nightfall, twenty thousand of Hadadezer's army had surrendered, the capture of some key officers accomplishing a rather easy victory. There were surprisingly few casualties on either side, Jonathan decided, considering the fierceness of the fighting.

Hadadezer and his superior general, Shobach, had both avoided capture. Scouts reported that Aramean units had struck out for Damascus, probably seeking reinforcements from the city. No doubt Hadadezer's army would regroup. There would be other battles in this campaign.

Joab exuded satisfaction at the outcome of the battle as he stood before his large field tent, receiving reports from his commanders. To Jonathan it seemed more arrogance than satisfaction.

"General," Jonathan asked after he had finished his account of the battle, "if you still intend to place a garrison in Damascus, I would like to be a part of it."

Joab's eyebrows lifted in surprise. It was no secret that Jonathan preferred to avoid city life whenever possible. He waited for his captain to explain.

"My armor-bearer was injured in the battle. He will die without proper care. In Damascus he could get it. The lad is the son of Ahiam, General."

"Ah, I see. I suppose that would be suitable. If the boy has the potential of being half the fighter his father is, we wouldn't want to lose him. I have placed Benaiah in command. You will report to him."

Joab had already turned his attention to another officer when Jonathan stayed him by placing a hand on his arm. "Sir, would it be possible to send word to Ahiam concerning his son's condition and whereabouts?" Joab shrugged. "Yes, of course. I can send a messenger to find Ahiam's scouting party and let him know."

Chapter Three

Ailea watched in dismay from her rooftop perch as the line of wounded, defeated soldiers poured back into the city. What a difference, she thought, from the proud army that had marched out of Damascus less than a week ago.

She searched for her father and brother among the returning troops but to no avail. Finally she gave up and went below to seek out her mother who was sick with worry.

She found Nariah in her chamber, the smell of burning incense heavy in the air. Her mother was kneeling before the statue of Nergal, the god of war and the underworld. Nariah had long ago chosen to center her worship primarily on this god, reasoning that Nergal would surely be inclined to answer supplications on behalf of such a great man of war as Eliada. Most of the people of Damascus, however, devoted themselves to Rimmon, the sun god, and had built a beautiful temple to him in their city.

"Mother?"

Nariah turned to her daughter, her eyes filled with tears. "Have you heard any word—seen them from the roof?"

"No, Mother, but I am sure they are well. You must try to rest tonight. You want to look your best when Father returns."

"How can I rest when I feel this terrible foreboding about

your father? Nergal may not be able to protect him against this invisible god of the Hebrews. Did you know that he is so powerful the Hebrews do not even speak his name? I will have to go early in the morning to the temple of Rimmon and make offerings there as well. And tonight we must take the best of our fruit and offer it to Sin, the moon god. His face is turned away from Damascus at this time. Surely that is not a good omen."

Nariah looked distraught for a moment, then went on anxiously, "Are there clouds tonight, child? I do hope the clouds will not hide us from the moon god. I will sing the chant to him that old Shua taught me. Come to the rooftop and sing with me."

Ailea was alarmed at her mother's increasing fanaticism. Although she believed there must be gods, Ailea sometimes wondered if they really heard the prayers of human beings. Surely there were so many people making so many requests of them that it was unlikely any of the gods would take particular notice of the supplications of two relatively unimportant women in Damascus this night. Still, Ailea was eager to soothe her mother and readily agreed to accompany her to the rooftop. Perhaps the cool evening breeze would calm Nariah, and she could be coaxed to take some nourishment.

When Malik brought a meal of baked fish and fruit, Ailea persuaded her mother to eat a little. Then she joined Nariah in her prayers to Sin, the moon god, looking down from time to time on the streets of Damascus, searching for any sign of her brother and father. At last, she led her mother down the stairs and sat beside her bed until she slept. But it was midnight before Ailea herself fell asleep.

~ ~ ~

Rezon rode alongside his father as the remnants of Hadadezer's defeated army made their way toward Damascus. He seethed with resentment and humiliation. That egomaniac

Shobach had nearly lost everything with his insistence that they stand and fight to the last man. Wisely, the king had finally taken the counsel of Eliada and the other commanding officers, overruling Shobach's careless disregard for the lives of his own men. The retreat had been sounded before the Arameans had been completely decimated. They would live to fight another day.

The whole thing had been impossible outside of a miracle! How had the Hebrew foot soldiers been able to win over a vastly superior army equipped with horses, chariots, and better weapons? Noticing a gesture from his father, he reined his gray stallion in alongside his father's great black warhorse.

"We will be in Damascus only briefly—to muster the remainder of our troops and to rest," Eliada told him. "Soon King David will be sending a contingent of troops to occupy the city. We must be safely away by then."

Rezon's expression was stormy. "Why don't we fortify the city and refuse to surrender?" He knew the answer, but leaving his home to an invading army was unthinkable.

Eliada sighed. He had already found it necessary to explain his strategy to Hadadezer and Shobach, who had both agreed to his plan. "King David is an expert at laying siege; we could not withstand if he came against Damascus. You have seen his army's strength—although it does not lie in numbers or weapons." He shook his head thoughtfully.

"No, our best hope is to head southeast. With the help of our allies—Ammon, Tob, and the desert chieftains—we can regroup and attack as the enemy returns to Jerusalem. We know the desert. We will have the advantage of choosing the time and place."

"If the king and the general had only listened to your counsel earlier, we would not be in retreat now!" Rezon's voice shook with the force of his anger. How could his father submit to such a leader?

Eliada eyed his strong-willed son skeptically. The boy was not known for his prudence. Glancing about to be sure they would not be overheard, Eliada dropped his voice, "Rezon, you must learn to take your place in the ranks, son, and curb that temper of yours."

Rezon did not respond to his father's comment. In silence they entered the city gates. It was after midnight when they arrived at the courtyard doors and found Malik asleep on a bench just inside the doorway.

~ ~ ~

In the middle of the night Ailea was awakened by the sound of muffled voices emanating from the inner courtyard. Immediately she pulled on a robe and went to see what was causing all the commotion.

Near the fountain in the center of the courtyard was her mother, clinging to a tall figure. Father! She took a step toward them, mouth open to call out a greeting.

A hand on her arm restrained her. "Don't disturb them just yet, baby sister." Ailea turned joyfully to greet the owner of the gruff voice behind her.

"Rezon!"

"Help me rid myself of a few layers of grime, and I'll satisfy your curiosity about the battle. Then you can speak with Father."

A wayward lock of hair had worked its way loose from her long braid as she had slept, and her brother pushed it behind her ear, giving her a crooked smile. "Sorry we disturbed your rest, little one."

Ailea tried to throw her arms around Rezon's neck, but he held her away from him. "Not yet, Ailea. I'm filthy. Go and fetch me a basin and cloth."

He sat down, dangling his long legs in the pool. When Ailea handed him the bowl, he dipped up some water. After moistening the cloth, he applied some potash soap from the small jar she had brought and began to wash his face and hands. When the water in the bowl was dirty, Ailea replaced it and returned the bowl to her brother, who repeated the washing process. He then removed his dirty blood-stained battle kilt and outer tunic and slipped into the soothing waters of the pool, wearing only his short undertunic.

Ailea had seen the lines of weariness around his eyes and waited patiently until her brother was revived enough to tell her what she was so anxious to hear. When he was finally seated beside her on the pool's edge, his curly black hair dripping, he accepted the drying cloth she offered and spoke bluntly.

"We're here only for a few hours. Then we go to join our allies in the eastern desert. Israel will send troops here to occupy the city. If we stay, we will be no better than slaves to that arrogant shepherd who calls himself their king. Hadadezer listened to the advice of that incompetent fool Shobach, and it cost us the battle. We hope to regroup and win the next fight. Surely Hadadezer will listen to our father this time. If not . . . well, I cannot give my allegiance to a man I can't respect, and I have no respect for Shobach!"

Ailea shuddered when she heard of an occupation force headed for Damascus. "But surely it would be wiser to prepare for a siege, concentrate all the troops here, and defend the city rather than go out and fight them in the open!"

His little sister echoed his own earlier thoughts, but now he snorted in derision. "And cower like some fox cornered in its den? I think not. We will not be vassals of the Israelites. We will drive them out. Just wait and see!"

They left at first light, having eaten little and slept but a few hours. Eliada patted Ailea on the head after pulling himself from the embrace of his weeping wife. Ordering his daughter to take care of her mother, he marched away without a backward glance, while Rezon kissed both women and followed his father with a jaunty swagger.

Nariah was distraught, and it fell to Ailea once again to act cheerful and unconcerned, although in truth she wondered if they would ever see her father and brother again.

Chapter Four

When Jonathan and his men entered Damascus the day after the battle, his first concern was for his wounded armor-bearer.

"I need a household staffed with plenty of servants to care for Isaac and an abundance of nourishing foods to strengthen him. Any suggestions?" he asked Benjamin, the warrior who had been sent ahead with the troops who were to secure the city.

Benjamin nodded. "The household of Eliada, a high-ranking officer in Hadadezer's army. The location is strategic, as well. However—" he paused, lifting a brow in dismay, "there is a small problem."

Jonathan noted a hint of mischief in the old campaigner's eye. "You mean there is still some resistance in the city you have failed to put down?"

At this, Benjamin laughed aloud. "The resistance is coming in the person of Eliada's younger child—a girl, to be precise. I have just received a report that she has wounded a couple of our men. The others are afraid to use force lest they harm her. Perhaps you would want to handle it personally?"

"Am I a woman that I must now discipline unruly girls?" Jonathan grumbled. When Benjamin offered no response,

Jonathan shook his head. "Very well. Where is the house of this Eliada? Isaac needs tending!"

"Follow me."

Benjamin led the entourage through the busy streets of Damascus to the wealthy section of the city. He stopped before an iron gate. Jonathan peered through the grillwork and was impressed with what he saw. In the courtyard was a fountain surrounded by stone benches. Beyond the fountain, a short flight of stone steps led to the arched columns of the white stone house.

Upon their arrival, a harried young soldier rushed up to meet them, his face red with chagrin. "Sir, I'm glad you're here at last. I didn't know what to tell the men after she—uh—sliced the last one with that cursed dagger. She's rather like a pesky little bee—too small and fast to swat! She is by the pool in the inner courtyard. We are afraid we can't get her down without hurting her, and—"

Jonathan interrupted the young man's litany. "Just show me to the best room in the house. After I've seen to Isaac's wounds, I'll take care of the little termagant myself."

The soldier opened his mouth as if to speak further, but the look on his superior's face silenced him. Following orders, Benjamin led the way to a chamber that opened directly onto the outer courtyard.

Stepping inside, Jonathan viewed the richly appointed room with approval. Heavy draperies, dyed a deep blue, provided stark contrast to the whitewashed walls. The rich fabric, drawn back from a large open window, admitted a flood of afternoon sunlight into the spacious chamber. In the center a raised sleeping platform was spread with linens and piled high with plush cushions.

Jonathan nodded with satisfaction. This would make a fine infirmary for Isaac, he mused. Striding to the bed, he laid the unconscious boy down before continuing his perusal of the room.

An intricately carved rosewood chair and a chest inlaid with ivory were a further indication of the family's wealth. Yes, this would do. It would do nicely.

A slight sound from an alcove at the far side of the room drew Jonathan's attention. There a woman swayed on her knees before an altar on which an ugly effigy rested. Carved in black marble, the figure held a battle-ax in one upraised hand. Two oil-burning lamps on either side cast the grotesque features in bold relief.

Jonathan crossed the room in a few long strides and swept up the idol, smashing it against the tile floor. He spoke to her in Y'hudit, the language of Judah. It was so similar to her own Aramaic idiom that there was no question she would understand him perfectly, and it would serve to emphasize that Israel was now in control—in Damascus and in Eliada's household.

"This house has been taken in the name of the one true God! There will be no more idol worship here. Understand?" he asked the trembling, middle-aged woman who rose quickly to her feet.

Evidently she had registered his subtle reminder, because she answered in Y'hudit. "Yes, my lord," she said softly, keeping her eyes downcast.

"We mean you no harm. But our God is a jealous God, and we observe His command that there be no other gods before Him. As long as you follow that dictate and help to nurse my armor-bearer back to health, we will not be enemies but friends."

Moving a little away, Jonathan turned to regard the woman, whose gaze was still discreetly lowered. "I understand that your husband is a military man. He should be returning soon under honorable terms of surrender. Until that time, my men and I—eight or ten of us—must impose upon your hospitality. Now, would you be so kind as to have one of your servants tend to Isaac there?" He gestured toward the prostrate form on the sleeping platform.

"He is the only son of my best friend, and I am responsible to his mother for his life."

The woman finally lifted her resigned eyes to his. "I, too, have a son, my lord. Knowing how this boy's mother must feel, I will care for him as if it were my own Rezon lying in that bed."

"Good. Good." Jonathan turned to observe Isaac, now tossing fitfully on the bed.

The matron pushed the young man's hair back from his forehead, testing for fever. After examining his wounds, she instructed an old woman to bring oil, water, and wine, along with a knife, heated over an open brazier.

"I must cauterize his arm and dress it, my lord," she explained, gazing at Jonathan with concern. "Since the lad is special to you, perhaps it would be best if one of your men assisted me. Also, I am afraid there is the matter of my daughter Ailea . . . in the inner courtyard. I'm afraid she is not taking this occupation of our home very well. She is a brave child and is only trying to defend her home."

She spoke up hastily, "If only I had not sent Malik, our chief steward, out of the city to seek word of his master, he could have disarmed her. As it is—"

Jonathan silenced her with an impatient wave of his hand. "If my men can't protect themselves against an angry child, they don't deserve to call themselves soldiers in Israel's army. I will hold Isaac still while you tend to him. When that is done, I will deal with your daughter. What name are you called by?"

"Oh, forgive me, my lord. I am Nariah, wife of Eliada." She dropped her gaze once more.

"There is no reason to fear, I assure you. My men and I will be here for only a short time . . . if things go as planned."

When the old woman returned with the supplies Nariah had called for, she turned her attention to the gaping wound in Isaac's shoulder and upper arm. She first gave him wine to dull his senses and then went to work. The lad regained consciousness briefly as she bathed the wound and remained stoic until she pressed the flat edge of the red-hot knife against it.

The boy's piercing scream and the smell of burning flesh brought the bile to Jonathan's throat, and he squeezed his eyes shut and turned away, wishing it had been he who had taken the spear thrust. When he opened his eyes a moment later, he saw that the boy had fainted again. Jonathan's lips curved in a hint of a smile. No, lad, he thought, I wouldn't begrudge you the glory. Just don't go and die on me. He pulled the soft fur around the boy and rose to his feet.

"He will sleep for hours now," Nariah told Jonathan. "I will stay with him. Get some rest, if you can, my lord. I will send for you if there is any change."

Jonathan looked down into her kind face and knew Isaac would be well cared for. "Now I shall attend to the matter of your daughter, madam."

Taking his leave, Jonathan went in search of someone who could tell him where he would find the girl. When he stepped into the inner courtyard, he had his answer. To the left, six of his best warriors flanked a wide ledge—a little higher than his head. Crouched there was a young girl, holding a knife with a long, wide blade—the kind used for household purposes. He was sure the child had not seen him emerge from the darkened corridor. She was turned in profile to him, her long black braid hanging below the ledge where she perched so precariously.

At her feet was a stack of disks. These appeared to be weights for measure. Apparently the girl had been wielding them successfully as weapons for when he glanced across the courtyard, he saw that one of his men was leaning against the wall, a bloody rag pressed to his forehead. Jonathan chuckled to himself. Poor Iddo would be taunted mercilessly by his friends for falling victim to a young girl. But then, perhaps not. Upon closer inspection, Jonathan saw that two other warriors were also wearing fresh bandages—one on his forearm, the other on his head. This child must be quite a fighter.

He looked again at the ledge. What age girl was he dealing with, anyway? Maybe fourteen or fifteen? He took in the well-defined contours of her face, then let his gaze drop to the generous curves of her body. This was no child! This was a woman, although still quite young. And very comely indeed. He shook his head slightly to gather his wandering thoughts.

Just then, her voice rang out mockingly. "What's wrong, oh brave servants of King David? Can it be you are afraid of a mere girl? Why don't you choose a champion from among you to fight against me? I will prove that one Damascene female can defeat the best of you cowardly jackals!"

Jonathan saw color flush the cheeks of some of his younger men. They itched to respond to the challenge, but Benjamin had ordered their silence with an almost imperceptible shake of his head. The seasoned warrior caught Jonathan's eye and raised an eyebrow in question. But he did not move from his relaxed stance as he leaned, arms folded, against a door frame, chewing on a piece of straw.

"Cowards!" the girl spat out again. "Are you men or women?"

A broad grin broke across Benjamin's face as he waited to see what his superior would do about this defiant whelp.

Battle-weary and irritated, Jonathan decided to bring this matter to a quick end. He jerked his head in Benjamin's direction, and the veteran knew immediately what he was being asked to do.

"We don't lower ourselves to battle with women," Benjamin called out as he uncrossed his arms and pushed away from the door frame.

Ailea, freshly angered, focused her attention on the approaching soldier. He was fearsome indeed. Cautiously she reached for one of the larger disks in case he attacked.

He moved slowly toward her as he continued, "But I might consider taking up your challenge, young lady. First, I'd want to know your weapon of choice for the duel."

Although she tried to hide her surprise, Ailea's eyes widened. In the hours she had held the Israelites at bay, none of them had addressed her directly, not even when she had wounded three of the dogs—one with her knife, two others with well-aimed missiles. Feeling a prickle of alarm, she squared her shoulders and called out, "I care not, Hebrew, as long as the choice doesn't give you the advantage of size or reach. Perhaps slings, or bows and arrows."

"Fair enough, but I haven't practiced with the sling in many years. A contest with bow and arrow is more to my liking." Aware that he had advanced while he spoke, Ailea drew back her arm. "Stop! Don't come any closer, or I will see that you join your comrades against the wall!"

So caught up was she in her sparring with Benjamin that Ailea failed to notice Jonathan, who had inched toward her until he was within arm's reach. Benjamin gave no sign that he saw what was happening, but took yet another step in her direction.

Ailea rose, ready to send the disk sailing through the air. But before she could toss her weapon, a powerful hand shot out and grabbed her arm, flinging her off the ledge. Airborne, she seemed to fly weightlessly, landing with a loud splash in the pool. She came up, sputtering and choking. Although she had dropped the disk, she still clutched the knife tightly in one hand.

There was another loud splash as Jonathan leaped in beside her. As he reached for her wrist, she slashed the back of his hand with her knife. But even as she watched a bright red line of blood appear, the tall soldier used his other hand to knock the blade from her grasp with a stunning blow that jarred her entire body.

Ailea launched herself at her tormentor with a furious hissing sound, clawing at his eyes with her long nails. But the warrior was too quick for her, manacling both her wrists with one powerful hand. In retaliation, she sank her sharp teeth into the tender web between his thumb and forefinger.

Jonathan let out a startled yelp and yanked at her braid, but her jaws clenched tighter. In a last desperate measure, he shoved her underwater. Finally, lungs nearly bursting, she released his hand, bobbed to the surface, and drew in great gulps of air.

"Now will you—" Jonathan began, thinking the pathetic little thing had surely had enough. He grunted in pain as a small fist connected sharply with his nose. For the second time in a brief span, the tiny girl had drawn blood! His blood!

The roar of laughter that went up from his men incensed

Jonathan. Didn't this foolish child know that he or one of the other warriors could have dispatched her with a single blow? If she had come across a less disciplined unit, she could be dead by now—or worse.

He did not waste another moment in useless conjecturing, but, heedless of her flailing fists, hoisted her over his shoulder like a bag of grain and headed for the corridor.

"Show me to this wild creature's chamber," he ordered an elderly woman. He asked her name as they walked along the passage.

"Shua, my lord. I am the maidservant of my lady Nariah."

"And who is servant to this little vixen?"

"Oh, she has no personal servant, my lord. Malik, Eliada's chief steward, looks after her."

When Shua opened the door to the room, Jonathan walked in and dumped Ailea unceremoniously on the tile floor. She immediately leaped to her feet, glaring at him, fists clenched.

"Unless you want to be trussed like a hart for the roasting, I would suggest you calm down and listen to me," Jonathan warned. She continued to scowl but made no move.

"I'm glad to see that you are not completely without wits," he told the lovely girl who stood before him, trembling as much from anger and dampness as from fear, he suspected. Of course this one would never admit to being afraid of anything.

Jonathan took in the well-defined curves of her body, molded by her wet clothing. Her braid had come loose, and her black hair, rich and lustrous as a raven's wing, hung past her hips. But it was her eyes that caused Jonathan to suck in his breath. They were jade green with a feline slant, large and luminous in the small, heart-shaped face. Somehow Jonathan was drawn to this young girl as he had never been drawn to another woman.

Ridiculous! he admonished himself. The girl was probably no more than sixteen and he nearing thirty. She was a heathen, his enemy. But his heart told him differently. He felt a physical attraction to her beauty; that was familiar enough for he was a grown man with normal desires. But this was something more. He felt at once the need to both protect and master her. He stared at her for another long moment before speaking gruffly to cover his discomfiture.

"I cannot believe that you are the daughter of the charming mistress of this house, the one who is even now bringing comfort to my wounded armor-bearer."

"You're speaking of my mother, of course. Well, she is docile. I am not!"

"You had better take lessons from her if you don't want to spend the next several weeks locked in this room and fed nothing more than water and bread."

The girl's chin came up. "Oh, and aren't you the brave one? Trying to terrorize helpless women and servants!"

Jonathan snorted. "Helpless?" He looked down at his hand, branded by the mark of her teeth, and could not contain a wry grin.

The barely suppressed smile softened the huge warrior's features until they were almost boyish, Ailea thought. It told her that her courage in fighting him had earned his respect. She continued to hold his gaze, unable to look away.

The spell was broken by Malik, who entered the chamber at a huffing run. "My lord, my lord, please forgive the child! She meant only to defend her home!"

Ailea stamped her foot in irritation. "I am not a child, Malik. I am nearly nineteen years old. And I will thank you not to make excuses for me to this . . . this invader!"

Malik continued to address Jonathan as if Ailea had not spoken. "My mistress finds her difficult, my lord, but I have returned now, and I promise you the girl will give you no more trouble!"

Jonathan turned to the faithful servant, noting the concern on his face. No doubt the man would give his life to protect his charge. Somehow the conclusion was gratifying. "If you can do a better job of controlling her than the rest of us, she is yours.

See that she stays in her room tonight, out of sight of my men. She managed to lay a few of them low, and they will need time to recover their pride. Please arrange for the household servants to meet with me after all their chores are done this evening." After giving this order, Jonathan turned on his heel and left the room without a backward glance.

Ailea listened to Malik's lecture with only one ear while her mind dwelt on the Hebrew warrior who had humiliated her. She recalled the steely grip of his powerful hand as it had closed around her wrist when he threw her from the ledge, her feeling of panic as he had held her underwater, the effortlessness with which he had slung her over his shoulder, the ripple of the powerful muscles in his back and arms.

Most of all, she could not forget his face, chiseled in harsh angles—thick black brows above an aquiline nose and a well-sculpted mouth—framed by a beard and mustache that were worn shorter than that of the other Hebrew soldiers. The thing that impressed her most about him, however, was the warmth of his eyes—light brown flecked with amber; they had shot sparks like fire when he was angry with her, had sparkled when he smiled.

The man was—a barbarian, her enemy! What did it matter that he was muscular and strong? Her cheeks burned as she reflected on the way he had treated her—like a child! Well, she would show him! She would exact her revenge against these aliens who had invaded her home. She need only to get rid of Malik for a while and form a plan.

Malik's brow lifted in surprise when Ailea agreed to spend the evening in her room and stay out of trouble. The Cricket must be up to something, he surmised, but he could not extract from her even one morsel of information.

He heaved his considerable bulk out of the chair and left the room. "Too old for this. Too, too old."

Chapter Five

"And where are you headed in such a hurry?"

Ailea halted in mid-stride at the sound of Jonathan's gruff voice. Plastering a smile on her face, she turned to greet her unwelcome guest. "With the extra mouths to feed, the servants will need my help this morning. I was on my way to supervise the cooking."

He gave her a curious, searching look. "I would think it beneath the spoiled daughter of the household to dabble in such menial affairs. What are you really up to?"

Ailea's temper flared. "You know nothing of me or my daily habits! I not only oversee the kitchen servants but all the others as well since my mother is seldom up to the task. Ask her if you don't believe me!"

Jonathan looked into the stormy green eyes and decided she was telling the truth. "Very well. You may proceed. Just take care to stay out of trouble, or I'll have you locked in your room." He walked briskly away.

Seething, Ailea went to the kitchen—a room at the back of the house that boasted a large opening in the ceiling to vent the smoke from the clay oven and coal braziers.

The cook, a man whose gaunt frame belied his culinary skills, did not bother to conceal his irritation with Ailea's intrusion into his domain. Although Nariah often left it up to her daughter to instruct the servants, Ailea had never before actually insisted on helping with the cooking, and it was an affront to his dignity.

This morning, however, despite the cook's grumbling, she would hear of nothing else than supervising the preparation of the stew for the soldiers. And when his back was turned, she added a few ingredients of her own choosing to the large pot bubbling on one of the braziers. Then, taking a bowl of stew and some broth she had ladled out earlier, she went to serve her mother and the wounded armor-bearer.

Making her way to her mother's suite with a tray, she tapped on the door with her elbow. It was opened by Jonathan.

Ailea's heart lurched at the sight of the one person who might be astute enough to foil her plans. But she hid her concern, brushing by him without a greeting. Let him get a taste of what it feels like to be ignored, she thought.

Nariah kissed her daughter, then removed the bowl of broth to feed her patient. Ailea came closer to gaze at the young man. She was surprised to see that he looked so young, surely no older than she. She helped her mother prop him up on a large pillow, unable to suppress a pang of sympathy when he gasped in pain.

"There now, Isaac," Nariah said soothingly. "You'll feel stronger with something warm inside you. Just lie still and open your mouth. I'll do the rest."

Ailea watched Nariah spoon out the broth, much like a mother bird feeding her young. It was good for Nariah to have something to take her mind off her own worries, Ailea decided. The tender-hearted woman was never so happy as when someone needed her. Ailea felt a little guilty that she herself was such an independent person with her need for a mother's nurturing long ago outgrown. In truth for some time their roles had been reversed with Ailea taking care of household matters and looking after her mother's needs.

"Who are you?" the boy rasped, jarring Ailea from her thoughts.

He was smiling at her, and she couldn't resist an answering smile. Surely one so young could not be held accountable for the attack on her people. After all, he was only an armor-bearer, not a warrior. There would be no harm in speaking with him.

"I am Ailea, the daughter of the lady who has been caring for you."

"I am Isaac . . . and most grateful for your hospitality. It is kind of you to take in a . . . stranger."

Ailea gave a sardonic laugh. "It's not as if we had a choice."

Isaac's face reddened. How thoughtless of him to remind his hosts that they were a vanquished people. To change the subject, he addressed Jonathan, who was standing at the foot of the bed. "My lord, I am feeling much better this morning. Perhaps by tomorrow I will be able to serve you again."

"No, lad. It has been only a few days since you saved my life. You deserve time to recuperate fully. Besides, your mother will deal very harshly with me if I fail to bring you home fully recovered."

Jonathan realized he had embarrassed the boy when Isaac's face reddened again. No young man wanted to bring up the subject of his mother in the presence of an attractive young lady.

Nariah evidently noticed this too and took pity on him, spooning the last of the broth from the stew into his mouth and asking if he would like more. Isaac nodded, and she obliged.

"My lord," she began, looking up at Jonathan, "why don't you finish what is left? I can get some stew from the kitchen later."

"No!" Realizing that she had almost shouted, Ailea modulated her voice. "I mean, you need to eat, Mother. You have been here, taking care of Isaac for hours. I am sure the captain will not mind eating with his men."

Jonathan took notice at this little speech but responded with a graciousness that masked his wariness.

"Most certainly, madam. You need the nourishment more than I. And your daughter is correct. I need to spend time with the men. Isaac, I order you to rest. That is all. And follow Nariah's instructions—to the letter—like a good soldier."

Jonathan made his way to the inner courtyard where his men were already wolfing down huge bowls of stew and chunks of crusty bread. Selecting a pomegranate and several figs from a tray of fruit nearby, he refused the bowl of the stew offered by a servant and sat on a bench, peeling the fruit and considering what to make of the fascinating daughter of Nariah.

~ ~ ~

Ailea sat near the young Hebrew's bed while her mother rested in the next chamber. They had spoken little since Isaac was still very weak and often drifted off into a light slumber in mid-sentence. Ailea, who had slept poorly the night before, was drowsing in her chair when the door slammed open. Her head jerked up, and she looked into Jonathan's face, explosive with anger.

Pretending serenity, she chided him, "My lord, you have awakened Isaac. Please enter quietly when you come to visit." Isaac's eyelids had barely fluttered open, but when he saw the captain's rigid stance and expression, he tried to sit up, thinking it was he who had somehow earned Jonathan's wrath.

"Lie back down, boy," Jonathan growled.

He crossed to Ailea in three strides and yanked her out of the chair by her arm. His grip was like steel, and she knew it would be useless to struggle.

"What are you doing?" she demanded.

He ignored the question and dragged her into the courtyard, where all ten of his men were writhing in misery. Some had their heads bent over bowls. Some clutched their stomachs and lay panting on the stone floor. Two ran toward the exit that led to the privy outside the back wall.

Sympathy battled with triumph as Ailea looked on. Jonathan's grip tightened painfully on her arm, and she made the mistake of looking up into his face. Her mouth went dry. He was furious, his jaw working in anger.

"You poisoned my men. Don't bother to deny it," he said, his voice ominously low. "I was the only one who refused the stew, and I am the only one who isn't sick. But if I had partaken, you would have poisoned me as well!" His voice rose to a throaty snarl. "Besides, you gave yourself away when you insisted your mother not eat any but the stew you brought to her. I can be thankful you spared Isaac more suffering at least."

He twisted Ailea's wrist savagely, jerking her toward him. "Now listen to me. You will care for these men. You will clean up after them, bathe their faces with cool water, and wash their soiled clothes. You, and only you—no servants may assist you. And you will have no food until they are able to eat again." His brows met in a frown, his voice pitched low once more. "If one of them dies—one—you will forfeit your own life."

Ailea knew it was foolhardy to taunt him, but her hurt pride loosened her tongue. "I didn't intend to kill them, only to make them sick. They won't die," she retorted. "I only regret that the main object of my plan escaped the consequences."

His hold tightened again on her arm before he got control of his temper and strode away. "See to it!" he called over his shoulder.

After Ailea gathered her supplies, she ministered first to the older soldier who had distracted her while Jonathan sneaked up on her that first night. Next, the commander. She hated this warrior most of all. Nevertheless, she set about bathing his face with cool water.

"What is this?" he asked suspiciously when she offered him a sprig of mint to chew.

"Only mint . . . to calm your insides." To prove it harmless, she took a slip of the soothing plant herself and began to chew.

Benjamin grunted and put the sprig in his mouth. "He should

have throttled you," he told her. "Jonathan is a just man, but his punishment is usually not tempered with mercy—not when the offense is cruel and deliberate."

"Cruel, ha! You dare call me cruel for trying to protect my home from marauding Hebrew barbarians?"

With that volley, she left Benjamin and turned to a very young warrior who was on all fours, his head hanging down. Just as she reached him, he heaved and threw up all over her sandals. The savoring of her small victory seemed very short indeed now.

~ ~ ~

Rising early after only a few hours sleep, Ailea made her way to the courtyard to see to her patients. Some of them seemed to be somewhat recovered and were sleeping peacefully—weakened but none the worse for having ingested the strong emetic she had put in the stew.

A few were still very sick, their complexions pasty. These men were seriously dehydrated, and she knew they must have fluids at once. She went to the kitchen and quickly prepared a thin medicinal broth to take back to them. She tried to resist feeling sorry for the soldiers, who for the most part seemed not to hold a grudge against her for the nasty trick she had played on them. Only one, the young man she had stabbed in the arm, had pushed her away, saying he had rather die in peace than have her tend him. She would just have to insist he take some of the broth this morning.

When she reached the courtyard, she found Jonathan with his ailing men. He looked up with a scowl on his face. "I told you to tend them. Where have you been?"

Ailea set the heavy pot of broth down beside the sick soldier who had occupied her thoughts in the kitchen. His eyes were closed, and he was moaning softly.

She did not reply to Jonathan's question until she had dipped the ladle into the broth and brought it to the soldier's lips. "I was preparing something they could keep down." She gave Jonathan a nod. "Would you mind lifting his head?"

When Jonathan did so, the young man opened his eyes and turned his head away. "No!" he croaked desperately.

"Easy, soldier. This will help you," Jonathan assured him. Hearing the familiar voice of his commander, the lad immediately obeyed. Ailea was not impressed. So the arrogant captain was accustomed to everyone jumping to fulfill his every order, she thought with disgust. Well, she would not be among them!

"Have any of them been able to eat yet?"

Ailea started at the resonant sound of the Hebrew's voice so near her ear.

She shook her head. "No, but I believe they will be able to keep down the broth."

"Then you will have nothing but broth yourself." He eyed her distrustfully. "You haven't had anything to eat, have you?"

"I remembered your decree, my lord. No—I have had nothing to eat." It was all she could do to restrain the sarcasm.

Jonathan dipped the ladle into the broth. "Then have some of this. You will need your strength today."

"I am touched by your concern," she spat, "but don't trouble yourself."

Ailea stooped to lift the iron pot, intending to move on to the next sick soldier. But she felt her arm gripped tightly as Jonathan placed the ladle at her lips.

"Drink it."

"I don't wish to," Ailea insisted.

"Why not? Does it contain more poison?"

"Of course not! It is merely medicinal—restorative but it does not taste good." She wrinkled her nose.

"Too bad. You will drink anyway. If it is good enough for my men, it is good enough for you." He saw the mutiny in her eyes and narrowed his own. "I can pour it down your throat but that would be very unpleasant for you. I suggest you obey." He placed the large ladle to her lips once more.

Realizing that he would make good his threat, Ailea drank the broth, choking over the salty, slightly bitter taste. She refused to look at him, knowing he would be laughing at her discomfort.

Thankfully, he soon left her alone with her charges, and Ailea did not see him again until late afternoon. By that time his men were feeling much better; some were nibbling on dry bread interspersed with sips of water. All of them were more congenial, after the hours she had spent nursing them. Even the young soldier whose arm she had cut offered her a smile. Only the crusty old soldier—Benjamin—continued to eye her warily. Not that she cared. She drew in a weary sigh and put a hand to her aching back. Would this day never end?

~ ~ ~

When Jonathan sought her out, Ailea was in the back courtyard, washing the men's soiled clothing in a huge washpot that bubbled over a fire of coals. The fire had warmed her until perspiration dampened her clothing and spun tendrils of hair about her face. She suspected that she resembled nothing more than the lowliest servant. Nevertheless, she lifted her head proudly at Jonathan's greeting and regarded him with a certain cool detachment never seen in any servant.

"Come. We are to sup with your mother and Isaac in her chamber." He gave her a sweeping appraisal. "That is, after you make yourself presentable."

Ailea was infuriated. "I don't feel like having dinner with you. And since your men are camped around the pool," she added pointedly, "I cannot bathe."

"True, but I have done you the kindness of having water sent to your chamber for bathing. You will join us when you are ready."

Refusing him the dignity of a reply, Ailea turned on her heels but was halted by his warning. "And don't be too long, else I will have to come and fetch you."

She stomped away without turning around. It was enough that she must endure the throaty chuckle that followed her all the way down the corridor, but a whole evening of him was unbearably impossible!

Jonathan did not know why, but he enjoyed baiting the girl. Today he had met with several of the city elders. Their shameless groveling had filled him with contempt. This tiny scrap of a girl had shown far more courage than any of the men he had come across in this conquered city.

It angered him when Ailea defied him, but he had to admit he admired her for it. Yes, he observed with a sense of wonder, he admired her very much.

Chapter Six

"The enemy is regrouping with other city state forces and is now amassing an army between here and the Euphrates," reported the messenger from Joab to the gibborim stationed in Damascus. "The commander has issued orders for all troops that are not essential in securing Damascus to prepare to join the main body of the army. He expects to see you by sundown tomorrow."

The messenger saluted, then spun smartly to leave when he added, "You will be pleased to know that the king himself had just arrived on the field when I left."

A great cry of excitement went up from these loyal men just as the messenger had known it would. The presence of their monarch on the field of battle always did wonders for their morale. "That will be all for now. Be prepared to leave at dawn."

The response to this announcement in the household of Eliada was anything but placid. Isaac threw a tantrum worthy of a two-year-old child when he learned he was to be left behind. Jonathan had to silence him with a stern rebuke which left Isaac sullen and Jonathan feeling guilty for being so hard on the boy.

Preparing himself for another unpleasant encounter, Jonathan went to seek out Nariah and Ailea on the rooftop. Ailea's eyes blazed when she learned that he would be leaving to fight her father and brother once again. "I am so certain I will never see you again, Hebrew," she taunted, "that I am almost tempted to give a farewell feast for you."

Nariah gasped at her daughter's impertinence. "Ailea, the captain is a soldier and must fight just as your father must fight. I'm sure we wish him and his men no ill, even though, of course, we will pray to our gods that our own army wins the ultimate victory." Ailea turned her back to them both and stared out over the city.

Jonathan turned to the delicate woman and took her hand. "Lady Nariah, you have been most hospitable. May Adonai grant that this war will soon be ended and all families reunited once again."

After Nariah had left the rooftop, Jonathan fixed his gaze on Ailea. "Instead of railing at me, little warrior, I would suggest you help your mother. This has been a difficult time for her, and she hasn't your strength."

"I don't need you to tell me about my mother, you overbearing barbarian!" Her hands were clenched at her sides as if she were resisting the urge to strike him. He couldn't keep the grin off his face, even though he knew it would only enrage her more. She turned and ran down the stairs.

He left without seeing her again but only after speaking with Malik, assuring the family steward that no harm would come to Nariah or Ailea, no matter what the outcome of the battle might be. He spoke with Isaac, also, leaving him in charge of the household, including two additional soldiers, untried recruits barely older than Isaac himself. A somewhat mollified armor-bearer saw the soldiers off at dawn the next morning and then sat in the courtyard for a while to survey his first command.

~ ~ ~

The armies of Aram-Zobah joined forces with their allies in the eastern desert. Scouts confirmed that Israel's army was busy garnering the booty from the previous battle and tending their wounded. It was also reported that the enemy had considerably weakened their forces by sending a number of their troops to occupy Damascus. All this boded well for the Arameans.

Eliada arranged for his impetuous son to be assigned to his command, hoping to forestall any trouble Rezon might have with General Shobach.

It was not to be. From his position in the vanguard of the assault against David's army, it became clear to Rezon that the smaller, less well-equipped force was fighting in a manner that would assure Israel the victory. When he reported as much to his father, Eliada was alarmed.

"The general's orders are clear, my son. We are not to retreat under any circumstances. Hold your line, no matter what your losses."

"But, Father, isn't it better to fall back now and live to fight again? I don't know what it is about the Hebrews, but I have seen enough to know that we will never prevail against them on an open battlefield."

Eliada replaced the crested gold helmet that proclaimed his rank. "Your idea may have merit, Rezon, but we will never know because Shobach will not sound the retreat. Now, let us rejoin our men."

The battle did not go well. At midmorning Shobach issued an order to Eliada's soldiers—including Rezon's unit—to attack the left flank of the army of Israel.

Once more Rezon argued for retreat. "Father, this is a hopeless maneuver. To attack means certain death. I beg you, refuse the order. Go above the general's head. Consult the king directly. But don't lead us into a slaughter!"

"I have no other choice, son." The general's expression was grim, but determined. "To disobey an order is treason. Perhaps your mother's prayers to the gods have prevailed, and we will win. Whatever happens, we must fight bravely and, if need be, die like men."

"I am no coward, Father," Rezon responded hotly. "But I am no fool either. I will fight the Hebrews my way and win." He turned and raised his voice so that the surrounding soldiers could hear.

"I, Rezon, son of Eliada, do hereby declare that I will leave the field—to hunt down and destroy the Hebrews until they are vanquished. Who goes with me?"

There was a moment of stunned silence before a cry of assent rose from more than a score of young men.

"You craven traitor! I will see your head mounted on the gate of Damascus!" It was Shobach, his face dark with fury, seated upon his black warhorse, his shield and helmet dazzling in the sunlight. "Cease this nonsense and mount the charge of the enemy's flank as ordered."

Shobach looked pointedly at Eliada who was quick to answer. "It will be as you have ordered." The general gave a nod and rode away.

Eliada, his mouth set in grim determination, gave the signal to advance, and most of the troops fell in behind him.

"Father!" Rezon called after him. "Do not go to your death! Come with us—" he motioned toward the small band that had assembled at his side, "—and live! We will attack and retreat until we have won the victory!"

"And betray my liege lord?" Eliada countered. "Rezon, think of your mother and sister. If I join you in this, they will suffer for it. Better that I die. Then they will receive honor. Whatever happens today, my son, take care of them." Eliada wheeled his horse and signaled to his men, knowing full well that his son would not be among them. Rezon watched his father lead the charge, disappearing into a cloud of dust that billowed up from the desert floor.

Motioning to his cohorts to follow him, Rezon spurred his horse, galloping to a rise that overlooked the battlefield. From that vantage point, he was able to see his worst fears unfold before his eyes. All took place as he had foretold. And before an hour had passed, Eliada had fallen, the elaborate helmet and shield distinguishing him from all others in the fray.

"Your enemies will die, Father!" Rezon vowed with a cry of rage. "By all the gods, I swear it!"

Then Rezon lifted his fist to the heavens and rode into the desert in the opposite direction, his loyal band riding hard on his heels.

~ ~ ~

As the battle raged, Jonathan wondered several times if he would have to fight against Eliada or his son. He hoped not, and as far as he knew, he did not personally engage either of them. But when the three-day battle was ended and the officers met to recount losses and victories, Eliada was reported among the dead. Jonathan could obtain no information about Rezon.

That night he slept as if made of stone, his body completely exhausted. His men did the same, most of them not even bothering to pitch their tents, merely wrapping themselves in their cloaks to sleep. Since they were located near the center of the encampment, it was not even necessary to post a watch.

The sound of shouting and the clash of swords woke Jonathan with a start. In a moment he was on his feet with sword in hand. Benjamin joined him as they ran toward the sound of the conflict on the fringes of the camp.

"How can they think to attack now when they are so totally beaten?" Benjamin asked as they neared the scene of the commotion.

"This is no organized attack by their troops," Jonathan answered as he motioned toward a group even now racing away on camels, Hebrew soldiers in pursuit. "It must be a band of robbers thinking to steal some of the spoils from the battle. These raiders showed more courage than sense," Jonathan remarked.

At the scene of the altercation, Joab was furiously upbraiding the sentries for failing to stop the intruders. Two Hebrew soldiers had been killed and several more injured.

Joab was still pacing furiously, impatiently awaiting word from the unit he had sent after the raiders. "It appears there may be more to it than just robbery. One of the sentries heard the leader shout something about avenging his father's death. Fortunately, one of our men shot him with an arrow. It is possible that it killed him. If so, that is the end to it. But if he still lives and has sworn vengeance, he will strike again.

"I want you and Benjamin to alert all the other captains that night sentries are to be set by each unit as long as we are in the field. The most the man can do is pose a nuisance. Still, I would not have the gentile dog nipping at our heels."

"Maybe the men you sent out will catch up with them tonight," Benjamin offered.

Joab grunted in disagreement. "I doubt it. They are not only bold, they are exceedingly fast."

~ ~ ~

Joab was correct. They were exceedingly fast. Before the sun was halfway into its journey in the sky, the *banditti* were in the city of Dan. They would have traveled even farther, but their leader, bleeding profusely from an arrow wound, had fainted from loss of blood.

Beor, his second-in-command, leaned over him in concern. "Rezon, what would you have us do?"

Rezon, his head swimming, answered in as strong a voice as he could muster. "We can't stay in Dan. The cursed Hebrews might send a troop after us. We head for the desert as soon as you get provisions." But after delivering this forceful order, the young leader lapsed into unconsciousness once more.

Beor shook his head as he looked up at the other rebels. "If we take him with us, he will die. There is a healer of some note in this town. Let's leave him in her care for the time being."

"He will be furious with us when he wakes," one of the younger men told Beor.

Beor nodded. "I know. I know. But better furious than dead."

~ ~ ~

For all those left in Eliada's household, the time crept by interminably. Ailea found herself spending more and more time with her mother and their patient. Nariah had asked her help in keeping the invalid as inactive as possible. He was still very weak from his wound although he would never admit it.

Ailea spent the hours teaching Isaac to play chess, a game her people had played for hundreds of years but which Isaac had never seen. He quickly caught onto the game of strategy, however. He was rather in awe of Ailea's beauty and often tongue-tied in her presence, so he seemed to appreciate the opportunity to cover his embarrassment by concentrating on the moves he must make.

Isaac also took charge of the two other recruits who were left to guard the household. He sent them out for daily forays to find out how the battle went. It was very awkward for him, wishing to receive word of an Israelite victory when he knew his hostesses were hoping to hear the opposite.

Ailea sensed his concern and was grateful for it. Isaac was truly thoughtful, completely different from that self-important, swaggering captain. She hoped she never had to see the man again, but then, that would probably mean he would have been killed in battle. No matter how infuriated Jonathan made her, she couldn't wish him dead. But the waiting was excruciating. Although Isaac sent his men out for word each day, she took the extra step of sending Malik into the city to find out what he could. Finally, they began to hear reports that the battle had once again gone in favor of the Hebrews.

When Malik entered the garden, Ailea and Nariah were pulling weeds around the saffron plants in an attempt to keep their minds off the disturbing news that had been filtering back to the city over the past three days. Hearing the old steward's footsteps, they glanced up. The look on his face confirmed their worst fears.

"What—?" Ailea managed to gasp out.

"I'm sorry." Malik swallowed hard, then reached out for the women, gathering them close. "I'm so sorry, my lady." He spoke to Nariah as a mother would comfort her child. "A captain in the general's brigade has just returned from the battlefield. He was with my master, Eliada, during the battle. Your husband fought bravely and slew many Israelites, but he was cut off from his men and fell late in the battle. They were unable to—to recover his body."

When neither Nariah nor Ailea moved or spoke, Malik made the mistake of releasing them and stepping back a bit to gaze into their faces. Immediately Nariah grew limp and crumpled toward the ground. Malik caught her in time, lifting her easily in his arms. Looking to the young mistress, he saw just what he had expected to see. Although she was reeling with shock, her face pale, she took a deep breath, lifted her little chin, and took charge.

"Take her to her room, Malik," Ailea instructed, surprised to hear the steadiness in her voice. She felt strangely numb, disembodied, as if she were somewhere else, hearing herself give orders. Then a terrifying thought struck her. "Rezon! Is there word of him? He wasn't—isn't—?"

"No, child. There is no word of him. I talked to a soldier who saw him alive late in the battle. I also heard—" Malik stooped to lay the unconscious Nariah on her bed. After doing so, he glanced anxiously at his mistress, then continued to address Ailea, keeping his voice low. "I heard one of the officers say that Shobach is furious with your brother. He claims that Rezon is a coward who deserted his post. The general is threatening to execute him if he gets the chance.

"One of the warriors who was near Rezon in the battle says

that is not true. Your brother fought bravely, but when Shobach ordered him to take a questionable position—one that would have meant the capture or death of his regiment—Rezon refused to follow orders and disappeared, taking most of his men with him. He hasn't been seen since, but I believe he still lives. What should we tell my lady when she wakes?"

Ailea thought for a moment. "We shall tell her that my brother is alive, but we mustn't tell her the whole story." She straightened her slim shoulders, as if accepting the full burden of the responsibility that was now hers to bear. "I will speak with her when she wakes. Go now and get some rest. I will take care of everything."

The next day passed in a blur to Ailea. As word spread that the general had been slain in battle, many people came to offer condolences. Nariah, seated in the open courtyard, greeted them for a while. But then she excused herself, saying she needed to rest.

Ailea understood her mother's desire to be alone. She felt the same need. Even after all the visitors were gone, Malik and Isaac hovered around her, urging her to eat, making idle conversation, anything to fill in the awful void. But nothing could fill it. Ailea's father, and perhaps her brother, were dead. She told them she needed rest and headed for her chamber.

On the way, she stopped at her parents' room. Her mother was staring out her chamber window. "Would you like me to sit with you?" Ailea asked.

Slowly Nariah turned to her daughter. Her eyes looked glazed. "No," she said after a long moment. "I wish to be alone now. Don't worry about me, child. I will be well." After kissing her mother, Ailea reluctantly withdrew.

~ ~ ~

Although a dozen candles gave off light in the chamber, their smoke, added to the heavy pall of burning incense, made the atmosphere dark and oppressive. Nariah knelt before a large image of Nergal. As soon as Jonathan left the house, she had removed the idol from a chest in the corner of her room. It was a bronze statue, overlaid with gold, used only for special occasions because of its value and size—more than two feet tall.

Now she chanted, over and over again, as she had for hours, "Come to me, O Nergal, lord of the underworld. Show me what I must do. You have power over the dead. Lead me to Eliada."

Nariah stumbled to her feet. Lack of food and sleep had reduced her to a trance-like state that caused her to sway when she walked. She reached with unsteady hands for a covered basket that had been placed beside the effigy of Nergal; then she turned and made her way to her bed. Dropping her outer robe to the floor, she sat on the edge of the bed with the basket balanced across her knees. Slowly, she lowered herself backwards across the bed, removed the lid from the basket, and turned it upside down. The contents—several large scorpions—spilled onto her chest, their deadly tails whipping viciously in protest of this unceremonious disturbance.

Nariah did not even flinch at the painful stings. She closed her eyes with an anticipatory smile. Surely, this night, she would be reunited with her beloved husband.

~ ~ ~

Ailea woke before dawn, strangely troubled. She lay still, wondering what had disturbed her sleep. All was quiet. Unnaturally quiet. She felt an urgent sense of foreboding. Rising, she wrapped herself in a robe and made her way to her parents' chamber. At the door, she coughed at the cloying smell of incense, straining to make out her mother's still form through the haze.

"Mother?" she called out as she approached the bed. But Nariah did not move. Ailea's heart began to pound as she called softly once again, "Mother?"

At that moment, Ailea caught sight of a slight movement. Her spirits lifted, then sank in despair as the veil of smoke cleared momentarily, just long enough for her to recognize the writhing creatures that covered Nariah's heart. Scorpions! The largest she had ever seen!

Ailea grabbed the basket lid that lay at her mother's side, using it to beat at the ugly creatures. Even as she shouted for Malik at the top of her voice, Ailea knew from the glazed, half-open eyes that stared into nothingness that her mother was beyond any earthly help.

Chapter Seven

Upon his return to Damascus, Jonathan found himself thinking constantly of Ailea. He had intended to take her the news of her father's death personally, but his military duties intruded. His men were kept busy cataloguing the spoils captured in the battle as well as artifacts taken from the temple of Rimmon and wealthy homes throughout the city.

He must oversee this work as there was only a short time to gather the treasures, arrange for their display in carts and wagons, and plan the great processional that would wind its way southward—through the cities of Kedesh, Hazor, Jezreel, Tirzah, Bethel, Raman, and finally, Jerusalem itself.

It was an enormous undertaking which really did take up most of his time, but he was secretly relieved to have an excuse to avoid seeing Ailea. He had been shocked and saddened when Benjamin had informed him of Nariah's suicide. He remembered well how he had felt when his own mother had been taken by a sudden fever. He was just thirteen.

Shageh, sunk in his own grief, had been little comfort to his son, and a few months later Jonathan had joined David, hoping to assuage his grief by raiding and fighting. He could not help but feel sorry for the girl who had lost her entire family in so short a time, but he had no idea how to express such an emotion as sympathy and knew that Ailea would reject it anyway. Consequently, he seldom saw Ailea, and when he did, their meetings were anything but pleasant.

The girl hated him even more since her father's death and her mother's suicide, and she made no effort to hide her hostility. Otherwise, she appeared perfectly composed. Isaac, his young face etched with concern, had told him that she had not yet shed a tear. Quite unnatural, Jonathan thought.

In Israel it would be considered an insult if family members did not weep and wail loudly for their deceased loved ones. In fact, professional mourners were sometimes hired by the wealthy to add their cries to those of the mourners in order to show respect for the dead. Jonathan was familiar enough with the Aramean culture to realize that, in general, the same customs prevailed here.

Still, he knew Ailea meant no disrespect. It seemed rather that she feared losing control of her fragile emotions. He could only rely on reports from Isaac as to her true state of mind. Ailea seemed not to hold the armor-bearer in the same disdain that she held Jonathan and his other men. Jonathan suppressed a twinge of resentment when he saw the two young people, their heads bent companionably over the chessboard.

As a means of personally gauging her mood, Jonathan urged her to share meals with him whenever he could arrange to return to Eliada's house. But she remained sullen and uncommunicative. Only when he told her that he was trying to learn what had happened to her brother did she behave in a civil manner toward him. Even then, when he asked her the names of Rezon's friends, she refused to reveal their identity. The girl's behavior was baffling and utterly unpredictable! Maddening!

"Ailea," he informed her one evening over dinner, "I do not care one way or another what has happened to your brother. I assume he is still an enemy of Israel if he is alive. But I had great respect for your mother, and for her sake, I am looking for

Rezon so he may be told of your parents' deaths and so I can convince him to return to look after you."

"My brother will not return to Damascus until he has successfully overthrown Hebrew rule!" said Ailea with a toss of her head.

"Be that as it may, your brother is responsible for you. I owe it to your mother to see that you are reunited with him if at all possible."

Jonathan couldn't help but remember the battle-cry shouted by the leader of the night raiders who had attacked the Israelite camp. He wondered if Rezon could be the man.

~ ~ ~

Before Jonathan could do more than make a few inquiries about Rezon, a visit from Joab changed everything he had in mind concerning Ailea.

Jonathan had just told Isaac he would be allowed to attend him today as he went about his duties. Hearing voices in the courtyard, he went to investigate. Joab stood with four of his men, questioning Benjamin. The commander stood straight and stiff as a lance. His features were that of a bird of prey—a curved beak of a nose and hooded, obsidian eyes that seemed to miss nothing.

He turned those eyes on Jonathan at his approach. "You allowed Eliada's widow, a valued captive, to die?" There was no mistaking the accusatory tone.

Jonathan answered defensively, "She was driven mad by grief and killed herself before I returned from our last engagement. Nevertheless, sir, I accept responsibility for the loss of the prisoner."

Joab gave a snort that conveyed his disdain. "And there is only one member of the general's family left?"

"Aside from a son who has been missing since the battle and is presumed dead, there is only the younger child, a daughter—Ailea."

Joab's eyes narrowed. "Could this son of Eliada be a fugitive? What is his name and where was he last seen?"

Jonathan thought quickly. If Joab were to learn that he had gone to the trouble of investigating Rezon's disappearance, he might suspect Jonathan's interest in Eliada's family—his daughter, in particular. In his quest for power, the commander might even remove Jonathan from the area where he could no longer supervise the girl. And if the general suspected that Rezon was possibly their midnight raider, he would surely treat Ailea with great cruelty.

So he answered as vaguely as possible. "I have heard that his name is Rezon and that he reorganized troops here in Damascus after the initial battle. His present whereabouts are not known, although he was not seen near his father at the time of Eliada's death."

Joab stared for a long moment at Jonathan, purposefully combing his fingers through his thick, short beard. "I would see the girl."

"She is mourning the death of her parents, my lord." Jonathan held little hope that this would dissuade Joab. The man had not an ounce of compassion in his body.

"So? That is of no importance to me. Bring her here immediately."

Jonathan motioned for Benjamin to carry out the brusque command. When Benjamin came back with the girl, Jonathan groaned inwardly. Her hair was unbound, flowing down to her hips. And instead of lowering those exceptional green eyes, she met Joab's questioning stare with defiance. When another long moment passed and Ailea still held his gaze, Joab laughed mirthlessly. He admires her courage, Jonathan thought.

"Come here, girl," the commander ordered.

When Ailea remained rooted to the spot, the general reached her in two long strides. He thrust out his hand and grabbed her by the throat, exerting enough pressure to lift her to her toes. "Never defy me, girl. Do you understand?" His grip tightened until Ailea's face turned red.

She reached up to pry at his hands but with no effect.

"Understand?" he asked again.

This time she managed a slight nod. He released her and made a circular motion with his hand. "Turn."

She turned slowly. He tilted her chin again, studying the fine features, then turned to Jonathan. "Unusual eyes, regal bearing. Although she's not of royal blood, she will make a fine addition to the king's harem. If he doesn't want her, she can be used for political gain—maybe given to one of the desert chieftains."

Addressing Jonathan as he was, Joab failed to see Ailea's reaction to his comments. But Jonathan took in the stiffening stance, the green eyes shooting fire. He only hoped she was wise enough to keep silent.

The general continued. "I'm not pleased that only this one girl remains of Eliada's household. Take care that nothing happens to her. She will be presented in Jerusalem as a trophy of war. The processional will leave Damascus within the week. You will escort her on the way."

~ ~ ~

For the next two days, Ailea avoided Jonathan. She couldn't bear to meet the mockery in his eyes over her humiliating interview with the general. When she finally decided that it was cowardly to hide in her room, she dressed carefully in one of her finest tunics and went to see what havoc the Hebrew was wreaking in her home now.

In the courtyard she found Jonathan and Malik speaking with a man who appeared to be of the wealthy merchant class. His mantle was colorful and the girdle at his waist was ornamented with garnets and lapis lazuli.

Malik spotted her first and pleaded with his eyes not to make a scene.

She glided forward, head high. "Welcome to my home," she

greeted the newcomer with ill-concealed disdain. "I hope my steward has seen to your needs and offered food and drink. What else may we do for you?"

The man shifted uncomfortably and turned to Jonathan with a shrug.

"Eli is a silversmith," Jonathan explained. "He has not been in Damascus long and has been a guest in the home of a friend while he establishes his trade here. As he will soon be married, he needs to purchase a home for his bride." Seeing the disbelief on Ailea's face, he rushed on. "Eli heard that your father's house will be sold since you—as you know—are to be taken to Jerusalem and are the only member of your family remaining."

"But Rezon—"

"Has disappeared and will likely never return to Damascus," Jonathan finished. "Even if he did, you realize that this property is forfeited to the king."

His heart plummeted at the array of expressions that tracked across her face—surprise, dismay, and finally fury. Trembling, she opened her mouth as if to flay him with her tongue, then snapped it shut, turned on her heels, and marched toward her room. He knew that the time had come to confront Ailea, to persuade her to accept reality. The life she had known here was over. It was time to put it behind her and face the future, whatever that may be.

~ ~ ~

In her room that night, Ailea lay upon her bed, focusing on every degrading and insulting thing that had been done to her since the enemy had invaded her home. That horrible general and his decision to display her as some war trophy! And the obsequious merchant who wanted to take over her home!

Life in Damascus had hardly changed at all since the Hebrew invasion. Some of its wealth had been plundered, of course, but for the most part the city was left intact, to continue in its prosperity and provide tribute for Israel's revenue. Very few hostages were to be taken back to Jerusalem. Why did she have to be one of them? Why couldn't they leave her alone? Hadn't they taken enough from her?

She hugged her resentment and rage to her, letting it all center on Jonathan, ignoring the small voice that told her that he really wasn't personally responsible for all that had befallen her. If she let her hatred for him fill her mind, then there would be no room for the grief, for the fear of what lay ahead.

Ailea finally fell into a fitful sleep. She was all alone in a desolate place. She had to go home, had to find her family, but as far as she could see, there was nothing. She walked for a long time, calling for Nariah and Eliada and Rezon. Then she saw something in the distance. A monolith—a great stone mountain. Ailea knew instinctively that if she could only reach that mountain, she would be at peace and she would no longer be alone. But she sensed just as instinctively that something was following her—something menacing. In her dream she began to run as fast as she could toward the sheltering rock. She ran faster and faster, but behind her whatever it was never lagged. She woke with a cry, her heart pounding.

Later that morning, after Malik had met with Ailea concerning the household, he lingered to tell her of a talk he had had with Jonathan the night before.

"The captain very kindly talked with the silversmith, Eli, who is willing to keep all the servants, even Shua and me." He smiled as he said this, which infuriated Ailea. Malik was her servant, and the Hebrew was even taking him away from her.

"I had thought to take you and Shua with me to Jerusalem, Malik."

"And I had thought to accompany you, Cricket. But the captain says it will not be possible. It is to be a military convoy, and only the, uh, prisoners will be accommodated. Besides, the captain is concerned that Shua is too old to make such a journey. He says. . . ."

Ailea turned away from her beloved servant. "Oh, go away, Malik. I tire of hearing you constantly prattle on about the captain!"

~ ~ ~

The next evening, Jonathan returned very late to Eliada's house after working long hours in preparation for the triumphal march. He told Benjamin not to wake him early. He planned to be well-rested when he met with Ailea. He had given her time to lick her wounds after discovering that her home was being sold, but it was past time to talk with her. She would not easily accept her fate. He must warn her that if she caused trouble and Joab heard of it, Jonathan might not be able to protect her from the general's wrath.

He also intended to tell her that the king was a kind and just man who could be persuaded to remand her to her brother's care, once he could be found. But Jonathan would wait for the most opportune moment to reveal to Ailea the evidence that Rezon was alive and now a desert raider. The sister, Jonathan knew, was as much a rebel at heart as the brother and would not hesitate to join him.

Furthermore, Jonathan suspected that Rezon was more concerned with making war on his enemies than with the fate of his orphaned sister. No, he would first track the young man down for himself and make it clear that he must give up his futile resistance and return to Damascus and assume his rightful duty as head of the household. In the meantime, Jonathan would continue to take responsibility for Ailea.

~ ~ ~

It was midmorning by the time Jonathan had dressed and was ready to leave his chamber. There was a discreet knock on the door. When he reached to open it, he found Malik standing before him, panting as if he had been running.

"Malik, my good man. What is the trouble?"

"She is gone, my lord. I have looked everywhere and cannot find her!"

"Ailea? When did you see her last?"

Malik became even more agitated. "As the sun was setting last evening, my lord. She has not been resting well and retired early.

"When Shua looked into her room this morning, it appeared that the young mistress was still sleeping. But when we checked on her a short time ago, we discovered only a mound of pillows under the covers." Malik wrung his hands, near hysteria. "We have searched the house and streets close by, but I believe she left the city many hours ago, my lord. I beg you to go after her! Something terrible could happen. I am sure she goes to find her brother."

Jonathan was already striding down the corridor in search of Isaac and Benjamin, the distraught servant trailing behind, when he replied, "Don't worry, Malik. I will find her. And when I do, she won't be running off again!"

~ ~ ~

Ailea wiped the sweat off her brow for the hundredth time. She was mounted on the sorriest excuse for a camel she had ever seen. But the beast had been all she could get in exchange for the small necklace she had used to barter for him. By the time she had dared slip out of her house, it was getting late, and she had been fortunate to find a camel driver who would deal with her, a woman.

For the past hour, she had been traveling due west, in the direction of the great number of vultures she had seen circling overhead. Other than the birds, she had seen nothing, either human or animal. She sniffed as she detected a stench in the air. Only about a half-mile away, on the other side of some low-lying sand dunes, she knew she would find the abandoned battlefield. She braced herself for the sight she was sure to encounter and urged her foul-tempered mount forward.

As she looked down upon the carnage a few moments later, her senses reeled at the sight of the great birds feasting on the corpses and the stench of rotting flesh.

How many men lay dead before her? Hundreds? No—thousands! She had some notion that if Rezon were alive, he might still be found not too far from the battlefield. She now realized that no one in his right mind would remain anywhere in the vicinity of this gruesome place. She would turn south in her search.

But first, something compelled her to look among the dead for signs of her father or her brother with the thought of burying them with some dignity should she find them. She owed her mother that at least.

Ailea urged the camel forward, but the stubborn beast balked. "I really don't blame you," she murmured, dismounting and tying the camel to a sturdy bush growing nearby.

Unwinding the long scarf she had worn over her head and now wrapped around her face to cover her nose, she hesitantly moved forward. She had to force herself to examine the bodies for some identifying feature. The dead, many dismembered or decapitated, were spread out as far as the eye could see. A week in the desert sun had left the remains so bloated and burned that she suddenly realized that it would be impossible to identify Eliada and Rezon, even if she came across their remains.

The bodies had been divested of all valuables. Obviously robbers had found the site, plundering what little the Hebrews had left behind. Other corpses had been stripped completely—a shocking sight. She prayed to her mother's gods that she would not find her father or her brother here.

Her stomach heaved, and she vomited. She had to leave this place of death before she went mad. If her father or brother were here, she never wanted to know.

As she turned back, she felt something strike her head. She

looked up as a large vulture swooped away. Ailea screamed and began to run back toward the rise where the camel was tethered. When she reached the place, she found that the animal had disappeared, taking her supply of water and her cloak with him! Only a bit of rope dangled from the large bush where she had tied him.

Turning in all directions, Ailea saw nothing but a searing sandscape. The sun beat down upon her mercilessly. I will die here, she thought as she stumbled from the grisly battlefield. I will die and the house of Eliada will be no more. Maybe it was fitting that she join the other members of her family in death.

Hours went by, and she wandered aimlessly, her feet burning from the sand, her forearms cooked by the sun. When she spotted a small outcropping of rock, she almost sobbed in relief and ran with the last of her strength for its shelter. At least she could die in the scant shade of the rocks, she thought. Her brain felt as if it were melting under the turban she had made of her scarf, the end of which she used to protect her face.

She curled up in the narrow shadow provided by the overhang of the rocks, realizing that as the sun moved farther west in the sky, she would once more be exposed. When that happened, she would surely die.

It seemed an eternity that she lay there, her tongue swollen in her mouth, her skin red and blistering, her mind wandering back to childhood and the wonderful pool of cool water in the courtyard. Then images from the battlefield appeared in her fevered brain, and she saw the vultures plucking at the eyes of the dead. She flung an arm over her face. "Please, no, don't let them be plucked out." It was her last thought before she lost consciousness.

Chapter Eight

It was late in the day before Jonathan left Damascus in his search for Ailea. He had combed the streets frantically all day before he at last found the camel driver who had traded with her. He had also come across a small detail of Hebrew soldiers who had seen a small figure mounted on a camel headed west into the desert—they had believed it to be a boy.

Jonathan wondered where Ailea would think to look for her brother, discounting the battlefield at first. Why would she visit the grisly scene more than a week after the battle? But since that was the last place Rezon had been seen, Jonathan knew he must look there. He turned his borrowed camel toward the circling vultures.

She wasn't there, he discovered after riding through the carnage for an hour. At least she was not on foot, he consoled himself. As the sun began to set, he despaired of finding her until the next day.

Dismounting, he raised his hands toward heaven. "O, King of the universe, Lord of Hosts, help me to find this lost child. She is not under Your covenant, but You are a merciful God. Show to her Your loving kindness."

When he finished his prayer, Jonathan felt a sense of peace.

But knowing that it would be futile to keep searching on this moonless night, he unfolded a blanket beside the camel and settled himself down for the night. In the meantime, he would simply have to place Ailea in the hands of the Almighty.

~ ~ ~

Jonathan was already underway when the sun appeared, suddenly, as always in the desert, bringing the day forth headlong. Moving south, he scanned the barren landscape for any small clue that would reveal Ailea's path—a camel trail, a footprint, anything. For some time, he met with only heat, wind, and sand.

Then, just ahead, he saw what appeared to be a small outcropping of rock. Maybe Ailea had stopped there to rest before moving on. As he neared the site, he saw no camel and almost turned back toward Damascus. But something prompted him to look more closely.

He leaped from the camel when he saw a dainty foot sticking out from beneath the rock. Ailea! He rushed to the prone figure and gently turned her over. She was badly burned from her long exposure to the sun, her breathing rapid and shallow.

"Ailea! Ailea! Do you hear me? You are safe now."

Jonathan took no comfort from his own words as he poured a skin of water over her arms and feet, where huge blisters had formed. He winced when he saw that even the soles of her feet had been burned, her worn sandals lying in tatters beside her. Apparently her mount had escaped, leaving her alone and helpless.

Unwelcome memories of the men he had seen die in the desert after being separated from their unit came to mind. And these were hardened soldiers. What chance of survival did such a fragile girl have? He tried again to cool her body, dribbling water from his pouch, drop by drop, into the mouth of the unconscious girl, then stroking her throat to coax her to swallow. But she was limp and unresponsive.

If he didn't find help soon, she would die. He took off his head covering and soaked it with water, then wrapped Ailea's head in it. He knew that cooling the head cooled the body faster than anything else. He also poured the water over the rest of her body. It dried almost instantly, as if he had poured it onto the sand. He picked her up and mounted his camel with her in his arms.

Just as Jonathan started back for Damascus, he saw Benjamin, mounted on a mule and riding hard, the desert dust swirling in his wake.

"The Lord be praised! You have found the girl!" cried Benjamin when he came abreast of his captain mounted on his camel, holding the unconscious Ailea. "Joab has been looking for you. I made excuses, put him off, but he was suspicious. Asked where the girl was. I told him she was with you. He sent me to order you to join the procession immediately. They departed Damascus before dawn."

"The girl needs help, Benjamin." Jonathan frowned, squinting into the sun. "Go to the city of Dan. From there it will be easier to join the others. Find a healer who can treat the girl. Be ready for us when we arrive. You and I will join the march as soon as possible. Go . . . quickly!"

Benjamin nodded. "Isaac is only a short distance behind me. I'll take him with me." He glanced at Ailea's still form, wrapped in Jonathan's cloak. "That girl is more trouble than she's worth, Jonathan. I hope you know it." Not waiting for a reply, he wheeled the mule around hard and hurried back across the desert.

~ ~ ~

At Dan, Jonathan found Isaac in the marketplace at the center of the town. "Benjamin went on ahead to join the procession, thinking he might need to soothe Joab's anger if he discovers you still missing," the young man told him.

"Were you able to find a nurse and a place where Ailea can rest?"

For a moment Isaac did not reply, his wide eyes fastened on the bundle cradled in Jonathan's arms. Then, clearing his throat, he croaked triumphantly, "Yes, my lord, I found an old woman who is skilled in the healing arts. Everyone comes to her from miles around to be treated. She lives at the edge of town with her widowed daughter. At first they refused me because they are already caring for a sick man in their home."

Isaac looked again at the small figure, then sensing Jonathan's impatience, rushed on. "But I finally persuaded . . . Jerioth—that's her name—that the girl would surely die without her care. She, in turn, convinced her daughter, Abishag."

"Quickly then, show me the way!"

Isaac, who was again trying to get a glimpse of Ailea, hesitated. "Sir? Oh, yes," he began, flustered, "the old one awaits us at her daughter's house. If Ailea is too ill to travel, we are invited to stay there until she is better. How is she, my lord?"

"Her condition is grave. Now, no more delays. We must get her out of this sun and into the hands of the healer."

Isaac led the way to a rather humble house at the edge of town. Although lacking in luxuries, the place was immaculate, its dirt floor swept and strewn with clean straw. The older woman waited for them inside.

Jonathan was immediately drawn to Jerioth. Unlike her daughter, she seemed not the least impressed or intimidated by the powerful warrior who had to stoop to enter the door. In fact, she almost ignored him completely as she fussed over her new charge.

"It would be better to wait a few days before moving her," she told him, after assessing Ailea's condition.

"Impossible. We must leave as soon as you have seen to her burns."

Jerioth gave him a disapproving look. "If you insist, my lord. I will give her water and treat her burns. If my ministrations cause pain, I can give her something to keep her from waking. But I think we need to worry more if she will ever wake at all. Some don't, you know."

"She will wake," Jonathan stated emphatically. "And as soon as she does, we will be on our way."

"Then I will treat her burns, and we can be off to wherever it is you're headed in such a hurry just as long as I eventually end up in Judah." She stood for a moment, waiting for him to object. When he did not, she left the room, grumbling about the foolishness of men.

Jonathan and Isaac left Ailea in the care of the women and went to purchase an ox and rough cart as well as a pack donkey. They lined the cart with straw and hitched it to the ox, tying the small donkey behind the cart. Then they returned to the healer.

Jonathan was eager to leave immediately, but Jerioth convinced him that Ailea would not survive the journey in the scorching sun.

"I will wait until sunset," he agreed, "but not a moment longer. Now where have you taken her?"

The two men followed the old woman into the chamber where Ailea lay. They stood by as she punctured the large blisters that covered the girl's arms. Ailea jerked occasionally, but remained unconscious.

"'Tis a blessing her face escaped the burns. She probably would have died if her head had been exposed to the desert heat." Jerioth continued to work as she talked, wrapping Ailea's arms in cloths soaked in herbs.

"Where she fell, a boulder shielded her face," Jonathan explained.

"It was the Lord's own mercy that saved her," Jerioth insisted. She punctured a large blister on the back of Ailea's hand. Isaac drew in a pained breath and left the room quickly. Jonathan felt like following but merely turned his head away.

~ ~ ~

They were not able to make the journey that day for Ailea's condition worsened. Jerioth told them, her brown eyes dark with sympathy and sorrow, that the girl might well die that night. Ailea's face was deathly pale—a strange sight in contrast to her reddened limbs. Her pulse was faint, so faint that when Jonathan tested it, the slight flutter was like that of a butterfly's wing.

Jerioth shook her head, laying aside the cooling cloths and herbs she had used as a poultice. "I have done everything I know to do," she said sadly. "Now she is in the hands of the Almighty."

"She will not die!" Jonathan insisted fiercely. But Jerioth just shook her head.

Isaac started from his place of vigil as a low moan sounded from another part of the house. Jerioth rose and turned to leave the room.

"Where are you going?" Jonathan demanded.

"The young man I have been tending is still very ill with a fever. I must go to him. Abishag will need me. Besides, there is nothing more to be done for the girl."

"Who is this man?"

"I do not know his name. Only that two friends brought him here with a festering wound. They told me nothing more."

When a louder groan reached them, Jerioth hurried off.

Jonathan followed her to the door, peering into the darkened chamber. The young man's face was turned away at first. Jonathan could only make out the outlines of his slim body beneath the blanket. For a moment he lay motionless; then he began to shake under the blanket, his head rolling from side to side as successive chills seized him. In the shadows Jonathan could only make out a mass of dark, dampened hair on the pillow. Something tugged at the back of Jonathan's mind but a whimper from Ailea ended his observations, and he returned quickly to her side. She was obviously dreaming. She whispered something, and Jonathan bent his ear to her lips to hear what she said.

"Rezon, Rezon," she called for her brother.

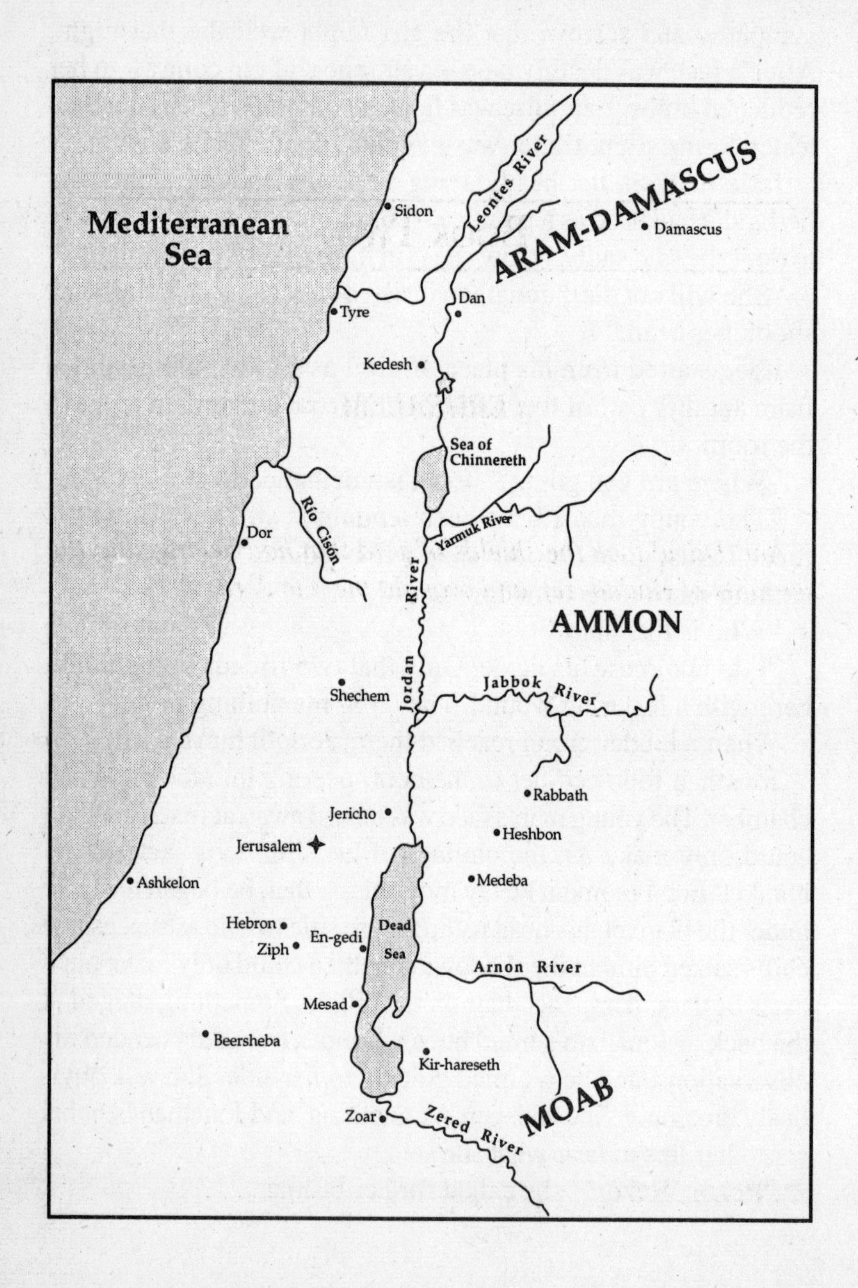
Mediterranean Sea
ARAM-DAMASCUS
Leontes River
Sidon
Damascus
Tyre
Dan
Kedesh
Sea of Chinnereth
Yarmuk River
Río Cisón
Dor
Jordan River
AMMON
Shechem
Jabbok River
Rabbath
Jericho
Heshbon
Jerusalem
Ashkelon
Medeba
Hebron
Ziph
En-gedi
Dead Sea
Arnon River
Mesad
Beersheba
Kir-hareseth
Zoar
Zered River
MOAB

Book Two

Jerusalem

And David took the shields of gold that had belonged to the servants of Hadadezer, and brought them to Jerusalem.

2 Samuel 8:7

Chapter Nine

The columns that made up the triumphal procession were already making camp for the evening when Jonathan's group caught up with them. They were spread out across the Transjordan plain some fifteen miles due south of Mount Hermon. Warriors moved briskly about setting up field tents and placing their cooking utensils and camp stools before them. There was no sign of Joab.

Jonathan maneuvered the cart bearing Ailea and Jerioth into position in the leading phalanx of the caravan, which was already arranged in order for its entry into Jerusalem. The treasure from the temple of Rimmon, lined up on flatbed wagons for all to see, was first in the order, followed by carts loaded with the gold shields and helmets taken from Zobah's army with the less impressive booty further back in the line. Fortunately, the commotion of unhitching the draft animals and setting up tents for the night caused their arrival to go unnoticed.

Jonathan was reluctant to leave Ailea, but he knew he would be expected to report to David's tent in the center of the camp where all the members of the gibborim gathered when on campaign with the king. He would do so just as soon as he helped Isaac set up their own tent.

Ailea was still unconscious when Jonathan removed her from the litter to the relative comfort of his spacious tent. She had awakened several times as they traveled but only briefly. His heart was touched again by the fragility of her small frame and the ravages that the sun had wrought on her arms and feet. She cried out as her arm brushed across the bedding when he placed her on the rough sleeping mat. But she did not awaken.

"I think she will need another potion soon," he whispered to Jerioth, who stood nearby. "Please keep her comfortable; I regret having to leave you to care for her alone."

The old woman had agreed to travel with them as far as Hebron where she would visit in the home of her son before returning to Dan. The decision had been made after Ailea had begun to rally a bit and when it was clear that Abishag could take over the care of the other patient in their home.

"Don't fret about the child," the healer said. "I will give her wine steeped in poppy leaves and bathe her arms and face with balm. Then I will wrap her poor feet in cloths soaked in aloe. She will not wake until morning, my lord. Go, and take your ease with the king."

Jonathan was not convinced. "Should I leave Isaac to help you?" He felt obligated to ask although he preferred not to leave the lad behind. Isaac was apt to grow even more attached to the little rebel. Once she recovered, she would be sure to attempt to involve him in her schemes, and Isaac could be hurt by her intrigues. Jonathan was thankful when Jerioth assured him that the youth would only be in the way. In addition, Isaac was too excited by the prospect of spending the evening in the presence of the king to insist on staying with the sick girl.

When Jonathan and Isaac approached the king's opulent tent, they found the men gathered outside in order to take advantage of the cool evening air. The gibborim were present, as were the king's advisors. Many sat on camp stools. Others sprawled about on the ground. In the center of the group was David himself, playing his ten-stringed *kinnor* made of intricately carved lotus wood.

The two newcomers accepted cups of wine and thick slices of bread from one of the several servants who were weaving in and out among the guests. With both hands full, Jonathan and Isaac made their way forward until they were near the king. Jonathan was relieved that Joab was not at the David's side; the inevitable confrontation with him over Ailea would be postponed for awhile longer.

Laughter rang out as the men, still heady with victory, jested and boasted of their exploits in battle. One of the young armor-bearers leaned down and whispered in the king's ear. David laughed and set his harp aside. When the king stood, Jonathan was struck again by the physical perfection of the man called "David the Golden" by his people. The short auburn curls framing the sculptured face shone like burnished copper in the rays of the dying sun. The unusual color—as surely as his skill as a musician, warrior, and ruler—set David apart from other men. While Jonathan lamented his lord's weakness for women, he could understand it because David, with his unusual good looks and prowess in battle, had always been extremely attractive to women, even in the early days when he was a servant in Saul's court. They had even written songs in his honor.

When David disappeared into the tent, Isaac gave a sigh of disappointment. "I had so hoped the king would stay and—"

Just then David reappeared with a broad spear that resembled a beam. Its tip, honed to a fine point, was made of iron. David balanced it easily in one hand, although the bulge of his biceps revealed the weight of the weapon to be substantial. In his other hand he held a small goatskin bag.

Isaac saw the knowing smile that flitted across his captain's face.

"This is Goliath's spear, my lord?" exclaimed the other young armor-bearer.

The king nodded and smiled indulgently. He pointed out Goliath's name, clearly chiseled into the iron head, then handed the spear to the youngster.

Isaac forgot himself and pressed forward. "May I see it too?" The other lad allowed Isaac to examine, then hold the spear. David frowned when he noticed the bandage on Isaac's arm. "You were wounded in the fight, son?"

"Yes, my lord, in the first battle of the campaign." Isaac's face flushed a deep red as his voice cracked, and the last half of his short speech was pitched an octave higher than the first. But neither David nor the other warriors mocked him. Instead, they showed him the deference earned by one who had shed his blood on behalf of Yahweh and the chosen people.

Jonathan stepped forward then. "This is Ahiam's son Isaac, my armor-bearer, my lord. He saved my life at the risk of his own."

"Then you have truly done service to your king, lad, for Jonathan is a man I value highly, as does your father. What you have done will make him proud."

David clasped Jonathan to him in an embrace. "I seldom see you anymore, my friend, except in the war council," he remarked in an aside. "That is my loss. Stay at court awhile this time. Ziph will fare well enough in the hands of your honored father. And how is the Rab?"

"As stubborn and as proud as ever."

"What is in the bag?" Isaac asked, daring to interrupt the reunion between the two men.

"Just an old sling and four stones from a small brook in the valley of Elah." The king pulled one of the rounded stones from the pouch and fingered it.

"The sling and stones you used in your battle against the champion, Goliath," said the other youth, who was attending the king, launching into the familiar tale. "Your strategy was to use the sling against Goliath while still out of range of his spear. Surely even the giant Philistine couldn't throw a spear of this weight very far. And you chose several stones, knowing you could get in another shot if you missed."

"Ho, young pup! I cannot let you continue to embarrass

yourself before the king with your ignorance." One of David's battle-hardened officers clamped his hand on the armor-bearer's shoulder, but his laughter and twinkling eyes belied his fierce appearance. This was Abishai, Joab's brother, and one of the top three commanders in David's army. While he could seek revenge just as ruthlessly as his elder brother, Abishai had a sense of honor and an ability to enjoy life that made him far more appealing than Joab. Jonathan couldn't help liking the man.

Abishai continued to tease the lad. "First, son, you must understand that this," he hefted the heavy spear in one hand, "in the hands of Goliath, was not a short-range weapon. He certainly could have thrown it far enough to skewer our king that day although my uncle didn't make much of a target, scrawny lad that he was." This jibe elicited laughter from the older warriors, but the two armor-bearers glanced at their king first; then, seeing that he was amused, they joined in the laughter.

"You're probably right about that, nephew," David admitted grudgingly. "Truly I was too angry that day for strategy."

Abishai continued. "And you mustn't think that the king picked up five stones that day because he feared he would miss his first shot. Not at all!" He clapped a hand on the boy's shoulder and leaned down to speak confidentially. "It's true that everyone in Saul's army thought the Philistine was too big to hit. But our king knew he was too big to miss!"

A roar went up from the gathering.

Isaac couldn't know he was falling into Abishai's trap when he asked innocently, "Then why did he gather the other four stones, sir?"

"Well, son, Goliath had four brothers down in Gath almost as big, just as mean, and just as ugly. The four stones were for them, of course. Only when they saw how skilled my uncle was with that sling, they went into hiding and have never been heard from since!"

The seasoned warriors, seeing the gullible looks on the faces of Isaac and the other armor-bearer, burst into loud guffaws once again.

David merely shook his head. "I am sure if Elhanan were here, he would challenge that statement, Abishai. Have you forgotten that he slew Lahmi, Goliath's brother, not long after my encounter with the giant?" He turned to the boys, putting an arm around each of their shoulders. "You must learn to distinguish fact from legend, lads, else Abishai will never stop spinning his tales for you."

Isaac had removed the leather sling from the bag and now changed the subject to cover his embarrassment. "My lord, would you mind giving me a demonstration of your skill with the sling?" There was a general chorus of agreement.

David looked dubious. "It has been years . . . but very well. We shall have a small contest—you and I, lad." He turned to the other youth. "What is your name?"

"I am Haruz, sire."

The king was beginning to enjoy himself. "You will join in our contest. And you as well, nephew. You started this."

"And you wish to humiliate me in return. Very well, I am always willing to serve my king." Abishai proffered and made a low bow.

He helped the two young men set up small clay pots on the slope behind David's tent. The pots were arranged in three rows, the last of which was at the peak of the hill, so distant as to be barely visible. Each contestant was to attempt to break three of the dozen pots in each row.

Next, the lads took several minutes to gather smooth, round stones from the hillside to use in the sling. They were allowed to take their turns first, honored to be using the very sling their king had used against the Philistine champion when he was their age.

Isaac and Haruz both hit three pots set up in the nearest row. Isaac broke one in the next set. Haruz missed the more difficult target. Then Abishai took the sling from Haruz and tested it carefully before proceeding to take out all his targets on the first two rows. However, he connected with only one in the most distant row.

The warrior received the congratulations of the crowd of soldiers who had gathered to watch the sport; then he handed the leather sling to David.

"The light is truly dim now. You are at a disadvantage, my lord." Jonathan suspected that Abishai was giving the king a way to save face if necessary.

The king merely laughed and loaded the sling with one of the larger stones the boys had selected. He stepped back, sending the sling whirring around his head, then letting it fly. With deadly accuracy, it smashed the first pot. All the remaining targets on the first and second rows quickly followed.

A low murmur signaled the admiration of the onlookers.

In the gathering dusk, torches were lit and campfires set ablaze as David once again loaded the sling and aimed for the distant targets that were now almost impossible to make out. The sling whirred again and the sound of the distant breaking pot could be clearly heard. The men gave a loud shout.

When the king quickly dispatched the last two targets, pandemonium broke out, the men praising their leader with the familiar songs they had written about him, wine and laughter flowing freely.

David summoned the gibborim to retire with him into the comfort of his tent, and Jonathan sent Isaac back to their own campsite, instructing the boy to return for him if Ailea took a turn for the worse. His mind was still on the girl as he seated himself among the large, brilliantly hued cushions strewn atop the thick rugs that made up the floor of the king's pavilion.

Under the heady influence of victory and potent wine, the king was in a magnanimous mood. "Most of you have been with me since the beginning," David told the group. "The Lord of Hosts has given us victory over every enemy, and we have taken many spoils, yet you have demanded little for yourselves. Now it is time to reward your many years of service. Sheva!" He motioned to the richly-robed man who was his personal secretary and official recorder for the kingdom.

The man came forward, carrying a leather scroll, reed pens, and a cake of solid blank ink, made from a mixture of gum and soot. After adding water to liquefy the ink, he was ready to record whatever the king dictated.

"Sheva, each of my gibborim will come to you—tonight or in a matter of days. You are to record each man's request for his share of the booty from this campaign. No request is to be denied."

Shouts of protestation were heard immediately.

"My lord, it is reward enough to serve you."

"Sire, we already live more than comfortably because of your generosity."

"We would dedicate the spoils to Adonai as always."

David raised his hand to silence them. "It shall be as I have commanded. And don't think to ask for some mere trinket, any of you, else I will choose your rewards myself."

As the men expressed their gratitude to the king, a plan began to form in Jonathan's mind. Maybe there was a way to thwart Joab's plans for Ailea after all.

~ ~ ~

It was late when Jonathan made his way back to his tent. Isaac was keeping vigil. He rose to follow Jonathan inside. When Jonathan raised the goatskin flap, he saw that the interior was lit by a single burning candle. Jerioth raised a silencing finger to her lips as Jonathan and Isaac came near Ailea's pallet.

"She sleeps fitfully, my lord. She cries out with fear and pain."

"Then give her another potion," Jonathan commanded with a frown.

"I gave her enough steeped poppy to render a large man senseless. I fear to give her more, Master, at least not until daybreak, or she may never wake." Just then the girl whimpered and flailed out with her arms.

Jonathan dropped to his knees beside the pallet and took her small hands in his. "Shhh. You are safe now, Ailea. It will be all right. Rest now. Rest." He smoothed the hair back from her brow—tendrils that had escaped the thick coil Jerioth had braided. His words seemed to have a soothing effect for she quieted into a deeper slumber.

"Is there anything I can do?" Isaac turned a worried look on his master and the healer.

Jonathan dismissed him with a gesture. "Just get some sleep. It will be difficult tomorrow with the girl so ill. You had best wrap yourself in a blanket and sleep outside so you won't be disturbed by her cries."

"And you as well, my lord," Jerioth spoke up, moving forward to stand by the pallet. "I will sleep beside the child and look after her if she wakes."

Jonathan shook his head. "No. I will sleep in the corner there. You may need my help."

And, indeed, Jerioth did need his help. Ailea dreamed she was in her bed in Damascus. It was hot, so very hot. The house must be on fire. Mother and Father and Rezon—they were in danger! She must get them out, or they would burn to death. She struggled to sit up, but strong hands held her down. Someone wanted her to die and her family as well. She screamed and clawed at the restraining hands, but to no avail. She was roasting alive.

Chapter Ten

Ailea lay swathed in a cocoon of cool dressings. To her fevered mind, the fire was not so hot anymore although she pitched restlessly. From somewhere in the distance came the sound of low voices, edged with anxiety.

"Soak another blanket in water. The fever is still too high."

"Here, take this. I'll see to another right away."

Suddenly Ailea realized that she was trussed in some way, unable to move her arms or legs. She fought in panic until she heard a soothing voice. "Easy, little warrior. We've wrapped you in a blanket soaked in water to cool your fever. Here's Isaac with another. Jerioth, just help me unwrap her. Isaac, take this blanket and soak it again, just in case we need it. Now, Ailea, does this not feel better? Answer me, Ailea. Open your eyes. I know you can hear me."

Emerald eyes blinked open and gazed up at him. "Of course I can hear you," she replied in a weakly disgruntled voice. "Why are you shouting at me?"

Jonathan laughed in relief. "The little warrior is back with us, Jerioth."

"Put me down," Ailea demanded when she realized that she was cradled in Jonathan's strong arms.

Surprisingly he complied, laying her back on the pallet. She tried to free her arms from the tight coverings.

"Lie still," Jonathan commanded.

Too weak to resist, for once she obeyed.

~ ~ ~

On the morning of the triumphant processional into Jerusalem, Jonathan stood pondering the nasty confrontation with Joab the evening before concerning the girl and how she would enter the city. After ignoring them throughout the week-long march, Joab had come to Jonathan's tent at dusk, asking how the captive fared.

The report on her condition had led to Joab's insistence on assessing the damage for himself. And when he viewed the girl's burns from the fierce desert sun, his eyes flashed with anger. "You allowed the escape of one of their most valued captives. It is very fortunate for you that she has not ruined her face," he observed, forcing the words through his teeth with a hiss.

It wasn't that the commander had been unaware of the incident, Jonathan thought testily. After all, hadn't he personally sought out his superior officer the morning after the celebration with the king in his desert pavilion and told him everything that had happened? Jonathan had received the expected dressing-down at the time, and now he was prepared for another. He was not surprised when he got it.

"You're slipping, ben Shageh. First, you let the mother do away with herself; then you allow the daughter to escape. It is fortunate for you that you were able to recover her. I would have you remember she is the king's property, and you are accountable for her. On the morrow you will dress the girl in her finest raiment, and you will lead her into Jerusalem in chains."

Hearing this, Ailea, who was reclining on her pallet, as was necessary several times a day, gasped and raised herself on her elbows. "I'll not be led about like an animal!" she shouted.

The general, with no more effort or concern than he would use in swatting a pesky fly, struck Ailea a powerful blow to the side of her head. She fell back, moaning in pain.

Jonathan had stepped forward, his fists clenched. "As you reminded me, Joab, the girl is the king's prize. You wouldn't want to mar her beauty."

Joab had stared at Jonathan a long moment before speaking. "You seem inept at handling captives. Perhaps I should take the girl with me."

Jonathan shrugged. "Do what you think best. Perhaps she will be more docile under your care." He heard Ailea's gasp of outrage and knew she did not understand his apparent callousness towards her. It wouldn't do for the general to suspect her fear of him. It would only fuel his determination to snatch her from Jonathan's care.

Joab gave him a shrewd sidelong long. "No, I think I will allow you to pay for all your former mistakes by leading the girl into Jerusalem tomorrow yourself. Make sure you take a position where she can be seen. And, Jonathan, you may be sure that I will notice if my orders are not carried out precisely."

Jonathan stood for a few moments after the commander's departure, lost in his own sense of relief that the encounter had been better than expected. A whimper from Ailea brought him back to the present. He dropped to one knee beside her pallet and felt a lump above her ear where Joab had struck her. "Does it hurt badly?"

Ailea jerked away. "Don't touch me!"

"You must listen to me, little one. The general is a very cruel and dangerous man. It would be extremely foolish to disobey his orders." Jonathan rose and paced the tent, hands clasped behind his back. "You may feel unfortunate to be under my control, but believe me, if you fall into Joab's hands, you will experience misery the likes of which are beyond your worst dreams."

He waited for a response, but when there was none, he continued, "It will be as he said, and you must not resist." With that,

Jonathan left the tent, praying that his mulish charge would be more docile on the morrow.

~ ~ ~

Jerioth woke Ailea quite early, pressing on her a gourd of milk and a round of cheese to break her fast. While Ailea was leisurely eating, the old woman brought a basin and cloth for washing and admonished her for her dawdling. Jonathan wished her to be dressed and ready to leave very soon.

She motioned to a pile of clothing at the foot of her pallet which Ailea recognized as her best tunic and robe. Jonathan must have recovered her own things from the contraband taken from Damascus. In addition, there was a pair of boots made of soft brown calfskin to protect her damaged feet. When worn, they would expose only the tips of her toes, otherwise covering the entire foot to above the ankle. He'll expect me to be grateful, I suppose, Ailea thought grudgingly as she donned the garments.

Her father had brought the rich linen cloth home to her from one of his journeys. Suddenly Ailea was struck by such a surge of loss and grief that she had to fight back tears.

"Hurry, child. The captain says you must come at once. It is time for Isaac to strike the tent."

Ailea took a deep breath to regain her composure and went in search of Jonathan.

He was standing beside a pale gray donkey. The animal was bedecked with a silver bridle. A small intricately woven blanket covered its back. There was no evidence of the ox or cart. Had he traded them for this?

"Come, Ailea. It is time."

Ailea stubbornly ignored his command.

He snorted in disgust and strode over to her, leading the donkey. In his other hand was a shiny object which he placed over her head. It appeared to be a gold hoop—a kind of necklace. Ailea put her hand to the metal warmed by his hand.

"It was made for an Egyptian princess—my reward for riding through a troop of Philistines to bring warning of an attack to the king."

As he spoke Jonathan was attaching a long chain of gold to the hoop. He made a loop of it about her neck, then around her waist. Finally, he fastened it through the thick gold bangle she was wearing on one wrist and lifted Ailea onto the donkey's back. With approximately three feet of the beautifully wrought chain still remaining, Jonathan threaded the end through his own studded leather armband.

Ailea castigated herself for having stood spellbound while he had put her in chains—no matter that as he led her forward to their place in the caravan, he appeared to be more her slave than she his.

"I hardly think this is what your commander had in mind when he ordered you to bring me in chains to Jerusalem," she said in a petulant tone.

Jonathan looked up at her with a tilt of his lips. "I'm following his instructions—precisely."

~ ~ ~

The king's entourage would enter Jerusalem with much fanfare. The road that led to the gate of the city was lined with cheering citizens.

David sat astride one of the war horses captured from Hadadezer's army. This was the first time the people had seen their king return from a victory mounted on such a steed, and the people were impressed with the powerful image he presented.

Jonathan felt a twinge of concern. In the past, his leader had strictly followed the admonition of the Lord through the word of Samuel that the king was not to acquire horses and chariots lest he come to trust in these more than in Adonai. Thus, any horses captured from the enemy had been hamstrung, making them unfit for battle. But this time David had saved a hundred chariots and at least two hundred horses for his own stables.

This compromise of the former strict adherence to Yahweh's ordinance was disturbing. It struck Jonathan that somehow all the glory was not going to the Lord but to the king and his army. Still, just as always, the majority of the spoils would not go to David's personal wealth but would be dedicated to Adonai to be used for the great temple the king had planned to build. The prophet Nathan had told David that the Lord would not allow hands that had shed so much blood to build His temple but that David's son would do so. So David was busy gathering all the necessary items for its construction.

Jonathan, leading Ailea seated on the donkey, marched at a distance behind the king and his bodyguards. Despite her lowly mount, she held her head proudly. Noting the crimson flush staining her cheeks, he was glad he had made the necessary arrangements to reduce her humiliation as a captive. Many of his fellow officers had cast admiring glances at the girl and envious ones at Jonathan as he marched with the other gibborim in this honored position directly behind the king.

He good-naturedly extracted himself from the embrace of a pretty young woman who had thrown her arms around him and kissed his cheek soundly. This was a common occurrence along the parade route during a victory march. Jonathan kept pace, neither breaking rank nor succumbing to the flattering chants of praise coming from the crowd.

He glanced at Ailea. She returned his gaze with a glare, and he found himself hoping that the admiring throngs had stirred her jealousy, particularly his enthusiastic welcome by the attractive young woman.

As they neared Jerusalem, Joab left his position beside the king to inspect the line of marchers, riding a beautifully outfitted camel. When he came abreast of Jonathan and Ailea, he scowled down at them from the beast's back.

Jonathan gave him a smile that did not reach his eyes. "Your orders, General. 'Led into the city in chains.'" Joab grunted and rode on.

Ailea got her first glimpse of the king as he rode ahead of them. Although she could not view his face, she was impressed with his appearance. Thick auburn hair curled at the nape of his neck. He rode his horse well, too, his broad shoulders straining against the fabric of his simple garment. Ailea was surprised that he wore no royal robes. In fact, were it not for his regal bearing, there was nothing of ostentation or pomp to announce the coming of the king of Israel.

As they made their way along the Kidron Valley, she heard his fabled voice for the first time as he began a chant of praise to his God.

> The Lord is my rock and my fortress and my deliverer;
> The God of my strength, in whom I will trust;
> My shield and the horn of my salvation,
> My stronghold and my refuge;
> My Savior, You save me from violence.
> I will call upon the Lord, who is worthy to be praised;
> So shall I be saved from my enemies.

Ailea heard other voices join in the chant and looked to her right as they continued to wind upwards towards the city. At strategic intervals along the path and on the wall of the city, musicians stood—a large choir of singers, trumpeters, and others playing instruments. The music they made was much different from that of her people. It seemed to revolve around the praise of the invisible God the Hebrews worshipped.

Despite her determination not to soften toward these people, Ailea could not help but admire their versatile king.

"What beautiful music!" she told Jonathan, raising her voice to be heard above the singing.

Jonathan nodded and called back, "David wrote most of it

and organized the musicians as well. They perform at victory celebrations and in our worship."

The song swelled to a crescendo, and it was impossible to continue their conversation. Ailea listened and took in the sights as the processional swung to the right and entered the city at the southern gate. She could not help but notice Jonathan's rich baritone as he sang along with the others.

> The Lord lives!
> Blessed be my Rock!
> Let God be exalted, the Rock of my salvation!
> It is God who avenges me,
> And subdues the peoples under me;
> He delivers me from my enemies.

These words of victory in battle brought Ailea back to reality with a jolt. What was happening to her? How could she possibly admire the boasting of the very people who had killed her father and mother and possibly her brother? Her mouth tightened into a thin line. They might have taken her captive, but they would never win her over. This was the enemy, and she must think of a plan to return to her people and find Rezon.

After they passed through the city gate, the procession was almost swallowed up by the throng in the marketplace. Here was a city that nearly rivaled Damascus in its commerce.

Traders from many nations hawked their wares, and people from all walks of life mingled together. Israel's king had brought prosperity to his people. Was it any wonder they loved him?

The procession came to a halt in front of the king's palace, which, Ailea could see, was still very much a construction project in progress. Men climbed up and down on the scaffolding that surrounded a whole new wing of the structure. The multistoried building was made of marble, its massive double doors made of oak, and very impressive. She noticed no statuary in the courtyard but then remembered the injunction against images that Jonathan had insisted be obeyed when he had entered her home.

There would be no images of gods or goddesses in this palace. But she did note that the huge doors were carved with beautiful lilies and pomegranates. Ailea's agile mind turned to more practical matters, and she began taking in the details of the structure, the number of guards, and any other information that might be useful in plotting her eventual escape.

Chapter Eleven

"You will be shown to your quarters to prepare yourself for the feast that will be held tonight," Jonathan instructed Ailea inside the palace, taking in her look of stubborn defiance. "Guards are posted everywhere, so it would be futile to try to escape."

Beckoning to an older female servant standing to one side, Jonathan ordered her to show Ailea to her rooms, then turned abruptly and strode off down the corridor.

Following the old woman, Ailea realized that the captain was right. Guards, muscular arms folded over their chests, stood at attention at every exit. She had to admit that escape from the palace would be nearly impossible. Besides, she had not yet fully regained her strength. She would bide her time.

Ailea's chambers were richly appointed, with a floor of fragrant cedar that had been polished to a lustrous sheen with oil and covered with several large, colorful rugs. The bed was piled with soft pillows. To her surprise, Jerioth was waiting for her in the far corner of the room. With a reminder to be ready for the feast at sunset, the elderly servant departed, leaving the two women alone.

Jerioth helped Ailea wash off the dust of the road, then

ordered her to bed. Ailea went willingly, realizing she was utterly exhausted. She sank into the soft bed and was almost instantly asleep.

It seemed that only minutes had passed when Jerioth awakened her. "My lady, it is time to dress for the king's feast. He has sent a most beautiful gown for you to wear tonight."

Puzzled, Ailea furrowed her brow. "He? Do you mean the captain?"

"No. I was speaking of the king. That is, one of his household stewards brought it," Jerioth went on, holding up the garment for Ailea's inspection. "The king is much too busy to think of such matters, of course."

Ailea ignored the elaborate gown. "Of course he's too busy! Too busy killing innocents and conquering people to have time for anything else!"

Jerioth clucked her disapproval but held her tongue.

In spite of her anger, Ailea was curious about the robe the king had chosen for her. The tunic was of a deep purple hue. Though her father had once brought her a girdle in that color, Ailea had never had a purple garment. The dye had been made in the city of Tyre, she learned, from sea mollusks found off the coast, and was extremely costly. The king's steward had also provided jewels—bracelets and a necklace of amethysts which she chose to entwine in the thick locks of her hair that was pulled up, off her face, and allowed to cascade down her back.

A knock sounded at the door and Jerioth opened it to admit Isaac. The boy stood gaping at Ailea for a long moment until Jerioth cleared her throat. He snapped his jaw shut and spoke up, croaking pitifully. "I have been sent to escort you to my lord Jonathan. You will have a place beside him at the banquet table—a great honor, my lady."

"Hmph! Not to me!" Ailea retorted. But she allowed the lad to lead her to the banquet hall.

The sounds of celebration were riotous as Isaac elbowed a path through the crowd to a table near the king's dais. Jonathan had been talking with Benjamin, who was seated beside him, and didn't see Ailea until she was only a short distance away. His wine chalice, on the way to his lips, halted midway, and his expression altered as he took in her appearance, head to toe. Then he broke into a wide grin—a disgustingly possessive grin, to Ailea's mind.

Isaac nudged her gently forward until she was standing before Jonathan.

"You do me great honor tonight, little warrior."

"I do you no honor at all, Hebrew, now or ever!" she responded in her most imperious tone, but Jonathan's smile only widened, and Benjamin gave a hoot of laughter.

Jonathan motioned for her to recline on the couch beside him, and she did so, being careful to hold herself as far away from him as possible. But it was not easy—his great bulk seemed to take up most of the couch.

Ailea tried to center her thoughts on her anger toward Jonathan in order to keep fear at bay. But when she looked up and saw Joab enter and take his place at the king's table, her thoughts spun out of control. What would be her fate this night? Would she be taunted? Ridiculed? What were the general's plans for her? Was she to be consigned to the king's harem, as he had intimated? Or would he give her to one of his men? Ailea shuddered as she contemplated what she might suffer before this evening was at an end. Jonathan had warned her that Joab could be unthinkably brutal. Shaking off her fears, she determined that she would meet whatever came bravely—then kill the man who defiled her.

"You tremble, little warrior. Are you chilled?" Jonathan's big hand grazed her bare shoulder, and she jumped at his touch. "On the other hand, you feel rather warm. What troubles you?"

You, she thought. But she was determined not to let him know it. She met his gaze with a level look. "What will happen tonight?"

"The king will arrive at any moment. There will be speeches

extolling his greatness and prowess. Then the spoils of war will be displayed."

"The spoils of war? That includes me, I suppose." Ailea was angry with herself when her voice quivered slightly. She dropped her gaze.

Jonathan cupped her chin in his hand and tilted it until she met his eyes. "No one will hurt you, little one. I make you my vow." Something in his expression infused her with a sudden confidence.

An excited murmur filled the banqueting hall. It rose to a roar as King David, accompanied by a darkly beautiful woman, took the place of honor reserved for him. The audience was on its feet in an instant, applauding wildly.

When the applause died down, Jonathan spoke into Ailea's ear, the gusts of breath causing Ailea to shiver. "The king's consort tonight is Maacah, his second wife. She is Aramean, as you are, and a princess—daughter of Talmai, king of Geshur. She is the most beautiful of the king's five wives, in my opinion, and the most proud."

Ailea nodded, her eyes fastened on the dais. The king wore a diadem of heavy gold—all the more stunning in its simplicity. He was dressed in a plain white tunic with short sleeves that revealed powerful muscles that bulged around the armlets he wore. His ruggedly handsome face—bronzed by the sun—was honed by years as a fighting man. Yet despite his warlike image, he was smiling and chatting with those around him, and Ailea reluctantly conceded that she could well understand why his people so adored him.

When the king signaled for the feast to begin, the servants who had been standing along the walls sprang into action, circulating through the banqueting hall, placing dish after dish on the tables until they groaned with abundance.

Before she could reach for the bread to dip into the bowl of minced fish and barley, seasoned with garlic, Jonathan held a sop to her lips. As in Damascus, she knew that this gesture was intended to honor her. She considered refusing but decided to save her resistance for later. She would doubtless need it.

As she accepted the morsel, Jonathan's fingers lingered at her mouth for just a second longer than necessary. It gave Ailea a strange feeling in the pit of her stomach. She caught Benjamin's knowing expression and felt her face redden.

Throughout the meal, Jonathan pressed the rich food upon her. Rather than the strong wine, he insisted that she drink the watermelon juice or mulberry juice sweetened with honey that was offered as an alternative. Finally she told him, "If you force anything else down my throat, I will shame you and myself, my lord, for surely all that has gone down will come back up."

Jonathan reluctantly agreed. "Very well. But you must begin to eat more, Ailea. You have become much too thin since you left your home."

"And whose fault is that, Hebrew?" she snorted, her voice rising in indignation.

"*Yours!*" he snapped. "I did not drive you out into the desert. You took yourself there!"

Benjamin leaned over to address them, speaking behind his hand. "I would suggest that you cease your verbal duel. Joab has risen to speak and looks this way. He will not appreciate it if you fail to show proper interest in his speech, which will doubtless be full of his own military exploits as well as that of his uncle."

"Joab is the king's nephew?" Ailea asked Jonathan, genuinely curious. "He appears much older."

"They are about the same age. Joab is the son of David's older sister, Zeruiah."

Ailea's heart sank. So Joab held the king's favor. Whatever Joab requested concerning her fate would be granted, and she knew the general hated and mistrusted her.

Joab, having gained the attention of everyone in the hall, launched into a lengthy recital of the battles fought against the Arameans in the latest campaign, carefully pointing out his own singular acts of bravery. When he wound down, he called for a display of some of the confiscated treasures of Zobah. Among these were the shields and helmets of gold taken from Hadadezer's high-ranking officers. One of the helmets was beautifully crested with white eagle feathers.

Ailea half rose, clutching her throat. Her father's helmet—or one identical to it! She pressed her fingers against her mouth to stifle an outcry, as once again the horrific panorama she had seen on the battlefield slashed through her mind. She was thankful when the military trophies were taken away and bronze items—bowls and incense burners from the temple of Rimmon in Damascus—were brought out.

Then Joab introduced an emissary from Hamath, a longtime enemy of Hadadezer. The man was Joram, son of Toi, the king of Hamath. Ailea was filled with dread. She had heard her father rail against Prince Joram many times. Eliada and Joram had met on a field of battle more than once, and Ailea feared that Joram would recognize her when she appeared before David. Ailea only half followed the speeches after the introduction of Joram. She studied his darkly featured face, looking for some sign of intent in it's deep-set, basalt eyes. The angular nose, set above a smallish mouth pulled back in a leering grin, gave Joram a decidedly wolfish appearance.

Joram, looking to his left at King David, suddenly turned and without searching the audience stared directly at Ailea. Her mouth felt parched and her throat tightened as if she were choking. Why had he singled her out? His eyes narrowed and the canine-like teeth disappeared briefly behind rigid lips only to reappear in an even more leering smile. A hand on her shoulder made her start with fright. It was Jonathan, leaning over to speak into her ear.

"The king has called for you. Shall I escort you to him?"

Her chin lifted proudly. "I need no help from *you!*"

She rose and moved forward until she stood directly in front of David. Ailea inclined her head in a mimiced bow. Joab's face registered anger at this impertinence. He murmured to the king and would have risen, but David shook his head.

From the corner of her eye Ailea could see Joab turn his head ever so slightly toward Joram and tersely whisper a comment. Joram's slate-gray eyes looked even more lifeless at this distance, and his expression took on a slight scowl in response to Joab's words. A shift in David's posture suddenly focused her attention fully upon the king who was now leaning forward, his elbows resting on the amply supplied banquet table.

For a long moment he studied her thoughtfully, a bemused smile on his lips. Finally, his eyes met hers. Ailea had made an effort to keep her expression bland, not wanting to appear either hostile or friendly. But David's beautiful, long-lashed eyes were filled with intelligence, and the smile was so inviting that Ailea found herself returning it.

"I have heard of your exploits, child, but now that I see you, I can scarce credit them. You are so very small. Can it really be true that you laid several of my trained warriors low and escaped a number of them set to guard you?"

Ailea was not sure how to reply. She did not want to boast, yet she could not deny the truth of what he had said.

He waved aside her silence. "No matter. You must truly have inherited the fierce heart of your father, the general. He would have been proud of you, child."

"Thank you, my lord," Ailea responded, speaking over the lump in her throat.

"Do you wish to stay here in the palace under my protection?"

"I am a prisoner, my lord, and have no choice in the matter. If I had a choice, I would prefer to be returned to Damascus, to my own people."

David chuckled. "Since that is not possible, you will stay here, at least until it is decided what will be done with you. We will have a private audience soon. Until then, you will be quite safe."

Grateful for a reprieve of sorts, Ailea bowed formally.

Neither Joab nor Joram had spoken against her, though both of them were glaring. The king was postponing his decision, though it seemed probable, from the way he was eyeing her, that he would choose to add her to his harem. Ailea knew that she should feel thankful. Her lot in life as a captive could hardly be expected to be better. But the thought of being locked away for life, perhaps occasionally summoned to satisfy the king's desires, repulsed her. Better death than such a captivity!

When she returned to her seat, Jonathan seemed pleased. "Good, very good."

"Good? I see nothing good in being held here against my will!"

"You will . . . soon enough. Be patient."

At the conclusion of the evening, the king departed the banquet hall, waving to the assembled officers and palace officials who responded with deafening shouts of tribute and admiration. The exhilarated mood, fueled by an ample supply of choice wine and years of soldierly camaraderie, diminished only slightly as the various guests clustered together in small circles that erupted in uninhibited laughter and backslapping.

Ailea stood at the edge of one such circle as Jonathan, Benjamin, and three other gibborim recounted episodes from their early services with David. Ailea was dwarfed by the circle of husky fighting men, but by moving slightly to one side, she could cautiously peek past Jonathan and observe the dais.

Joram and Joab were making their way toward the doorway, ostensibly smiling at the numerous guests who impeded their exit but clearly anxious to leave the assembly. Joram surveyed the reception hall with an intense glance, unable to find the object of his interest. For the first time ever, Ailea felt safe in the shadow of the gibbor and lightly rested her tired head against Jonathan's arm.

~ ~ ~

For the next two days, Ailea was kept in suspense as to what her fate would be. The king had not called for her nor had she seen Jonathan. She tried to convince herself that any feeling of disappointment in his absence was only because he could have supplied information about the king's intentions.

To relieve her boredom, Ailea went for a walk in the palace garden. She had been there for some time, seated beside a fountain, when she heard voices. She looked up and saw a woman and boy approaching. Ailea recognized the woman as the wife who had accompanied David to the banquet. The boy wore his thick auburn hair in a braided style she had never seen before. Still, he looked vaguely familiar.

The woman stared at Ailea. "You are the new captive, are you not?" she asked in a condescending tone.

"I am Ailea of Damascus," she replied with a proud lift of her shoulders. "I was brought here with the treasures taken from my people."

"And you are now my husband's concubine." The statement was made with a trace of resignation mixed with resentment.

"No. I have not been called before the king. I have been given guest quarters."

Appearing somewhat relieved, the woman continued in more congenial tone. "I am Maacah, and this is my son, Absalom."

Ailea turned her attention to the boy. He was smiling at her—a dazzling smile—and Ailea was struck by his extraordinary beauty. He was probably no more than twelve or thirteen years old, yet he was tall and well-built. Ailea now realized why he had looked familiar—the hair and the smile were identical to that of the king. "You look very much like your father," she observed.

The boy made a face. "You are not the first to tell me so."

"And you always take it as the highest of compliments," Maacah reminded him.

"Of course I do, Mother." But there was an air of petulance that did not escape Ailea's notice. Not wishing to intrude on their outing, she took her leave and returned to the guest wing of the palace.

When she entered her chamber, she found three servants waiting. Jerioth quivered with excitement. "You have been summoned to appear before the king this afternoon!" she told Ailea. "Come. There is so little time to prepare."

Ailea was taken to a room with a bathing pool with rose petals floating in the scented water. Two young servants stood ready to attend her. She was bathed and dried, and her skin rubbed with scented oil until it shone. Her freshly washed hair was combed, the top braided and arranged in a coronet while the rest was brushed out to ripple down her back in silken strands. She was dressed in a flowing white robe but given no head covering.

"The king will wish to see your hair," one of the servants timidly explained.

~ ~ ~

Ailea tried to mask her nervousness when she entered the king's audience chamber at last. She drew in her breath at the opulence of the room. Everything seemed to be overlaid with gold, and the light from the late afternoon sun ignited the room until it glowed with an inner fire.

By contrast, David was dressed quite simply, as was his custom. His fine linen tunic was embroidered at the neck and sleeves with gold and silver, but other than that, he wore no ornamentation except his signet ring.

The king was standing at a large open window, looking out over the city. Ailea waited to be acknowledged, since the servant who had escorted her quietly had already left, backing out unobtrusively and closing the great doors behind her.

Just as Ailea was wondering if she should cough discreetly to gain his attention, the king turned and smiled at her. "Come and join me," he invited.

She stood beside him at the window, and after he had inquired about her comfort, they turned their attention to the scene outside. From this vantage point Jerusalem lay spread out before them. Directly below, dozens of workers were busy on the palace construction. On a rise a short distance away, a low wall enclosed a courtyard. Ailea could see priests coming in and out, some burning incense, others performing unknown rituals before an unusual tentlike structure.

Ailea could not contain her natural curiosity. "What is that?"

"It is the tabernacle of the Lord," he explained.

"But it is so plain," she blurted out. "In Damascus, the temple of Rimmon is so much larger and more beautiful." When it occurred to her that she had just insulted the Hebrew god, she quickly apologized. "Forgive me. I meant no insult."

The king waved aside her concern. "You are right. It *is* plain. I have often thought so myself. You see, this tabernacle is patterned after the one my people were instructed to erect in the wilderness when we left Egypt. Materials were not plentiful then. It was enough that the Almighty chose to dwell among His people." David paused, his rich voice rising in his enthusiasm. "Inside the innermost chamber of the tabernacle is the ark of the covenant—the symbol of His pledge to us as His chosen people. For many years the Philistines possessed it. But Yahweh was gracious enough to give us victory over our enemies, and we recovered the ark.

"When I made Jerusalem my capital, I had the ark brought here and a more permanent tabernacle constructed. It is more elaborate than the original, but I agree with you—" he squinted against the sun streaming through the window, "it does not do justice to the Almighty. Just the other day, as I oversaw the construction of the new wing of my palace, the thought struck me that my house is finer than His. Someday I intend to remedy that."

The king turned and, motioning Ailea to follow, took a seat on one of the many couches scattered throughout the room. For some time they continued to discuss matters of interest. David told her how important music was to him and how he had appointed a chief musician to oversee the choirs and orchestra that led his people in their worship. "It has become so popular with the people that they are beginning to come to Jerusalem for the religious festivals instead of holding them in their towns and villages," he explained.

He paused, gazing at her intently. "As for music, the servants tell me your voice is as clear and sweet as a songbird's. Why don't you teach me a song you would sing in Damascus, and I shall teach you one of the songs I wrote when I kept the sheep for my father in Bethlehem. I will go first." Picking up a lyre, only one of several instruments in the room, he began to strum.

"The Lord is my shepherd, I shall not want. . . ." The words were so beautiful that tears came to Ailea's eyes.

At first Ailea was nervous, but the king's cordial manner soon put her at ease. After he had taught her the shepherd song, she sang for him a lullaby her nurse had taught her as a child. In turn, he sang another worship song he had composed. She marveled at his gifts—composing, playing, singing.

At last the king laid his instrument aside. "I suppose we must decide what to do with you, child." The term was spoken so fondly that Ailea began to believe that his feelings for her were more paternal than lustful.

"I could always bring you into my harem," he mused, and a pang of apprehension seized Ailea once more. "You would be well cared for, lavished with gifts, and regarded well. But I must also point out the drawbacks of such an arrangement."

When Ailea raised her eyebrows in question, David laughed. "Shall we say only that I have my doubts that you could find happiness as one of my concubines?"

Though he seemed most gracious—even friendly—this man was the king, with the power of life and death over Ailea. She felt she must at least placate, if not flatter him. "Oh, my lord, I am sure you could make any woman happy. You are kind, and—and very attractive. . . ."

At this the king threw back his head and laughed heartily. "And you, my dear, are ravishingly beautiful . . . and very young. If I took you into my harem, I am afraid you could not expect to see me often, if ever. I might never even give you a child." He seemed genuinely saddened. "Do you understand what I am telling you?"

She nodded, eyes wide. "Yes, my lord."

"You are lovely and intelligent, Ailea. I believe you deserve a man whose loyalties are not . . . divided. You should have many children. Why don't we look for a husband for you who could give you these things?"

Her lashes fluttered as a flush heated her cheeks. "It is very kind of you to take an interest in my future, my lord."

The king rose to pace the length of the room, sorting out his thoughts. "Now, tell me what kind of man you desire—a gentle man or a man of war like your father?"

"Oh, not a soldier, sire!" Ailea couldn't help herself. The thought drained the color from her face. "My mother loved my father very much, but she was a very unhappy woman . . . and very lonely. My father was always off making war, you see, and she would often be sick with worry over him."

"Go on, child. What else do you look for in a husband?"

Gathering her courage, she spoke honestly. "I do not wish to wed a young man, my lord. Young men are not as kind—not as thoughtful of their wives. Nor do they have the wisdom of an older man. If I must be given in marriage, I would prefer someone your age, or even older."

Again, to Ailea's dismay, the king burst into uproarious laughter. "I am sorry, little one. It's only that—" he struggled unsuccessfully to control his mirth. "It's just that you are such a lively little thing. I have a picture of the life you would lead with an elderly groom. I am afraid that keeping up with you might prove too much for an older man, and you would soon find yourself a widow."

"Well, as to that, my lord . . ."

Seeing that the prospect of her future husband's demise was anything but distressing to Ailea, David once again succumbed to a volley of laughter. Then he assured her that he would try to choose someone who would please her, promising that she would remain a welcome guest until that time.

As she made her way down the cool dark halls of the palace, Ailea heard a sound behind her. She turned quickly but saw no one. This had happened several times during her stay. It must just be the echo of her own steps, she assured herself.

She turned a corner and was suddenly jerked into a dark alcove. A hand clamped down over her mouth, and she started to struggle, but a raspy voice whispered into her ear.

"Be calm, my lady. I have word of your brother. But we dare not talk here. I will seek you out in the marketplace tomorrow."

Suddenly she was released, and the man who had appeared out of nowhere disappeared through a nearby doorway. All his shadowed profile revealed was his short stature and a pronounced nose.

Chapter Twelve

It was late when Jonathan was ushered into the king's private audience chamber. He had hoped that Sheva would be in attendance, but only David greeted him, motioning for his old friend to sit beside him on a cushioned window seat. There was a moment of silence while both men surveyed the skyline of the city—a dusky sun swallowed up by the encroaching night.

"You requested an audience with me?" At Jonathan's nod, David continued. "Ah, yes. It has been far too long since we have had a conversation—just the two of us." David let out a long sigh. "One should never become too busy for one's friends. What can I do for you?"

Jonathan would have preferred to have worked up to his request more gradually, preferably in Sheva's presence. But that was apparently not to be the case. He would bring his petition, but he would proceed with caution. "You know of my great loyalty for you, my lord. I have been your man without question since I was a lad of fourteen."

"I know, my friend. In that you remind me very much of that other Jonathan. . . ." The king glanced out the window once more, his eyes misting over.

"Your loyalty to friends long past is well known, sire."

There was another long pause as David struggled for composure. "There will never be another friendship in my life like the one between Jonathan and me. Though it was all too brief, I was blessed to have such a friendship."

"I never met King Saul's son. I wish I had known him."

"You would have liked each other." David sighed deeply, then waited for Jonathan to get to the point.

"I wished to speak to you about Eliada's daughter. I believe you have seen her recently . . . perhaps even today."

David smiled. "A very interesting audience indeed. Did you know the girl sings like an angel?"

Jonathan frowned. "No, my lord, I did not . . . though for most of the time she has spent with me, she has not felt much like singing, I'm afraid. First, there was the matter of her anger over the defeat of Hadadezer's army. Then, her preoccupation with the death of both her mother and father and possibly even her brother. She ran away from me into the desert, looking for him, I presume. She was almost dead from exposure to the sun when I found her. Did she speak of it?"

"No, she didn't mention it. But it doesn't surprise me. She is a most unusual young woman."

Jonathan dreaded the answer to his next question. "So, after meeting her . . . have you decided to keep her for yourself, my lord?"

David eyed Jonathan keenly. "I have made no decision as yet. When I asked the girl what she desired, she told me that if she could not return to Damascus, she would like to be given to some rich old man on his last leg." The king's hearty laughter rang out through the vaulted hall.

Jonathan tried to hide his curiosity. "And do you have anyone in mind?"

David arched a quizzical brow. "Were you thinking of applying for the job, Captain?"

Jonathan rose and paced nervously. "I had considered it, yes."

The king's intelligent eyes widened. "You are the last man I would expect to take an interest in a foreign woman. What will the Rab think?"

David's question was one Jonathan had never truly pondered. There had been much on his mind these past weeks. Not the least of them was his worries over Ailea—and Joab. Now he found that he must consider his father's opinion when he appeared in Ziph with an Aramean bride. He justified the matter easily. "I don't believe he will condemn it out of hand. After all, the Law allows such marriages."

"Then what if the girl objects? You don't exactly meet her criteria."

Jonathan grinned and returned to the couch. "I am many years older than she, it is true, though not on my last leg, I hope."

David's laughter echoed once more. "Far from it, my friend!"

At the sound of a muffled cough, they turned to find Joab at the threshold. "Forgive the interruption, but I have one or two urgent matters to discuss with the king concerning the distribution of gifts and rewards. After viewing all the gold and bronze Prince Joram brought from Hamath, I wanted to ask you about a suitable gift for him in appreciation for his alliance with us. Such a gesture might be worth the trouble."

"Hmmm." David stroked his chin thoughtfully. "What did you have in mind?"

Jonathan worked to stifle the resentment welling up within his chest. It was common knowledge that the king's nephew and closest advisor was kept apprised of everyone to whom the king granted an audience. Joab had known Jonathan was with David; therefore, it was certain he had planned his entrance accordingly. Before the words were out of Joab's mouth, Jonathan knew what he would suggest.

"I thought to give Joram the daughter of Eliada." Joab's tone was deceptively calm. "He showed an interest in her at the banquet the other night. If we give him the girl, we will not have to part with anything of value to us."

Jonathan could see Joab studying his reaction through narrowed eyelids. He would not give the wretch the satisfaction of seeing his discomfort. He clenched his jaw, his hands fisted at his sides. It was too soon to speak. For now, at least, he would simply listen.

"I, too, saw Joram watching the girl last night," David replied, weighing his words carefully. "I also heard some of the comments he made concerning her father. King Toi and Prince Joram considered Eliada their enemy. I have a feeling Joram would seek revenge were he to get his hands on the daughter."

"Is that really our concern, my lord?" Joab continued smoothly. "After all, she is of no importance—" Joab slanted him a look of cold appraisal. "Since you did not send her to the women's quarters, I assumed you did not want her for yourself. Of course if you do, that certainly changes —"

David interrupted him with a cool smile. "I was not aware that you had such an intimate knowledge of my dealings with women, nephew."

Jonathan was amazed to see Joab's face color with embarrassment. "You know that women are not a primary concern of mine, uncle, whether they be yours or anyone else's."

"Ah, yes, it is no secret that you are far more concerned with fighting and killing than with loving. So I am left to wonder why you are concerning yourself with the matter of one orphaned girl. You haven't made any promises in my name without consulting me first, I hope?"

"Of course not!" Highly offended, Joab's tone became briskly impersonal. "But if you do not want her for yourself, I would recommend you send her from the kingdom at once. The Aramean alliance may be temporarily subdued, but they still seek to throw off our yoke. We have intercepted messages between Damascus and Ammon. If the girl stays in Israel, she won't hesitate to spy against us. If you have no other plans for her, I suggest you resolve this matter quickly by giving her to Joram."

David rose from his seat and faced his nephew, towering over the shorter man. "But someone else has spoken for her, and I am seriously considering his request."

Joab looked startled, then narrowed his gaze on Jonathan. He turned back to the king. "My lord, such a decision would be disastrous. With Jonathan's high military rank, there would be great risk of valuable information falling into enemy hands."

"Do you think me so weak I would let a woman use me so?" Jonathan took a menacing step toward the general, and Joab reached for his dagger. "You insult my honor, Joab—something I will not let go unchallenged!"

As David stepped between his two officers, a soft voice diverted their attention. "Ah, sire, if I may say so, I believe you already settled this matter some three weeks ago."

Sheva, the elderly scribe, was slight of stature but carried an aura of authority. In his hands he held a parchment scroll.

"How could that be?" David quizzed him. "I was unaware of the young captive until just this week."

"Allow me to remind you, my lord." Sheva unrolled the parchment and spread it out on a low table, using two onyx statuettes to weight the ends.

David and Joab bent over the scroll. Jonathan, who was aware of the contents, stood with arms folded, trying to suppress a look of triumph.

Leaning over, arms braced on the low table, David read silently for a moment or two, then stood, smiling at Jonathan. "So you chose her that night in my tent? I see that Shammah chose three of the gold helmets from Hadadezer's officers—a small fortune. Most of the other men made similar choices. But you chose the girl." Jonathan merely nodded. "Then you shall have her."

Beneath his swarthy tan, Joab paled. "But, my lord, surely some other gift could be exchanged!"

David held up a silencing hand, anger flaring in his eyes. Jonathan realized that he had seen the king this angry at his nephew only once before—the day Joab had murdered Abner. "I have given my word. So be it." He turned his back on Joab in dismissal.

After the general had stalked out of the room, David reached into a drawer of the table and brought out a parchment tied with red cord. "A gift for the Rab the next time you see him. Will you take it to him with my warmest regards when you return to Ziph?"

With a swift motion Jonathan loosened the ties and three scrolls made of very fine parchment spilled onto the table.

"I can think of no more suitable gift for the Rab, my lord. My father loves the Torah as much as you do."

"I remember that Shageh stood for me when all the other elders of Ziph voted to turn me over to Saul." There was a reflective tone in the king's voice. "I'll never forget his kindness."

"Yes, my lord, you never forget a kindness. That is why your people feel such loyal love for you."

The men parted with a kiss on each cheek.

~ ~ ~

Joab left the king's audience chamber with one thought in mind—to seek out one of his most trusted aides, Uriah the Hittite. Uriah, already numbered among the gibborim, had recently been appointed by Joab as an armor-bearer—one of five aides who acted more as bodyguards. With many enemies, it was expeditious that the general choose carefully those who would be most loyal to him—and to the king, of course.

He found Uriah in the barracks, polishing his shield. Seeing the well-muscled young man, Joab congratulated himself again on his choice.

Uriah was an ethnic Hittite. His ancestors had been living in Israel at the time of the conquest, having migrated southward from the Hittite empire. Uriah himself, however, was a strict follower of the Law and an ardent believer in Yahweh. Even his name—"God is Light"—proclaimed his belief. It was his only weakness, in Joab's opinion. Men who were too religious had scruples that sometimes got in the way of military or personal goals. So far, in the case of Uriah, this had not been a problem.

When the young man saw his commander approaching, he quickly laid down his shield and stood at attention.

Joab came straight to the point. "I have an assignment for you, Uriah. It will take you to the east side of Jordan, into Zobah and perhaps Ammon. I want you to stay until you gather the information I need."

A look of disappointment flitted across Uriah's rugged features. "At your service, my lord."

Joab's sharp eyes missed nothing. "Does something about the assignment give you pause, Uriah? If so, tell me now. I will countenance nothing but complete dedication to a mission once it is undertaken."

"Sir, my hesitation is not due to any doubt as to my ability or desire to serve you. It is only—" the young man paused, shifting uncomfortably. "It's only that I am to be married the first week of Sivan."

Joab lifted a brow. "I hadn't heard. And who is the fortunate young woman you have chosen as your bride?"

"Bathsheba, sir—the daughter of Eliam. He told me about her when we bivouacked together on campaign. And when I finally visited his home and saw her for myself, sir," Uriah's face flamed, "I found her to be more beautiful even than he had said. I offered for her at once."

Joab chuckled appreciatively. "A good choice, I'm sure. Eliam is a soldier as worthy of the title gibbor as you are. His daughter should breed you fine warriors to serve the king, and with Eliam's father, Ahithophel, as their great-grandfather, they should be as wise as they are fierce."

"If the Lord permits, may it be so." Uriah dipped his head in a nod of acknowledgment, blushing furiously.

The general was suddenly all business, not a trace of a smile lingering on his stern countenance. "As to the assignment, your impending marriage should be incentive enough to speed you on your way and accomplish your mission in record time."

"As you wish, sir." Uriah was not surprised that his plan to wed had not swayed Joab to give the assignment to another. Indeed, Uriah was proud of the fact that his superior had anticipated that he would put his military duties first. It was the quality that had raised Uriah, not born a Hebrew, to the coveted ranks of the gibborim.

"Now, I wish you to seek information about an Aramean named Rezon. He is thought to have been killed in the last battle with Hadadezer. I want you to find proof, either of his death or that he still lives. Start your questioning with Zobah's military. Rezon is thought by most to be a coward and a deserter. I believe Hadadezer has put a bounty on his head. Also, question his friends in Damascus. Shammah is in charge of our garrison there. He will be glad to assist you," Joab smiled with a gleam in his narrowed eyes, "in using any means necessary to obtain information from them."

Uriah felt a tingle crawl up his spine. The commander relished the thought of inflicting pain on anyone he perceived as an enemy. While Uriah was not at all squeamish about hacking a man to death in battle, he had no stomach for employing torture. But he was careful not to let his distaste show on his face as Joab continued to brief him on the mission.

"What shall I do with Rezon if I find him alive?" Uriah asked when Joab had finished at last.

"Do? You are to do nothing. Merely come back and report to me."

When Joab left, Uriah prepared for his journey. He would send a messenger to the home of Eliam, explaining his absence and informing Bathsheba's father that he was anxiously awaiting the date of the wedding. He fervently hoped that it would not be delayed. He only hoped his bride-to-be would understand.

~ ~ ~

Ailea receive another summons for an audience with the king the next morning. The same elderly woman servant who had first shown her to her chamber appeared to take her to David. Ailea was nervous and afraid, even though the king had proven to be all charm when she had spoken to him before. She knew that he had called for her this time to announce what her future would be. She supposed she should feel flattered that he would take the time to tell her personally, but she felt nothing but foreboding. She was sure she would not like what he had to tell her.

She was led up the stairs that led to the third story, then up again to the rooftop of the palace. It was an exceedingly beautiful spot, a garden where all manner of flowers bloomed, even more lovely than the outdoor garden where she had met Maacah and Absalom.

A cool morning breeze blew, ruffling Ailea's tunic and hair. She turned to ask the servant where to wait for the king, but the woman had disappeared. Ailea wondered if the servant's only duty was to lead people about the palace.

Casting about for a sign of the king and not seeing him, Ailea explored the enormous rooftop. Interspersed with the plant life were sitting areas with gorgeously upholstered couches and chairs, as well as cushions large enough to use as beds. Impressed by the opulence, Ailea tried to tell herself it would not be so bad to live here in the palace for the rest of her life. But her heart cried out that she wanted something different. She wasn't sure what, but she was certain it was not to be found in Israel.

To quiet her nerves as she waited, she decided to distract her thoughts by looking out over the city. She mounted two steps that led to a bench where one could look down on the city below. Up here one could see even farther than from the window in the room where she had stood with David three days ago.

"This is my favorite spot in the palace. I wanted to show it to you." Ailea started at the king's voice. David was dressed in a military uniform this time. His scarlet tunic was almost completely covered by a leather coat of mail held together with bronze loops.

The king, noticing her attention to his attire, explained. "No,

I am not headed off to battle. I have been training with my men since daybreak. See the barracks down there?" David pointed to a group of buildings next to the palace. "And that larger one. That is the house of the Gibborim. It is a place where my thirty greatest warriors stay when we are in council. Have you heard of their exploits?"

Ailea rolled her eyes. "I am afraid that is all I have heard from Isaac, Jonathan's armor-bearer. His father is one of them."

David nodded. "Yes. I met the lad. He fought bravely and was wounded in the last campaign. He might very well take his place in the ranks of the gibborim himself someday."

He abruptly changed the subject. "Were you enjoying my rooftop?"

"Oh yes, my lord. It is beautiful."

"You should see it decorated during our Feast of Booths. That takes place in early fall. It is a time of thanksgiving to the Lord God, both for the harvest and for His care of our people during forty years when we wandered in the wilderness—in the Negev and the Sinai."

"And you build booths?"

"Yes. On this rooftop and all the others in Jerusalem, to keep off rain and sun while we live out-of-doors for seven days. As I said, it commemorates our nomadic past and gives us a chance to take time to rest after the harvest."

David looked out over the city with a smile. "It is the happiest time of the year, with neighbors shouting greetings to each other and visiting from rooftop to rooftop. Such feasting you have never seen. Perhaps you will be in Jerusalem for this year's celebration."

At Ailea's indrawn breath, David paused and looked at her keenly. "I suppose you are not as interested in where you will be in the fall as you are in knowing without further hesitation what I have decided about your future."

Her heart hammering, Ailea managed a smile. "That would be most kind, sire."

"Very well. I must tell you that though I was unaware of it

when we spoke yesterday, I had already made arrangements for you some weeks ago."

"But how . . . ?"

David held up his hand. "I will explain. After my last campaign, I promised my chief officers a reward for their faithful service. You see, generally our army does not loot and plunder as is customary for other victorious armies. Instead, we dedicate most of the spoils of war to the Lord God. My warriors are honored and cared for by the people, and of course, they are paid for their services. But some members of my war council deserved . . . special recognition for their valor."

Ailea's heart sank. She was to be given to one of the king's soldiers to be used—maybe even to be passed around among them! All kinds of horrible possibilities flashed through her mind.

So troubled were her thoughts that she almost missed David's next words. "And so, each of the Thirty chose what he would have as his reward. . . . Jonathan of Ziph chose you."

"I beg your pardon, my lord. I wasn't attending."

"I said, Jonathan ben Shageh chose *you.*"

"The captain? He chose me?" The truth crashed against her consciousness like a rare clap of thunder in the desert sky.

"Are you deaf, girl? That is what I said. It was all recorded properly by Sheva on the scroll. Only yesterday did I learn of Jonathan's choice."

Ailea was still reeling from the shock of the king's disclosure. She sprang from her chair. "But, my lord. That is impossible! Jonathan . . . the captain . . . *hates* me."

"No, no, you are mistaken, my child. He doesn't hate you. He wants you. He told me so himself last evening."

Ailea threw herself at the king's feet and grasped his ankles, mindless now of the proprieties. "You must reconsider, sire. You can't give me to Jonathan! Please, my lord, let me stay in your household. Jonathan will abuse me! He killed my father and my brother! I don't wish to go with him! Oh, please . . ."

David took Ailea firmly by the shoulders and drew her to her feet. "Calm yourself and listen to reason. The captain did not kill your father. They simply fought on opposing sides in a battle, and your father's side lost. Jonathan had no direct part in his death. As to his abusing you, that is ridiculous."

The king dropped his hands and took a few paces from her, turning to regard her with a scowl. "I have known Jonathan ben Shageh for nearly twenty years. He is fierce in battle, but he is a just man. He will treat you well. Besides all that, I have given my word, and my word is law. Even Joab, my nephew and closest advisor, could not persuade me to change my decree, and I certainly won't change it for you—a mere child and a captive at that!"

Ailea could see that the king was angry with her, and she dared not argue further.

As if reading her thoughts, David resumed his pacing, hands clasped behind his back. "General Joab's reasons were not really that complex. First, he did not want Jonathan to have you; there is no love lost between my nephew and the captain. Second, Joab thought you should be given to Joram of Toi for political reasons."

When he saw Ailea shudder at the mention of the prince of the minor kingdom, David nodded. "If the captain had not intervened, reminding me of my promise, I might have listened to Joab. You have Jonathan to thank for saving you from the prince, whose reasons for wanting you are not pleasant to contemplate."

Ailea said nothing, knowing it would do no good. The only thing remaining was to try to convince Jonathan that it would be a terrible mistake to keep her. She would never submit to him—she would fight him forever, if necessary.

The king motioned her escort, who had at sometime reappeared on the roof and sat some distance away. Ailea knew that the king was at an end of his patience and was dismissing her, but she could not resist one last timid question. "What does Jonathan intend to do with me?"

The king eyed her appraisingly. "That, little one, is entirely up to him," David said before he turned abruptly and strode away.

Chapter Thirteen

Ailea circulated among the stalls in the marketplace, fingering a jade amulet, then pretending interest in some fine linen cloth. She glanced behind her and saw that Isaac was busy haggling over the price of a scabbard for his knife. It was the first time she had been able to slip away from her unwelcome escort all morning.

She had made the request to be taken to the marketplace through the king's servants and had hoped one of them would be her escort. They would not be likely to care if she slipped away from them for a moment or two.

But somehow the arrogant captain had gotten wind of her request and sent his armor-bearer to keep an eye on her. Though she personally liked Isaac, she had no doubt where his loyalties lay and that he would give his master a full report of her every move.

She had ventured an attempt to charm Isaac when they had first started out this morning. But she soon found that although he blushed and stammered and apologized, he steadfastly refused to let her out of his sight. "The captain charged me with your safety," he explained.

So she sent another furtive glance at Isaac, realizing that this was probably as far away as she would get from him on this outing.

Was her strange visitor of the day before watching? Ailea hoped so—because she wasn't sure when she might get another opportunity to talk to him alone.

At that very moment she heard a hiss from the side of the stall where she was standing. A familiar beaked nose appeared first, then the man's head. He beckoned her with the crook of a finger. Isaac was still arguing loudly with the merchant. Seeing her chance, Ailea quickly slipped into the alleyway behind the cloth stall. "What do you wish to tell me?" she whispered anxiously. "I am watched all the time. Speak quickly, before we are seen."

"I am Akim, and I am here to tell you that your brother lives."

"Rezon lives?" Ailea gasped. "Take me to him at once!"

The man shushed her, tugging her into a darker corner of the alley, and spoke hurriedly in a low tone. "No, my lady. Your brother gave strict instructions that you were not to come to him. It is not safe. I am with a group of men who joined him as renegades rather than surrender to the Hebrews. The Arameans of Ammon and Moab will soon throw off the yoke of the shepherd king. And when that happens, we will be ready to march into Damascus and destroy the minions he has left in charge of the city. In the meanwhile, the life we live as bandits is an extremely hard and dangerous one. You must wait for him to come to you. Or better still, try to persuade your captors to return you to Damascus."

Ailea's countenance fell. "He will never consent to it."

"He?" The dark-skinned man leaned forward, his interest quickened. "Then the Hebrews have decided who your master will be?"

She nodded. "He is Jonathan, a captain in King David's army, from the village of Ziph in Judah."

"That is most fortuitous. Had you been consigned to the king's harem, it would have been difficult to free you."

"But I don't know how long we will stay here. Or where we will go from this city. How?"

Akim silenced her with a gesture. "Never fear. Rezon will find you wherever you are." He paused, throwing another quick glance over his shoulder at a shopkeeper who had stepped into the alley to throw out a pail of dirty water. "Your brother will free you, then the Hebrew dog who has dared touch you will die!"

Seeing the shopkeeper's curious stare, Akim lowered his head, allowing the folds of his head covering to shield his face. "I must go now before we are found out. Is there a message for your brother, my lady?"

"Just that I anxiously await the day I can join him. Akim, does my brother know about our mother?"

"Your brother's spies have told him everything. Watch for me. You will see me again before many days have passed." Whirling about, Akim ducked back through the stall and into the milling throng, vanishing from view.

~ ~ ~

It was late when Isaac and Jonathan retired for the night, leaving Benjamin to guard Ailea's door. The head of the palace guard had been highly insulted at this demand for extra precaution, but Jonathan had won over his protests. He had instructed Jerioth to send word immediately if Ailea behaved in a suspicious manner. The old nurse—wise in the ways of women—would be quick to detect any attempt to escape, Jonathan suspected.

Now he turned to Isaac, eager to hear his report of the day's events, including some awkward moments during Ailea's excursion to the marketplace.

The lad was red-faced with shame. "We went into the village today, as you know, sir. I was negotiating over the price of a scabbard when Ailea pointed to some linen in the next stall and said to meet her there. Since I could keep an eye on her, I saw no harm in it. I was lax, my lord. I . . ."

Jonathan waved away his apology. "Just tell me exactly what happened, Isaac."

"When I noticed that she was missing—only a few moments, sir—I went to look for her inside the merchant's tent. I had moved near the rear of the stall when I heard voices outside—in the alley behind the stalls. Through a small opening, I was able to see her talking with an older man—from Ammon or Zobah from his garments, I suspect."

"Yes, yes, go on."

"I'm sorry, sir. I could hear nothing of their conversation. But the lady did not act as if she feared him, and he did not try to restrain her. Then the man slipped through the crowd and disappeared. I wanted to follow him, but—" Isaac spread his hands and hunched his shoulders helplessly. "I knew you would not want me to leave the lady."

"Well done."

The captain's scowl, Isaac decided, was not intended for *him*. "There *is* one fortunate thing, my lord," Isaac said, hoping to cheer his captain. "She did not try to leave with him!"

"I'm afraid that doesn't mean she won't try it in the future." Jonathan paced the spacious room, deep in thought. "We will have to watch her very closely, Isaac."

Isaac retired to his small bed in the corner, but Jonathan found it impossible to sleep. He sat for a long time in the window alcove of the room, staring out into the darkness.

He was furious with Ailea. It seemed he was nearly always furious with her. The girl could anger him more quickly than anyone he had ever known. Couldn't she see the danger she would face if she ran away and left his protection? First, there was the threat of Joab. And hadn't she learned anything from her near-fatal experience in the desert?

He planned the lecture he would give her in the morning. Then another disconcerting thought struck him—a blistering reprimand would only fire her rebellion. No, he wouldn't lecture her. Nor would he let her know that he was aware of her clandestine meeting. Instead, he would take her away from Jerusalem. That would remove her from the intrigue of the capital and Joab's influence. He would take her where he could guard her more carefully, protect her . . . even from herself if necessary.

~ ~ ~

The next morning, while it was still dark, Jonathan woke Isaac. "Come, boy. We will start for home today. Go and rouse the men from Hebron who said they wished to travel with us. Tell them to be ready in an hour. I will fetch Jerioth and Ailea."

Isaac needed no further prompting. He was thrilled to be going home. Visions of a hero's welcome swirled in his head as he went to wake the soldiers.

Neither Ailea nor Jerioth was as pleased as Isaac. Both grumbled that an hour was not sufficient time to prepare for such a journey.

"Be ready within the hour, or you will be brought along in whatever state you are found at the time," Jonathan warned them crossly.

The two women were ready when Isaac came to fetch the few belongings they had hurriedly folded into heavy woven travel packs. Ailea's hastily braided hair was tucked under a head covering which hung over the shoulders of her richly ornamented outer robe, a final present from the king delivered with his regards by a servant.

As she waited for the baggage to be secured, Ailea glanced around at the palace, remembering the purple robe and exquisite jewelry she had worn, the finely appointed palace chambers, and the fragrant scent of rose petals and perfumed oils. For a few short days she had felt a princess, but now this life, like her life in Damascus, was ended, and the despair that she had kept at bay during the past days struck with such ferocity that she fought to keep from tears.

"Evidently the captain believes an early morning walk will

do us good," Jerioth interrupted. "Jonathan may indeed be a true son of Abraham, but I doubt if the blessed Sarah herself was ever pulled from her bed and force marched like a galley slave as these two daughters of Israel."

Jerioth, having grown fond of Ailea, had absentmindedly misspoke herself of course. Ailea knew that she had meant nothing by her comment. It was in fact the first time Ailea had seen the normally imperturbable healer out of sorts. But she was wrong. Ailea wasn't a daughter of Israel, and her foreign descent would be all the more obvious outside the capital city. Her treatment in the palace had been far better than expected, but there she had been the king's prize.

Now that she had been given to the Hebrew, what did he intend to do with her? Even if he were more kindly, what of the Israelites who would, without a doubt, despise her? They were to stop for the night in Hebron and stay at the home of Isaac's parents. On the second day they would travel to Ziph, Jonathan's home village. Once there, would he still protect her from the revenge of those who had lost husbands or sons in the war?

Her despair engulfed her as she walked silently at the end of the small procession, only catching snatches of the boisterous conversation between Jonathan and two other travelers in the lead. Where was he? Where was Rezon? Why couldn't she join him now? Ailea smiled to herself when she realized why her brother had given instructions not to betray his location. Rezon knew her so well, knew that she would strike off the instant she learned where he might be hiding. Well, the next time she saw Akim, she would just have to trick him into revealing Rezon's whereabouts.

Jerioth would be leaving them when they reached Hebron. She would be staying for a time with her son who lived in the countryside. Ailea had grown accustomed to Jerioth 's scolding and ordering her about. She would miss the old nurse's companionship.

She would probably never see Shua or Malik again either.

She felt so desolate that her mouth trembled as she fought back tears. To release the terrible emotions she felt, she gave a long, hopeless sigh.

The sound drew Jonathan's attention and pricked his conscience. Ailea looked so miserable. He removed the heavy bundle from the back of the small donkey, securing it to his own by a thick, heavy strap. Then he grabbed Ailea by the waist and lifted her onto the donkey's back.

"You are tired," he told her in a gruff voice. "You will rest at the home of my friends tonight, and things will seem much better in the morning." With that, he handed Ailea the reins and strode ahead to join the other two warriors who were traveling with them.

If it was an attempt to comfort her, Ailea thought, it was a useless effort on his part.

~ ~ ~

It was midafternoon before they reached the town of Hebron in what Jerioth explained was the "hill country" of Judah. As they approached the city, perched high atop a long slope, Ailea understood the designation, for all along the horizon to the south and east the earth dipped and swelled in a series of rhythmic undulations. Served by an abundance of wells and springs, the area blossomed with lush vegetation. Ailea was surprised to see a city of such size that was not walled. But then she guessed its location atop a hill made it as secure as any wall could.

The town, Jerioth informed Ailea, was associated with the Hebrew patriarch Abraham and with a man named Caleb, who had been a great warrior at the time of the settlement of the land. Caleb and his family had been given this area as a reward, and his descendants were still proudly numbered among its inhabitants. In addition, David had ruled Judah from Hebron for seven years. As the capital and king's residence, Hebron had prospered and grown in size and was now a bustling city.

"Greetings, Jonathan ben Shageh!" called an elder as Jonathan and his entourage passed through the city market. "Ahiam has told us of the exploits of your young armor-bearer."

Jonathan raised his hand in greeting. "All you have heard is true, Caleb. Isaac saved my life—put himself between me and a heathen javelin."

There were murmurs of approval from the crowd that had gathered to witness the arrival of their heroes. There was much backslapping and merriment as the warriors were welcomed.

They continued past the marketplace, following a street up a gradual incline. Ailea did her best to hold her head high, despite the speculative glances cast in her direction.

Finally, Isaac entered a door in a wall, and Ailea found herself being led into a lovely courtyard—not as grand as her own in Damascus but filled with carefully tended flowers and shrubs.

A woman maybe ten years older than Ailea—short and rather plump—was drawing water from a cistern. Seeing Isaac, she quickly set down her waterpot and threw herself at him with a glad cry. This must be Judith, the mother of whom Isaac had spoken so fondly.

Threading her arm through her son's, Judith turned then to Jonathan, standing on tiptoe to kiss his cheeks in greeting. As she did so, her gaze fell on Ailea, who waited, eyes averted.

Ailea looked up. This was the moment she had feared. But the woman's eyes were luminous and kind, and her smile lit up her pretty round face in honest welcome.

"I see you have brought a guest with you, Jonathan. Come, child. Our home is your home."

Ailea, not knowing the custom of these people, merely inclined her head in acknowledgment. But she felt a small weight lift from her spirits.

Judith called for her husband, Ahiam, a tall, stocky man with a booming voice, and the greetings and introductions were repeated. Ahiam was unabashed in his pride when he greeted Isaac. He gave the boy a hug so fierce that Judith intervened.

"Careful, Ahiam. He's been wounded, remember."

"I remember well. I was worried when I first heard the news, son. I argued with Benaiah long and hard to get leave to come see you, but he flatly refused me. Insisted you were in good hands with Jonathan, and I see he was right."

"Jonathan took care of me, yes. But it was really the care of Ailea and her mother that brought me back to health so quickly."

Ahiam turned his attention to Ailea. He bowed. "Judith and I are in your debt, my lady. I am deeply grateful for what you did for my son and honored to have you as our guest."

Ailea shook her head. "I did very little. It was my mother—" Ailea felt her throat clog at the memory of Nariah. Ahiam looked exceedingly uncomfortable and turned to Jonathan with a question about the army.

Bustling about, Judith called out instructions for a meal to be prepared for the guests and sleeping arrangements to be made.

Jerioth stepped forward, expressing her thanks for the hospitality but eager to be on her way. She must reach the home of her son before nightfall, she explained.

Ailea hung back, fighting a feeling of unreality and depression. The land and people of Judah were so different from Aram-Zobah, and yet somehow this home called up a haunting image of her own lost family. And now with Jerioth's departure, she felt newly bereft.

And the little scene in the courtyard later—Isaac, Ahiam, and Jonathan discussing military matters while Judith supervised the baking of bread in an outdoor oven—served only to heighten Ailea's sense of isolation.

At that moment a little girl about five years of age appeared at the gate. When she caught sight of Isaac, she ran immediately to his side, tugging at his tunic. Isaac was deeply involved in recounting for his father some detail of the battle in which he had been wounded and paid no heed to the child. This must be the little sister Isaac had spoken of, Ailea surmised.

The child continued to vie for her brother's notice, finally resorting to climbing up his side. A memory of Rezon and herself flashed through Ailea's mind. How many times had she struggled to capture her hero's attention, only to be ignored?

"Adah, get down! Your brother has been injured," Judith scolded, stepping forward to remove the clinging child.

Isaac noticed his little sister at last, kneeling to hug her. "And who is this beautiful young lady? It can't be my little Adah. She was much smaller when I left three months ago." To illustrate, he lifted the child with an exaggerated groan.

"Isaac, be careful," Judith admonished, but the youth swung the little girl above his head, bringing forth excited giggles.

Ailea smiled at the touching scene, recalling Rezon's gruff demonstrations of affection toward her in those long-ago days.

"What is this? I thought you belonged to me!" Ahiam teased, taking Adah from Isaac and tossing her into the air.

"Oh, I do! I do, Father!"

"Well, don't you forget it, my pretty one." He gave his daughter a smacking kiss and set her on her feet.

How strange, Ailea thought. Instead of scolding the little girl for being a nuisance, her father and brother teased her affectionately. Eliada would never have been so demonstrative in front of guests, Ailea recalled sadly. Nor would he have countenanced such an interruption.

Ailea was silent during the meal shared with Ahiam's and Judith's family. She was aware that in most Hebrew households the women would not have sat down with the men to eat. But this, of course, was a special occasion. In addition, theirs was a very loving and close-knit family with Ahiam giving his wife much honor.

As Ailea looked on, a knot formed in her throat. Would she ever be a part of such a loving family? Maybe . . . someday. In the meantime, however, she was subject to one who had been responsible for destroying the only family she had known. Never—not for an instant—must she forget that. Nor would she allow herself to surrender to tender feelings for the Hebrew who had proven himself to be her enemy.

But long after Ailea had retired to her small pallet in a corner of Adah's room, she fought the warring emotions within her own heart, this strange affinity she felt for Isaac's family and her desire to have one like it in stark contrast to her hatred of the Hebrews—and one Hebrew warrior in particular.

~ ~ ~

Once the servants had been dismissed and the younger people settled for the night, Ahiam, Judith, and Jonathan sought the cooling breezes of the rooftop to continue their reunion.

Judith wasted no time in voicing the question that had been on her mind since her guests' arrival. "Why on earth did you bring the Damascene girl here, Jonathan?"

Jonathan shrugged and turned to gaze out over the distant hills. "I'm not quite sure myself," he admitted honestly.

"She is beautiful, of course," Judith observed. "But there are many beautiful women in Judah. And I could not help noticing that she seemed less than happy to be accompanying you."

"She is a captive, Judith—my prize from the king. Of course she isn't happy about it now." Jonathan rose to pace nervously, his hands clasped behind him. "But she will adjust . . . eventually."

"Adjust? To what? What are your plans for her? Will she be a bondslave? A concubine? Or do you intend to wed her?"

"Yes, I do intend to wed her," Jonathan answered without hesitation, his words as much a shock to himself as to his friends. "But I think it best she not be told just yet. There is plenty of time."

"We would say nothing to Ailea, Jonathan. I just hope you will ponder long and hard before you carry through with your plan. But enough of our interference." She threw Ahiam a warning glance. "Are you two going to visit old Caleb before you leave tomorrow, Jonathan?"

"I am afraid I need to be on my way early. Maybe next time."

Ahiam was disappointed. "I had rather promised the old man I would bring you by. He will want news of Shageh and the village."

Jonathan thought of the old friend of his father's who had greeted him in the marketplace the day before. "Well, since the old fellow gets up before the cock crows, I guess we could visit him very early in the morning."

"You had better get some rest then," Judith said in her practical way.

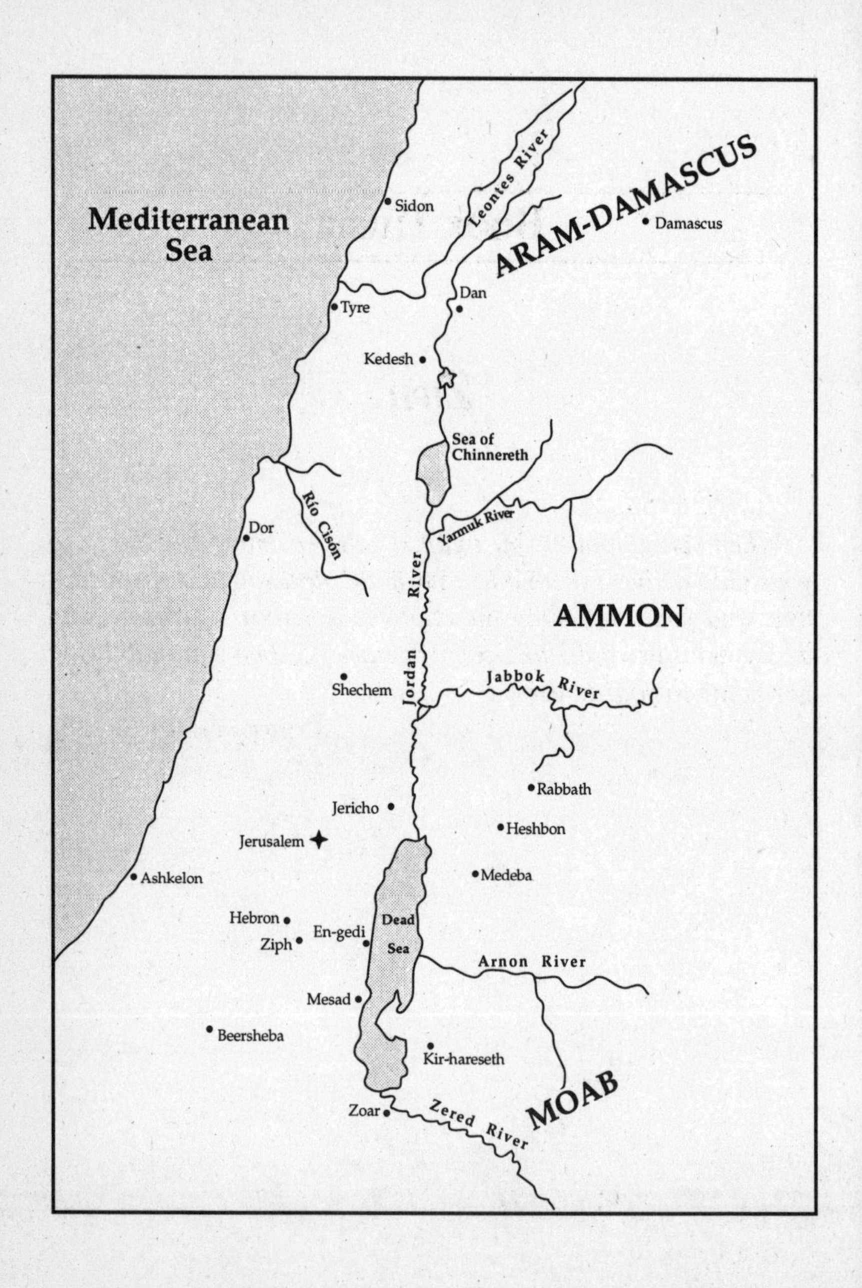
Mediterranean Sea
Sidon
Leontes River
ARAM-DAMASCUS
Damascus
Tyre
Dan
Kedesh
Sea of Chinnereth
Río Cisón
Yarmuk River
Dor
Jordan River
AMMON
Shechem
Jabbok River
Rabbath
Jericho
Heshbon
Jerusalem
Ashkelon
Medeba
Hebron
Dead Sea
En-gedi
Ziph
Arnon River
Mesad
Beersheba
Kir-hareseth
MOAB
Zoar
Zered River

Book Three

Ziph

When you go out to war against your enemies, and the Lord your God delivers them into your hand, and you take them captive, and you see among the captives a beautiful woman, and desire her and would take her for your wife, then you shall bring her home to your house. . .

Deuteronomy 21:10–12

Chapter Fourteen

Ailea slept poorly in the strange house and awoke very early the next morning, full of dread. Today Jonathan would take her to Ziph where she would surely be hated by the villagers who would not be likely to tolerate an Aramean in their midst. She would be a slave or, at best, a concubine to Jonathan, and she would never see her home or Rezon again.

Impulsively she decided that if she were ever to escape, it must be now. She rose in the predawn light and quietly slipped on her tunic and cloak, taking care not to awaken little Adah.

On one side of the room a window opened onto a narrow lane behind the house. She wasn't sure where it lead, but it would have to serve as her escape route.

Cocking her head, Ailea listened for any sounds of the household stirring. Nothing. Still, Judith would soon be rising to prepare food for her guests. She must hurry.

Most of Ailea's clothes were in packs in the courtyard where they had been unloaded yesterday. She did not dare take the time to go for them. Instead, she took off the beautiful cloak David had given her—it would draw attention—and used it to wrap her meager belongings. There was only a comb, a dagger, and an extra pair of sandals—items Jonathan had unpacked for her except for the dagger, which she had managed to secret under her tunic.

Pushing aside the shutters, Ailea stuck her head out the window. She looked up and down the lane which was no more than an alleyway. Not a soul in sight.

Throwing the bundle into the alley, she hoisted herself out the window. She stood for a moment, trying to decide which direction to take. Choosing to go in the opposite direction of the marketplace, she took the lane in the opposite direction. She had no plan really, only a rising sense of panic. She must flee this unfamiliar place, find Akim, and force him to take her to Rezon.

As she hurried down the narrow lane, Ailea neared a cross street. She quickened her pace, fearful of being seen. Just as she did so, two men turned from the cross street and stepped directly in front of her.

"Umph!" one of them cried out as she jammed into him. "Why don't you watch where you're going!"

The big man Ailea had plowed into grabbed her arm to steady her. He recognized her at the same instant she realized that she had just had the misfortune of running into Ahiam! Nor did she need a second glance to know that his companion was Jonathan! Instead, she kicked Ahiam in the shin as hard as she could. He released her with an oath, clutching the injured limb in both hands.

Ailea took off running—this time choosing to rush out into the main thoroughfare, hoping to lose herself among the increasing number of vendors and tradesmen who were beginning their day early. She ran down a narrow twisting lane, through a poorer part of the city, until, at last, it opened out onto a vista of a countryside heavily dotted with trees. Surely if she reached the safety of the forest, her captor would not be able to find her. Perhaps he would decide she wasn't even worth the effort. She paused for a minute to look behind her, but no one was following her. Feeling a surge of hope, she sprinted ahead, putting the city behind her as quickly as possible.

She had gone only a few yards, however, when she heard footsteps pounding behind her. When she looked over her shoulder, she saw Jonathan bearing down upon her. She screamed and darted to the right, but it was no use. A huge hand clamped down on her shoulder, and Jonathan spun her around to the ground.

Ailea pulled herself into a sitting position and covered her face with her hands. Something warm and thick touched both cheeks, and she pulled her hands back. Both palms had caught the weight of her fall and were oozing red.

A sob began deep in her chest, pulling her head forward and then back as it made its way upwards, gathering force and rage as the sound neared her lips. Jonathan was bending over her, his hand extended to pull her to her feet, when the full measure of her fury broke upon him like a storm wave on a barrier rock.

Before he could react, Ailea was on her feet, screaming and flailing at him with both hands gathered into fists, catching him on both sides of the face with bloody imprints from the heels of her palms. He instinctively stepped back, caught off guard by the intensity of the attack but was instantly prepared to fend off successive assaults by simply holding her at arm's length.

Her futile blows fell well short of Jonathan's body, a fact that enraged Ailea even as it amused Jonathan who wiped at his face with one hand while holding Ailea at bay with the other. He laughed and was about to point out the futility of further resistance when a fierce kick from Ailea caught his left shin bone. He momentarily lost his grip. Ailea took one full step forward for the second kick, hitting the same shin slightly higher and more painfully.

Jonathan step back again, but this time as Ailea advanced, he swept to his left, pulling his right leg forward and knocking her to the ground face forward. Before she could reach her feet, Jonathan had covered her with his body. Using his far heavier weight to hold her still and pinion her hands on either side of her head with his arms, he held her fast.

Ailea struggled for a moment, her yells subsiding to hoarse

groans coming between gasps for air. Jonathan eased some of his weight onto his knees but kept his forearms firmly in place. Ailea's eyes were tightly closed, and her head rolled from side to side against the leather bracelets on Jonathan's wrist. With only one means of resistance left, Ailea took in one long draw of air, raised her head as far forward as possible, and began to strike her head against the rocky ground, again and again.

"Stop it! Stop it, Ailea!"

Jonathan captured both her hands in one of his and held her head against the ground with the other. Ailea squirmed under the pressure of his hand against her forehead but finally lay still, drained of her will to fight and left only with enough strength to weep softly.

Jonathan was afraid to loosen his hold but eased even more of his weight onto his knees and finally dropped her hands from his grasp. He had never been comfortable with women in general, much less a grief-stricken girl whom he had wrestled to the ground in hand-to-hand combat. He would indulge her a few more minutes of weeping while he considered what to do next.

He reached to wipe her tears away, but Ailea jerked her head to one side, exposing a blotch of dirt-thickened blood against her raven hair.

"You've injured yourself, you foolish girl!" he scolded her to cover his dismay.

She made no outcry when Jonathan lifted her in his arms and carried her back to the house. But the tears continued to flow. When he entered the courtyard, Ahiam and Judith were waiting.

"It didn't take you long," Ahiam called out jovially. "I told Judith not to worry, that you—" he stopped short when he saw the blood.

"What happened?" Judith gasped.

"She hit her head. I don't think it's serious. Get some water to cleanse the wound."

He sat down with the girl on a bench, and Judith quickly fetched a pail and drew water. The tears were still running from the corners of Ailea's shuttered eyes.

"Oh, Jonathan, see how she weeps!" Judith's voice was filled with compassion. "She must be in pain. Is she conscious?"

In answer, Jonathan spoke to the girl in his arms. "Open your eyes, little warrior. You are frightening Judith." When she did not respond, he shook her gently. "Open your eyes, Ailea."

Much to his surprise, she obeyed. But when he gazed into those deep green pools of despair, Jonathan wished he had not insisted. "Enough," he said as he dabbed at the moisture with the clean, dry cloth Judith handed him. But the tears continued.

They flowed silently while Judith cleaned Ailea's cuts and those she had inflicted on Jonathan with her sharp nails during the struggle. They continued all afternoon until Judith and Jonathan were truly frightened for the girl's sanity.

At last, when everyone had tried without success to appeal to Ailea's reason and Isaac's little sister had been sent to a neighbor, Jonathan felt forced to take sterner measures.

"That is enough, Ailea! You are making yourself ill and distressing the entire household. Stop crying, at once!"

She did not respond to his command. Frightened for her, he took her in his arms and held her. "Please, Ailea, please."

Ahiam, Judith, and Isaac ate the evening meal while Jonathan stayed with Ailea. Afterward, Judith came to insist that Jonathan eat something. She tried to tempt Ailea as well with an offering of broth from a chicken. When she refused, Judith persisted. "Is there something I can get for you, my dear? Anything you want?"

Judith had not expected a reply. The girl had not spoken all day. Now she murmured something inaudible before changing to a thin, high-pitched wail. "I want my mother! I want my f-f-father! I want to go ho-o-o-me!"

Jonathan lightly stroked her hair as she cried on the bed, and Judith's own eyes filled with tears as Ailea's grief, finally given voice, wracked her body. She sobbed, calling out for her lost family. It seemed to go on for hours, Jonathan, Judith, and Isaac trying to offer comfort while Ahiam stood by in abashed silence. Finally, the sobs subsided, and Ailea slept.

"We should watch her closely tonight, but I think she will feel better now that she has grieved for her parents," Jonathan whispered to his friends.

Later, Ahiam called Jonathan aside. "My friend, I do not wish to interfere, but I must share with you an observation." He paused to see if Jonathan would be open to his counsel.

"Speak your mind, friend."

Ahiam combed his fingers through his beard, weighing his words. "In my day I have seen many wild things tamed. But there are some that cannot be tamed. If they are not set free, they eventually die. I fear that Ailea is such a creature."

Jonathan made no reply but waited for Ahiam to gather his thoughts.

"Surely you do not really intend to marry this girl, for what would be the basis of such a marriage?" Ahiam sighed. "Think it over, my friend, before it's too late. I know you feel pity for the girl. If you care for her at all, take her back to Damascus and see her safely settled among her own people."

Jonathan nodded, promising to consider his friend's words. But within himself, his decision was firm. He would not insist . . . for now. But the day would come when he would make Ailea his wife.

~ ~ ~

Ailea was pale the next morning, her eyes puffy from the crying, but she was composed as she and Jonathan broke their fast with Ahiam's family. She had slept next to Adah, the little girl cuddling close to her all night, as if realizing Ailea's pain. This morning, Ailea had exchanged a few words with her though she had said little to anyone else.

When Jonathan had finished loading the donkey's panniers, he thanked his hosts for their hospitality. Judith embraced Jonathan and kissed Ailea good-bye, leaning near to whisper in her ear, "Jonathan may be a hardened soldier, but he is a good man. Do not be afraid of him. He will be good to you."

Judith stepped aside at Jonathan's approach. "I need your promise not to try to run today, little warrior." He appeared a little uncomfortable. "I don't wish to bind you, but I would not have you injured."

She looked at him for a long moment before she answered, her eyes dull and lusterless, lacking their usual fire. "You would trust my word?"

"Until you prove to me I cannot," he answered wearily.

She gave a little sigh of resignation. "I will not try *today*. I don't have the strength."

Her emphasis did not escape his notice, but he decided to let it pass. They began their journey to Ziph side by side, Jonathan leading the donkey.

While they walked, he told her about his family, about the life they had lived together, about the villagers. His sister, who was a childless widow, lived with him and his father, who was the village wise man and teacher. His name was Shageh, and Jonathan's voice filled with pride as he spoke of the man's kindness and wisdom.

"He will teach you our Law, Ailea. And you must not hesitate to bring your problems to him. He will never ridicule them, no matter how small. I remember the time when I was a little boy and . . ." During the six-mile journey, Jonathan revealed more of himself to her than he ever had to any other woman. He found himself wondering why, when she remained so aloof, holding herself carefully erect, staring straight into the distance with unseeing eyes.

~ ~ ~

Jonathan quickened his pace as the village of Ziph came into view. It was much smaller than the bustling city of Hebron, though walled for fortification from marauding bands. The gates were opened for the daylight commerce, and Ailea could see inside as they drew near. The structures appeared humble, entirely unimpressive, she thought—simple dwellings of wood and plaster and native stone.

The Ziphites greeted Jonathan even more enthusiastically than had the people of Hebron. It was apparent that he was the local hero. As in Hebron, the old men called out questions about the battle while the women inquired about his health. Small children clamored for attention, grabbing at his arms. Scooping up two of them—a plump little girl and a grubby boy of about four—he swung them onto his shoulders. The children squealed with delight, and Ailea had no choice but to follow.

Ailea slowed her pace so that she now walked beside the donkey. Jonathan's attention was diverted by the milling crowd that pressed in on both sides of the road. She could see the smiling faces of the women change to surprise and then disdain as Jonathan moved past and they suddenly caught sight of his captive.

Out of his hearing, they made no doubt as to their feelings regarding the dark-haired stranger whose fine fabric robe was decidedly out of place among the simple everyday outfits of the village women.

"Make way for the princess."

"What's she doing here?"

"We've no place for an idol-worshipping harlot here."

The women were evidently speaking what the men were thinking. While none spoke to her directly, she could see them turn to one another with hurried comments, not trying to contain their ribald laughter.

An attractive woman fell into step beside him, and he smiled down at her. "Have you been well, Dinah?" The woman's reply, uttered in a low, throaty tone, could not be overheard.

At last they came to a stop in front of the finest house Ailea had seen in Ziph, and the crowd following all the way into the courtyard.

A tall, rather dour middle-aged woman came out of the house, evidently curious about the commotion. Her stern countenance softened somewhat when she saw Jonathan. She hurried to greet him, and he deposited the two children on the ground so that he could engulf her in a hug. Ailea noted a resemblance between them and surmised that this was Ruth, the sister he had mentioned on the way.

After she had embraced her brother, the woman looked up into his face. "We didn't expect you to return so soon. The Rab thought you would want to stay in Jerusalem for a while longer."

Jonathan shook his head. "You know I would rather be home than in Jerusalem. Speaking of the Rab, where is he? There are matters I must discuss with him."

"He is still at the teaching rock, tutoring a group of young village boys."

When Jonathan stepped aside, Ruth noticed Ailea for the first time. She broke off speaking and stared at the strange girl for a long moment, then turned a questioning gaze on her brother.

Jonathan took Ailea's arm and drew her forward. The crowd hushed. "This is Ailea of Damascus. I have brought her back as a prize from the king." There were several audible gasps at the news.

Ruth eyed Ailea as if she were a bug crawling on freshly baked bread. "You intend to have your concubine live here—in my home?"

Jonathan scowled and braced his hands on his hips. "I intend for her to live here—in *my* home. It will be hers as well."

Ruth quickly masked her look of shock and disapproval. She turned without another word and reentered the house. The crowd, sensing the tension in the atmosphere, quietly dispersed.

Jonathan did not follow his sister into the house but led Ailea up the outer stairs to the rooftop. She was surprised to find here comfortable couches, potted trees, and flowering plants—much like she had left in Damascus. An upper room had also been added, occupying nearly half the space of the rooftop.

Jonathan motioned her to enter, and she stepped inside, blushing when she realized that this was his sleeping chamber—a chamber as richly appointed as any in the house of Eliada. A raised platform was spread with pillows and furs. And to one side a large chest, constructed of acacia wood and inlaid ivory, rested upon a thick rug fringed in blue.

Jonathan moved to the chest and deposited the heavy pack he had brought with him. Seeing the look of alarm on Ailea's face, he hastened to explain, "These are *my* quarters. You will sleep below in the small room next to my sister's." The look of relief on the girl's face was almost comical.

"Come, I'll show you. Then we will go find the Rab."

Thankfully, Ruth was nowhere to be seen when Jonathan helped Ailea place her belongings in her new room before leading her outside the walls of the village.

From there, they made their way toward a large sycamore fig tree that dominated a small rise. Under the tree, sitting on a boulder with an indentation forming a bench, was an old man whose hair and flowing beard were the color of a newborn lamb. At their approach he left his students and came forward to greet them.

Ailea noticed that the Rab was very tall, like his son, and not nearly as frail as he had appeared from a distance. Indeed, his shoulders were broad and straight—not bent at all—and his skin was burnished from his many years in the sun. He might be a holy man, she mused, but he had not spent all his time poring over manuscripts or meditating in the darkness.

As he drew near, Ailea could see that his eyes were amber—like Jonathan's—but deeper set and almost translucent and seemed to penetrate into her soul.

He embraced his son, kissing him on both cheeks. "Welcome home, my son. I have offered many prayers for you in your absence."

"And I, for you, Father. I have missed you."

Jonathan stepped back and Shageh's gaze fell upon Ailea once again. Her heart raced. For some reason she could not fathom, it was important to her that this man's opinion of her be different from those of his daughter Ruth and the other villagers.

"Father, this is Ailea of Damascus. Her mother and father died during the campaign, and I have brought her back to live here," Jonathan hastened to explain, ready to argue his case should the Rab object. "She was brought to Jerusalem among the captives, and the king gave her to me as a prize of war."

Shageh's smile crinkled the corners of his eyes. "I can see that you are indeed a prize, child. I welcome you to Ziph. You will find peace here."

Ailea wanted to tell the Rab that she doubted his words—not while his exasperating son controlled her life—but she decided not to bring the old man into her struggle with Jonathan. The rabbi was, after all, the only person in the entire village who had greeted her warmly.

When they returned home with Shageh, they found Ruth busily preparing the evening meal. The older woman completely ignored Ailea's presence and answered only when someone spoke to her. She hates me, Ailea groaned silently. But no more than I hate being here!

Wishing somehow to ease the tension she had created, Ailea decided to be useful. She picked up the two large, rounded loaves of freshly baked bread and broke them, in order to arrange them in a nearby basket.

Suddenly, to her horror, bread and basket were knocked out of her hand. "How dare you touch the bread with unclean hands?" Ruth hissed. "Now it is unfit to eat!"

Completely baffled, Ailea looked into the woman's angry face. "But my hands are not dirty. See?" She held them up for Ruth's inspection.

Ruth angrily batted her hands aside, picked up the bread, and went to throw it away. Ailea glanced at the two men. Surely one of them would offer an explanation as to what rule of etiquette she had breached.

Jonathan kept silent, but Shageh walked over to a bowl and pitcher that sat on a chest against the wall. "Come here, child." Ailea obeyed.

"Now hold out your hands." She did as she was told, and he picked up the pitcher and poured the water over her hands into the bowl before handing her a clean cloth.

"In this manner, we Hebrews cleanse our hands before eating. It is a ceremonial washing, to remind us that Lord God desires that we be clean and pure. You must pour the water over the hands as I have just done before you handle food. Do not pour it in the basin first, else your hands will not be bathed in pure water alone but in their own filth. Do you understand what I have told you?"

Ailea shook her head. "No, I do *not* understand. I am not a Hebrew. Nor do I wish to be one." She scowled at Jonathan, then plopped down on one of the cushions arranged around the low table, her growling stomach signaling her hunger. How foolish to throw away perfectly good food!

Ruth returned to the table with the leg of lamb that had been roasting on a spit outside and some crusty bread—several days old from the looks of it. When Ruth was seated, the Rab took the bread, broke it, and holding it heavenward invoked the blessing of the Hebrew God, whom he called Adonai. They ate in silence.

Immediately after the meal, Jonathan ordered Ailea to her room to rest. "You have still not recovered from all your escapades, and this day has been difficult."

Determined not to dignify his remarks with a reply, Ailea turned her back on him. He immediately brought her around to face him, his strong fingers digging into her shoulders. "And you will obey Ruth. She will be as a mother to you. You may think her harsh, her ways strange to you, but in time she will accept you if you do as she says." When Ailea only glared back defiantly, he dropped his hands and left her.

~ ~ ~

For a long time Ailea lay awake, thinking of Rezon and the messenger he had sent. Had Akim followed her to Ziph? Surely he would come for her soon. Ailea did not know how long she could bite her tongue and pretend submission. Jonathan was bad enough but now that obnoxious sister of his! How could a man like the Rab have fathered two such children? He was not at all judgmental; indeed, he seemed to understand her plight. Ailea sighed and fell asleep with a vision of the deep, kindly eyes locked with hers.

Chapter Fifteen

Ailea's first days in Ziph were just as she had imagined they would be—loathesome. While her arrogant captor kept to himself, his sister was about night and day, never letting Ailea forget that she would just as soon have the plague in her house as she would a foreigner!

On Ailea's second day in the household, Ruth pointed to a large waterpot that stood in the courtyard just outside the door of the house.

"Take this to the spring and fill it with water, and be quick about it!" Ailea wondered if she would be able to lift the large vessel in its present empty state, much less when it was filled with water. Nevertheless, she obeyed.

When she got to the spring, several of the village women were there ahead of her, their light chatter and gay laughter fluttering through the air like a flock of birds. But the women scattered when they saw Ailea, not wishing to sully themselves with her presence, she supposed.

She was leaning over, drawing up the leather bucket filled with water to pour into the pot she had brought with her when she heard a mocking voice behind her. "So Jonathan's harlot is making herself useful. What's the matter? Has he already grown tired of you? If the Law did not forbid it, he would have brought you back as his slave. But as his concubine, you will find your lot much the same. When he marries *me,* I'll have you fetch my food and wash my clothes. Jonathan will have no more use for you in his bed."

Ailea turned, coming face to face with Dinah, the woman who had greeted Jonathan with such familiarity on their first day in the village. Now her pretty features were distorted with a venomous scorn.

Ailea felt a rush of anger. She wasn't surprised to find that the villagers were whispering behind her back about her captivity, thinking that the captain used her shamefully. But hearing this hateful woman insult her honor was past endurance. "If you want him, you're welcome to him! There are no real men except in Damascus!" she called out, making no effort to conceal her contempt.

Infuriated, Dinah hurled more insults. "Wanton offspring of an uncircumcised heathen!"

Pretending to ignore her, Ailea picked up the waterpot, suppressing a groan at its heaviness. She would sooner die than let Dinah see any weakness in her. Balancing it on her shoulder with one hand, she moved gracefully toward the house of Shageh.

After that incident, the women of the village gossiped openly, speaking distinctly whenever Ailea was within hearing distance. They speculated on her parentage, on Jonathan's probable use of her, and on how long he would keep her before he grew tired of her. A few times she was pelted with mud and small stones, a fact that only fueled her resolve to escape as soon as she could find a way.

~ ~ ~

Three blasts on the shofar, or ram's horn, heralded the beginning of the most important day of the week to the Hebrews. It was sundown on the sixth day of the week.

Ailea put away the cloth she had been using to clean the house. She had already been warned by Shageh that in Israel no work would be done until after sundown the next day. It was one of Adonai's commands.

Just then, all three members of the household appeared. Ruth scowled at her; Jonathan gave her an enigmatic look and then glanced away. Only Shageh smiled at the stranger in their midst. As Ruth lit the candles of the sabbath, he told her of the seven days of creation and how the Lord God rested on the seventh day.

Jonathan was at home for the entire twenty-four hours, and Ailea was more miserable than ever. Ruth seemed to think it necessary to point out every fault Ailea had and every mistake she made. Her brother fluctuated between scolding his sister for her contentious ways and scolding Ailea for deliberately provoking his sister. By the end of the sabbath, she felt as if she had anything but a day of rest.

~ ~ ~

After a week of conflict between the two women in his household, Jonathan was more battle-weary than he could ever recall and sought refuge with his father and the others at evening circle—a time after the last meal of the day when the men of the village gathered to share news and swap stories. He bid a curt goodnight to Ailea and Ruth, then went to settle a matter with Habaz before heading for the open plaza near the city gate.

When Jonathan arrived, he stood on the fringes of the group under a tamarind tree. They were seated around an open fire, listening to Shageh's story about a Philistine raid that had taken place when he was a boy.

"And so they took all our sheep and anything else they could carry out of Ziph and headed back to Gath. We followed them, of course, and waited until they had consumed the wine they had stolen. Soon they were all sleeping like dead men."

"They were drunk on the wine?" The question came from a smooth-faced youth who had yet to fight his first battle.

"Ha! They were *drugged* on it. When we got word they were coming to raid us, we put poppy juice in half the wine we had in the village and buried the rest."

There was a round of hearty laughter before the young man spoke up again with an air of bravado. "The Philistines are such fools! It is no wonder our people vanquished them!"

Shageh drew his heavy brows together in a scowl. "Only a fool puts his trust in the sword. If not for the favor of Adonai, we would have lost the battle, and the victory would have belonged to our enemies." Glancing up, he saw Jonathan standing in the shadows. "Here is my son, recently come from both the battlefield and the palace. Come, tell us how it was, my son."

For the next hour, it was Jonathan's turn to speak of matters of state and of the latest campaign, finishing with an account of his arduous trek across the desert. He sighed wearily. "After so many months away, I am glad to be back with my people."

Drawing a ragged breath, he got on with the important news he must share with the men of Ziph. "As you know, I brought with me a girl of Damascus. . . ."

An elder nodded knowingly. "Your concubine."

"No, Eli, not my concubine. I mean to make Ailea my wife."

There was stunned silence before the elder spoke again. "Surely you can't mean what you say! You will marry a Judahite girl and make this foreigner your concubine. Is that not true?"

"Ailea will be my wife—my *only* wife. We will wed next week." Jonathan glanced toward the Rab, scrutinizing him closely. Shageh met his gaze, pausing only for a moment.

"He speaks the truth. I am pleased to invite you all to the wedding of my son seven days from today. Come, my friends, make merry with us."

There was a murmur of acceptance; no one would have dared refuse the Rab's invitation outright. But the lighthearted jesting and congratulations that usually accompanied such an announcement were conspicuously absent. Apparently, the men of Ziph doubted the wisdom of his decision, Jonathan mused.

As they walked home under the stars, Shageh was the first to speak. "How did you persuade the little rebel to become your bride so soon, my son? She still kicks like a donkey." He chuckled softly. "I had expected it would take some time to win her over."

An uncomfortable silence descended upon them while Jonathan phrased his confession. "Ailea does not yet know I am making her my wife. In fact, she believes that I plan to make her my concubine. Maybe Eli told her—you heard him at circle tonight."

"More likely it was his daughter who started the rumor."

"Dinah?"

"The girl has been tormenting Ailea all week, making her life miserable. So I have been told."

Jonathan frowned. "All the more reason we should be married soon. I have seen how the villagers treat her, though I wasn't aware that Dinah—"

"And why have you kept your intentions from the little one?" the Rab interrupted him. "Have you asked what she thinks of the idea?"

"There is no need." Jonathan snorted. "I *know* what she would think!" A pang of guilt struck him, but he shrugged it aside. "Besides, it matters not. I won her. She is mine, and that is all there is to it!"

Shageh halted at the gate of the courtyard. "Son, I would counsel you to reconsider your decision to wed the Damascene."

Jonathan ground his teeth. How humiliating that his father still had the ability to reduce him to the status of a naughty boy. But he was no longer a boy. And his decision was final. "The wedding will take place next week."

~ ~ ~

Habaz was late. Outside the gates of Ziph, Jonathan paced impatiently. The man knew well that he was supposed to travel to Hebron with Jonathan to purchase stock. Jonathan did not tolerate delays. He himself was always punctual, conducting his affairs with military precision. And these days he had much to occupy his mind. There was the wedding to plan—after he told Ailea, of course. At some point, he would have to return to Jerusalem, at least for a while to meet with the war council. And there was always the threat of being called up to engage in one of the many skirmishes that plagued this land. As one of the gibborim, Jonathan was never off duty.

Today, however, he had business with the chief shepherd of Ziph—the acquisition of some new rams. As the town's wealthiest citizen, Jonathan often provided the means for the villagers to improve their own lot.

As for telling Ailea of his plans for their marriage, his long hours away from home were a convenient excuse to further delay the dreaded confrontation. Far better to hear Habaz praise his generosity than to hear Ailea's sharp rebuke when she learned the truth about the forthcoming event!

While Jonathan consulted with the chief shepherd, Ailea met Shageh under the sycamore tree for her third lesson. The Rab seemed particularly anxious to begin the session today as he settled on the teaching rock. Ailea, on the other hand, was disheartened and listless and took her seat at his feet, distracted by her own concerns.

She was lonelier than she had ever been in her life. For one thing, all the villagers spoke Y'hudit, and though Ailea could understand it—for it was so similar to her own language—it seemed unnatural never to speak in her own tongue. And there were so many rules! She was always making mistakes and feeling the harsh criticism of Jonathan and his sister. Only Shageh took pains to explain the strange customs to her, kindly enlightening her on each point of the Law. She sat straighter, determined to listen carefully.

"Today we will learn about the Law of the captive bride," Shageh told her.

She arched a sable eyebrow. "You have a Law for everything!"

Shageh chuckled. "So we do, child. And since this portion pertains to your own situation, I thought you might find it interesting."

Her attention piqued, Ailea leaned forward.

The Rab closed his eyes for a moment, recalling the ancient passage. He did not use the scrolls David had sent him when he taught; these were stored in a special chest in the house and brought out only for Sabbath study with the elders. Instead, he opened his eyes and recited from memory.

> When you go out to war against your enemies, and the Lord your God delivers them into your hand, and you take them captive, and you see among the captives a beautiful woman, and desire her and would take her for your wife, then you shall bring her home to your house, and she shall shave her head and trim her nails. She shall put off the clothes of her captivity, remain in your house, and mourn her father and mother a full month.....

The old man paused at the look of dismay on the beautiful face of his pupil. "You are telling me that Jonathan is going to cut off my hair?"

"No, child. Perhaps you didn't listen closely. The Law says only that the captive may cut off her *own* hair. I doubt if Jonathan even recalls this passage, for it has not been widely used since the time long before the kings."

"Then why are you telling me about it?"

"Because I am teaching you the Law of Moses, my child." He regarded her with narrowed gaze, observing her wide-eyed innocence. It was clear that Jonathan had not yet revealed his intentions. "Perhaps, someday, you will find the information useful."

~ ~ ~

Jonathan did not go to evening circle with his father. Instead, he remained at home after the meal. The time had come to tell Ailea of her future.

Inviting her to join him on the roof, he gestured toward a couch and then began to pace in front of her.

"There was something you wished to tell me?"

As usual, when she was alone with him, her voice was full of tension, tinged with fear. Jonathan could not abide the sound of it. But his anger was born of his own guilt, and he spoke more sharply than he had intended. "For the remainder of this week, there will be much for both of us to do. In six days, we are to be married, and—"

"Married!" Ailea, putting aside all restraint, jumped to her feet and grabbed his arm. "I am your slave. You can't make me your wife!"

He smiled benignly. "You belong to me. I can do whatever I please. But you are not my slave."

"No? I am free to return to my people?"

"No."

"Then I am your slave—for now—but I will *never* be your wife." She tossed her head in defiance, green fire glittering dangerously in her eyes.

Jonathan grasped her by the upper arms and dragged her close to him. "You will be whatever I want you to be." He stopped in midsentence. This was not going at all the way he had planned. He was torn between the desire to yell at her and the desire to kiss her.

He took a steadying breath. "I see no need to discuss the matter further. You are entirely unreasonable."

"And you are *mad!*"

"Perhaps, but know that we will be wed in six days. And now I bid you a good night."

With one last lingering look, Jonathan released her. He turned and went into his sleeping chamber and closed the door, leaving Ailea sputtering in indignation.

~ ~ ~

Jonathan was quite surprised when she stopped him the following morning before he left to join Shageh at the teaching rock. "Jonathan, I would speak with you."

He looked down at her strained face. It didn't look as if she had gotten much sleep. Good. Neither had he. "Do you have something to add to our conversation of last evening?" he asked flatly.

"Yes, I think I have, if you will hear me out."

"Very well." He motioned to the bench that sat before the door of the house. As they sat down, she fussed unnecessarily with her loose, flowing tunic, tightening the girdle around her waist and worrying the fringed ends of it.

She is very nervous, Jonathan thought as he watched her. Perhaps she has changed her mind afterall.

"I must be on my way soon, Ailea. What did you wish to tell me?"

She looked up with a weak smile. "I have been thinking about your desire to marry, my lord, and it occurred to me that you may not be aware of something regarding your prospects in that matter."

He frowned. "My prospects?"

She rushed on as if this was a speech that had been rehearsed. "I know it is important to you that the mother of your Hebrew children be above reproach. I don't think you have considered that if you married me, our children would always be considered outsiders. Half Aramean."

"Ailea, I have considered that and—"

She held up her hand. "Just hear me out, Jonathan. There is someone much more suitable right here in Ziph. It has occurred to me that because you have been away so much, you may not have thought of her. But I happen to know from conversations with her that the lovely widow, Dinah, the daughter of Eli, would be very amenable to wed with you. And I am sure her father Eli, as a village elder would be more than proud to call you son . . . What are you laughing at?"

She looked so befuddled that Jonathan made a valiant but hopeless effort to keep a straight face. But it was no use. He shook his head and let out an unrestrained laugh.

"Ailea, you must truly hate me to wish me bound to Dinah for the rest of my life! Lovely widow indeed." He lifted her chin with his forefinger until her eyes met his.

"I am nearly thirty years old. Old enough to notice when a woman throws herself at me. I have no desire for Dinah nor any other woman but you. I suggest that you get used to it."

~ ~ ~

Uriah was bitterly disappointed. He had found no helpful information in all of Damascus nor in any of the cities that made up the Zobah alliance. He did not know where else to look for Rezon, and he was running out of time. The month of Sivan was approaching. He had to get back to Jerusalem, or his wedding would have to be postponed.

Having no further ideas, Uriah returned to Damascus and inteviewed Rezon's former military friends once again. This time, he noticed that one of them seemed uncomfortable with the pointed questions. Believing that the man knew more than he was letting on, Uriah ordered Shammah to have the soldier brought to the garrison headquarters for further questioning. He would meet them there at midnight.

As Uriah had expected, the fellow was unnerved at being dragged out of his house without warning in the middle of the night. The experience loosened his tongue.

In answer to the questions Uriah fired at him, the soldier hunched his shoulders and spread his hands. "Rezon is anywhere. Everywhere. He and his band of men raid the caravans on the trade routes, especially the King's Highway. He prefers to strike Hebrew targets."

"How many men are with him? Name them!"

The soldier knew only that the band numbered over fifty and cited two of Rezon's closest friends who had joined him in exile. Uriah was not disappointed with the information. It was at least a start. He set off thc same day, confident that he would easily find Rezon, observe his movements, and still make it back to Jerusalem in time for his own wedding.

Chapter Sixteen

Jonathan was disturbed by Ailea's unaccountable air of serenity since his startling announcement that they were to be married. She seemed to make an effort to pacify Ruth. She even smiled at Jonathan once when Shageh told the story of his son's encounter with an angry hive of honey bees. Of course it was probably the thought of the painful stings he had suffered that made her smile. Still, it had taken his breath away to see her lips curve invitingly and her eyes sparkle.

Ailea was still unusually calm on the day of the wedding—an event that would be celebrated with fewer than the usual formalities, considering the fact that Ailea was a captive bride and without father or mother.

Jonathan had sent word to Hebron, and Ahiam's family arrived that morning. Judith went to work at once helping Ruth, who had grudgingly baked bread and made fig cakes for the past three days. Jonathan tried to banish his sister's surly mood by pointing out that they had plenty of wine and that when the food was all gone, the feast would be over. "Everyone knows this is an unusual marriage, anyway," he assured her.

Ruth turned an accusing glare on her brother. "Unusual? It is disgraceful! No one can understand why you are going through with this. If you had to bring her here, why didn't you just make her your concubine? The shame of it—making a foreigner your *wife!* You will regret it for the rest of your life. And I am supposed to join in the merrymaking. I tell you, I won't."

"Silence!" Jonathan ordered in a harsh voice. "I expected resistance from Ailea, but she has been on surprisingly good behavior. Now my own sister lashes me with her sharp tongue. I will hear no more." He stalked off to make his own hasty preparations for the wedding.

~ ~ ~

When he had gathered all his guests in the courtyard—a rather disappointing crowd, as many of the villagers had made their excuses, wishing to show their disapproval—Jonathan went to fetch his bride. He found Shageh waiting outside her closed door. "Go and join the guests, my son. I will bring the child to you in a few moments."

Maybe it was best this way, Jonathan conceded to himself. She seemed to get along with the Rab better than with anyone else. Jonathan returned to the wedding guests. He was glad Ahiam and Judith had come. He knew they had reservations about his decision, but they offered him their full support, and Judith had helped prepare the bridal bower. Maybe her thoughtfulness would help overcome the bride's reluctance, though he doubted it.

When Shageh paused in the doorway a few minutes later with Ailea beside him, she was not wearing the customary richly embroidered bridal robes, nor was she bedecked with jewels. She was dressed in an unadorned tunic Ruth had given her. Her hair was pulled back from her face and hung in two long braids.

Jonathan supposed she had purposely tried to make herself less attractive. All Ailea had succeeded in doing, however, was to display the lovely lines of her body, molded against the starkly simple design of her garment. And the raven-black hair, pulled away from her face so severely, only framed her perfect features.

Jonathan's heart soared. She looked so young, so tender. Today this fascinating creature would be his!

He made a move to join them, but Shageh shook his head slightly and lifted one hand to silence the crowd. "I welcome you all here today, my friends, to witness the marriage of Ailea, daughter of Eliada of Damascus, and my son Jonathan. As you know, she was brought here as a captive after our victory over the Arameans and has . . . consented . . . to be his wife."

The Rab lifted one of the precious scrolls and opened it. "I will read to you concerning the Law of the captive bride." His voice rang out deep and resonant while Ailea followed mentally, repeating the words she had committed to memory. Jonathan was only half listening, stirred by the sight of the lovely young woman who would soon be his wife. His pulses quickened at the thought that he would claim her before night's end.

". . . she shall mourn her father and her mother for a full month," the Rab was reading. It had been at least a month since Jonathan had fallen heir to Ailea as a prize of war. A very long month, fraught with frustration. . . .

"And it shall be if you have no delight in her," Shageh continued, "then you shall set her free."

Jonathan smiled to himself. Ailea was maddening, but she was thoroughly delightful. She would be even more so . . . when she belonged to him fully. He would never let her go. His imagination wandered. Everything was in readiness. . . .

A sudden motion caught Jonathan's eye—something glinted in the light of the many torches.

Ailea grabbed one of her long braids with one hand, holding in the other a slender object. Before it registered in Jonathan's clouded brain that the object was Ailea's dagger, she had severed the braid near her scalp.

There were gasps and cries of alarm from the onlookers. Jonathan took a step toward her, but Ailea stepped back quickly, and before he could reach her, she had severed the other braid. "Ailea! What—"

"I am following the Law, Hebrew! *Your* Law!" There was triumph in the emerald eyes.

Jonathan felt himself grow pale, his knees weak. A strong hand steadied him. "Leave her alone, my son. It is her right."

Jonathan was tempted to push Shageh aside and haul Ailea off as he had on the day he had met her, but a soul-deep respect for the Rab and the knowledge that the villagers were watching broke through even his anger and obsession with his captive bride.

When his eyes met hers, she threw the braids at his feet with a fulminating glare. Stupidly, he stared at them, then back at her. "Why?" he mouthed.

The Rab answered for her. "She mourns her family and her humiliation. Since she has chosen it to be so, she will have a full month—from this day—before you can take her as your wife."

The stunned crowd made no further outcry as they stared at Ailea's shorn head. Jonathan, too, was silent, numbed by the sight. Her hair, her beautiful hair. A slow rage began to build, replacing his shock.

Prostitutes, he knew, were sometimes forced to cut their hair as a sign of shame. And occasionally a woman who had been raped or had lost her husband in some great tragedy would cut her hair in sorrow. But this act was not required. Jonathan wondered if the villagers would now believe that he had raped Ailea—had murdered her family?

As the thought of his father being an accomplice in this, his anger boiled over. "You . . . you," he sputtered, jabbing his forefinger under the Rab's nose, "*you* put her up to this, just to thwart me! I tell you, it won't work! It has been well over a month since she was taken captive, and I demand my rights!"

He was reaching for Ailea when the Rab again stayed him, clasping his son's arm. "The child cannot be punished for following the Law," Shageh said under his breath. "I am the teacher of the Law in this village, and I say her month of mourning begins today. It would be most unfair to count the time when she was distraught or unconscious. She is only just now recovered. If you cannot deal calmly with Ailea, I suggest you join your guests and leave me in charge of her."

Too late, Jonathan saw that Ailea had taken advantage of his distraction to finish the prescribed ceremony. She was paring her nails with the sharp blade of the dagger. But her hands trembled so—what with the spectacle she was making and her captor's strident anger—that the blade slipped, and she cut her thumbnail to the quick, causing it to bleed.

Jonathan saw it happen. "No!" He jerked the knife out of her hand. "No more!" he thundered as he took off his cloak and covered her head. He dragged her up against his side, heedless of her struggles, and addressed the crowd.

"Go home now. There will be no marriage feast. But spread the word far and wide that one month from today, you are all invited to the biggest celebration ever given in Ziph—the wedding that should have taken place today!"

The guests drifted away, too stunned for conversation, murmuring polite good-byes to their hosts.

Jonathan looked down at Ailea who was still squirming in his grasp, her face partially obscured by his cloak. "Get inside before I give in to the temptation to throttle you," he said through gritted teeth and gave her a push toward the door.

For once, Ailea did not resist. She wanted nothing more than to leave his presence.

Ahiam and Judith, the only guests who remained, had been discreetly waiting to one side. "Is there anything we can do?" Ahiam asked quietly.

Apparently they had sent Isaac on ahead of them. For that, Jonathan was grateful. "No. There is nothing you can do. But I should have listened to you when you tried to warn me." He gave a short, bitter laugh.

"Then we will leave for home now. Later, when the time is right, we will speak again."

When his friends were gone, Jonathan stooped down and picked up the braids that lay at his feet in a forlorn heap. How could she have cut her glorious hair? In the past weeks he had dreamed many times of sinking his fingers into these thick tresses. He felt as if he had been robbed of a treasure. He could not explain to himself later why he did such a thing, but he took the braids to his chamber and put them in a kid-skin bag.

When he went below, still shaken, he found Shageh applying a healing ointment to Ailea's thumb. She sat stoically as he bandaged it.

Ruth was placing food on the table, her countenance as dark as his spirits. "We have twenty loaves of bread and enough fig cakes to feed the army," she muttered. "I gave most of the roasted lamb to Eleazer's family since there are eleven of them. The rest we can eat today and tomorrow. Such a waste I have never seen. And the scandal—today's debacle will be food for the gossip-mongers for years to come."

"I have told you before, Ruth," Jonathan said in an ominous tone, "I am tired of hearing your complaints."

Ruth pursed her lips and glared at both her brother and the girl who had caused all the trouble, but she said nothing more.

As they ate in silence, Ailea waited for Jonathan to unleash his anger on her. But he remained silent. He must be planning her punishment. She wondered what it would be and could not repress a shiver of apprehension at the thought of the exquisite torture he was probably devising for her. Even the Rab could not protect her now, she feared.

~ ~ ~

Ailea lay on her pallet unable to quiet the thoughts and images that vied for her attention. Without Shageh's help she would have been married to Jonathan and become a wife as well as a prisoner. *Shall mourn her father and her mother.* The words caught her unprepared. Their force struck her like a blow to the face. Her father, her mother, dead. They would never see her wedding, never hold their grandchildren. Rezon might never come as well. She was truly alone with no one to see her, to know her hurt, and to care. Burying her face in the pillow, she muffled her cries until they exhausted her, and then she slept.

The night repeated the events of the day, however, as a dream played itself out in the darkness of the sleeping chamber. Ailea was walking from the house into the courtyard where the wedding guests were assembled. Torches were burning on all sides, but the light was wind-blown and shadowy, distorting the forms and faces.

Ailea searched among the company for someone familiar, but the closer she approached the further they seemed to retreat. Then from the far back, at the seam of light and darkness, a figured moved forward, parting the crowd to either side, a dark presence whose eyes caught the yellow light of the flames and intensified them in its stare.

She was running, running in the darkness, not knowing where she was going but running from it, from the dark presence until she could run no more. Something cool and hard seemed to hold her, and she hugged at its rough surface for safety.

Ailea awoke to find herself wedged against the cold stones of the rear wall. It was still dark, and she could hear the steady breath of Ruth in the next room. She had rolled from the low pallet and was facing the wall, her arms drawn to the front of her body and her hands clasping the uncut surface of the field stones. Reaching behind her to the pallet, she pulled her blanket off the bed and covered herself, one hand clutching the rough weave of the wool cloth while the other rested in a small cleft of stone near the floor.

Ailea was awakened by a rough hand on her shoulder, shaking her.

"Get up. Dress in your plainest tunic—your wedding garment will do." Jonathan sneered, turning to leave the room. "Meet me outside. And wear your sturdy sandals." He left, slamming the door behind him.

Ailea decided it would be wise to obey, but she took her time dressing. Before leaving the room, she reached for her comb and had passed it once through her short locks before remembering that her hair was gone. She fought back tears of regret. How ugly she must look now! Then, stiffening her resolve, she dashed away the lone tear that had escaped a corner of her eye. It was worth it, she reminded herself. At least she was not Jonathan's wife!

When she joined him a few minutes later, Jonathan did not greet her but motioned her to follow him. He led her outside the town walls to the large, low building that was the permanent sheepfold. A wall formed the outer part of the enclosure, and an open, arched doorway led into the roofed building where both sheep and goats were kept at night and in bad weather.

A young shepherd still lay sleeping across the entrance. He sat up, rubbing his eyes when Jonathan and Ailea stepped over him, but Jonathan ignored him and addressed a short, wiry man who rose from a sleeping pallet nearby.

"Habaz, I would speak with you."

Even in the predawn light, Ailea could see that the man's hair was well-streaked with gray and knew he must be the overshepherd.

"Whatever it is must be quite important for you to be here so early in the morning, my lord. Even the sheep and goats are still asleep." The man chuckled at his own jest. "Did you perhaps want to view the new rams you had delivered from Jerusalem?"

"Not now, Habaz. I have come to ask a favor of you—one that will require a great deal of you, I'm afraid."

The man made a formal bow, touching his forehead with the tips of his fingers. "Anything, my lord. After all you have done for me, you may ask anything."

"I would like for you to take charge of the girl," Jonathan said, indicating Ailea, whom Habaz had pretended not to see.

"Since you were present in our courtyard yesterday and saw what happened, you know that I can't leave her among the women. Now she looks like a prostitute or a boy, and the women will shun her. They already resent me enough for bringing her here. I would not make them any angrier."

"But she grew up as the pampered daughter of a wealthy man. The life of a shepherd would be too rough for the likes of her. Besides, I have all the help I need with the sheep. And another problem occurs to me. Most of the shepherds are no longer children but young men. It is possible that they, like the women, will look on her as a harlot. I won't be responsible for what may happen to her if she is placed among them." Habaz finished this speech with a look of relief on his face, as if congratulating himself for avoiding the dilemma.

Jonathan pondered his objections for a moment. "What about the goats?"

Habaz shook his head firmly. "Goats are difficult animals. They like to graze on the hillsides, and their keepers must follow them up and down all day. They don't even rest during the hottest time of the day as the sheep do. And they are more venturesome and less manageable."

"The girl is also difficult and hard to manage. She should get along quite well with them. And since you use the younger boys as goatherds, she should be safe enough among them. Surely you can find a place for her." Habaz shrugged, sighing deeply. "As a matter of fact, the oldest boy among the goatherds has been begging me to make him a shepherd. And as the other two boys are young—only seven and nine years of age—I suppose I could use her to look after them." Habaz still seemed skeptical.

"Very good, my friend. The ideal solution for us both." Jonathan extended his hand to shake on the matter. "Treat her just as you would the others. And don't hesitate to be stern with her. She is stubborn and rebellious and will require a firm hand."

Ailea seethed inwardly as she listened to this exchange. Her nose twitched in disgust at the smell of the animals, and she did not relish the idea of spending her days following them around while tending two little boys. On the other hand, she thought, she would be free of Jonathan and his odious sister.

Ailea was gratified to see the look of puzzlement in Jonathan's eyes when she did not protest. But her pleasure was short-lived. He turned to her and made an announcement. "I have to go away for a time, and I do not want Ruth to have the worry of watching after you. Since you look like a boy, I have found you a boy's job. When I get back, it will go badly for you indeed if you have caused trouble."

Without a backward glance he left her standing there with the chief shepherd and his smelly animals. And when he departed for Jerusalem the next day, he didn't bother to say good-bye.

Chapter Seventeen

Shageh took advantage of Jonathan's absence to accelerate Ailea's training in the ways of Israel—the hundreds of commandments that Adonai had given to Moses, all of which the Rab knew by heart. Each day, after her duties with the goats, they would meet at the teaching rock, and he would patiently tutor her.

Despite the enormity of their task, Ailea could not resist the kind persistence of the wise teacher. Although she thought many of the laws quite arbitrary, Shageh did not seem to take offense at this and encouraged her questions.

"Why is the hart considered a clean animal while the hind is not?" she asked one day. "Venison is venison. Is this another example of how your God rejects the female in favor of the male?"

"I have tried to explain to you, dear child, that the Lord God loves all people equally," he explained patiently. "But let us return to the subject of the hind and the hart. The Lord allows us to kill and eat the hart, the male deer. But He protects the female. I believe the reason is clear. If we killed the mother, her fawns would die. Soon there would be no more deer."

"I see, Rab. But all the laws are not so easily understood."

He shrugged. "Perhaps not. But those we don't understand we are to accept, believing that the Lord God in His wisdom, knows what is best for us. He has given us the Law because He loves His people, not because He wants to burden them."

"You really believe that Adonai cares about small things?"

"Without question." Shageh took the fig Ailea had picked and paused to take a bite before continuing. "I think it is time for me to tell you the story of Hagar, my child. There are some similarities between her and you. She was also a foreigner, the handmaiden of Sarah, wife of our father Abraham."

"The slave who bore Abraham the child your God rejected?"

The Rab glanced at her, a small frown worrying his brow. "The boy's name was Ishmael—but Adonai did not reject him. He had already decreed that the son of Abraham's true wife would be the heir. That is a good place to begin our story."

Ailea settled more comfortably on the grassy knoll under the sycamore tree, listening intently.

"After Hagar had been a handmaiden in the household for some time and Sarah had still not conceived, Sarah decided to send Hagar in to lie with Abraham so that the male heir Adonai had promised might be born. But Sarah loved her husband and soon became very jealous . . . especially when Hagar conceived. Now when Sarah began to complain to Abraham, he pointed out that this had been Sarah's idea in the first place and that she must settle the differences between them. Instead, Sarah began to treat the girl harshly."

"But that wasn't fair!" Ailea interrupted. "Hagar had no choice—she wasn't free!"

Shageh chuckled. The child was always so impatient, her mind racing ahead. "No, it wasn't fair. Hagar was at the mercy of others, just as you have been. You see why I said the story brought you to mind? Now, what would you have done in Hagar's place?"

Ailea's green eyes blazed. "I would have run away, of course!" She thought of her painful experience in the desert and amended, "But first, I would think of a plan."

Again Shageh chuckled. "I am afraid Hagar was too upset for thinking of plans. She ran into the wilderness, not knowing which way to go."

"Poor Hagar."

"Yes. She felt quite sorry for herself, too, until she heard a voice speaking to her." Here Shageh paused, the suspense mounting.

Ailea held her breath. "Who was it?"

"The angel of the Lord, child. He asked her where she was going. She replied that she was running away. Then the angel told her to return and submit to her mistress for the truth was that Hagar had a little trouble with submission." Again the old man paused, giving Ailea a pointed glance before continuing the story.

"The angel told Hagar that she would have a son who would be the leader of a great people. She was to name her son Ishmael, meaning 'to be heard,' for the Lord had heard her cry.

"Hagar listened and obeyed. Afterward, when all came about as she had been told, she called the Lord *El Roi,* 'The God Who Sees,' and the place of this miraculous encounter came to be known as 'The Well of the Living One Who Sees Me.'" Shageh leaned forward to peer intently into Ailea's eyes. "Do you understand what I am telling you, child?"

She pondered the idea. "You are saying that if God saw and heard the Egyptian handmaid, He sees and hears me, too?" Strange. She had never believed that the gods could see her or would care if they did. It was hard to believe that the Lord of Hosts, the Almighty, might actually know of her plight and care what happened to her.

~ ~ ~

The sun was just past its zenith when Ailea reached an outcropping of rock on the hillside. She sat down to rest, taking off her sandals and massaging her aching feet. The soles were still tender from the deep burns inflicted by the desert sun, and she had been climbing the hills all day, tending her restless herd of goats and her equally rambunctious young helpers!

For the moment, at least, the herd was grazing on the succulent grasses that grew on this slope. Strange that they had never ventured here before.

Shading her eyes with her hand, Ailea looked for Ari and Joel, who usually scampered just ahead of her, as lively and exuberant as the young kids themselves. She spotted them now. Right after their noon repast, the boys had sought the shade of a large boulder and fallen asleep, innocent in their repose, tousled heads pillowed on their hands. She hadn't the heart to wake them to be about their duties.

She shrugged and gazed up at the playful clouds, forming images in the sky. For a few moments she watched the pictures shift and change as if stirred by a great breath from the heavens. Who lived behind those clouds?

Rimmon, the sun god? Nergal, the god of war? Angels? Or was it Adonai, the One True and Living God who had spoken the world into existence, as the Rab claimed? *Was* it true? Did He listen when people spoke to Him?

Ailea had often come upon the Rab in the early morning, kneeling upon a small rug, his face turned toward the rising sun. She could hear him plainly as he said his morning prayers. "Hear, O Israel, the Lord our God, the Lord is one. You shall love the Lord your God with all your heart, with all your soul, and with all your might." He would go on to speak to Adonai as one would speak to another person—as if Shageh could see and hear Him.

Her mother had been equally convinced that her gods were real. Yet there was a vast difference. The Rab exuded calm confidence that his prayers would be answered while her mother had been drawn into madness. Perhaps the gods of Aram-Zobah were not as powerful as this Hebrew God.

Then there was the prayer of blessing that both Shageh and Ruth always said at mealtime. Shageh would break off a large piece of bread, lift it toward heaven, and proclaim his gratitude,

"Blessed art Thou, Lord God, King of the Universe, who causes to come forth bread from the earth for our benefit." She never tired of hearing his strong, resonant voice. What would she have done here in this foreign land without his guidance? He filled the void left by the father she had lost.

Almost timidly, Ailea lifted her hands toward heaven as she had seen Shageh do so often. "Adonai?" she whispered hesitantly. "I am Ailea. I don't know You, but the Rab tells me that You know me. If You are truly there—" she held her breath, "then show me."

An unusual thought struck her as she waited. Suppose she asked Him for something very special, something that no one else could know or suspect? Then if he answered her petition, she would know that Adonai was truly there, that He was real and cared about her. The Rab had warned her that one should not tempt the Lord God. Therefore, she would not presume to ask for a large favor. She did not wish for riches and did not greatly miss the luxuries she had left behind in Damascus. What she missed most was her family.

She pondered for a moment. Loneliness welled up inside once more. A friend! She would ask for a friend—someone she could confide in, someone with whom to share her fears and doubts about her new life in this strange land.

When she had finished asking the Lord for a friend, she opened her eyes. Nothing was different. Yet everything seemed changed. Perhaps Adonai had heard her.

Just then Joel and Ari darted up to her, their cheeks flushed with heat and excitement. "The goats! The goats! They've wandered away, and one of them has fallen!"

Quickly tying on her sandals, Ailea jumped to her feet, following the boys to a distant rock on the far side of the hill. How thoughtless of her! Praying to an invisible God when she should have kept both her eyes open! What would Ruth think if one of her animals should be injured . . . or worse? Ailea berated herself for her foolishness.

"There! There she is—one of the mama goats!" cried Joel,

pointing to a crevice where a doe was firmly wedged between two boulders. She was bleating piteously, and Ailea's heart wrenched at the sound. This was one of the pregnant nannies, prized by the village for her healthy offspring.

Moving quickly, Ailea assessed the problem and discovered that one hind leg—the left one—was likely broken. "Careful, Joel, Ari. We must not hurt her if we can help it. You, Joel, take her front right leg; Ari, the left and pull gently, very gently. I'll support her middle."

Scrambling over the rocks, the three did their best to heft the heavy goat, swollen with her advanced pregnancy. The animal continued to bleat, more weakly now. With one final burst of strength, they lifted her free of her stony prison.

Ailea carried her over the rocks, the two boys waving the rest of the herd toward home. They were met by an angry Habaz, who took the wounded goat from her and proceeded to lecture her all the way home.

"I'll get something to bind her leg," Ailea volunteered.

"Don't waste your time!" he told her bluntly. "She will have to be destroyed. It looks as if she will give birth early, brought on no doubt by the fall," he shot Ailea a scathing look, "but we will let her live—long enough to see if she can bring forth live young. After that, she will be slaughtered and roasted. If her babies are accepted by one of the nursing mothers, they will live; otherwise, they, too will be slaughtered."

The stricken look on Ailea's face gave even the tough old shepherd pause. "It is a kindness. The kids would only starve to death—a terrible way to die. As for the mother, everyone knows that no beast can survive a broken leg. Death will release her from her suffering."

~ ~ ~

The last light of day was fading in the western sky when Ailea reached the house. Ruth and Shageh had already finished their meal and sat on cushions—Ruth, with her sewing; Shageh, repairing an ax handle.

"What kept you so late?" Ruth asked in an irritated voice. "Did you lose one of our flock?"

Ailea almost groaned aloud. How had the woman guessed? Drawing in a deep breath for courage, Ailea decided to confess. Ruth would hear about it in the morning at the latest. "I'm afraid I did. I sat down to rest—just for a little—and one of the goats wandered away. We found her but she has suffered a broken leg. I am so late because she was heavy with twins, and it took so very long to carry her back to the village."

"You let harm come to a prize goat?"

Ailea nodded miserably.

"Stupid, ignorant girl!" Ruth railed at her, delivering a sharp slap to Ailea's right cheek. "You are not fit for even the most menial task. You have destroyed not one goat, but three!"

Ailea put her fingers to the reddened spot. "Forgive me, Ruth. I . . ."

She glanced at the Rab. Was he disgusted with her also? His sinewy hands rested on the ax handle, his head bowed as if in prayer. He spoke to Ruth in a quiet voice. "You should return to your room now, daughter. Surely you must very tired and not yourself, or you would not have struck Ailea. You must never do such a thing again."

Ruth had the grace to look embarrassed. She did not apologize to Ailea, however, but merely hurried from the room.

Ailea waited to see what admonition he would give her.

"Go, child," he said without looking up. "Get some rest. Tomorrow will come soon enough."

Ailea sighed. As she passed by the Rab's chair, she put out her hand tentatively and touched his arm. "Forgive me. I *am* trying to be a good goatherd. Truly I am." Her voice broke.

"Be at peace, little one," Shageh said as he reached out to smooth the tangled hair from her face. "You are learning."

She smiled weakly and left him, her shadow preceding her in the flickering candlelight.

Shageh sat for endless moments, thinking of the proud girl who had come here from Damascus and reflected on the great changes that had already taken place in this fiery little stranger. What had happened today out on that hillside? It was more than the accident with the foolish animal. Something had broken in another of God's dear creatures—the proud, lovely girl who now made her home with them. The girl who would become his daughter-in-law if Jonathan had his way.

No harm must come to her in this fragile state. He would protect her from Jonathan, if necessary. And as for Ruth, he had waited long enough for his daughter to come around, the Rab decided. From now on, he would see that she treated Ailea with respect.

~ ~ ~

Ailea insisted on helping Habaz with the birth early the next morning. The first kid was born dead. "Probably killed when the mother fell," he said as he laid the still form aside. Habaz pulled the second kid from its mother just as she died. Ailea felt tears sting her eyes. Her failure to look after the animal had caused her death, and the baby would probably soon follow. Despite its vigorous bleating, it appeared too tiny to survive.

"The little one will probably die soon unless I can get one of the nursing mothers to accept it," Habaz told her. They took the kid in turn to each of the goats with young, but none would let it nurse.

"Habaz, let me take it home with me and care for it. I'll feed it until it's strong enough to live on its own."

"You have no way to feed it. And it is so small; I am not sure it would live even if you could. It is kinder to end its suffering before it begins."

She had never understood the logic of that argument. Wasn't life worth the risk, the pain?

"Please, Habaz. Let me try."

Habaz looked into the brimming green eyes and found it impossible to refuse. "Very well, take a day to work with the kid, but I expect you back at your duties the day after tomorrow. If the little thing still lives, you will have to carry it with you. It will not be as easy as you think."

"Perhaps. But I have to try. Thank you, Habaz." Ailea favored him with a smile, then threw her arms around the astonished man's neck in an enthusiastic hug before setting off for home with the baby goat.

Ruth did not welcome the new member of the household. "Goats stink!" she declared. "I won't have the smelly creature in my house!"

"But Ruth, it is just a tiny baby. It doesn't stink. It smells sweet and new. Come and see for yourself."

Ruth peered at the small animal for a long moment. Ailea placed her little finger in its mouth and it sucked, pulling fiercely. "See? The will to survive is strong. I know I can keep it alive, Ruth. Please . . . let me try."

Like Habaz, Ruth could not resist the appeal in Ailea's eyes. Over the past weeks she had grudgingly come to respect the girl who had continued to do her duties at home before she left in the mornings and after she returned exhausted from following the herd all day. Though Ruth had tried to harden her heart against pity, she couldn't help but feel sorry for Ailea. The villagers taunted her whenever they saw her—especially the women. Ruth had even seen Dinah deliberately trip her one day while the women were washing clothes in the stream. It had surprised Ruth when Ailea had not challenged Dinah. Perhaps she was simply too tired from all her labor.

"I suppose, if you want to try to save the kid, I would have no objection," she began, then added a warning note. "But when it is old enough, back to the herd it goes."

The radiant smile, breaking like morning upon Ailea's face, coaxed an answering one from the usually dour Ruth.

~ ~ ~

"Good morning, Ailea. I am surprised to find you at the sheepfold. I had feared I would have to search the hills for hours before I found you." Ailea looked up from feeding her baby goat to see the pretty round face of Ahiam's wife, Judith. Her mouth dropped open in surprise at the appearance of this unexpected guest.

"Habaz is following the herd today, and I am nursing this motherless little one and two sick ewes. What are you doing here?" she asked, then realized how rude and unfriendly the question sounded. "I mean, I am glad to see you again, Judith, but I wondered what brought you to Ziph today."

"Me?" Judith nodded and sat down on the crude bench that provided the only seating for the sheepfold. She began to stroke the kid's soft coat. "I knew that Jonathan was very angry with you when I last saw him. I wanted to come and visit you before, but I just couldn't get away. How are you, Ailea?"

"As you can see, I am now a goatherd. But, in truth, it is not such a terrible thing. In fact, if Jonathan will just stay away, I will probably do quite well."

"Oh, Ailea, I had hoped that your feelings toward Jonathan might have changed!" Judith's large expressive eyes conveyed genuine concern.

"No. They have not changed. And I think it would be better if we talked of other matters." Ailea watched the wife of Jonathan's best friend closely. Would she be offended and go away?

But Judith just smiled. "You're right. We should not waste our time talking about men. Tell me instead how the women have been treating you. If that shameless Dinah has been unkind, I will deal with her myself.

So they spent a very pleasant day together, each telling the other about their childhood and family. They shared the delicious raisin bread that Judith had brought with her, and the time passed so quickly that they were both surprised when it was time for Judith to return to Hebron.

It wasn't until that evening, when she was sitting with the Rab on the rooftop looking at the shimmering stars, that she remembered her prayer to Adonai. He had heard and answered her! She knew it just as surely as she knew that the sun would rise tomorrow.

"Rab, I have something to tell you. You won't be at all surprised, but I have to admit that I am amazed . . . and very happy. The Lord God has answered my prayers. I asked him for a friend, and he sent me one—Judith."

"You are right, child. I am not surprised at all. So you have come to trust in Him?"

"Yes, Rab. But I still don't understand many things. Why have you and Judith accepted me when everyone else despises me so?"

The Rab patted her hand. "There are several reasons, little one. Ziph is a small village, rather remote. Any stranger here comes under suspicion and scrutiny. They don't have much to talk about, so they gossip about anything or anyone who is new or different.

"Then, of course, there is the fact that you are not of our people."

Ailea nodded knowingly. "And Adonai has forbidden you to befriend anyone who is not of the covenant."

"No, Ailea, He has not. But many people are convinced that that is the teaching of the Law. They know that the Lord God has told us not to be like the nations around us—not to burn our children as sacrifices to false gods and such as that. And He has told us not to marry with some of the people of Canaan, the Amalakites and the Amorites and others. But Adonai has specifically commanded our people to be kind to the pilgrims and foreigners among us. It is very clearly stated in the Law of Moses. It says 'You shall not oppress a stranger, for you know the heart of a stranger, seeing you were a stranger in the land of Egypt.'"

"Rab, I do not want to sound disrespectful, but you must have forgotten to teach the villagers this precept."

Shageh chuckled. "I have not forgotten to teach it, little one.

But like many of the commandments, it is much easier to teach than to follow. But perhaps you are right. I should remind them."

Ailea was skeptical. "I am not sure you can change their minds, Rab. They are very stubborn."

Shageh nodded. "As stubborn as Habaz's goats."

The next time Judith came to visit, Ailea told her about how she had been the answer to Ailea's prayer and about her conversation with Shageh about why Judith and he had accepted her while the others had not. "You must have been taught about this Law of the stranger."

Judith shook her head. "No, I do not recall hearing it. But it is implied in many other teachings of the Law. And, after all, our father Abraham is called a 'wandering Aramean.'"

Ailea chuckled as they followed her herd up yet another hill. "A wandering Aramean—that is definitely what I am." They continued in silence for a few moments before Ailea spoke again.

"There is something in the Law that puzzles me, Judith. It seems to me that Adonai does not care for women much, especially in connection with childbearing and the things that surround it. This is a concept unknown to my people. Why, there is even a goddess of fertility. Her name is Ashteroth, and in her temple there are women who—" Judith's hand came over her friend's mouth, interrupting her monologue.

"Please, Ailea, we mustn't talk about false gods. Adonai would not be pleased."

"Oh, yes, as I was saying. It seems that Adonai punishes women for bearing the children. You know, the laws concerning uncleanness and the injunction against a woman appearing in the congregation until several weeks after giving birth."

"Believe me, Ailea, if for some reason the Lord were to tell us that a woman need not keep those laws if she did not wish to, most women would choose to observe them."

Ailea's eyes widened in surprise. "Really? Why?"

"If you were either a wife or a mother, it would not be much to explain. Let me use myself as an example. You know I love

Ahiam very much. But there is a certain time of the moon when I am very pleased that he is not to come too near me."

"I understand. There are those days when it is best to leave me alone as well."

"Exactly. Adonai made us. He knew that we needed that time alone. And when you have a child, you will understand even more. Those last months of carrying the child are very difficult. Then when the baby is new, you feel almost overwhelmed with love and with your duties as a new mother. The husband has been under a strain, and. . . ."

"Why?"

Judith looked a little embarrassed. "You will understand when you are married. Anyway, the Law excuses a woman from attendance at public worship and from her . . . obligations as a wife. It is a chance to regain strength and give all her attention to the baby for a while.

"I don't mean to say that the laws of uncleanness are only for a woman's benefit. No, they are also meant to remind all of us that we are born sinners, that from our mother's womb we need the Lord's mercy and atonement in order to be acceptable to Him."

"The Rab has been teaching me about the Day of Atonement. At first I did not understand it. My people make sacrifices to appease the gods, but that is not the same as atonement or the forgiveness of sins. It is sad that an innocent animal has to die for the sins of people, but the Rab has explained that it is necessary. And now you have explained that Adonai does not hate women. I have come to see these laws in a whole new light now. Thank you, Judith."

Her new friend's face was wreathed with a smile. "You are becoming one of us," she said as she gave Ailea a hug.

Chapter Eighteen

Jonathan told himself that Ailea had not deserved a good-bye from him. Let her work for Habaz for a month tending goats. Then she might appreciate the benefits of being his wife! He would just put her out of his mind, concentrate on training new army recruits and planning strategy in the war council.

When he reached Jerusalem, word was waiting for him that he was not to stay in the House of the Gibborim but at the palace. The king commanded an audience with him as soon as possible. As two servants helped him to bathe and don robes the king had provided, Jonathan wondered what the meeting could possibly be about. Well, the sooner he was there, the sooner he would find out. He was ushered into David's presence a short time later.

He stopped short when he saw that Joab and the Prince of Hamath were seated with the king. David saw him and motioned. "We have been waiting for you, Jonathan. Come and join us."

The king extended his hand, motioning Jonathan toward a chair on his right. Joab met Jonathan's glance with a surly stare while Joram bent slightly forward from his chair and tilted his head, a slight attempt at a smile fighting to make progress across his face. His eyes fixed upon Jonathan's and followed him as he settled in the chair and turned toward David.

"I thought to ask you how it has gone with you these past weeks, my friend. I wonder if you may have tired of your prickly prize by now. Would you prefer to have gold in exchange for the girl?" Jonathan's mouth went dry as David paused for an answer. A suggestion such as this by the king was tantamount to an order. Any wise subject would at this point show a willingness at least to negotiate.

"My lord, if you wish to have the girl back, it would ever be my privilege to serve you. But if the king would grant that I keep Ailea, it would be my earnest desire. It is true that she is strong-willed and troublesome, but I find I enjoy the challenge, and in fact, wish to convey my father's invitation for the king to come to a wedding feast on the fourth day of Tammuz. Ailea will become my wife. So you see, my lord, your gift is certainly more highly treasured than any amount of gold." Even as he answered, Jonathan was calling himself a fool to risk so much for a girl who rejected him at every turn.

There was a muffled sound of outrage from Joram, and he spoke in an audible whisper to Joab. "But you vowed I would have—" Joab made a hissing sound and the prince was silent.

David answered slowly. "I see. Then you shall keep the girl you so highly treasure and make her your bride. Please convey my regrets to your father concerning the feast. I would like nothing more to travel to Ziph for your wedding, but the affairs of state will keep me in Jerusalem."

"I understand fully, sire."

"I cannot believe that you have not explained more fully to him the reasons he should give the girl back!" Joab exploded without attempting to mask his anger.

"You heard what Jonathan said, nephew. The matter is concluded," David replied with a cold civility.

Joab, never afraid to gainsay David even though he was the king, ignored the dismissal and turned to Jonathan.

"The king has given his word and won't go back on it, even to his own harm, but I hold you—"

David interrupted. "Joram, I am sure you wish to refresh yourself in your chambers. We will talk at the banquet in your honor tonight." He clapped his hands and a steward appeared to usher the prince out of the audience chamber.

After he was gone, David turned to Joab. "You may continue now, since you are so intent upon speaking your mind. But in the future refrain from such discussions in front of foreign emissaries."

"I was just about to inform the son of Shageh that he has put you in a very embarrassing position politically." Turning to Jonathan, the general continued.

"Joram has refused all other offers of favor from Israel. He wants the daughter of Eliada. He claims that an alliance with her would help bring peace between Hamath and Damascus. According to the prince, King Toi believes that, aside from joining his family to Hadadezer or Shobach, making Eliada's daughter his wife would smooth relations between Hamath and the southern Arameans more effectively than anything else."

Jonathan snorted his disagreement. "I have my doubts that King Toi ever said such a thing. It would take more than an alliance with a rich and respected family of Damascus to change the hatred that has always existed between Toi and Hadadezer. Joram's interest in the daughter of Eliada is strictly a matter of vengeance."

"The reasons for his request are not really the point. The point is that the strategic location of Hamath is important to us, being on the Orantes River as it is and controlling our shipments of bronze from Cun, Berioth, and Tibhath."

"What does that have to do with Ailea?"

"Joram is threatening not to give us his complete support as an ally. He says that without an alliance in Damascus, he will not be able to supply the military support he had promised nor pay the expected amount of tribute because of the expense of military operations. In other words, he is threatening to withdraw from his alliance with us unless he gets what he wants."

"He would not dare!"

"He would dare, and if you saw fit to put the affairs of the kingdom before your own desires, we would not have this problem at all. A loyal subject would release the king from his promise." Both Joab and Jonathan had risen from their chairs and stood face to face.

"We have had this conversation before, Joab. If you continue to accuse me of disloyalty to the king, I will have no other choice than to challenge you to personal combat!"

"Enough, now!" David shouted, his handsome features twisted in anger. He stepped between the two military men and addressed them both.

"This sniping will stop now, and I had better not hear of it again. We have enough enemies without fighting among ourselves. Joab, the prize I gave Jonathan is between him and me. If I thought it necessary, I would ask for the girl back. But that pompous young peacock poses no real threat to us. Tonight at the banquet I will make it clear to Joram that I will not take kindly to any shirking of Hamath's commitment to our alliance. He will come to heel. Now leave my presence, both of you. I don't wish to see either of you until the gibborim convene tomorrow."

For the rest of Jonathan's stay in Jerusalem, David remained cool to both Jonathan and the general. But on the day that Jonathan returned to Ziph, David had a donkey loaded with spices, richly colored cloth, and beautiful ornaments for both Jonathan and his bride. Jonathan's gift was a heavy signet ring of topaz. For Ailea, the king had chosen a thick gold bracelet etched with a floral design.

Before he left Jerusalem, Jonathan stopped by the barracks to question the soldier who had promised to keep an ear open for word of Rezon.

"The robber is still very much alive," the man told him. "But he won't be for long. Joab has his men dogging Rezon. Our general doesn't like to be bested by anyone and most especially not by a desert bandit."

As he traveled, Jonathan argued with himself over whether he should tell Ailea. He could imagine the joy that the news would bring to her. But as much as he wanted to make Ailea happy, he was afraid the news would only make her want to run away again. No, he decided. He would not tell her until after he made her his wife—until after he had bound her to him.

~ ~ ~

When Jonathan arrived back in Ziph, he sought out his father and received a full accounting of all that had taken place in his absence. Then he went in search of his betrothed.

From his position on the hill above the stream, Jonathan watched Ruth and Ailea join the other women of the village in performing their daily chores. As they washed their clothes in the stream, Ruth gossiped with the others, but Ailea hung back, ignored and unwelcome.

She stood alone, holding a basket—soiled clothing, Jonathan assumed. Wandering over to a more isolated part of the stream, she set the basket on a flat rock. Something caught her attention, and even from this distance he could see her amused smile. The object of her amusement—a young kid, its black coat shining—came bounding up to her, butting her legs playfully.

Ailea lifted the little black goat into her arms and sat down on the rock. He could hear her laugh out loud as her pet licked her face.

Something about the scene tugged at Jonathan's heart. The ridiculous little goat was the only friend the girl could claim in the entire village of Ziph. No, not quite true, he reconsidered. The Rab was her champion, having taken her part in the altercation about the Law of the captive bride. Though that affair still rankled him, a part of Jonathan was grateful that Shageh had stood up for the stranger when everyone in Ziph had opposed her.

He asked himself for the thousandth time if he was doing the right thing in marrying this foreigner. He knew he was drawn to Ailea and that it was much more than the stirring of his passion, though he wanted her to bear his children. They would be comely—and brave. No, he also wanted to protect her, to give her a home and family to replace all she had lost. Further, he coveted her proud spirit—for Adonai. The Rab had told him of her willingness now to learn the ways of the Lord and how she even seemed inclined to trust in Adonai for herself, to embrace Him as her only God.

Until now, however, Jonathan mused, it seemed she had rejected all of his efforts to make her accept him. She had fought him at every turn. She refused to forgive him for the death of her father. Very briefly Jonathan considered returning her to Damascus, then immediately discarded the idea. He had already defied the wishes of both a prince and a king to keep her, and he wasn't about to alter his course now. He had won her in battle, and the Law allowed him to take her. And he would.

He strode down from the hill, surprising her with his presence on the opposite bank of the stream. "Even with your hair cut like a boy, you are beautiful," he told her in a voice roughened with desire.

"Jonathan!" She gave a little cry and rose, clutching the goat tightly in her arms. "You're back!"

She looked so appealing standing there—the sunlight filtering onto her face, her curly short locks catching glints of gold—that he could not resist her. Crossing the stream in a single bound, he gathered her to him—the little goat between them. Before she could protest, he cupped her head in one hand, bent over her and kissed her—gently but thoroughly.

She pulled away at once, heart pounding, head swimming from the impact of his lips on hers. She was stunned at the feelings that flooded her. Such yearnings as she had never known. A yearning to be held by him as she had been when she was sick and after her attempted escape at Hebron. A yearning to have him always look at her the way he was looking at her now—with admiration and longing. And a yearning to feel the soft touch of his lips against hers.

Then the memory of all she had lost because of him hit her with incredible force, and she stepped back in anger, her hand going to her shorn head. "No! You are lying! I'm not beautiful! Because of you, I'm *ugly!* You've taken everything from me, and now you expect me to fall at your feet in gratitude? Never. I hate you!" Leaving her basket, she fled back down the path toward the house, past the other women who were finishing their work and glanced up after her curiously.

Obviously she had not changed her attitude in his absence, Jonathan thought as he picked up the little goat she had left behind. He started to follow her but halted at the sound of a low chuckle. Whirling around, he saw his father emerging from a cluster of trees. "How long have you been standing there?" he demanded.

"Long enough to know you need advice in dealing with the girl you have vowed to make your wife."

Jonathan gave a snort of disgust. "And what makes you think you know the secret? As far as I can tell, no one else has been able to do so—not her parents, not her servants, not I, not even the whole Hebrew army!" He sat the goat down and threw up his hands in exasperation. "She is stubborn and rebellious and—"

"Young and lonely and frightened, no matter how bravely she hides it," Shageh finished for him. "You are a warrior, accustomed to overpowering your enemy, and you seek to conquer Ailea in the same way. But a woman can never be won by such tactics, my son. You do not wish a slave who does your bidding because you demand it. You desire, rather, a soul-mate, a helper, a partner. Am I not right?"

"Well, yes, though I had never thought of a wife in that way." Jonathan eyed his father quizzically. "I only know I want her, and she is the *only* one I want . . . though I don't know why. There are any number of women I have known who would be overjoyed to be my bride. But this one *refuses* me! It is unheard of! She is but a woman—and from a conquered nation at that! How dare she!"

The Rab held up his hand to end the tirade. "There. You are doing it again, son. You are thinking of Ailea as the enemy who must be subdued. As long as you do so, you will not find happiness. Ailea is unlike most other women. She has spirit, and she would fight you to the end."

"If she is so determined to fight me, then I have no choice but to fight back." Jonathan folded his arms over his chest and set his jaw, his lips thinning.

"Then you will lose her."

Slumping onto the rock recently occupied by Ailea, Jonathan looked up at his father. "Then what should I do?"

The Rab looked off into the distance as if calling up all the wisdom of a lifetime. "Refuse to become angry when she challenges you. Instead, show her that you care for her, that you understand her fears. Give her time to learn our ways. Love her. Remember, the Lord God formed the woman from the part of man nearest his heart."

A look of mischief crinkled the old man's eyes. "And, most of all, allow her some choices. Oh, I know a man doesn't have to listen to his wife, but on occasion, he would be well advised to do so. I discovered this when your mother and I were very young, and that is why we were both content—why there was more joy and laughter in our home than most."

Jonathan looked pensive. "It is true that you and my mother seemed very happy together. I had always thought to have such a marriage." Standing to his feet, he appeared determined. "I will try, Father, but I'm not sure it will work. After all, Mother was reasonable and compliant—not at all like Ailea!"

The Rab's laughter echoed through the stillness of the grove, long since deserted by the women of the village who had returned to be about their household chores. "If it pleases you to think so, my son, I will not try to convince you otherwise."

~ ~ ~

Jonathan tried over the next week to follow his father's advice, being careful not to issue arbitrary orders nor to deliberately incite her temper. He gave Ailea the rich cloth the king had sent, instructing Ruth to help her make a suitable wardrobe. He presented her with several small gifts he had brought back for her from Jerusalem.

He even asked her to teach him the game of chess. She rose to the challenge—relishing the thought of defeating him. This she accomplished time after time.

Quick learner that he was, he soon began to lower the margin of victory until he was certain that soon he would win a game. Then what? Ailea would probably never play chess with him again. Briefly, he considered losing purposely for the pleasure of spending more time with her, but he knew this ploy would only succeed in igniting her fury if she ever suspected. Besides, his pride would never allow her to continue to best him in anything—not even a game.

The games took place after the evening meal, in the hour before sunset while the other men gathered at the village gate for the evening circle. When Jonathan had failed to appear several nights in succession, the men began to tease him unmercifully. Jonathan was a little embarrassed by their taunts but not enough to give up his chess games with Ailea.

Finally one evening, the game came to checkmate, Jonathan's favor. Ailea tried to cover her chagrin. "You played very well this evening," she reluctantly admitted.

He could not resist a gloating smile. In truth, he had deliberately distracted her, interspersing comments about her ignorance of Hebrew custom and her weakness as a woman with compliments about her beauty and intelligence. Flustered, she had been unable to concentrate on strategy. Even now she blushed becomingly, and Jonathan longed to take her in his arms and kiss her and have her respond to him as a woman responds to the man she loves. But he had vowed not to force himself on her. He would be patient.

"If I play well, it is because I have had an excellent teacher. I have enjoyed these evenings with you very much, little warrior. I think we will make it a custom in our household." He paused to gauge her response to his blatant reference to the fact that she would be his wife. It was obvious that his words had disturbed her, but she said nothing, only continued to hold his gaze. He leaned toward her ever so slightly and was secretly thrilled that she did the same, unconsciously tilting her head back in expectation of his kiss.

Suddenly, he laughed. "You please me, Ailea. You please me very much." He stood, tousled her halo of ringlets as he would have Adah's and walked away, whistling.

Chapter Nineteen

Upon Jonathan's return, Ailea's duties as a goatherd were over. She had grown quite fond of Joel and Ari and missed their antics. She even missed the animals to some extent. She had given many of them pet names. But mostly Ailea missed her duties on the hillsides because now she had to spend most of her time with sour-faced Ruth, even though there was a slight thawing in the older woman's attitude, attributable, Ailea suspected, to Shageh's intervention on her behalf.

Judith visited several more times, and Ailea was coming to value her friendship. But it was irritating to hear her new friend go on and on about how wonderful it was that Ailea would soon be married to Ahiam's best friend. And wasn't it wonderful that Jonathan had brought back such wonderful gifts from the king? And wasn't it wonderful that Jonathan was doing so much for the little village of his birth?

Jonathan himself had changed. It seemed he issued fewer orders these days and no longer baited her. Why, she hadn't had a good excuse to yell at him since his return. He even looked at her in a new and very disturbing way. She found herself wishing she could have her old belligerent taskmaster back.

She was to get an unexpected reprieve from Jonathan's

presence during the week before the wedding. Because Israelite custom required that the groom fetch his bride from her father's house, it had been decided that Ahiam would serve as surrogate father for Ailea. He arrived at the house of Shageh three days before the marriage was to take place. Ailea was shaking out one of the several fine rugs that were booty from one of Jonathan's campaigns. Ahiam approached and greeted her cheerfully.

As much as she had tried to maintain her hostility to Jonathan's best friend, the burly warrior was so cheerful and good-natured that she found it impossible to keep from smiling at him, and besides, he was the husband of her best friend..

"Good afternoon, Ahiam. I am afraid the Rab is teaching and your friend is out for the day with Ziph's shepherds," she said as she welcomed him into the courtyard. "Ruth is inside. May we offer you some refreshment?"

"Yes, I would find a raisin cake and a cool drink of water very pleasant, thank you. I am sorry to say that Judith was too busy to come with me. She has come to enjoy your company very much in the weeks since you have become friends, but she had to stay at home and prepare a room for a guest, or, I should say, a daughter." Ahiam chuckled as if he had made a joke.

"A daughter? Adah?"

"No, you, to be precise. It is the custom of our people for the bridegroom to fetch his bride from her father's house. Jonathan has asked me to act in that capacity, so I have come from Hebron, my child." He laughed as he emphasized the last two words.

At first, Ailea was alarmed. She was to be taken to Hebron? Hebron was only some six miles distant. Still, it was one more confusing occurrence in the progression of events that was inexorably binding her to her Hebrew enemy and his people.

Later, as she served Ahiam the water and raisin cakes he had requested, the idea became more appealing. It would be good to put distance between her and her prospective bridegroom. She was finding it harder and harder to hate him. And she certainly found Judith's company more pleasant than Ruth's. The only person from this household she would miss was Shageh. Also, since Hebron was a town of some size, maybe Rezon would find it easier to somehow rescue her from this travesty of a marriage.

So she prepared to leave with Ahiam, accepting from Ruth the package that contained her wedding regalia, something Ailea had refused to view. When Ahiam told her they must leave immediately if they were to reach Hebron by sunset, neither Shageh nor Jonathan had returned. She was relieved. She didn't care to see Jonathan at any time, and she was afraid that a farewell to Shageh might bring on the tears that she seemed to battle constantly. He had been the only good thing in her life in this place, and it was a bit frightening to leave him.

She chose to focus on the possibility of escape as she walked with Ahiam and a group of other people who were returning to Hebron. Perhaps Rezon would take this opportunity to rescue her. She was to be disappointed on that score, however, because there was not a moment during the next two days that either Judith, Isaac, or Ahiam were not with her. Even at night, Ailea slept in the chamber behind that of Judith and Ahiam. It had no window, and Ailea bristled with resentment, noting that they had not made available the chamber from which she had escaped before but had stuck her in this one that was like a prison cell.

She had to admit to herself, though, that it was the only spare sleeping chamber in the house, the one she had stayed in before belonging to Isaac. Judith had mentioned other guests who had stayed in the room, trying to make her feel better, Ailea guessed.

She had briefly considered trying to slip past Ahiam and Judith as they slept, but assumed that Ahiam, a seasoned soldier, would be a very light sleeper. Besides, she had seen no caravans in the marketplace, and she knew that she had no chance of making it back to her people on her own.

When the morning of the marriage day arrived and there was still no prospect of avoiding it, Ailea began to fear that she would indeed become the wife of Shageh's son. It was impossible! He was a Hebrew—and a soldier. He had killed her father or might have. Even as Judith chattered on about the great feast Shageh had planned to celebrate and even as she was led by that kind lady to a pool in the courtyard of a neighbor for a bath and even as she was dressed in her wedding finery, she kept repeating to herself that it wasn't going to happen.

Judith dressed her in a scarlet tunic, secured it with a golden girdle, and covered her short shiny curls with a thin veil of fine linen that fell to the floor, front and back. Her vision was only slightly inhibited by the sheer material. Jonathan had recovered several of her own gold bracelets, and along with David's impressive gift and the ones he had given her, the jewelry covered her nearly to both elbows. Small golden hoops for her ears were also a part of her bridal gift from Jonathan.

As soon as the sun was set, Judith and Ahiam urged Ailea to go to their rooftop with them to watch the trail between Hebron and Ziph for signs of Jonathan and the wedding party.

They did not have long to wait. Ahiam chuckled when he sighted the lights held in the hands of the groomsmen. "I knew he could scarce wait till the sun set before coming for you, little warrior," he teased Ailea.

"Don't call me that, Hebrew," she snapped.

Judith agreed with Ailea. "She is the honored bride, husband, and you should accord her due respect. You can go down to the courtyard to let them in. We will wait here. We don't want to seem too eager, do we, Ailea?"

"Eager is not the word I would use to describe my feelings at this moment," Ailea assured her as Ahiam descended the stairs. But as she watched the bobbing torches and heard the joyous singing and laughter of the approaching entourage, she realized that she had not been completely truthful with her friend. Eager might, after all, be an appropriate term for her feelings. At least excitement would be—her heart was beating like that of a captured bird. And that is what I am, she reminded herself, a captive. But she couldn't seem to keep the happiness of the occasion from eroding the resentment she had carefully nourished over the past months.

When Jonathan and his friends bounded up the stairs to the rooftop to claim his bride, she was reluctantly impressed. He was magnificent. His hair and beard had been trimmed, and he smelled of spices from the ritual bath. A totally different fragrance than her own perfume—stronger but not unpleasant at all. On his head was a woven band of many colors. It looked like a crown. His woolen cloak covered his linen tunic, its snowy whiteness a startling contrast against his bronze skin. He wore a thick gold armband and a ring on his right hand. It was gold, set with stones of deep amber. He extended his hand to her, along with a dazzling smile. "Come, little warrior, it is time to go. The wedding feast awaits us."

What else could she do? She took his hand, and the laughing, singing crowd began the six-mile parade back to Ziph. Shageh greeted them at the gate and escorted them to his house. He stopped at the doorway and raised his hand to hush the crowd. Then he turned to Ailea and said in a voice loud enough to be heard by all, "Welcome home, daughter."

He opened his arms wide, and Ailea rushed into their safety, knowing his words of acceptance were from the heart. She stood a long moment in his embrace, fighting back tears as his gnarled hands patted her head as if she were a small child. Then the spell was broken by Ahiam who, as chief of the wedding feast, bade everyone to join him in celebrating the marriage of his friend.

Of course the house was not large enough to contain all the inhabitants of Ziph, so the feast was held in the open air. The outside ovens of several neighbors had been borrowed to roast the lamb and bake the bread. Raisin cakes and fig cakes were plentiful as were honeyed wine and apricots stewed with almonds. It was a celebration the likes of which Ziph had never known. Judith stayed nearby, and even Ruth seemed friendly although the remainder of the village women, while not impolite, treated her with cold formality.

At one point a ram's horn was sounded, and Ahiam, in a voice loud enough to be heard by all, announced that the Rab, Shageh, father of the groom, would bless the couple. He stood in the doorway once more, announcing the marriage of his son to Ailea of Damascus and offered a prayer of blessing. The marriage was official.

When the hour was late and many of the children and elderly had gone to seek their beds, Judith and Ruth came and took Ailea by the hand. "It is time to prepare for your bridegroom," Judith explained.

They took her into Jonathan's rooftop room. It had been prepared as a bridal chamber. Fresh rushes covered the floor. Lilies in a pottery vase filled the room with fragrance, and the bridal bed was covered in snow-white linens.

Ruth sounded self-conscious as she explained. "The linens are new. My bridal gift to you and Jonathan."

Ailea looked at her new sister-in-law. Where once the older woman's eyes had glared with resentment, she saw a faint offering of friendship. As much as Ailea hated the thought of belonging to the Hebrew warrior and spending her life in servitude in this forsaken village, she couldn't harden herself against the appeal in Ruth's eyes. So she mustered a weak smile. "They are—very lovely. It was thoughtful of you, Ruth."

"I knew you had been accustomed to nice things. I thought perhaps you would like them."

"I do. Very much."

Judith came forward to remove the veil. She folded it carefully and put it in Ailea's chest. Ailea wondered absently who had moved it to the roof chamber from her room. Then Ruth was removing her tunic, and Judith was slipping her arms into a soft white robe and belting it with a beautiful girdle of the same fabric woven with gold and silver threads entwined.

Then the sound of male voices in low conversation came from

just outside the door. "They come!" Judith's cheeks were rosy with excitement as she hurriedly pulled a comb through Ailea's short curls.

"Who comes?" Ailea asked, unable to keep a tremor from her voice.

"Be calm. It's just Ahiam escorting Jonathan to the bridal chamber. It's a—"

"Custom of the Israelites. I know." Ailea finished, trying to inject disdain into her voice in order to keep the fear at bay.

"The groom awaits permission to enter." Ahiam's voice boomed jovially. "Are you ready in there, Judith?"

As Judith and Ruth rushed around the room making sure all was in readiness, Ailea's heart began to beat faster and faster in panic. She quickly went to her clothing chest and opened it, searching frantically for her ceremonial dagger. She didn't really have any idea of what she would do with it; she just felt more secure knowing she had some means of protecting herself from her captor—*your husband*, a small voice reminded her as she heard Ruth and Judith slip from the room.

There was complete silence in the room as Ailea closed the chest and slowly rose from her knees and turned around. Her husband was standing just inside the doorway.

Ailea quickly concealed the dagger behind her back, already embarrassed by her impulsive decision to get it. Had Jonathan already seen it? He raised a thick black brow in sardonic question. Ailea took a step back and tightened her grip on the small weapon, but surprisingly Jonathan made no move to take it from her.

Instead, he unwrapped and removed the long, elaborately woven girdle that secured his outer robe. After folding it, he then removed the woven headband and turned his back on her as he knelt to place the clothing in the chest. This chore finished, he rose and took a step toward Ailea. She was backed against the wall—no retreat possible, so she raised her chin defiantly, having no idea that the pose did not irritate her bridegroom but gave him a sense of pride that such a brave and proud creature now belonged to him.

"Small warrior, the battle is over now. The treaty has been signed. We are allied—the time for peace has come."

"Never, Hebrew," she replied in a low, desperate voice.

"Tonight, my little warrior, you will cease fighting me. You will yield for you will become my wife."

She shook her head vehemently. "I won't, I can't!" Why could he not understand that to become his wife was a betrayal of her own people?

"You will." He took two large strides and was standing toe to toe with her. Ailea could feel the heat emanating from his body and see the implacable will in his gaze as it pinioned her like some small creature run to ground by a great mountain lion. In desperation, she drew the dagger from behind her back. She really didn't mean to do more than try to hold Jonathan at bay with the threat of it.

But when he merely chuckled and started to reach for her, she was suddenly so furious that she drew the blade back and lunged forward to strike him with it. He caught her wrist in a powerful painful grasp. She pounded on his chest with her free hand and struggled mightily to free herself. But he continued to tighten his grip until her hand went numb and the dagger clattered to the floor. Then he released his gip and stepped back.

Ailea knew he would win this battle, just as he had all the others they had fought. "Jonathan, please let me go."

"Ailea, I will never let you go."

"I won't be your wife!"

"But you are my wife."

Jonathan lifted her in his arms, and Ailea was astonished at the gentleness this powerful warrior displayed as he carried her to the marriage bed and showered her with lingering kisses and murmured reassurances. For some reason, all her well-constructed defenses crumbled at this gentle assault when they had held firm in all their other battles. And when he had finally, irrevocably sealed their bond, he did not gloat as she had feared, but soothed and petted, and wiped away the tears that stained her cheeks.

Enfolded in Jonathan's arms, Ailea slept so deeply that the accustomed nightmares of wandering in search of her family did not come. The sun was just risen and the room suffused with pale light when she was awakened by a pounding sound. At first she just turned into the warmth that pillowed her head and sought the comfort of sleep once more. Then the pillow moved, and she realized that it wasn't a pillow at all, but Jonathan's shoulder! He sprang up from the bed and covered himself in an old, unbleached robe that hung on a peg by the door.

"Who is it?" she asked in alarm as he returned to the bed and began to rummage for something among the covers.

"It's only Judith and Ahiam. Go back to sleep."

"But what do they want at this hour?"

"Only this," he said with a grin as he held up a large square of white cloth with a dark stain.

Ailea gasped in outrage and snatched at the cloth, but Jonathan held it out of her reach and turned toward the door. "I'm coming. I'm coming." He opened the door just a crack, and Ailea could hear the murmur of a distinctly feminine voice and an indiscernible response from Jonathan before the door was closed again. Her face was red with both anger and embarrassment when her gaze met Jonathan's.

He shook his head. "No, little warrior, don't get ready to do battle. This is not meant to humiliate you. It is a vindication of your honor. Judith and Ahiam will act in the place of your parents to display the proof of your virginity."

When he saw that her shoulders were still slumped in shame, he went over to her chest and removed her robe, handing it to her. "Come with me, wife."

Hearing him address her as his wife caused a lump in Ailea's throat, and she pulled on the robe with trembling hands, allowing him to lead her outside to the corner of the rooftop that overlooked the main street of the village. There were a dozen women there, waterpots or baskets in hand getting ready for the day. They were gathered around Ahiam and Judith, and the sound of Judith's earnest voice wafted up to her as Ailea saw the white cloth held aloft in her hands.

"See, even at this very moment your standing in Ziph is rising. The Law of Moses provides this as a means to silence slander against a chaste woman. Now the women will treat you with the respect due my bride, and if they do not, they will answer to me."

Ailea wanted to respond that she could take care of the hostile village women without his help, but before she could, she felt his strong arms encircle her as he drew her back against him. His warmth was so welcoming in the cool morning air that she succumbed to it willingly and rested quietly against him.

There was another day of feasting, and it became apparent almost immediately that her husband's prediction of her improved status was correct. As she sat beside her husband, receiving the praise and gifts that came from every family in the village, she saw new respect in everyone's eyes for the bride of their most illustrious citizen.

But the most precious gift was the praise of Shageh. He told all who would listen of his new daughter's spirit and beauty, bragging that with two such capable daughters as he now had to take care of him, he would undoubtedly live many happy and prosperous years.

Chapter Twenty

In the weeks following her wedding, Ailea felt more and more at home in Ziph. It was impossible not to. Shageh continued to teach her daily, but now he was even warmer and more affectionate toward her.

Ruth seemed sincere in her efforts to be more pleasant, and as they went about the household chores, Ailea gradually learned things about the older woman that made her understand Ruth's harsh demeanor.

Ruth spoke of her husband, Sered, who had been killed by the Philistines. She had loved him very much and in the years immediately following his death had persuaded Shageh to refuse several offers for her. She would rather remain a lonely widow in her father's house, she said, than replace her beloved Sered with another man.

Though Ruth never said so, Ailea had the impression that her sister-in-law regretted her decision not to remarry. Ruth spoke wistfully of her tiny son who had died. Now she would never have children. Ailea could not keep her tender heart from taking pity on Ruth, and they gradually became friends although the older woman would never express her affection in words.

The change in the village women was even more dramatic.

Ailea was now the wife of Ziph's most prominent citizen, and they accorded her due respect. It was almost embarrassing to see the way they bowed and scraped. At first some of them, Dinah particularly, were afraid she would retaliate for their cruel treatment of her when she had first come to the village, but Ailea no longer wanted to fight them. She wanted peace.

Her relationship with Jonathan was not improving so smoothly as her other relationships, however. As the days went by, Ailea found herself more and more in love with her groom while he seemed to ignore her for the most part until they retired to their rooftop apartment in the evenings.

There, he made love to her—sometimes tenderly, sometimes fiercely—giving her no doubt that he desired her. But words seldom accompanied these intimate acts of marriage, and Ailea was left to wonder if Jonathan felt more than physical attraction towards her. They seldom even had a rousing fight anymore. He just took her for granted.

Jonathan's time was spent helping improve nearly every enterprise Ziph was involved in. He purchased more sheep and goats, adding to the production not only of meat but also cheese and cloth. One of his favorite projects was the establishment of an excellent pottery in the village. One of the families of Ziph had for years held the secret of creating durable crockery with an attractive design. The Hebrews did not glaze their pottery as did the Phoenicians and Egyptians, so the process was much simpler. Jonathan helped the family extend their production by adding on an extra building and hiring several of the town's young people to learn the trade. Jonathan assured them that one day the pottery works at Ziph would be well known throughout Israel.

Ziph was prospering, Jonathan thought one afternoon as he returned from a day spent with the shepherds. He wished his marriage was going as well. He didn't seem to know what to say to his new bride. Did she still count him her enemy? She seemed to be adjusting to her new life, but how could he be sure she wasn't just biding her time, waiting for the opportunity to escape? That's foolish, he thought. She is no longer a captive. She could just walk away. She's not being guarded.

But even as he sought to reassure himself with these thoughts, Jonathan knew, and he knew that Ailea knew, that if she left him, he would follow and bring her back. He needed her as much as he needed food and water. He wondered what his wife would do if she realized how important she was to him. One part of him wanted to tell her.

Another part was wary, afraid it would somehow weaken him to admit vulnerability to a woman. Certainly many of his friends in the army would laugh at his tender feelings toward a mere woman. Of course Ahiam would not laugh, but he was the exception.

Jonathan thought about the embarrassing incident that had happened just that morning. He had been at the pottery works, discussing his plans for expansion with some of the men, when that little demon goat his wife was so fond of came bounding up with something dangling from his mouth. Ailea, trailing several yards behind the animal, called out, "Jonathan, stop him. He has your pouch, the special one you keep atop your chest."

Jonathan stepped in front of the goat, but it ran between his legs. Dangling from its mouth was the kidskin pouch that contained Ailea's braids. He caught hold of the dangling drawstring and pulled. The goat pulled in the opposite direction. There was a ripping sound as the pouch tore open. Out tumbled his wife's hair! Jonathan thought to pretend he didn't notice the braids lying there, but Ailea, with her goat now in custody, stooped down and picked them up.

"My braids," she observed, puzzled. "What were they doing in your pouch?" Jonathan's face turned red. "Oh . . . you saved them. That's very sweet." Her battle-hardened husband was mortified to hear mocking laughter from the group of men gathered in front of the pottery.

"Yes," one of them said. "He is such a sweet fellow." The other men laughed.

Jonathan took Ailea's elbow as she cradled her pet and turned her toward home. "I will be back later," he snapped to the men. "First I must tend to the roasting of a goat."

"He is only jesting," Ailea called to them over her shoulder.

"Amal!" Jonathan said as the animal bleated up at him.

"Amal—Trouble. Jonathan, thank you. I have been trying to find a name for him. Amal is perfect."

As he went about Ziph that day, he knew that word had spread about the incident because people kept commenting on how "sweet" he was. They all thought him obsessed with his wife to the point of folly. He could not let that continue. Still, as he hurried home, he found his heart beating faster as it always did at the prospect of seeing her. He loved the time spent with her at the evening meal. She seemed genuinely interested in his plans for the village and also talked easily with his father and sister. After the meal, Jonathan went to the evening circle, staying until the last man left for home.

He did this not because he wished to. No. What he wished to do was retire to his rooftop apartment with his bride—to have her alone to himself, to feel that finally, she truly belonged to him. But because he did not want to look foolish, he tried to stay away as much as possible during the following week. And the effort was driving him mad.

After several such nights, Jonathan tired of the effort of keeping his distance from his wife. He wanted nothing more than a peaceful night at home, but complications with the birthing ewes kept him away far later than usual.

"Ailea!" he called as he entered the main room of his house. No one answered him.

Then Ruth appeared. "Oh, Jonathan. You were so late. We have already eaten. I put some food aside for you. Why don't you go upstairs and wash up? I will bring your meal up in a few minutes."

"Where is my devoted wife?" Jonathan asked, sounding more sarcastic than he really meant to sound. He felt strangely hurt that Ailea had not been the one to greet him.

Ruth gave him a questioning look. "Why, she is above stairs, awaiting you. Where else would she be?" Jonathan grunted and went to seek his wife.

Ailea was playing with her irritating pet, singing some little nonsense song to him, and only glanced up at Jonathan, acknowledging his presence with a smile as she continued humming a goat lullaby.

To cover his uncomfortable feelings, Jonathan turned his back on Ailea after a terse greeting and took longer than necessary to wash. He felt something butting his leg as he dried his face and kicked out.

"Don't! Amal just wants to play." Ailea knelt with her arm about the animal. "Why are you so cross, anyway?"

"Perhaps if my wife showed me as much kindness as she does that smelly goat, I wouldn't be."

Her eyes narrowed. "Perhaps if you were half as nice as the goat, I would."

There was the sound of quickly smothered laughter. They both turned to see Ruth standing with a tray of food. "Excuse me for interrupting. Your dinner, Jonathan."

"Very well, just set it down and leave."

"No, Ruth. Don't leave. I would like some pleasant conversation," Ailea said. Ruth glanced at her brother's stormy countenance and quickly made her departure. Jonathan ignored his wife's glare and finished his meal in silence.

When his belly was full, Jonathan found he was in a better mood. Ailea had returned from putting her pet in his pen and now stood looking at the clear night sky. The stars were brilliant, and the moonlight reflected off her upturned face, adding a soft luminescence that drew him to her.

"Come to bed," he said. "It grows very late." He laid a hand on her shoulder, but she shrugged it off. It was the first time she had rejected his advances since their marriage, and it cut him deeply.

"Ailea, I want you to come to bed."

She turned on him angrily. “And what will you do if I don’t wish to come? Will you force me?”

Jonathan sucked in a breath. He had wondered how she felt about being his wife. Now he had his answer. She still thought of herself as a prisoner. She didn’t want him. He stepped back from her.

“If you don’t wish to come to bed, I certainly won’t force you. I have no desire for an unwilling wife.” He stalked into the sleeping chamber, slamming the door.

Tears filled Ailea’s eyes as she turned back gazing at the sky, Jonathan’s remark still ringing in her ears, “I have no desire for an unwilling wife.” Her husband had already tired of her. He was staying away from home so much because she bored him. That was why he was so mean to her, so impatient. He regretted bringing her to Judah. What was she to do?

After a few moments, she pulled herself together. One thing she would not do was grovel. She would not come begging to him for little scraps of attention. She would ignore him just as he ignored her.

She stomped into the darkened sleeping chamber, making as much noise as possible as she prepared for bed. She knew he was awake, but he lay on the far edge of their bed, turned away from her, not moving a muscle. When she got into bed, she lay just as still and stiff on the edge of her side. And so they both lay awake for a very long time, within arm’s reach of each other, but as far apart as Jerusalem and Damascus.

~ ~ ~

The next morning, Isaac arrived with a message for Jonathan. There was trouble with the nation of Ammon. David had sent ambassadors to that country when their king, Nahash, had died a month ago. Hanun, the son of Nahash and newly appointed king, had been persuaded by some of his advisors that the men were spies. He had sent them back to Israel with their robes cut off immodestly short and half of their beards shaved. It was a grave insult to their dignity and manhood and to David, whom they represented.

"A messenger from the king arrived in Hebron yesterday," Issac continued. "He wants father and you to report to Jerusalem as soon as possible. Father says we will leave tomorrow."

It was midmorning. Shageh and Ruth had been helping Jonathan and Ailea clean the cistern in the courtyard. It had been Ailea's suggestion that the family attend to this chore today. She had awakened before Jonathan this morning and gone below to prepare a delicious meal to break his fast. She had thought of cleaning the cistern as a plot to keep him near her. And it had worked. Now he was going away again. She welcomed Isaac as soon as he had delivered his message.

"Come and refresh yourself. You can stay here tonight and leave with Jonathan in the morning."

Isaac nodded, "That is what I . . ."

"We will leave as soon as I have gathered my things. That way we can get an early start from Hebron in the morning," Jonathan said gruffly. Ailea watched him mount the stairs to get his things. She wanted to go after him—to tell him she would miss him—to beg him not to go. But she did not. He could have stayed one more night with her, but he didn't care to. She felt miserable as she watched him descend the stairs with his pack.

"If you are rested enough, we will go now, Isaac. Good-bye, Father, may Adonai keep you well. Come and kiss me, Ruth."

After saying his good-byes to his sister, Jonathan at last turned to Ailea. She couldn't read his expression, but she was certain her own longing and unhappiness must show clearly on her face. "Come here, wife," he said quietly.

She should just ignore his command, Ailea thought, after the way he had treated her lately. But her need to be held by her husband was greater, so she came forward until she stood before him. Then she held out her arms. He crushed her to him for a long moment before tilting her head up and giving her a passionate kiss. Then he unwrapped her arms from around his neck and left without a word.

~ ~ ~

They had no way of knowing how long he would be gone. Ailea was surprised at how much she missed him. Jonathan filled her thoughts most of the time, even though Shageh tried to distract her with discussions of the Law and tales of the early days when the Philistines frequently raided the village.

On the second week of Jonathan's absence, Ailea was in the town market when an old man carrying a basket of pomegranates came through the gate. Funny, she thought. Although he was bent over and his hair was white, he moved quickly for an elderly person. Ailea looked more closely. It was Akim! She looked at some other wares for a few minutes before seeking him out.

"Good day, sir. You have lovely pomegranates today. How much do you want for them?" She picked one up and pretended to consider it while Akim spoke in a quiet voice.

"Rezon will soon cross the Jordan and camp not far from here. You must slip away unnoticed. The Hebrew who captured you would have him killed if he found out you are meeting your brother. It is unlikely that Rezon will be able to take you with him at this time, but he wishes to see that you are well. I will get another message to you soon to tell you where to meet him."

"Tell my brother I will come."

"Remember, you must be careful not to be observed."

Ailea nodded. "If your pomegranates are as good as you say, I will take three." Ailea placed them in her market basket and then turned back toward home.

Neither she nor Akim noticed a thin, darkly clad man standing just inside the city gate. He watched Ailea until she was out of sight, then followed Akim as he left Ziph. By late evening, Joab had a full report on the meeting between Ailea and her brother's messenger.

Chapter Twenty-One

When Ahiam, Jonathan, and Isaac arrived in Jerusalem, word had just come that there was to be another battle. The Ammonites, knowing that David would not let the slight to his diplomats go unpunished, decided to mobilize their forces for a preemptive strike. They sent one thousand talents of silver to hire Aramean warriors to fight with them. Twenty thousand foot soldiers from Beth Rehob and Zobah, one thousand soldiers of King Maacah, and twelve thousand warriors from Tob were on the march.

Jonathan was surprised and disappointed to find that David did not plan to lead the army himself for this engagement. As he discussed it with the gibborim, David explained his reason. "They have so insulted my emissaries, I refuse to honor the Ammonites by personally leading the army against them. Instead, Joab will act as commander-in-chief. Abishai will be second-in-command."

When the army crossed the Jordan, scouts found that the Ammonites were dug in around their capital city of Rabbath, while the Arameans were arrayed some thirty miles south at Medeba. After meeting in council, it was decided that the larger contingent of troops would march north to Rabbath while Joab would take the smaller force to Medeba and face the Arameans. They would send word to each other if the battle turned against them, and the troops would be sent where they were needed most.

Jonathan immediately volunteered to serve under Abishai. Joab readily agreed. The army was camped outside Rabbath-ammon the next day. There was a fierce but short battle. The Ammonites retreated into their capital by sunset. Abishai personally rode up to the city gate and flung insults at the enemy before ordering the troops to march to Medeba.

Joab awaited them at Medeba. He had also put the enemy to rout. "They are headed to Hadadezer, just south of the Euphrates. I don't doubt they will regroup eventually and attack us again. I'll not tire our troops by chasing them. Let's return to Jerusalem and see what David wishes to do."

Back in Jerusalem, David decided to keep the army in readiness. As soon as word came that Hadadezer's forces were on the move, he personally would lead the army against them. As for the Ammonite dogs, it was decided to let them cower in Rabbath while David devised a plan to lay siege and take the city.

Jonathan and Ahiam requested leave and were granted it with the understanding that they would be called back immediately were hostilities to break out again.

~ ~ ~

Ailea had hoped that Akim would contact her again while Jonathan was gone. She was afraid her husband would find out about her clandestine meetings. At the very least he would forbid them. He would probably be furious with her.

She waited for Akim for several days, but he didn't appear. Neither did Jonathan, and she was very concerned about him. Early one morning she set off for Hebron, planning to spend the day with Judith. Her friend would understand Ailea's concern about her husband's safety.

As soon as she entered Hebron, Akim joined her on the

crowded street. "My master cannot meet you yet. He joins the forces of Ammon against the Hebrew army. Even now a great force is gathered at Rabbath. He tells you not to worry. He will come for you as soon as the Israelite dogs are defeated."

"There is to be a battle?"

"Yes, but don't fear. Your brother is under the command of no army. He fights under his own banner. If the Ammonites are too weak to throw off the oppressor, Rezon will slip away to fight another time."

Akim did not understand. Ailea's first thought had not been for her brother's safety but for the safety of her husband. She no longer even felt guilty about that. She was Jonathan's wife now.

"I will pray to the God of heaven for my brother's safety."

He snorted in disgust. "I doubt the God of the Israelites will look to the health and welfare of the likes of Rezon. Best not ever let your brother hear you call on their God."

Ailea made no response. In a moment, Akim disappeared into the crowd.

Judith was glad to see her. "Have you heard any news about our husbands?" she asked Ailea almost immediately. Without thinking, Ailea told her that there would soon be a battle at Rabbath and that they must both pray that the Lord of Hosts would allow a swift victory and send their husbands home untouched.

Ailea remained with her friend until midafternoon, then began the six-mile walk back to Ziph. She knew her family would worry about her if she didn't arrive well before dark. She smiled when she realized how she had changed over the past months. She now thought of Shageh and Ruth as her family and Ziph as her home.

~ ~ ~

The sun was setting, turning the sky into a tapestry of violet, rose, and gold when Ahiam, Jonathan, and Isaac reached Hebron. Jonathan had hoped to arrive earlier. He had wanted very much to arrive home by sunset, but now he realized it would be wiser to rest the night at his friend's home and continue on to Ziph at first light.

He was disappointed that he was not going to see Ailea until tomorrow. With every mile his desire to be with her again had grown greater.

Judith had welcomed them and soon had a hot meal set before the three starving men. "Guess who spent the early part of the day with me?" she said to Jonathan with a sparkle in her eyes.

Jonathan swallowed the large bit of bread he had just taken whole. "My wife?" he asked in a rusty voice.

Judith nodded. "It's a shame she did not stay a little longer or that you didn't arrive sooner. As it was, we spent our time together talking about nothing but our men. I have been worried sick. No word at all had reached me about the battle. At least Ailea was able to tell me you were fighting at Rabbath and that you should be home soon."

Ahiam raised startled eyes to Jonathan, and he knew what his friend was wondering—the same thing he was wondering. Maybe Judith had a simple answer. "How did Ailea know we were fighting at Rabbath?"

Judith shrugged. "She didn't say, exactly. Maybe a traveler from Ammon was passing through Ziph. Whatever the source, she was certainly right about your being home soon."

As he set out on the short trip to Ziph at dawn the next morning, Jonathan still wondered how his wife, in a remote hill-country village, had learned about military operations. He determined to find out. But the closer he got to home, the more he forgot his questions. He just wanted to see his wife—to assure himself she was all right.

Surprisingly, she was at the city gate when he came through it. She ran straight into his arms. Jonathan lifted her off the ground in an embrace. This public display was quite shockingly improper, but he knew the people of Ziph had become used to breaches of propriety by Jonathan's Aramean bride. Whereas before they had seized on her lapses to condemn her, now they used her foreign origins to excuse anything she did that was not according to Hebrew custom.

Ailea was so obviously thrilled to see him that Jonathan forgot to question her about the knowledge of the battle for the entire first day he was back. It seemed that everyone in the village stopped by to hear word of the battle that had just been fought with the Ammonites.

When at last they were alone in their rooftop apartment, the battle with Ammon was the last thing on their minds. Jonathan and Ailea did not discuss the fight they had before Jonathan had been called away. They were too glad to see each other, and their reunion was very sweet. But the next day brought an opportunity for Jonathan to bring up the subject.

The next morning, Ailea woke from an unpleasant dream to find Jonathan asleep beside her. She rose up on one elbow to study the familiar, and now, she admitted, beloved face of her husband in repose.

He had not trimmed his beard while in the field, and by all objective accounts looked more fierce than ever. But to Ailea, he looked almost boyish with his face relaxed in sleep, his breath coming in soft, gentle rhythms through slightly parted lips.

As if he sensed her watching him, Jonathan opened first one eye, then the other. "What woke you so early, little warrior?"

She decided to risk revealing her feelings. "A dream. I dreamed you were still gone. I was so happy when I woke to find you here beside me. I was very worried about you."

This reminded Jonathan of what Judith had told him, and although he hated risking this sweet interlude between them, he decided to ask Ailea about it—get the question answered now rather than later.

"Ailea, how did you know we were deployed to Rabbath?"

"What?"

"You told Judith that we were sent to Rabbath. We were only told after we got to Jerusalem. So how did you find out?"

For a moment Ailea looked disturbed. She sat up in bed,

pulling the covers securely around her before answering. Then she looked at him with clear green eyes and said with perfect honesty, "A vendor came to the village. He was selling pomegranates. He told me that the Hebrews and Ammonites were fighting at Rabbath. His pomegranates are very good. See—there are two of them left in the bowl there on the chest. I want you to taste them." She started to get up, but Jonathan's fingers closed around her upper arm, staying her.

"Who was this man? Where was he from? Where did he go?"

"I . . . I had never seen him in the village before. He wasn't a Judahite. I believe he was from beyond Jordan. And I have no idea where he is now," Ailea said, quite truthfully. After staring at her for a moment, Jonathan released her arm and settled back on his pillow.

~ ~ ~

Jonathan believed that some of what Ailea had told him had been the truth. Still, he could not help feeling she was holding something back. He wondered if he could wholly trust her. His wife was still very much a mystery to him, a riddle with an ever elusive answer.

He sought out the Rab that afternoon. The old man had one of his precious manuscripts spread out on the table in the courtyard and was deep in concentration.

"Father?"

"Umm-hmm."

"I would talk with you."

"Hmmm."

"Father, please. It is important."

Shageh reluctantly looked up from his studies. When he saw his son's worried face, he motioned for him to take the stool on the opposite side of the table.

"So, what burdens you today, Jonathan?"

"It's nothing really specific. At least, I don't think so. I'm not sure. Father, how has Ailea seemed to you? Do you know how she feels now about me? I mean . . . about living here among us? Does she seem happy?"

"Son, she is your wife. Why do you ask me the answers to such questions? I am merely her father-in-law."

"But in many ways you are much closer to Ailea . . ." Seeing the raised eyebrow, Jonathan continued clumsily, "As her teacher, I thought you might have insight."

Shageh nodded. "I have spent much time with the child. Hours. I have taught her the Law. And I have asked her opinions, her feelings. I have listened carefully to her. Have you?"

"Have I listened? . . . Well, yes, some. But when we talk about certain things, we always argue. And I don't want to argue with my wife. I want . . ." Unable to articulate just what he did want, Jonathan raised his shoulders in an eloquent shrug.

"I was just reading the Torah." Shageh found the place and began to read.

> And from the rib which the Lord God had taken from man, He made a woman, and brought her unto the man. And Adam said, "This is now bone of my bones, and flesh of my flesh. She shall be called Woman, for she was taken out of Man.
>
> Therefore shall a man leave his father and his mother, and shall cleave unto his wife; and they shall be one flesh.

Shageh studied his son's reaction. "Son, a man has to cleave to his wife in order to get to know her. The rest of his family must come second. He must trust his wife more than he trusts another soul, and he must inspire trust in her. Oh, I know that many men don't bother to do this. They reason that their wives are weak and of little importance except for breeding children. But these men are not following the precepts of Adonai. And they are cheated of the greatest joy a man can know—true oneness with the woman the Lord God made especially for him. I have known this joy, Jonathan, with your mother."

Jonathan felt a lump in his throat and cleared it. "I realize that, Father. That is what I wish in my own marriage. But it is so difficult. Ailea resents the way I forced her to come here—to marry me. I am not sure that can ever be overcome."

Shageh laughed. "Are you not aware of the circumstances that brought your mother and me together? I can assure you that neither of us were pleased when we found out who our parents had chosen for us. Even though it is rare to be like our ancestor Jacob and choose a wife because we love her, I had my eye on a young girl in the village. You needn't ask—she married a man from Moan many years ago. You have never met her, and none of the family remains in Ziph—and all that is beside the point.

"What I want you to understand is that I did not want to wed your mother. As you know, she was from Beersheba, many, many miles away, and she did not wish to leave her family and her town and friends. When I went to fetch her, she cried all the way from Beersheba to Ziph. She was very young and knew that she might never see her mother and father—who were not in good health—again, so it was understandable. But I was young and not at all understanding. I told your mother—on our wedding night, mind you—that I wanted no sniveling bride and ordered her to stop her weeping. It did do the trick. Miriam stopped crying—started throwing things. The wedding guests heard the commotion, and my father actually came to see what I was doing to my gentle bride. Imagine his surprise when he entered my tent in time to see her throw a candlestick and hit me right in the eye." Shageh broke into laughter.

"You never told me this story before," Jonathan said with a broad grin.

"Of course not! What man would admit being brought low by his bride on his wedding night? Besides, by the time you came along, I was the Rab. It was beneath my dignity to admit to such a thing."

"But I never remember you and Mother fighting. What happened to change things?"

"First of all, your grandfather, who was a man not to be contradicted, declared that we were excused from attending the remaining three days of the wedding feast. This was to serve two purposes—I would not have to explain my black eye, and Miriam and I, with only each other's company, would learn to get along."

"Did Grandfather's decree have the result he desired?"

"I will say only that it did not take us long to discover that there are better things for a man and wife to spend their time doing than throwing things at each other. But I would have you understand, Jonathan, that it took time for us to gain the unity we finally achieved in our marriage. It is not easy. Do you think it worth the effort to strive to have such a marriage?"

"I know it is worth the effort. I want a home like the one I grew up in—like Ahiam and Judith have. But is it possible?"

"Oh, it is possible, if you are willing to pay the price. I want you to read what Moses said. I think it will help you to understand what I am asking of you." Shageh lifted the top two scrolls and pointed to a passage in the middle of the third. "Here. Read this."

Jonathan carefully read the scroll.

> If a man has recently married, he must not be sent to war or have any other duty laid on him. For one year he is to be free to stay at home and bring happiness to the wife he has married.

"That is impossible," he murmured.

"Of course it is not impossible. It is the Law of God. You are to have the freedom to spend time with your wife."

"But no one does that! Are you saying I am to do nothing for a year, but, but . . ."

"I am not saying you are to take an entire year to pay attention only to Ailea. What I am saying is that the Law of Moses allows you to take *some* time to establish your marriage, and if it is important to you, you will do so."

"But I am a sodier. The Arameans may launch another campaign. I may have to fight."

Shageh shook his head and pointed to the manuscript on the table. "Moses particularly mentions exemption from the army. Why don't you ask for a leave of absence? Let the army know where you will be."

"Where I will be?"

Shageh gave his son a long-suffering look. "This is a small village, son. You can't expect to stay here and spend any time alone with your bride. You know how everyone looks into everyone else's affairs."

"So you are telling me to take a leave of absence from my military duties and take my wife away somewhere until she is satisfied with this marriage?"

"I would never presume to tell you, a grown man, the most important citizen of Ziph, what to do, Jonathan."

"I can just imagine Joab's reaction when I tell him why I want time off. I don't suppose you would like to accompany me to Jerusalem to get his permission?"

Shageh sighed as he bent back to his scrolls. "I would love to go with you, son, but I am an old man, as you know. I don't think I could tolerate such a rapid trip as I imagine you'll be making."

Once Shageh had made the suggestion, it became more and more appealing. By evening Jonathan had informed Ailea that he was returning to Jerusalem, that he would be back in three days, and that she should prepare for a trip as soon as he returned. At first he refused to tell her where they were going, but his instructions and the provisions made it clear it would be a lengthy journey. Ailea was intrigued. She begged to know their destination until he finally told her.

"En-gedi, where we often lived when Saul, the former king of Israel, was chasing us. It is beautiful there, Ailea. There are trees and springs and caves . . ."

"Why are we going there?"

"Because . . . because I wish to, that is all. Now go to sleep. I leave at dawn for Jerusalem."

~ ~ ~

Joab was even more incensed than Jonathan had thought he would be when he heard the request. Jonathan could have gone over his head and appealed directly to David, but avoiding conflict with his nemesis did not fit his idea of manliness, and it would only make Joab angrier if Jonathan went directly to David. Besides, Jonathan decided he would much rather face Joab's wrath than the amusement he was certain he would see on the king's face.

At first Joab flatly refused the leave. "You must have lost your mind. You are asking leave when we may have to march against Ammon, not to speak of Aram, any day? And you wish this time in order to take your Aramean woman on a tour of Israel?"

"She is my *wife,* general. And Moses allows that as a newly married man, I have the time off. If you need to call a priest to confirm it, feel free to do so."

Joab waved his suggestion away. "I know the Law, son of Shageh, even if I don't go around spouting it as certain others do!"

"I assume you insult me and not my father or our king, Joab."

That implied warning had the desired effect. "Very well, you are granted the leave, if you can assure me this was all your own idea."

"What do you mean?"

"Did the girl suggest this little trip?"

"Certainly not."

"What is your destination?" When Jonathan did not answer immediately, Joab let his anger show. "As your commander, I demand to know where you may be reached in the following weeks!"

"I am taking her to En-gedi."

"En-gedi. Ah, yes. Isolated and beautiful. And not too far from the royal stores at the stronghold. It is possible she wishes to find out more about Mesad and the arms and gold that are kept there."

Jonathan laughed derisively. "Only a few of the Thirty know about those stores. They are virtually inaccessible and no longer of much importance to the king anyway. My wife knows nothing about Mesad and had no idea of the destination I picked. Besides, I told you we were going to En-gedi. Mesad is more than ten miles south."

"Just see that your *wife*," Joab spat out the word as if it were a foul taste in his mouth, "doesn't learn any military secrets during your tender moments together."

Jonathan held his fist to keep from striking the man. One day he hoped to have a final reckoning with the general, but now was not the time. He was brusquely dismissed and left immediately for home.

He made only one stop on the way. He found Ahiam and Judith at home in Hebron. Isaac was also there—disappointed to hear the Jonathan was taking a leave from the military, which meant Isaac wouldn't be called on to serve in the near future either.

"Don't worry, lad. We will see battle together before the year is out. Just see that you practice the arts of war that I've taught you. I don't want you to grow fat and lose your skill! Now, Isaac, would you excuse us for a little while? I have a private matter I wish to discuss with your parents."

Ahiam and Judith were already near to bursting with curiosity over their friend's announcement. They were anxious to hear whatever else he had to impart. Their curiosity turned to an amusement they could hardly conceal when their battle-hardened friend finally stammered out the reason for his visit.

Judith, aware that her husband was struggling to keep from laughing aloud, took pity on her friend. "Let me see if I understand this, Jonathan. You wish Ahiam and me to tell you what to say to Ailea when you take her to En-gedi?"

Running his fingers through his thick, black curls, Jonathan couldn't look at Judith directly. He stared out the window and nodded. "I have been busy in war and haven't had time to learn the . . . gentle phrases that women like to hear. I can talk of battle and weapons, but I don't think that is what Ailea would want to hear during our weeks together."

Judith couldn't suppress a giggle. "You are right, Jonathan. But there are really no special words or phrases."

Ahiam interrupted, unholy glee in his eyes. "Of course there are, dear. He should tell Ailea that her ears are like perfectly matched, tiny shells. Her eyes are like emeralds, her lips as soft as . . ." He broke off when his wife drove a small fist into his stomach.

"Pay no attention to Ahiam. You will be glad to know that he was just as confused as you when he first tried to speak of love. Don't worry about what you will say, Jonathan. Just tell Ailea what is in your heart—that you love her, that you're glad she is your wife, that you will always be together—those kinds of things. Now go home. Your wife is waiting for you. And Jonathan, as a woman, I know. She cares for you—deeply."

Jonathan finally escaped the uncomfortable encounter with only a small measure of teasing from Ahiam and a hug and kiss from Judith.

~ ~ ~

While Jonathan was gone, Akim appeared again. Ailea was alone at the stream, filling a waterpot, when he appeared.

"Follow me," he said quietly.

He led her to a secluded spot a mile or so from the village.

"Your brother may be able to come for you soon. Be ready."

"But my husband is taking me away tomorrow."

"Where are you going?"

"He is taking me to En-gedi."

"That is near the Dead Sea. We have heard that the Hebrews have hidden treasure near there—in a place they call the Stronghold. See what you can find out about it."

"You want me to spy?"

"Certainly, why not?"

When Ailea didn't answer, Akim asked another question.

"How long will you be gone?"

"For at least two weeks."

"Oh, that is not so long. Rezon would probably not have been able to make arrangements to come for you by then anyway. Go with your . . . Hebrew. But when you return, look for the signal that Rezon has come. The day after you see the signal, you will know to meet him here at noon. Make sure no one sees you leave."

A few minutes later, Ailea watched Akim go. Strange, just a few weeks before, she would have been elated at this news. Now it filled her with confusion. What was she going to do?

When Jonathan reached Ziph a short time later, Ailea wasn't there. "She said she was going to gather dead branches in the hills," Ruth told him. "She took the goat with her, of course. I'm sure she would not have gone if she had known you would be back so soon. But we do need more firewood, Jonathan." Ruth had seen the disappointment in her brother's face when he hadn't found his wife at home. She hoped to excuse Ailea's absence.

Jonathan went to the hills in search of her. In a short time, he saw her—coming toward him from the east, the goat gamboling behind her. She had no firewood in her arms.

"Where have you been?"

"Oh . . . this naughty thing ran away. I had to go after him. Ruth needs firewood. Would you help me gather some?"

Jonathan knew Ailea was trying to distract him. He decided to let her think she had succeeded. When they finished gathering the wood and depositing it in the small shed beside the house, Jonathan excused himself, telling Ailea he had business to attend to if they were to leave early on the morrow.

He followed the tracks his wife and her pet had made until he came to a sheltered spot on the leeward side of the tall hill. There he saw not one set of human footprints but two. His wife's small ones and a much bigger set—a man's. He followed these prints for another mile to the northeast, toward the Jordan. Were they Rezon's tracks or maybe an emissary's? If so, why hadn't Ailea told him? He knew the answer. She didn't trust him. He intended to change that. The sooner they could start on their journey, the better.

Jonathan did not seek his bed until it was late and he was sure his wife was asleep. He was brooding—trying to find a reason to trust her, trying hard not to believe Joab's implications that she would spy against him. Surely Ailea would not do such a thing. No. The most she might attempt was to go back to her people. What tortured his mind was the thought that she might still want to do that. In the next three weeks he had to make sure he bound her to him in a way that would insure that even if Rezon appeared, she would choose to stay with her husband.

Chapter Twenty-Two

As promised, Jonathan woke Ailea early, and in the gray light of dawn, they said their farewells to Ruth and Shageh. Jonathan had filled the panniers of his camel with the supplies they would need. Ruth and Ailea had packed food and bread, cheeses and olives, dried raisins and figs.

"Is there still room for us?" Ailea asked skeptically. She was not looking forward to the camel ride after her previous experience with the one that had left her in the desert.

In answer to her question, Jonathan gave a low, guttural command and tapped the animal with a stick he held in his hand. The camel dropped to its knees, then on the joints of its hind legs, then leaned forward on its chest. Finally, the hind legs folded completely, and the animal was ready to mount. Jonathan climbed aboard the saddle, which had two high pommels in front and two in back. He held out his hand to Ailea, who looked doubtful.

"Are you sure you know how to handle this beast? I have never seen a camel in Ziph. I thought you hill dwellers never used camels."

"If I need any instruction, I will be sure to ask the plains dweller who is traveling with me." He was referring to the fact, of course, that the Arameans made far greater use of the desert animal than the Hebrews did.

"If you are depending on me to control this mount, I have to warn you that the last one I rode left me stranded."

"Get on. Between us we will manage the animal. We need his size and strength to carry our supplies and to get us to En-gedi as quickly and comfortably as possible." Ailea shrugged and joined her husband, turning sideways in front of him, with her legs resting across one of his knees. Jonathan silently congratulated himself on thinking of this intimate way to travel, then tapped the animal sharply with his stick. Ailea laughed aloud as the animal rose in the opposite manner than he had knelt, hind quarters coming up first, which threw his riders forward. Then the front of the beast came up, and they were thrown backwards. Finally, the camel lurched forward and they were thrown forward once more. Jonathan moaned, "Did I say 'comfortably'?"

They were both laughing as they waved good-bye to Ruth and Shageh. They could see his nod of approval as they rode past him.

The ride was not comfortable for the first few miles for the camel was not well-adapted to traveling in the hills. "In another mile or so, we will begin descending to the plains, and the going will be easier," Jonathan assured her as they bounced along.

"What villages will we pass through?"

"None."

"We won't see any towns or villages?" she asked, turning her face up to his.

Jonathan shook his head. "There are none between here and En-gedi."

"We won't see any other people, then?"

"I hope not, because if we do, they will likely be bandits. They sometimes hide out in the caves and hills we are headed for. In fact, I used to hide out there myself when I was a fugitive."

"You were a fugitive? What crime did you commit?"

"The crime of giving my allegiance to David. Saul, the king at the time, felt jealous of David and accused him of plotting to overthrow him. David had to run for his life many times and his friends with him."

"And you were one of those friends."

"Yes. I still am."

As they descended to the desolate plains that led to the Dead Sea, Jonathan told his bride about his early years as a warrior and their battles with the Philistines. Of course he told the tale of Goliath's death and of taking Jerusalem as the capital.

He also told her stories about Joab that made the hairs on the back of her neck stand up. She reached up and touched his cheek. "Jonathan, you must promise me that you will be careful in your dealings with Joab. You should never trust such a man. Try not to make him your enemy, or I am sure he would stop at nothing to destroy you."

He looked down, intently studying her face. "And would you care?"

"What do you think?" she asked. Then she teasingly pinched his cheek before turning around.

They rested in the heat of the day in the shadow of a huge redstone outcropping, then continued their journey by the light of the moon. Ailea fell asleep against Jonathan's broad chest, but the rocking gait of the camel kept jarring her awake. Jonathan stopped at a series of low-lying, barren hills. Ailea sleepily spread out their blankets as Jonathan tended to the animal.

"Jonathan, don't you dare tie that camel to a bush. Find a boulder and wrap his lead around it several times."

"I think you do not trust my knowledge, wife."

"I do not trust your camel, husband." They both laughed, but Jonathan did tie the camel to the rocks. When they lay down to sleep, Jonathan, turning on his side, drew her against him, circling her waist with his arm. But he said nothing, nor did he make love to her. There would be time for both when they reached En-gedi. He could hardly wait to get there.

Shortly after daybreak they started out again. If they rode hard, they would reach En-gedi before sunset. As they traveled toward their destination, Ailea raised her hand and pointed to a massive rock formation many miles away. "What is that mountain called?" It reminded her very much of the monolith in her dreams, and she felt drawn to it. It was magnificent.

"Actually it is more of a massive rock than a mountain." Jonathan answered. "It is called *Mesad,* the stronghold."

"Are there any people there?

"No. The top is almost inaccessible. I often went there with David in the early years when we were on the run from Saul."

"Will we go there?

Jonathan's mind flashed back to his conversation with Joab, and he was somewhat disturbed by her question. "Of course not. Why would you ask?"

Ailea didn't want to tell her husband about her disturbing dreams of running toward a mountain or a great rock. Not when this was to be a time of happiness. So she answered lightly. "Oh, I guess I just thought it would be an exciting place to explore. Maybe we would even find buried treasure."

Having no idea how much her response had disturbed Jonathan, Ailea continued her chatter, asking many questions about the area and about Jonathan's experiences here.

He answered them, but his mind dwelt on her interest in Mesad. Finally he told himself that he would not let suspicion mar their time together. It was only a coincidence that she had asked about the stronghold and mentioned treasure, but Jonathan wished she had not mentioned Mesad.

They reached En-gedi in midafternoon. They were hot and tired. Ailea groaned when Jonathan had them dismount from their camel and climb a narrow, twisting path up into the sandstone hills. After several minutes they reached a place of remarkable beauty. There was a large waterfall with a clear pool at the bottom. Around the falls grew ferns and moss and many varieties of trees, some bearing fruit, such as the large luscious figs that Jonathan reached out and plucked for her. As they approached the pool, they startled a large wild ram. He turned his bearded face toward the intruders, dipped his magnificent curled horns at them, and bounded away.

"There are large herds of wild goats around here. I will kill one tomorrow so that we will have fresh meat," Jonathan told her. He led her further up the cliff face to a spacious cave. When he lighted a pitch torch that had been left near the cave's entrance and held it aloft, Ailea could see that it had been used as a dwelling before. There was a large supply of dried wood and dung for building fires. And there was a leather pallet, stuffed with straw.

"A few travelers know of this place; mostly the gibborim. Whenever anyone stays here, he tries to leave behind supplies for the next occupant. See, the fire is already laid."

After they had their things settled into the cave, Jonathan and Ailea both felt awkward and embarrassed. They had been married for several weeks, but this was their first opportunity to be completely alone with no distractions.

Jonathan observed his wife's sudden shyness and reserve. He cleared his throat and said, "I think we should cool off in the pool." She agreed, and they made their way down the steep, rocky path to the foot of the waterfall.

Jonathan unceremoniously divested himself of his clothing and dived into the cool, crystal-clear waters of the pool. When he bobbed to the surface, he saw Ailea still standing uncertainly at the edge.

"Well, wife, are you coming?" he grinned at her.

"It's the middle of the day," she said timidly, stating the obvious. Jonathan knew what must be troubling her.

"We are alone here, Ailea. No one will see us. Come." Then he swam away toward the falls, to give his wife some privacy.

She stepped tentatively into the water, letting it lap at her feet. Then in a quick motion, she pulled off her robe, tossed it over her head, and plunged beneath the water. She swam toward Jonathan, coming up under the cascade of the waterfall. The rushing waters were so cool and refreshing, she felt the uneasiness drain from her.

She was swimming lazily about when Jonathan suddenly came up under her, lifted her high in the air, and tossed her back into the pool with a splash. She came up sputtering, trying to catch her breath. She was angry for just a moment, but when she saw the playful smile on Jonathan's face, she had to laugh in spite of herself.

"You look just like you did when I first met you," he remarked with a grin. "Only this time you are in a much better mood."

"Oh, you are very bad to remind me of that day." Ailea hit the water with open palms, splashing his face with water.

"But I like to think of that day. If it hadn't been for that day, I wouldn't be here with you now." Suddenly the playful look in his eyes turned to ardor. He swam to his wife and wrapped his arms around her. "Ailea . . ." Jonathan's mouth worked as if he wanted very much to say something. He started to, several times, then shook his head in frustration. With Ailea's arms wrapped around his neck, he swam to the mossy bank of the pool. There he made love to her, trying to convey without words how he cherished her. They fell asleep on the shady bank.

Something woke her later. Jonathan was tracing the contour of her ear with his finger. Through her half-closed lashes she watched him.

"They really are like tiny matching shells," he murmured. Ailea, who had never heard her husband say anything so poetic, giggled.

He looked startled that she was awake and embarrassed that she had heard him. She was sorry she had laughed for she would have liked to hear more. But the mood was broken. Jonathan sat up, crossing his arms on his raised knees. He placed his chin on his arms. "It won't work," he said dismally.

"What won't work?"

"The pretty phrases. I'm just not good at them."

"I thought the one about the matching shells was very good, husband."

He snorted. "Ahiam gave me that one." When she giggled again, he grabbed her arms. "It isn't funny. I have to tell you—and yet I can't!"

"Tell me what, husband?"

"That . . . that I don't want you to think of yourself as my captive anymore. That I want you to be my true wife—for always. That I—that I love you."

Ailea framed his face with her small hands. She smoothed her thumbs across his cheekbones. She smiled into his eyes. "I love you too, husband," she whispered.

~ ~ ~

On the third day at En-gedi, Jonathan took her to see the source of the falls at the springs in the limestone cliffs high above. As they made their way up the steep path, Jonathan stayed behind his wife to protect her if her feet should slide.

"There is a story surrounding that rock just above us," he said after they had climbed for a half-hour. "Let's rest there, and I'll tell you."

The rock slab he spoke of was completely flat and rectangular. "Why, it looks just like a table," Ailea exclaimed, hopping up onto its smooth surface.

Jonathan gripped her arm suddenly. "No, don't go out on it. This rock is precariously balanced. Even your puny weight could cause it to topple if you were to go out on the edge. We will sit on this end to have our rest. You are right, though. It does look like a table, which makes me hungry." He opened the bag he had tied around his waist and handed her a bunch of grapes.

"Tell me the story about this place," she reminded him after her hunger and thirst had been slaked with half the fruit.

"Well, once the king's men—I refer to King Saul's men—had chased us through the whole land of Judah, and we ended up here with three thousand of them hot on our heels. Ahiam and I found this place. We decided that if they cornered us up here, we could send this rock crashing down on them. Make the fight a more even one. The large branch, tree trunk actually, that you stepped on to climb on this rock, we dragged up here and placed it so we could use it as a lever to dislodge the stone."

By leaning sideways a bit, Ailea could see that the rock, if it fell, would land on the path some thirty feet below. She shuddered a bit at the thought of what would happen to a person who happened to be standing under it.

"Obviously, you never had to use the ploy," she observed, "or the rock would be down there and not up here."

"No, we never had to use it because our leader had a meeting with the king that was both daring and touching." Jonathan went on to tell her of the day David had followed Saul into one of the caves in these hills and cut off the end of his cloak without the king's ever being aware of it, later showing Saul the evidence that David was not his enemy.

"Did the king believe him?" Ailea asked, fascinated with David's compassion on a man who had hunted him like a wild animal.

Jonathan nodded. "That time, he let us go. Took his three thousand troops back to Gibeah. But that wasn't the end of it. I think a kind of mad jealousy overtook Saul from time to time, and he was driven to do things he was ashamed of in his more lucid moments. A sad story."

"Then let us have no more of it. Show me the springs." So they climbed higher until they came to the springs. There was a large herd of wild goats drinking from them—large rams with magnificent horns, mother goats with nursing kids.

"I understand now why this place it called En-gedi," Ailea remarked.

Jonathan nodded, *"The Spring of the Goats."*

"Oh, look at that one, Jonathan. He is just the size of Amal."

Jonathan groaned. "Don't remind me of that mangy animal."

"Mangy! What a thing to call my pet."

They continued the teasing banter for the rest of the afternoon.

It was wonderful, this new closeness between them, Ailea thought as she lay enfolded in Jonathan's arms that night.

They spent more than two weeks at En-gedi. Ailea thought it must be the closest thing to the Garden of Eden that Shageh had taught her about. Just the man and his wife—with nothing to spoil their happiness. Of course it wasn't really the Garden of Eden, and the day came when they had to go. But now they felt secure with each other. They had declared their love and their loyalty to one another, and they felt sure that nothing could ever separate them.

Chapter Twenty-Three

~

Ailea knew she should tell Jonathan about Rezon as soon as they returned to Ziph, but she was afraid he would be angry that she hadn't told him sooner. Also, she feared that if Jonathan knew that Rezon was still alive, he might not only forbid her to see him, but his loyalty to David might also require that he report Rezon and have him captured.

Ailea couldn't bear to think of that happening. The contentment between her and Jonathan had been so hard won and was still, she believed, so tenuous, that she dared not risk it at this point. She decided that she would have the arranged meeting with Rezon—and then tell Jonathan about it after her brother was safely away.

~ ~ ~

At the same moment Ailea was formulating her plan to meet her brother, Jonathan was in the home of Ahiam in Hebron, talking to Joab and Uriah. He had received an urgent message to meet them there. Ailea would have been shocked to know that her husband not only knew that her brother lived but that he was now receiving a detailed report on Rezon.

"The man has been raiding Israelite convoys for months. He has already gathered a large band of fighters around him. If allowed to continue, he will only get stronger and cause more trouble," Uriah reported.

"That has nothing to do with my wife. She is not responsible for her brother's actions," Jonathan said heatedly.

"Is she not?" Joab asked. "You know, don't you, that they have been in contact all along? She was probably trying to join her brother when she got lost in the desert."

Jonathan said nothing. He did not want Joab to know what he knew—or suspected. If Joab had proof of Ailea plotting against Israel, they would not be having this conversation. The general would have merely had her arrested—or assassinated. Since Jonathan had no proof, only her suspicious behavior the day she had gone missing and her inexplicable knowledge of the king's stores of silver and gold at Mesad, he would remain silent and see what Joab would do.

One thing Jonathan was certain of—Ailea might scheme to see her brother, she might even plot to leave Jonathan, but she would not spy for Rezon against Israel. Jonathan believed her conversion to Yahweh was real, and he loved his wife. He would never doubt her, no matter what Joab said.

Jonathan looked at the dark eyes staring at him from behind narrowed eyelids, trying to decipher some hint of Joab's intentions, but there was no sign of an emotion, nothing on the impassive face etched like stone from years of wind and sun. It was the same expression Jonathan had seen before on the battlefield, the one Joab carried into the fight like another piece of armor, that hard, impenetrable look from the depths of a tomb. This is how he looks when he kills, Jonathan thought. No guilt, no pity, nothing. Wait, Jonathan told himself. Keep quiet.

For a long moment Joab remained fixed, poised for the next move as if calculating what game piece to play. Jonathan's evenings with Ailea over the chess board has taught him to think his strategy through in advance—four moves, five moves, looking for the vulnerable opening. How many moves ahead was Joab?

"She met with Rezon's emissary, Akim, several weeks ago. Akim went straight to Rezon. We believe that Ailea will meet with her brother soon, and we have to know what information she has passed or will pass on to him."

"My wife has no information that could be harmful to Israel. I never speak of military matters to her, and she has not left Ziph except in my company."

"Except when she sneaks off to meet with her brother or his messenger! Tell me this, did you tell her about the storehouses at Mesad?"

The question pushed Jonathan past his limit of patience. "Do you accuse my wife of treason?"

"One must be a Hebrew to commit treason against Israel. I suspect her of spying, and if she is, I intend to catch her at it no matter how hard you try to protect her."

"Ailea is now a Hebrew. She follows the Lord God and has taken instruction from the Rab to become one of us."

The general shook his head. "And it never occurred to you that it could all be a ruse to get you to trust her, the better to find out military secrets for that bandit brother of hers?"

Jonathan's hands clenched involuntarily into fists, and he felt a heat rising from his chest to his neck. His head was pounding with anger, yet he fought to remain calm. He had to keep control. Don't let Joab get the upper hand, he reminded himself, or he'll move in for the kill.

"General, if I might offer a suggestion." Uriah interjected Jonathan had forgotten about the armor-bearer who had been standing against the wall next to the door of the small inner room. "It seems that the captain is firmly convinced of his wife's innocence, as any good husband would be. He would have no reluctance to prove her loyalty beyond a doubt, I'm sure."

Jonathan listened, but watched Joab, not turning his back on the general. "What do you have in mind, Uriah?" Joab asked.

"A simple plan. Jonathan will provide her with information that would be of use only to Rezon. False information, of course, but tantalizing enough so that he'll take action. If he does, we'll know she's a spy. If not, then she is innocent."

Joab stepped closer to Jonathan, not looking at Uriah but studying Jonathan's reaction as he moved in a deliberate circle to Jonathan's right.

"A brilliant idea, my good man. Perhaps Rezon will be as foolish as his late father. We will give her information that appears so vital to our people that only a true enemy would divulge it."

Jonathan turned slowly, following Joab's steps toward the door. "And when she is caught, there will be no question that she is guilty. And then," he said with a pause as if playing his last move, "you will turn her over to me."

Jonathan looked at Uriah whose face appeared soldierly, impassive, but not hardened like Joab's. The man gave him a glance—of compassion or contempt?—and then looked forward as if standing at attention. Uriah's suggestion had been given in the same official tone as his scouting report. Had he thought of the plan himself or was someone else using him like a pawn, holding Jonathan like a helpless king awaiting checkmate? Jonathan had never doubted the man's loyalty to Israel and to David, but how far would he go to serve Joab?

Jonathan had one piece left to play, the only one left to him. "What do you want me to tell her?"

~ ~ ~

"Tell me about your meeting with Joab." Ailea asked when Jonathan returned to Ziph.

Jonathan sat down on the bench by the door and unfastened his sandals. Ailea brought a basin and jug of water and knelt down, lifting his foot into the basin and washing it with fresh water. Jonathan leaned back against the wall and watched her. It was the first time she had done this for him, a routine thing he had always done for himself in a house without servants. Ailea looked up and returned his gaze with a smile. His wife, his very heart—he couldn't imagine his life without her. Ailea dried his feet with a cloth and looked back with a questioning gaze.

"Did it go well, husband?" she asked.

"It went well. There is to be a large shipment of gold from Medeba to Jerusalem. I will meet the convoy after it crosses to the west side of the Jordan and escort it to Jerusalem. I will have to be gone for at least a week."

"When is this to happen?"

"The convoy will leave Medeba in two weeks, so I must leave here in one."

She leaned up and placed a kiss on his cheek. "I will miss you, my love."

His amber eyes studied her intently, "Will you, wife?"

"Yes, of course," she replied. "When you return, perhaps we will have more time together, husband. I—" Ailea stopped as if the words caught in her throat. Something in Jonathan's eyes—a sadness she had not seen before—frightened her, and she sat silently on his lap, her arms encircling his neck and her head resting on his chest.

"You were saying, my love?" he asked.

"I will be looking for you to come home."

"Yes, when I come home."

Jonathan was very busy for the next few days, so it was easy, when the signal came, for Ailea to sneak away without his knowledge. But she was disappointed, because it was Akim once more who met her.

"Rezon has business to take care of first, then he will come for you."

"But that is what you told me before. I need to talk to my brother in person. Why can't he come now?"

"Because he is to lead an important raid. But he will be here before the month is out, so be ready."

Ailea returned to Ziph feeling guilty for hiding this from Jonathan. In the days before his departure, she tried to make it up to him. They both clung to each other on the morning he had to leave.

≈ ≈ ≈

Jonathan, Ahiam, and Benjamin met Joab and Uriah in Medeba. "This is a waste of everyone's time," Jonathan told them, as they sat on a hillside overlooking the formation of the fake convoy.

"Not if Rezon shows up," Benjamin remarked.

"He won't," Jonathan bit out.

Jonathan's spirits began to rise as the convoy got underway and advanced unmolested. Most of the warriors were hidden in the wagons. Only Joab, Jonathan, Benjamin, Ahiam, and Uriah hung back. They were mounted on mules and camels.

They were in a flat stretch of terrain a few miles east of Jordan when Rezon's raiders swooped down on the wagons, mounted on swift camels. The men hidden in the wagons fought but could do little damage to the mounted raiders.

Rezon had realized immediately that it was a trap, and when he saw Joab and the others approaching on their mounts, he retreated. The Arameans were on much swifter mounts, and though the Hebrews gave chase, they quickly disappeared into the desert.

As they camped for the night, Joab gave instructions. "I am sending Benjamin back to Ziph with you, Jonathan. I believe now that the trap has been sprung. Rezon will know his sister has been found out and will come for her. It may still be possible to capture Rezon. On the other hand, he may care more for his own neck than he does for his sister. If that is the case, I want her brought back to Jerusalem. I want to question her before she is . . . punished."

Jonathan sat staring at the campfire. "And, Jonathan, it is

important that when you first return, you give the girl no clue that you know she has betrayed you. Is that understood?"

Jonathan nodded.

~ ~ ~

The month was drawing to a close, and Ailea was watching from the rooftop for the fifth night when she saw the signal—five short flashes of a torch followed by two long ones. She was to meet Rezon at midday tomorrow.

"What are you looking at?" The harsh voice made her jump. Jonathan had been different in the two days since he had returned from his military mission. He wouldn't talk about it, but something must have happened to upset him. He was withdrawn and short-tempered. He seemed to be trying to avoid her, and though he made references to their time at En-gedi, somehow there was a bitterness in his voice when he spoke of it. Just last night he had said, when they retired to their room, "I'll never forget the promises of loyalty you made to me at En-gedi. I know now how much those promises meant to you." Ardent words, but his eyes had not reflected love.

"I said, what are you looking at?"

She jumped again. "I . . . oh, I'm sorry. My thoughts were somewhere else. I was just enjoying the night sky."

"A remarkable feat on a night that is so overcast with clouds."

Ailea could think of no answer to that. He knew she was hiding something from him. That was likely the reason he was behaving so strangely, she thought. She opened her mouth to tell him about Rezon, to explain that she had to see her brother at least once so that she could persuade him that she had found a new life now and that she couldn't go with him, as much as she loved him. But Ailea was afraid for her brother and afraid for her husband. She was sure he would insist on confronting Rezon. And Rezon's hatred of all the Hebrews was so strong—much stronger than Ailea's had ever been. She feared they would try to destroy each other, her husband and her brother, and she loved them both.

So she remained silent. And Jonathan remained silent, even though he came to her that night and held her body to his as if he was afraid she would disappear. But he said nothing at all.

~ ~ ~

Jonathan had gone to Hebron with Eleazer to get supplies for the pottery. Ailea was glad she didn't have to tell her husband any falsehoods in order to slip away. She took the soiled clothing in a large basket, as she did on the third day of each week, and told her sister-in-law that she was going to the stream to do the wash. She sat the large basket down by the stream before heading for the appointed place to meet Rezon.

At first she thought he wasn't there, but then he stepped out of the deep shadows cast by the large oaks that grew at the base of the hill.

Rezon smiled at her, and she ran to him, throwing her arms around her brother, who looked and felt thinner than he had before. His beard was untrimmed. He truly looked like a dangerous bandit. But she loved him.

"Brother, I am so glad you are safe. Have you been well? You didn't come alone, did you? Are some of your men keeping watch for you?"

"Slow down, Ailea. You are asking too many questions at once. My men are watching my back, so you needn't worry. I have been well, and I have come to take you with me."

Ailea drew back in surprise. "But I can't . . . I mean, have your circumstances changed, then? Have you decided to disband your raiders?"

Rezon laughed. "Not at all. But I now have contacts who will care for you when I have to be away, and I am negotiating with someone to arrange a marriage for you."

"But I can't come with you. Jonathan would be furious. He

would come after you." Ailea knew better than to tell her brother that she now wished to stay with her husband, that she had accepted Jonathan's God and his people. Her brother would never understand, so she had to try other means to convince him.

"Rezon, you must go away now. We must not meet again. I fear for your life."

Her brother laughed aloud. "Your Hebrew warrior is no match for me, little sister. He couldn't trap me with that false shipment of gold. By the way, what did you find out about the stores left at Mesad?"

"Your sister knows nothing of that, because no matter how enraptured by her charms I might have been, I would never be such a fool as to divulge military secrets to a woman." Ailea's eyes were wide with fear and shock as Jonathan appeared behind Rezon, and his words didn't really register.

Rezon whirled around on the balls of his feet, ready to fight. "I came for my sister, whom you abducted and ravished. But I am glad you came. I will take great pleasure in killing you."

Jonathan stood, impassive. Then he shrugged. "Take her."

"What?"

"I said, 'Take her.' She is nothing to me, not even worth fighting over. And if I kill you, I will just have to find someone else to take her off my hands."

"Jonathan?" Ailea spoke in a whisper, reaching out a hand to him, confusion and hurt written plainly on her face. Then comprehension dawned in her eyes, and she took a step toward him. "But I wasn't planning to go with Rezon, Jonathan. I want to stay with you." She wrapped her arms around his neck, intending to tell him right here in front of Rezon that she loved him, but he roughly pulled her arms loose and shoved her violently toward her brother.

"Get her out of here. There is a contingent of soldiers even now coming to capture you and execute her for spying. If you go now, they won't be able to catch you."

Rezon keenly studied the Hebrew warrior. He cared for Ailea.

That was why he was letting her go. And his sister had been well and truly caught in a web of love for the man. As much as he hated Jonathan, this was not the time to fight him. His sister would hate him if he killed the man, and it was entirely possible that Jonathan had spoken truly about the danger of being captured.

He backed away, pulling his weeping sister with him. "Very well, Hebrew. I will kill you another time. I want my sister safe."

Jonathan said nothing, only turned to go. Suddenly Ailea began to struggle in her brother's grasp. "Jonathan, don't. Please. I want to stay. Please!" But her husband had already disappeared over the crest of the hill.

Rezon shook her. "Stop it, Ailea. Where is your pride? He doesn't want you. He used you, and now he is through with you." Ailea grew very still, then wiped the tears from her eyes. Numbly, she let her brother lead her away.

Jonathan returned to the village slowly, his heart filled with a pain so great he was certain it would fell him. He squeezed his eyes shut, trying to block out the image of Ailea, her face pale and streaming with tears, begging him not to send her away.

Ahiam had received Jonathan's message that this was the day of her meeting with Rezon and would be waiting to join him in capturing them. A message had also been sent to Joab, who was en route from Jerusalem.

Just as Jonathan expected, Ahiam stood in the courtyard, talking to the Rab. He could tell by the look on Shageh's face that Ahiam had informed him of the plan to trap Ailea and that he disapproved. Jonathan groaned inwardly—he needed his father's support.

As he approached his friend and father there was a commotion behind him, and he turned to see Joab and Uriah riding up at full speed on their mules. Benjamin followed them with a contingent of about a dozen warriors.

"We were detained at Hebron," Joab explained after he had dismounted.

"I just got back myself. Rezon escaped with his sister just a short while ago. I tracked them for a while. If we hurry, we might be able to catch them."

The general stared at Jonathan with eyes as cold as the snows on Mount Hermon. "You let them escape, didn't you?"

Jonathan ignored the question. "I have come to lead you to them. Come, let us be going before the trail is cold." And he did lead them to the oaks where the meeting had taken place; of course Rezon's band had disappeared. Joab, still suspicious, returned to Jerusalem with all the warriors except for Benjamin, who remained with Jonathan.

They were seated on cushions in the main room when Benjamin brought up the subject of Ailea. "Why did you risk Joab's wrath to help her escape?"

Jonathan did not bother to dissemble with his friend. "Because she is my wife—or was."

"She is," Shageh said from across the room.

"Leave us now, Father. We will talk later."

Shageh rose from the stool where he had been seated. "Yes, we will talk later." He left he room deliberately, with a slow dignity that silently rebuked the curtness of Jonathan's command. Jonathan lowered his eyes as his father paused briefly at the doorway, looked directly at his son, and then passed through into the late afternoon sun.

Benjamin let out a slow breath. "You need to make up your mind about your wife, friend, else you will not be of use to anyone. Least of all yourself. Decide if you believe she had truly betrayed you."

"There is little doubt of that. I saw it with my own eyes and heard what they said. I have no choice but to believe she's betrayed me."

Benjamin shook his head. "No. If you were really convinced, I wouldn't see that look in your eyes."

Jonathan had no response to that, and Benjamin, realizing his friend had no intention of confiding in him, soon left.

Jonathan breathed a sigh of relief. He wanted to be alone to lick his wounds. But that wasn't to be. Shageh sought him out immediately.

"How could you send your wife away with that robber brother of hers?"

"Don't upbraid me, Father. I am not the one at fault."

Shageh was not to be deterred. "What kind of man sets a trap for his own wife?"

"A man who has reason to believe she can't be trusted!" Jonathan snapped. "And she fell right into it. Don't you see? I had no choice!"

"Then I suppose you would like for me to write you a bill of divorcement."

"I . . . no, not just yet. I will wait for a while."

Shageh's stern expression finally eased. There was even a hint of a smile in his clear amber eyes. "Yes. I think it might be wise for you to wait awhile."

To Jonathan's surprise, even his sister defended Ailea. "I know that Ailea loves you," Ruth said as she served him his bread and lentil soup the next evening. "If she gave her brother information—well, she feels loyalty to him as well. I don't see why that is so unforgivable. Find her and ask her to come back where she belongs."

"You don't understand the situation," the Rab interjected. "Ailea did not leave with her brother willingly. Jonathan forced her to go. He banished his own wife."

Now Ruth glared at her brother. "How could you do such a thing?"

Jonathan pushed aside his bowl of soup—he wasn't hungry anyway. He escaped to his chamber on the roof.

~ ~ ~

When they arrived in Heshbon, Rezon's men scattered throughout the city to find lodging. Rezon, Ailea, and Beor were welcomed into the home of a prosperous widow. At least Rezon was. The attractive woman, several years older than Rezon, had obviously looked forward to having him to herself. Still she made his companions welcome as well.

When Ailea was left alone in a small, comfortable room to rest, the import of what had happened finally hit full force. But she did not cry. Tears did not seem strong enough to express her despair.

She lay on her pallet trembling as she remembered Jonathan's words, "She means nothing to me. Take her. It will save me the trouble of finding a place to send her." Why had he said those cruel things? Had their time at En-gedi meant nothing to him? Or was he so angry that she had slipped away to see Rezon that he had spoken harshly? Perhaps he had truly believed she meant to leave him, to go with her brother.

But she had told him she didn't want to go with Rezon. Why hadn't he believed her? She vaguely recalled some mention of a shipment and spying, but that made no sense to her. Her face flamed when she remembered the way she had clung to him, begged him not to send her away—and how he had roughly pushed her at Rezon, saying he didn't want her. And still she had called after his retreating back, pleading with him not to leave her.

Never again! If she ever saw the Hebrew again, she would act just as cold and uncaring as he had. She would show him that she did not need him, that her life had continued quite nicely. She planned all the spiteful things she would say to him.

Then pain pierced her heart just as surely as if she had been stabbed with a dagger. What was she thinking of? She wouldn't have an opportunity to say those things to Jonathan. Most likely she would never see him again. Never look into his golden eyes. Never feel him lift her effortlessly in his strong arms. Never again hear him call her "little warrior." She squeezed her eyes shut, trying to keep the tears from coming.

Rezon left her with Meshil, the widow. It had been obvious

almost immediately that the woman was his mistress, but as the days went by, Ailea came to realize that Meshil loved Rezon. Consequently, she was very kind to Ailea. Ailea knew that her parents would never have allowed her to associate with a woman of such low birth and loose morals. However, everything was changed now. She had no parents, no husband to care what happened to her. She didn't care anymore either.

A month went by, and Ailea's depression deepened. She ate little. After awhile, even the little she ate would not stay down. One day, after she had been sick, Meshil came to her room.

"Ailea, how long has it been since you last had your woman's courses?"

Ailea shrugged. "I don't remember. I guess it was the week before I went to En-gedi."

"And how long ago was that?"

"Oh, it must be more than two months." Ailea stopped when she saw the knowing look on Meshil's face. "Why does it matter?"

"Your woman's courses haven't come. You are sick every day. Don't you know these are the signs that a woman is with child?"

"No! It couldn't be!" But even as she protested, Ailea knew that it was true. She was to have a child—Jonathan's child. But he did not want them. He had sent them away. Ailea's resentment grew even greater.

But she could not hold back the maternal love that grew each day as the child within her grew. She could not be sorry for its existence, even though it complicated her life drastically. She made Meshil promise to keep her condition a secret. Meshil agreed but counseled Ailea to tell Rezon as soon as he returned.

When Rezon returned to Heshbon, he was alone. He had left his men at Medeba under Beor's command. "We are joining with all the Aramean nations and with Ammon, and within a month we will have vanquished the Hebrews," he told Meshil and Ailea confidently. "As soon as that happens, I will come for you both, and we will return to Damascus."

Ailea had never felt so torn. She was furious with her husband and knew there was no hope that he would ever want her back, so she should be elated at the prospect that she might be restored to her home. And she did look forward to seeing Malik and old Shua and finding out how they had fared under their new masters.

But as Rezon talked of the great battle that was to come, with more than fifty thousand soldiers amassed by the Aramean-Ammonite alliance, she shuddered to think of Jonathan in that battle, of the brave and handsome king of the Hebrews perhaps being killed, of Isaac, and, of course, of Rezon, being hacked to death or possibly maimed in battle. She had nightmares almost every night of the horrors she had beheld months before in the desert. She couldn't sleep for worry.

In a few days Rezon left them again. Ailea had not told her brother that she would have a child, and Meshil had held true to her word that she would not tell him. But when Rezon returned, she knew she must. Her condition was already evident to anyone who observed her closely.

Thankfully, Rezon was too caught up in his own concerns to have noticed thus far. Ailea wondered what his reaction would be. He certainly wouldn't be able to make a suitable marriage for her, even if she wanted it. Perhaps she would tell people she was a widow when she returned to Damascus. For all she knew, the coming war might make that a reality. One thing she knew. This child would be a Hebrew. He must be brought up in the ways of Adonai and learn the Law of Moses. She realized that her determination to do so would surely cause trouble between her and Rezon. She would just have to deal with that when the time came.

The time would not come as soon as she had expected. Word came that a huge force was marching south from the Euphrates. All the nations east of Jordan would join together to overthrow Israel. Ailea knew from what she had heard after the previous battle at Rabbath that this time David would personally lead his army. She found herself praying for his safety and Jonathan's and for all his comrades that she had come to know. But she also entreated the Lord's mercy for Rezon. She found herself hoping that if anyone had to die, it might be the ruthless generals of the two armies—Joab and Shobach.

Chapter Twenty-Four

Jonathan sat drinking wine in the barracks in Jerusalem. He knew he was headed toward intoxication but did not feel inclined to stop. He had drunk too much wine only once in his life—shortly after joining David at the age of fourteen. He had wished to impress his leader with his manhood. Instead, David had laughed until his sides ached when Jonathan had been miserably ill.

That experience, combined with his father's teaching about the dangers of strong drink, had kept Jonathan sober, even when others overindulged due to boredom on campaigns. He felt a soldier needed to be disciplined and alert at all times.

But tonight he felt like drowning his sorrows. A lovely spy haunted his thoughts day and night. He went from wanting to punish her to worrying desperately about her safety. Was she accompanying her brother and his raiders? Had Rezon married her to some Aramean or Ammonite?

Since Rezon was out of favor with his own people for his apparent desertion, Jonathan doubted he would be able to procure a respectable bridegroom for Ailea. Jonathan raised the wineskin to his lips once more at the thought of his wife given to another man. In his mind he knew she would always be his wife.

He argued with himself that the Law allowed him to send her away. The Law was righteous, and he had followed it. So why was he still tormented? He had treated her more than fairly by letting her go to her brother. He would have been justified in having her executed. She had, after all, divulged information to her brother that at the least would have seen Israel robbed and perhaps some of his comrades killed. Why had she done it?

The wine was halfway to his lips again when a large, roughened hand stopped him. "Good evening, friend. I see you are trying to make yourself merry. But I must say, from the expression on your face, that the wine doesn't seem to be doing the job. Maybe some good news would serve better."

Benjamin sat down, took the wine from Jonathan's hand, and raised it to his own lips. He quickly spat it out. "You must be miserable to be drinking this swill. Come for a walk in the night air. It will clear your head."

"But I don't want a clear head."

"You will when I tell you the interesting news I heard. Now come with me." Benjamin led his friend outside and along a deserted side street. He stopped and sat down on a large stack of bundles that a merchant had left for the night and motioned Jonathan to join him.

"I hope you aren't too drunk to understand the import of what I am about to tell you, friend." He drew in a huge breath and expelled it forcefully. "Ailea did not give her brother the information about the supposed shipment of gold."

"Of course she did. Don't you think I want to believe otherwise? But Ailea was the only one who knew. And she met with Rezon."

Benjamin plucked a straw from a nearby pile and chewed on it for a moment before responding. "No, Jonathan, she wasn't the only one who knew."

"Well, of course I knew, and Joab and Uriah, but . . ." There was dead silence for a moment before Jonathan breathed the name—"Joab!"

"Uriah and I were on duty together the other night—training the new recruits, you know. He casually let it slip that Joab had sent his bond servant to visit a certain, er, friendly widow whom Rezon often visits. She lives in Heshbon."

"You're telling me that Joab planted the false information with the woman and that Rezon got it from her?"

"I'm saying that Joab knows very well that your wife is not a spy. But since he has no use for you or for Ailea, he saw it as an opportunity to get rid of one or both of you and perhaps capture Rezon at the same time."

Jonathan jumped to his feet with a roar. "I'm going to kill that misbegotten . . ."

"Not tonight!" Benjamin pushed his friend back down. "Has the wine robbed you of your common sense, my friend?"

"Let me up!"

"I really hate to do this, but . . ." Benjamin's huge fist connected with his friend's jaw, and Jonathan fell back on the bundles.

". . . you'll thank me in the morning," he finished before walking off, shaking the pain from his knuckles.

If Jonathan didn't actually thank the soldier the next morning, he was at least clearheaded enough to know it would be suicide to take on the second most powerful man in Israel. Far better to find Ailea first, then deal with Joab.

Where could she be? He would go to Damascus and seek out Malik. If Ailea had returned to the city, her faithful servant would surely have heard from her. But before he went after his wife, Jonathan decided to visit the widow in Heshbon. He might need her testimony if Joab gave him trouble. But Jonathan had a feeling that Joab wouldn't pursue the issue. He would most likely wait for another opportunity for revenge.

Perhaps she could tell him of Ailea's whereabouts. Had she been another of Joab's unwitting pawns or a collaborator? Could he trust her information? What if Joab had taken steps to silence her? The sooner Jonathan reached Heshbon, the sooner his wife could be found. He would take his chances there.

While Jonathan was in the barracks preparing to go to Heshbon, orders came calling not only the standing army but also the militia to active duty. David was going to make a preemptive attack on the combined Ammonite-Aramean forces.

The morale of the troops was high, because this time David would personally lead his army. The last campaign, under Joab's leadership, had been a close call. Joab had nearly gotten overpowered by the chariot corps of the enemy. If it had not been for his brilliant strategic move of splitting his army in two, he would have surely been defeated.

David had no intention of giving the enemy the advantage of having time to prepare. He would personally lead his troops in a lightning sweep up the valley of Succoth and catch the enemy by surprise.

Within a matter of hours, Jonathan was marching out of Jerusalem with the army.

It was sometime during the march that Jonathan made up his mind that if Rezon was among the allies against Israel, he would seek him out. He felt almost sure that his brother–in–law would lend his marauders to the cause of defeating the Hebrews. Jonathan decided that the quickest way to get Ailea back would be to get Rezon to tell him where she was.

They made a forced march across Jordan and up the Succoth Valley. Just outside Helem, which was about forty miles east of the Sea of Kinnereth, not far from where David's triumphal march had passed months ago, they engaged the enemy.

Just at dawn, David led the charge. His men were armed with lances, javelins, spears, and swords of iron or bronze. Their long swords were worn, in most cases, in a sheath strapped to the left hip for easy access by the right hand. Few wore the heavy bronze mail that the Philistines and Ammonites favored, but most did have leather armor covering the upper part of the body. And they carried leather-covered wooden shields, some round, others larger and rectangular. Most of the conscripts were not as well outfitted. Many of them were armed with ox goads from their homes and with axes they used in their labor. But they were just as eager for the battle as the regular army.

The spearmen led the charge, with the archers staged to the rear, firing their arrows over the heads of their frontline troops.

While directing his troops, Jonathan kept his eye on the periphery of the battleground, for that was where he expected to see Rezon. At midday he scanned the hills surrounding the battle and saw a band consisting of fewer than a hundred men. They were not dressed in the regalia of either army but wore the long flowing robes of the desert people. Most of them were mounted on camels. Somehow Jonathan knew that they were led by Rezon. He left Benjamin to direct the troops and, despite that man's objections, rode off to confront his wife's brother alone.

He knew when Rezon spotted him because he motioned his men to fall back and brought his camel forward a short distance toward Jonathan. There he waited on the crest of the hill. He did not dismount, of course. He would not want the disadvantage of looking up at his brother-in-law. Let him keep his pride, Jonathan thought, just as long as he gives me Ailea's location.

Finally, they were face-to-face again; Rezon dressed like a nomad, and Jonathan arrayed for war. Rezon's outer robe was held in place by a cord of deep scarlet. In his hand he held a long sword.

"I've dreamed of this pleasure but I had not thought to experience it so soon. I must thank you for giving me an opportunity to fulfill the promise I made you when last we met." Rezon smiled, and his teeth shone very white in contrast to his dark face.

"I will not fight the brother of my wife," Jonathan told him quietly.

Rezon's face twisted in fury, and he slid from his camel, not even taking time to have the beast kneel. "Never speak of my sister again, Hebrew, or I shall cut out your tongue! She is no longer your wife!"

"I really wish to be at peace with you, but I am afraid I shall speak Ailea's name each day for the rest of my life. And she is certainly still my wife for I never gave her a bill of divorcement."

"Ha! How can she be your wife when I, her guardian, have given her in marriage to another?"

Jonathan's mouth went dry, but he tried to keep any sign of his reaction to Rezon's words from showing on his face. "Then tell me this man's name and where I may find him for I will fight him to the death if I must to get my wife back."

"You will never see Ailea again, Hebrew, and you will never see the light of another day." Rezon spoke softly, as if he commented on the weather, but suddenly raised the curved sword in an arc above his head and attacked Jonathan with lightning speed.

Only his extensive experience as a warrior kept Jonathan's head connected to his body as the deadly blade slashed toward Jonathan's neck with a rush of air. But Jonathan's own double-edged broadsword came up to stop its descent in the final split second, and there was a jarring sound of iron meeting iron.

The two men fought with deadly concentration. Jonathan had a grudging respect for his wife's fierce brother. He was younger and thus less experienced. He was also much shorter and greatly outweighed but seemed unaware of his disadvantage as he pressed the fight. Jonathan was aware of it. He deliberately passed up two opportunities to deliver the decisive blow to Rezon, choosing instead to wear down the younger man. But Rezon did not seem to be tiring. Then Jonathan's foot slipped on a stone, and he fell backwards.

Rezon was on him in an instant, his blade nicking Jonathan's ear just as he rolled out of the way. He sprang to his feet. It was time to bring this duel to an end. The next time Rezon's sword swung toward him, Jonathan put all his strength behind his parry, and Rezon's weapon went flying from his hand.

Jonathan lunged forward quickly, and Rezon was so intent upon avoiding the expected death-dealing thrust to the heart that he failed to see Jonathan's kick that knocked Rezon's feet out from under him, sending him sprawling. Out of the corner of his eye, Jonathan saw Rezon's men running toward them. Still, he planted his foot on Rezon's chest and nudged his neck with the sharp point of his sword until he saw a crimson drop of blood well up.

"Tell me where she is, and you may live."

Rezon's answer was to fling sand at Jonathan's eyes, but the ploy did not work. Jonathan turned his head in time to avoid being blinded, then calmly stepped on Rezon's outstretched hand with his other foot.

"Tell me where I may find my wife," he repeated.

"Never!"

"I have no doubt of your relation to Ailea. She is the only person I have ever known with a more stubborn spirit than you. I hate to end this pleasant encounter, 'brother,' but your henchmen approach. We will meet again." With that parting remark, Jonathan turned and headed down the slope to rejoin his men.

As the battle continued, it soon became apparent that it would be an even greater slaughter than the first campaign against the alliance. Shobach led his troops personally and was soon engaged in a pitched battle against some of David's gibborim. They cut him down with a great cry of victory.

In the midst of the fray Jonathan once caught a glimpse of Rezon's raiders swooping down on units of Israel's infantry, then riding swiftly away before they could be engaged by a larger force.

He knew that tonight Joab would have a watch set just as he had since Rezon's first raid. He told himself that it was none of his concern. His only interest in Ailea's brother had been to try to get him to tell where she was. Why should I care if Joab rids the world of the arrogant troublemaker? But Rezon might be his only means of retrieving Ailea. For her sake Jonathan hoped Rezon survived despite himself.

~ ~ ~

It was the middle of the night, and Uriah fought back sleep. He had slept only a few hours earlier in the evening after the battle, and now he was stationed with some fifty men along a series of sand embankments to the east of the camp. Joab reasoned that Rezon would follow a similar pattern—strike at the enemy on the night after the battle when they would be enjoying the victor's sleep.

Joab's orders had been clear—he wanted Rezon but he wanted him alive. Uriah and five others were to focus on the lead camel which would undoubtedly carry Rezon. Two of the soldiers carried ropes with weighted ends. These would be used to snare the camels legs and topple Rezon to the ground. Then he would be overpowered with staves and cudgels but no swords.

Only half a moon lit the low hills whose tops rose out of deep shadows. Uriah rubbed at his eyes, trying to keep the horizon line in focus, but in the waning light the shadows seemed to join one another and creep up the hillsides.

To his left Uriah caught the briefest flash of silver in the shallow gully between the dunes. A blade of some kind? He waited, looking into the darkness for another reflection. Careless, he thought. Someone was carrying an unsheathed sword. In a moment he caught another glimpse of gray light and made out the barely-perceptible line of camels just inside the shadow of the hill. Uriah passed the word left and right in a low whisper, "On my signal, advance."

With only partial moonlight Joab had correctly guessed that Rezon would avoid the hilltops. By stationing the ambush party in a semicircular valley between the last hills before the camp and the dunes, Rezon could quickly be outflanked and surrounded.

When the lead camel was within distance of the snare ropes, Uriah gave the signal—a loud war cry that startled the raiders and their mounts. From both sides of the narrow valley, soldiers rushed the dozen or so raiders who struggled to wheel their camels about in the darkness and retreat. Several were knocked off with spear shafts, and their riderless camels galloped off into the night. Several eluded the attackers and broke through the line to the far hillside and disappeared over the ridge.

Uriah's detachment successfully brought the first camel to the ground before it could escape the snares. The rider leaped off in time to avoid being pinned underneath the animal and quickly rolled to his feet. Rushing toward Uriah with an outstretched sword, he screamed at the top of his lungs and pulled the blade back high above his head, preparing to divide the Hebrew from shoulder to waist in one fierce slice.

From the corner of his eye, however, he caught sight of another Hebrew, coming from behind and to his left. There was a blur in the darkness and the war club connected with the back of his head. The Aramean fell face forward in the sand and lay still.

"Turn him over and get him up. Let's take a look at our prize."

Two soldiers grabbed the limp figure under each arm and pulled him to his feet. Uriah grabbed the man by the beard and bought his face up the light. Across one cheek was a rough scar, and the forehead was creased with age lines. It was not Rezon.

"Where is Rezon? Tell me or I swear I'll cut your throat!"

The man's only response was to spit directly at Uriah's anger-contorted face only inches away. Uriah wiped the spittle away and struck the man backhanded across the right cheek, following through with a fist to the stomach that doubled him over to the ground.

"I should have killed you, dog! You will talk, believe me."

Uriah looked back to the east. A mile or more away he could see the faint dust cloud of the retreating band of raiders backlit by the first light of sunrise. Whatever the man said when Joab made him talk would be of little use anyway. Uriah had failed, and one thing he knew beyond a doubt—Joab did not forget a failure.

~ ~ ~

It was a week after the battle before Rezon and his band appeared. Word had already reached Heshbon of the battle's outcome, but Ailea was thrilled to know that her brother was safe.

Rezon had lost none of his arrogant swagger. "At least the battle ridded me of one of my greatest enemies," he told Meshil and Ailea as he wolfed down the first good meal he had in a week. He gestured with the bread he held in his hand. "Shobach was surrounded by a high ranking Hebrew officer and his men. I must say the Hebrews did fight fair.

"The officer fought Shobach hand to hand. Hah! I could have won the fight easily, but the Hebrew cut Shobach down in minutes. I think it may have been Joab—David's general. You saw the man in Jerusalem, did you not?" he asked Ailea, who nodded in response. "Wiry, rather tall, with a face like an eagle?" Again Ailea nodded. "But then, I guess a lot of men would fit that description. Still, I can thank whoever it was for killing Shobach."

Ailea knew that her question would anger Rezon, but she could not keep from asking. "Did you see . . . Have you word of, of . . ."

"Your illustrious husband?" her brother sneered. "I am sorry I cannot bring you certain news of his demise. But I may have seen him in the battle."

"What happened?" Ailea asked, torn between hope and dread.

"Our chariot corps overran one of their battalions. There was a soldier who looked like the Hebrew dog who captured you. He had taken up a position directly in front of one of our chariots. It ran him down. I remember hoping it was not the son of Shageh, for I would like to kill him myself. Still, it was gratifying to watch the bones of the Hebrew being crushed under the wheels of our chariot, and I couldn't help but hope it was the man who dishonored my sister."

Rezon looked at Ailea as she paled and sank back onto one of the cushions that surrounded Meshil's eating mat. He had no qualms about lying to her. She had to get over her obsession with the Hebrew. Better that she think he might be dead.

Ailea was more and more disturbed by her brother's fanatic thirst for vengeance, by the joy he took in fighting and in killing. Though Jonathan had been a hardened warrior, she had learned that he took no satisfaction in shedding blood. For that matter, she was sure that David himself longed for peace, not war. Even Eliada had not shown the same intense pleasure in battle. His fulfillment had come in being a good military man and the tactical aspects of warfare.

As she listened to his tirades against his enemies, Ailea feared more and more telling her brother about her condition. Amazingly, he still had not noticed.

Meshil whispered one morning as they ground barley. "Tell him soon, Ailea. He will be all the angrier if he finds out on his own." Ailea knew that Meshil was right, but somehow she just couldn't bring herself to do it. She hoped that her brother would go away again, and she wouldn't have to tell him. If he came back and found that she had a child, what could he do but accept it? But Rezon did not go away without her. Instead, he announced that he was taking her with him.

He told her that their destination would be Kir-hareseth, a city on the southeast bank of the Dead Sea. After hasty preparations they soon took their leave from Meshil and headed south. As Meshil kissed her cheek, she whispered, "Tell him." But somehow fear paralyzed her. She knew her brother's reaction would be violent.

When they stopped for the night, Rezon came to help her dismount from her camel. His face stiffened into an angry mask. He left his eyes there for a long moment, as if to convince himself that he wasn't imagining what he had discovered.

Then his eyes grew cold, and he struck her a blow that knocked her to the ground. "You filthy . . . You have ruined everything, giving yourself to that Hebrew dog!"

Ailea staggered to her feet, reaching out to her brother. "But I did not give myself to him—at least not at first. I had no choice. Won't you try to understand?"

Rezon slapped her, but this time the blow was not as hard. Ailea tried to take heart from that. Maybe his anger would dissipate.

"I understand that because of you, I have lost an important alliance," Rezon said furiously.

"Piram of Kir-hareseth has already agreed to take you as his wife, providing my description of you was accurate. I assured him of your great beauty, not knowing, of course, that you were with child. I needed Piram's wealth and men to advance our cause. Now he will refuse to have you, and I will have nothing!"

Ailea should not have been surprised at her brother's plan to marry her to a desert chief, but she was. She felt even worse than she had when the Hebrews had taken over her home and dragged her away to a strange land. This was her brother, the only relative she had left, and he thought of her as nothing more than a commodity to be traded. She wept bitterly as she lay on her pallet that night.

The next day, Rezon sent a messenger to his friend Piram. He did not tell her what was in the message. He refused to speak to her at all. They traveled a short distance to a small village where Rezon and his men seemed to be well known. He found a place for Ailea with a large family that lived in a rather small house.

"I will pay you well to keep her," he told the obese wife of the household. "She can sleep outside, and you can use her to help you with your work. You have my permission to beat her if she does not obey you."

So began several weeks of misery for Ailea. Because of her condition, the woman, Timnah, thought her no better than a prostitute and continually heaped abuse on Ailea. She had led Ailea to the rooftop the first evening and handed her a mat of woven grass to sleep on. "Unless it is raining you will sleep here," the woman told her, still panting from the climb up the stairs.

The next morning Ailea was awakened by a foot thrusting sharply into her side. "You won't sleep your days away while I put food in your mouth," she said harshly. "Now get up. There's wash to do."

There was wash for a family of seven plus Ailea's own. But she preferred doing the wash to looking after the four younger children of the household who were just as bad-tempered as their mother and never obeyed her.

Timnah's husband and grown son were more of a problem because they held the same low opinion of her, and she had to continually fight off their advances.

Finally, Rezon appeared to tell her of her fate. He still looked at her with disgust as he spoke. "I have received a reply from Piram today. It seems that all is not lost. Of course he refuses to have you as a wife, but he says he will consider taking you as a concubine. After the Hebrew's child is born, I am to bring you to Piram. If you please him, he will keep you. There will be no bride price, but he will ally himself with me, and I will have his protection and the use of his fighting men if I should need them."

"But what will happen to my baby? Surely Piram does not want to raise a Hebrew child?"

"Perhaps I will give it to someone who wants a slave, or maybe I will do the world a favor and just dash its brains against a wall as soon as it is born."

Ailea was sickened by the cruel smile on Rezon's face as he said this. She didn't believe that he was capable of killing a baby, but she knew he would sell her child as a slave without blinking. She had to get away from him. But where could she go? She had no other family, and she couldn't return to Israel or Damascus. In either place she would be found out as the wife Jonathan had put away. She would be treated worse than she had been by the family she was now with.

Rezon gave the family money to keep Ailea and went off to raid and harass the Hebrews. When he had been gone for two months and Ailea had grown very large with the child she carried, she knew that somehow she must escape. She would have to prepare herself as best she could.

By the front door the man kept a bow and a quiver of arrows next to a heavy staff. The only other weapon in the house was an ax which he kept in the sleeping chamber. At best Ailea could only hope for some leftover bread and a few pieces of fruit as provisions. The woman had taken Ailea's clothes and sold them shortly after Rezon left. Fortunately, Ailea had hidden her dagger underneath her robe and later wrapped it carefully in her bedding. She would leave tonight after midnight as the household slept. She could carry food in a woven sack she secreted out of the kitchen and hid under her sleeping pallet.

Ailea was lying restlessly on her pallet when she heard footsteps on the wooden stairway. They paused at the top, and then there was silence. Ailea raised on one elbow, attempting to sit up when hands grabbed at her in the darkness. A hand covered her mouth, and she struggled against the weight of a man's body holding her against the mat.

"Stop it! Don't scream, you fat harlot." It was the oldest son of the household. Ailea could feel his free hand fumbling at the hem of her robe. She couldn't reach her dagger under the mat. Using her only possible defense, she bit suddenly with all her strength into the fingers covering her mouth. In an instant she tasted the warm, salty blood as her incisors struck the smooth hard surface of a bone.

The man screamed and rolled to the side, holding his bleeding hand. When he reached his feet, he came at her, cursing and kicking at her. Ailea pulled her knees against her abdomen to shield the baby and covered her head with both arms. She rolled away from the attack just as several kicks landed against the back of her legs. One caught her in the side, knocking the wind out of her. She wanted to scream but fought for just one breath of air to squelch her rising panic. Gasping for air, she pulled herself together as tightly as possible and waited for the next blow.

None came. Ailea could hear a voice below, a sleepy, aggravated voice threatening whoever was disturbing his sleep. Ailea felt the round outline of her womb and realized that no kick had found its mark. Her baby was safe. She waited for some time, listening for any movement or sound but detected nothing.

It was painful to stand. Both legs felt bruised and stiff. Her left side hurt with each breath, but she could walk. Retrieving the bag and her dagger from beneath the pallet, Ailea moved cautiously across the roof and down the stairway. Pausing at the table, she loaded the meager leftovers of the evening meal into her pack and made for the door. Removing the short bow and quiver of arrows from their peg, she slipped silently through the door and into the early morning darkness, walking close by the houses until she reached the edge of town. Then she headed south because she believed Rezon would assume she would go to Heshbon and Meshil and then Damascus. She hoped her keepers would not come after her. They seemed too indolent to bother, especially since she had taken nothing that belonged to them. And she hoped she would be well away before Rezon found out.

She found a small caravan and joined it, giving the master a gold bracelet to take her. She told them she was from Damascus and that her family had been killed in the fighting with the Hebrews. They assumed she was a widow and were very sympathetic.

The caravan was headed for Egypt, and she traveled with them until they reached the town of Zoar at the southernmost tip of the Salt Sea. By then she knew where she must go. She had no choice. There was only one person on earth who would welcome her with kindness. She would go to the Rab, and he would tell her what she must do. For now she refused to think what her husband's reaction would be when she showed up again.

She made her way north, alone in the wilderness, the shore of the Salt Sea on her right and the monolith of Mesad before her. She knew that ten miles north of the stronghold was En-gedi and due west of En-gedi was Ziph. It would take her many days, but then she had some experience traveling in the wilderness, and the kind caravan master had left her with two large waterskins and food. He had no idea how far she intended to travel, or he would never have allowed her to set off on her own. At first Ailea had thought mainly of reaching Ziph, but as she walked she began to think more of En-gedi.

She told herself she was stopping at En-gedi first in order to get her bearings before heading west to Ziph. But deep down, she knew there was a more important reason. Before she faced her husband again, she had to spend time at En-gedi—to remember the loving, gentle man Jonathan had been there. At En-gedi they had ceased to be strangers to one another. Perhaps the spirit of their love still lingered there.

Chapter Twenty-Five

As she traveled over the rough terrain in the bright moonlight, Ailea realized she was not alone in the wilderness. She heard the lonely call of a desert owl and the scurrying of small nocturnal animals that hurried to get out of her way. She was not afraid except for a horror of stumbling onto a bed of scorpions. Since Nariah's death, scorpions had been a recurring nightmare. Even though she knew it wasn't completely rational, she kept glancing at the ground where she stepped, thankful for the bright moonlight.

With her attention mostly directed at the ground, her shock was all the greater when she neared an outcropping of rock and glanced up to see the moon reflected in the feral eyes of some creature watching her. She jumped back with a small, involuntary scream. The eyes disappeared. She stood frozen for long moments but neither heard nor saw anything disturbing. Finally, she started out again, quickening her pace, more anxious than ever to reach En-gedi. She thought of the time she had spent with Jonathan there and looked forward to bathing in the cool waters of the pool, gathering the dates and other fruit that could be found, and sleeping in the safety of their cave.

As had become her custom, she prayed to the God of Israel as she went along. "Oh, Adonai, King of heaven, I praise You for giving me the strength to return to Judah. Please give me the wisdom I need to face Jonathan again and admit that I want to be the wife of his heart, to bear his children and worship his God."

Surely her husband would take her back for the child's sake even if not because he cared for her. Why had he so suddenly rejected her? she wondered for the thousandth time. The child moved, and she passed a hand over her distended abdomen. "Do you grow restless too, little one? We will be there soon. You will meet your grandfather. He is a great Rab, a wise man, and he will teach you many things. Your Aunt Ruth will love you, and you will fill the empty place in her heart that was left by her lost son. And, best of all, you will see your father. He will love you and teach you how to be strong. Maybe you will look like him, my son—tall and comely. I know you are a son, don't ask me how."

Ailea murmured aloud as she went along, conversing as if her unborn child could understand. Occasionally she would laugh at herself, thankful that no one else was about to think her a crazy woman.

Suddenly something—a sound, a premonition—caused her to stop again. She stood very still, listening intently. Faintly, she heard the sound of a waterfall. Silhouetted against the burgeoning dawn, she could see the outline of the date palms that lined the oasis of En-gedi. Ailea quickened her pace, almost running now. She had arrived! After a brief rest of perhaps a day, she would strike out on the two- to three-day journey to Ziph. Her spirits soared, even though she was exhausted from walking all night. As she neared the pool at the front of the waterfall, all her memories of the time spent here with her husband returned, and tears ran down her face. She missed him so. Soon, she prayed, they would be together again, all the strife and unhappiness forgotten.

She bathed in the pool, then slowly climbed the steep rock

face to the cave where she had stayed with Jonathan. Exhausted, she gave the cave a cursory examination for unwelcome residents, then slumped to the cave floor. She was sound asleep in no more than a moment.

She woke at midday, feeling surprisingly well rested and full of energy. She was almost at journey's end, she thought.

She took her quiver and bow out of her pack with the thought of having some fowl or small animal to break her fast. Or perhaps she could somehow catch one of the lazy fish that swam in the pool. At the very least, she would have dates to eat for the date palms were abundant here. She left the cave with her mouth watering.

It was a disappointing afternoon of futile hunting and fishing. She lost one of her five precious arrows shooting at a large bird and another when, in desperation, she shot into the pool, trying to catch a fish.

Even the dates were not that easy to obtain. It was impossible to climb the tall trees in her condition and frustrating as well because it would have been a simple matter only a few months earlier. Fortunately, she was able to reach fruit from one of the trees by climbing to a rock ledge that jutted out close to the top of it. Still, she had to lean precariously across a twenty-foot drop to reach the cluster nearest her. She ate a few of the dates, then decided that she should gather some of the wild berries, fill her waterskin from the pool, and start out for Ziph tonight. She started to make her way back to the cave for a few hours of rest.

She was nearly back to the cave when she felt the first labor pang. Ailea had experienced mild contractions periodically over the past month, but this one was different—stronger. She sat down to allow the pain to pass, speaking to the child again. "Oh, little one, please don't come now! Wait a little longer. Just two more days and we will be home. The Rab can intercede with Adonai for our safety. And your aunt will be there to help the midwife ease your way into the world."

She slowly made her way back to the cave, deciding that she

should stay with her plan to rest. If she were really in labor, she certainly wouldn't be able to stand the scorching sun.

But as she lay in the cave, her fears nearly overcame her. She had never seen a birth—except that of animals. And she didn't know what to expect. How quickly would the baby come? How far apart would the pains be when the time was near for the birth? Would her labor last hours, or days?

Over the next two hours, the pains were infrequent but strong. When the sun was still a full hour from setting, she gathered her pack and made her way back to the oasis. She gathered wild berries, filled her waterskin, and started walking towards the northwest.

Only twice during the next hour did the pains come strongly enough that she had to stop. Maybe, she thought, this would continue for several days before the baby was truly ready to be delivered.

The sunset was beautiful, and its red glow was still discernible in the sky when she heard them.

Ailea had tried not to think of the possibility that she could be attacked by man or animals, but the fear was always in the back of her mind. After all, robbers came to hide at the oasis. David had fled there from Saul years ago, and desperate men occasionally came to the area. Hadn't Jonathan said so? As for wild animals, even bear and lion were a possibility, though most of the large animals lived in the more wooded Judean hills.

The yipping sound that had made her stop was the call of either hyenas or jackals. As she stood, trying to determine what distance the sound came from and how many animals she was hearing, she decided she would rather face a pack of hyenas than a pack of jackals.

The hyena was a larger animal but more cowardly. A pack of hyenas would choose to eat carrion rather than risk the danger of killing prey. They would probably attack only if directly threatened or starving. Jackals, on the other hand, hunted in packs. They enjoyed the thrill of the kill. They were the size of a large dog but had sharper teeth and stronger jaws. A pack of five or six could easily kill a small or weakened person.

Ailea shivered as the yipping grew louder. The animals were coming nearer, and night was falling. The howls were coming from at least half a dozen creatures.

She quickly searched for stones that were large enough to do damage to the jackals or at least drive them away. She looked around for a place to position herself for their attack, but there was only flat terrain. The yipping grew louder, and Ailea saw the pack several yards away. The leader was easy to discern. He was much larger than any of the others, and he was bolder. He approached her with ears laid back, and she waited as long as possible before flinging her largest rock at his head.

She hit her mark and the leader yelped, veering away. The rest of the pack scattered. But Ailea knew they would return. She had only hit the large jackal with a glancing blow.

She realized that the pack was out there somewhere in the darkness, following her. Between her and the hill country lay many miles of open desert—impossible to find a place of shelter there. Even as she thought of the difficulty of continuing toward Ziph, Ailea was stricken by another birth pain. There was no choice now. She had to return to En-gedi.

She turned back, walking quickly, tamping down the impulse to run. She knew the pack would move in on her all the more quickly if she did. She was thankful for the bright moonlight which allowed her to catch sight of them several times. They stayed several yards back, silent now. It was almost worse than the yipping noises they had made before.

She was almost at the cliff face of En-gedi when they rushed at her again. She quickly picked up a fallen branch and managed to hit two of them—the leader and the animal closest to him. It was enough to temporarily discourage their attack. They stayed back, snarling.

Ailea took advantage of the distraction to scramble up the steepest route of the cliff face and into the cave, hoping the pack would find it difficult to follow. If only she could build a fire and keep it going, she could keep them at bay. Her hands shook as she tried again and again to strike a spark from her flint rocks to ignite the pile of straw and small sticks left by Jonathan on their previous trip.

Fortunately, Jonathan had left a large supply of wood and dried dung at the back of the cave. She finally ignited the straw and went to get wood to build the fire up.

As the fire gathered strength, the jackals advanced through the cave entrance with the dominant male in the lead. He came at her with his head held low and teeth bared, a low continuous growl echoing into the depths of the cave behind her. The other jackals held back, pawing at the dirt just outside the circle of firelight, but the leader moved forward, eyeing the fire while tracking Ailea's quick movements close to the center line of the flames.

Ailea thought of the bow, but she would never be able to reach it, much less notch an arrow before the jackal caught her. Suddenly, Ailea lunged forward and grabbed a branch from the fire just as the jackal leaped at her, catching her shoulder with both forelegs but missing her neck with a snap of the jaw. As Ailea rolled backward in the dirt she felt claws rake the soft underside of her left forearm. In an instant she swung the firebrand in her right arm forward catching the jackal directly under its muzzle before he could grab hold with his teeth. The smell of burning fur stung her nostrils, and the jackal retreated with a yelp of pain.

She let out a bloodcurdling scream and advanced on the jackals, brandishing the burning log. They retreated in the face of her aggressive attack. She stood at the mouth of the cave, holding the fire aloft, looking and listening for the pack. There was no sign of them, but they would be back.

Ailea sat down to assess the damage done to her arm. It was only when she saw the two sets of marks, made by the animal's two forward claws, that her wounds began to throb almost unbearably and pour blood. She poured water over the wounds. After cutting a strip from her cloak with her knife, she made a bandage for her arm, wrapping it around the damaged flesh and pulling the ends into a knot with her free hand and her teeth. The puncture wounds were deep. She hoped that infection would not bring on a fever.

She wanted to build a huge bonfire, but she knew she had to conserve her precious supply of fuel. At the back of the cave, she found two pitch torches. She lit them and wedged them in rocks at the cave's entrance, then went back to tend the fire.

Another labor pain brought her to her knees, taking her mind off her throbbing arm. When it passed she realized she had to prepare to have the baby here—in a cave. All alone.

"Oh, God, please help me."

Suddenly she saw Shageh's face in her mind. She could hear his voice. *The God who sees me*. That is what Hagar called him. She was a woman alone and desperate in the desert, and Adonai had spoken to her, promising to bless her son.

"Oh, Adonai, please, please help my son. Help him to be born safely. Save us from the jackals!"

The pains increased in strength and regularity, but somehow Ailea was not as frightened anymore. She talked to God; she talked to her baby. She even talked to Jonathan. Her words to her absent husband were not kind.

"Oh, Jonathan, why did you send me away? What did I do to deserve this? You got me with child and then abandoned me. Ohh . . ." She drew out the word on another powerful contraction, then went right back to castigating the man who had gotten her into all this trouble. "Just wait until I see you again, you stubborn man! I will make you beg my forgiveness before I take you back. Ohh . . . No, I won't. If I could just see you now, I wouldn't even mention what you did . . . Ahhh . . . If you would only come for me. But you don't even know where I am, even if you wanted to come for me!"

Ailea had started to cry as the pains grew more severe. Tears ran down her face as she purified her dagger by placing the blade in the fire. She cried and prayed and talked aloud as she spread her cloak near the fire. She went back and forth to the rear of the cave, bringing the logs, one at a time, to have them in readiness. Somehow moving about helped her get through the birth pangs. She had only one waterskin, but it was full. Still, it seemed very little. She would have to cleanse herself and the baby after the birth.

Once she thought she saw a shadow move at the cave entrance. But the torches still burned brightly. As long as they did, the pack would not enter. At least she hoped they wouldn't. If worse came to worst, she had her dagger.

The torches burned out just as the dawn lightened the cave entrance. Ailea didn't notice—she was crouched on her knees, asking God for the strength to give the final push that would bring her child into the world. As a loud moan escaped her lips, the baby slipped from her body, his loud wail telling Ailea he was strong enough to survive and that God had heard her prayer.

Ailea lost consciousness for a short time, but her son's cries brought her back to herself. She attended to cutting the cord and did her best in her weakened state to cleanse herself and the baby, wrapping him in the long strip she had torn from her cloak. When she put him to her breast, he quieted and was soon asleep.

She was asleep herself and dreaming when she sensed a presence. Her eyes flew open. At the cave opening, the burned-out torches still smoked; suddenly, a jackal appeared. Ailea recoiled in shock. The animals were nocturnal, and she had thought they would withdraw with the rising of the sun. But the smell of blood and the newborn's cries had emboldened them.

Ailea piled more wood on the fire and kept watch all day, afraid to sleep. When night came, she built the fire even higher and made sure the small pile of stones and her dagger were within her reach. She kept terror at bay by singing to her newborn—the song David had taught her about Adonai as Shepherd. She repeated the words

. . . yea though I walk through the valley of the shadow of death, I will fear no evil . . . . Already the Lord had taken her through the valley of childbirth safely. She prayed He would keep her from the evil of the ravening pack.

The moon slowly moved in its journey across the night skies, and Ailea succumbed to sleep. She woke to the sight of three jackals on the other side of the fire. The leader's yellow eyes gleamed in anticipation, or so it seemed to Ailea. She rose to a sitting position, screaming and throwing stones. They slinked away. She pick up her torch and jabbed it at them

All the next day she fought sleep, and by nightfall she was almost overcome with fear, pain, and exhaustion. She knew that in order for her and her son to survive, she had to drive the pack away. Her supply of water and food was almost gone. Tomorrow she would have to go to the pool. But in the open she would be easy prey. And there was the baby to consider. She couldn't risk taking him out into the open with her, nor could she leave him alone in the cave. She had to think of a way to escape.

She found another torch and now lighted all three, placing them near the entrance. She built up the fire until it was roaring, even though she knew that her supply of fuel would soon be gone. But she had no choice. She had to get some sleep. In the morning she hoped to be rested enough to formulate some kind of plan. She could only sleep fitfully, awaking with a start and unable to determine if she had been dreaming again of running in the darkness, of running for the shelter of the rock, or if she was merely reliving the events of the night before.

When she woke, sunlight was streaming through the cave opening. There was no sign of the animals. Still, she knew they waited not far away. She had no idea what to do. She fought down a vision of the jackals tearing her baby apart. As if sensing his mother's distress, her son began to wail. Quickly she put him to her breast, afraid his cries would attract the pack. As she nursed him, she crooned the song of David again. *The Lord is my shepherd, I shall not want . . . .*

The vision came to her when she was near the end of the song. At least that is what she would call it later. She was singing the words, *Thou preparest a table before me in the presence of my enemies . . . .*

As clearly as if she were standing there, she saw in her mind's eye the table-rock that was high above the cave. And she heard Jonathan's voice as he had told her about the days when King Saul was chasing David's band.

"If Saul's men ever had us trapped up here, we thought to topple the boulder onto as many of them as happened to be on the path below . . ."

Was it possible for her to lead the jackals to the spot and crush them under the rock? *"Thou preparest a table before me in the presence of mine enemies."* Had this idea come from Adonai?

She certainly hadn't been able to think of another. She had no choice but to try it. But how could she climb up the steep cliff path? She had to try for her son's sake. She looked down at his sleeping face. Each time he exhaled he blew a tiny bubble of milk.

She kissed his mouth. If this plan was to work, she couldn't take the baby. It would be difficult enough to climb even without a baby in her arms. She shuddered to think what would happen if the pack caught up with them on the path. Without the baby in her arms, she might stand a chance of fighting them off using her dagger. No. As frightening as the prospect was, her son would be safer left in the cave.

Ailea went to the back of the cave, to a ledge that was about shoulder high to her. There was an indentation deep enough that the baby could not fall out, and she hoped desperately he would be safe from the jackals. He was full and sleeping soundly. She prayed he would continue to sleep while she went on her mission to save them both. She wrapped what remained of her cloak completely around him to make a soft bed and to further hide him. "Sleep, baby. I will be back," she promised him.

Ailea took off her sandals. She would be more surefooted without them. She would carry only her dagger. She was tempted to carry a torch also, knowing how the jackals feared fire. But she knew that it would be impossible to climb with it in her hand.

Outside the cave opening, she stood for a moment, looking for them. They were right where she expected them to be—about a hundred yards below at the pool. She waited for them to see her. Her plan depended on their following her. Then another thought struck her and she dashed back inside the cave for a moment, emerging with a small bundle that she tied to her waist—discarded rags from the birth. She knew where she would leave it.

Again she waited, gazing down on the half dozen jackals, easily distinguishing the leader by his size. Finally, he looked up, right at her she knew, even though at this distance she couldn't make out his eyes.

As soon as he moved, Ailea did too. She ran up the cliff path, sliding, slipping, but not slowing, despite the pain and weakness.

Her heart beat heavily with both fear and hope—until she heard her baby's cry. It was loud, but it was not a cry of pain. At least it did not seem to be. Surely the pack could not have reached the cave yet, much less gotten to her son. But if he continued crying, would they abandon their pursuit of Ailea and go after the sound of his voice?

"Dear God, should I go back?" she prayed, stopping for a moment. The cries continued unabated. No. It would do no good to go back. If the pack had indeed gone after him, it would be too late already. But if they were still after her, she could defeat them.

Hoping the leader would keep in pursuit of her, she scrambled on, skinning her hands and knees but not slowing until she reached the flat, broad area of the path that was directly below the table-rock. She untied the bloody bundle and dropped it in the middle of the path, praying it would distract the animals long enough.

Before the last turn in the path, she looked back and saw no animals. When she reached the table-rock, she struggled with the branch until it was poised as a fulcrum under the boulder. She wondered if she would have the strength to tilt the boulder with it. But first she had to see if the jackals were there beneath her. She cautiously tiptoed out onto the edge of the rock and looked straight down. They weren't there. What had happened to them? Dear God, her baby!

Then they appeared. The whole pack was coming up the path. The first ones to reach the spot did just as she had hoped. They stopped and began to worry the bundle, growling as they fought over it, including the leader. He looked up and saw her, and she knew that the bundle wouldn't stop him for long. He would be coming for her.

She turned to leap off the rock, but even as she turned, she felt it. The rock trembled. Then it tilted and began to slide. The weight of her body had unbalanced it, and now it was falling. It poised in midair for a moment before it went over. In that instant, Ailea leapt free, landing hard enough to knock the wind out of her. Then she heard the awful thud of the boulder landing below.

When she had her breath back, she crawled to the edge and looked over. She saw nothing but the huge rock. No jackals. No sign they had been there. Had they all been killed, or only some of them? Or had they all gotten away?

Ailea was terrified to venture back down the path, not knowing what awaited her. But then she remembered the words that had almost miraculously come to her: "*Thou preparest a table before me in the presence of mine enemies*," and she started cautiously back down the mountain. When she reached the boulder she had to climb over it, for it completely blocked the path. On the other side she saw part of a tail and a foot sticking out. She had destroyed them! No, God had destroyed them.

She raced back to the cave, to her son's makeshift bed. There he was, sleeping peacefully. She lifted him gently in her arms and carried him to the warmth of the fire. Only then did she allow the tears of relief to flow.

Chapter Twenty-Six

A month passed, and Ailea and the baby grew stronger each day, but the wound on her arm had been slow to heal, so she waited until she could be sure she was strong enough to make the journey to Ziph. Even though the jackals were gone, she never left the baby alone. She feared that some other predator could threaten him.

She used one of the long strips she had cut from her cloak to fashion a sling to carry the baby in. Each day, she tied it around her neck and laid the baby in it, close to her breast. In this way he slept most of each day, lulled by his mother's motions and by the beating of her heart.

He was such a good baby, Ailea thought with the typical pride of a new mother. She provided for their survival by spearing fish—a skill she had finally learned after much practice—and by bringing down small birds with her arrows. Ailea knew she needed to build her strength so that there would be milk for her son and so that she could safely make the trip back to Ziph. This time, they would travel in daylight when predators would be less likely to attack them. Besides, it was now the winter month of Tebeth and much cooler, even here in the wilderness. It was the time of the latter rains in the hill country, and Ailea feared more that she in her son would suffer from damp and chill than from the sun and heat.

With each day she felt stronger, and now she began to plan their return to Ziph. Ailea felt a combination of anxiety and elation when she thought of seeing Jonathan and Shageh and Ruth. She didn't know what kind of welcome she would receive from Jonathan or his sister, but she never doubted for a moment that Shageh would open his arms wide to her.

Ailea took the still-unnamed baby to the pool for a bath. She laughed at her son's reaction to the water. It was cool, and for a moment it took his breath. He puckered his mouth to cry, but as she swished him back and forth through the water, he changed his mind about the new experience and smiled at his mother. As he kicked his hands and feet happily, she wondered at the wisdom of binding a baby with swaddling so that he couldn't move. But it was supposed to make the limbs grow strong and straight, so she would continue to do it.

She dried them both on the third of her cloak she hadn't cut up and wrapped him in a long strip of swaddling, which seemed to quiet him so that he almost immediately fell asleep. She gathered dates and returned to her cave.

When she reached the entrance and paused to survey the land spread out below, a movement in the distance caught her eye. Someone was coming! It appeared to be a man alone, leading a donkey. She ducked into the cave quickly, her heart pounding. Should she make herself known to the stranger? He might have compassion on a woman with an infant. It would be so much easier to return to Ziph on the back of that donkey than on foot. Even if the stranger was not that kind, he might provide protection as they traveled.

But what if he were a thief or murderer? What if he was a Hebrew who hated all foreigners? Did she dare take a chance with her son's safety? She looked down at the sleeping infant. Placing a kiss on his tiny rosebud mouth, she took him to the back of the cave and laid him on a ledge. She would break her custom of keeping him with her at all times. She would slip down to the pool where the man would undoubtedly refresh himself and his animal. She would hide herself and watch him. If he appeared trustworthy, she would chance asking him for help.

Ailea made her way quickly to a ledge that jutted out above the pool. She knew she could see but not be seen from this position. The man came around a bend, and she could see him more clearly, though he was still too far away to tell if he was young or old, rich or poor, forbidding or friendly of countenance. She watched him ascend the trail toward the falls. Something in the way he moved was familiar. She stared harder as he drew closer, then covered her mouth with her hand to keep from crying out.

Jonathan! It was impossible. It couldn't be. But as he came nearer, she knew it was true. She was torn between elation and fear. Why was he here? Was it in answer to her prayers? Was Jonathan coming for her? But how could he be? There was no way he could know she was here. What would he do when he saw her? Would he take her back? And what would his reaction be to the baby? Surely he would want his son. But what if he still didn't want Ailea? Would he take her child away from her?

In a sudden panic, she whirled about and made her way up the steep cliff face. She couldn't face Jonathan, not yet. And she had to get to her son.

~ ~ ~

Jonathan looked up when he heard the sound of small rocks falling from above. Rock slides were common, so he didn't necessarily expect to see anything. But he did—a blur of movement. Was it a person? He thought so, but he had only had a glimpse of something. He couldn't be sure. He was tired and thirsty. He decided to take time to water the donkey and drink from the falls before investigating.

A few minutes later he made his way up the hillside. He saw no sign of man or animal. Still his heart began to beat faster as he neared the cave that held so many memories of Ailea. He wondered again why he had felt compelled to come here. His heart tripped faster as he reached the cave's entrance and could smell the evidence of a recent fire. Someone had been staying here. His grip tightened on the cudgel he carried, though he sensed no threat. But he did sense a presence.

"Ailea?" he called out softly. No one answered. *If she is here, she might be frightened,* he thought as he remembered how they had parted. "Ailea, if you are here, don't be afraid. I won't hurt you."

He heard some movement from the back of the cave, and Ailea stepped into the light. Jonathan stared, speechless, as it struck him how long it had been since he had seen her and how she had changed. She was thinner, and her hair, which had been a halo of curls about her face, now fell to her shoulders. He thought she was the most beautiful creature he had ever seen. He promised himself then and there that they would never again be parted for so long a time.

"Why are you here?" The question was high and breathless.

Jonathan raised an eyebrow. "I might ask you the same question."

"I asked you first."

Jonathan smiled, and something unknotted inside her. "True, you did ask first. I've been looking for you."

"Why?"

"You're my wife."

The firm little chin came up. "Am I? You sent me away. I thought you had divorced me."

"I didn't. Rezon told me he had wed you to another man."

"He told me he thought he saw you slain in the battle."

Jonathan snorted. "He knew well that I wasn't. I saved his miserable hide."

"He didn't tell me."

"No. I didn't expect him to. It would hurt his pride too much to admit it. Now answer my question. Did Rezon give you in marriage to another man?"

She gave a small, bitter laugh. "He tried to arrange it, but the bridegroom decided at the last moment that he didn't want me after all."

"I find that hard to believe," he said, thinking that surely no man could resist her beauty.

"You, of all people, should find it very easy to believe. It is what you did yourself, is it not?"

Jonathan's guilt felt as heavy as a huge boulder. He was anxious to get rid of it. He had misjudged her badly, and now he must swallow his pride and ask her forgiveness. "Ailea . . ."

A lusty cry echoed through the cave, and Jonathan's mouth went slack with surprise. "What's that?"

"I'll show you," Ailea said calmly. She turned and walked back into the darkness. Jonathan heard crooning words, and then the cries ceased abruptly. She reappeared again with an infant in her arms.

Jonathan's throat went suddenly dry. His mind was not functioning, and he asked a ridiculous question. "Where did that come from?"

Ailea couldn't help it, she laughed. "Where do you think babies come from? And it isn't a 'that,' it's a baby. A boy."

Jonathan stared hard at the infant. "Is he mine?"

Anger flamed in Ailea's eyes, and she raised her hand as if to strike him. Then she let the hand drop back to her side, and her eyes filled with tears.

It cut Jonathan to the quick, and he reached out and cupped her face in his hand. "No, no, my love. I did not mean that the way it sounded. It is just that we have been apart for so long. And I don't know what might have happened to you since I sent you away with Rezon. I meant no slur on your honor."

"He is your son, Jonathan."

Jonathan felt his knees go weak. Tears filled his own eyes,

and he had to swallow a lump in his throat before speaking. He asked gruffly, "When was he born?"

"A month ago."

"Why did you bring him here? How long have you been here?"

"A month." She let Jonathan have a moment to absorb the information before continuing. "He was born here, in the cave, Jonathan."

"But, who helped you?"

Ailea smiled softly, "The God who sees me; the Lord, my Shepherd."

Jonathan shook his head in disbelief. "You are telling me that you gave birth to my son in a cave, with no one to help?"

"I had no choice," Ailea said defensively. "Besides, as I told you, the Lord was with me. He really was. And I even heard the Rab speak to me a few times. Of course that was only my imagination, I'm sure. Now, would you like to hold your son?" She thrust the infant into his arms before he could frame a response. Again, he fought a manly battle to hold back tears as he looked into the face of his sleeping son.

When she handed him the baby, Jonathan saw the scabs on the inside of her arm. "What happened to your arm?" he asked.

She hesitated. "I will tell you later. Let's walk down to the pool so you can remove the dust of the journey. The baby and I have already bathed today, but we will keep you company. And I can catch some fish for our dinner."

How calm she is, Jonathan thought. She is proposing we spend a quiet afternoon together as if we have never been apart. Was it a sign that she had forgiven him, or a sign that she just didn't care anymore?

They went in silence down the path that curved by the waterfall to the pool. There, Ailea proudly displayed her newly acquired skill of spearfishing and fed the baby while Jonathan refreshed himself. After a while, he came to sit beside her under the shade of an olive tree that grew near the edge of the water.

"What happened to your arm?" he asked, taking up the conversation where it had left off.

"I was scratched by a jackal."

"Jackals don't travel alone. Where was the rest of the pack?"

"They attacked us too. But Adonai gave me a plan to defeat them." She sighed deeply. "Do you mind if I tell you that story another time? It is quite a long one."

"If you wish. But I can't stand to think of you here, injured and weak from childbirth. . . ."

"That is why I decided to stay here for a while instead of . . . . No matter."

"No matter?" Jonathan shouted. "You are telling me you and my son were attacked by a pack of jackals, that you were badly bitten, and it does not matter!" He jumped up and paced in front of her. "What is it about you that makes you want to run around in the desert all the time? Why could you not have stayed with Rezon until the child was born?"

"Because he did not want me after he knew I would bear a Hebrew child and after I ruined all his careful plans to ally himself with a powerful desert chieftain. And because I had already decided that. . . . Never mind."

Jonathan sat back down. "I am sorry I shouted at you, Ailea. I just couldn't bear to think of the danger you were in." He stroked the baby's soft cheek with his forefinger. "What is his name? I didn't even ask."

"He has no name yet. I wanted the Rab to name him."

"The Rab? You were headed for Ziph?"

Ailea nodded. She did not trust her voice.

"You were coming back to me, little warrior?" She kept her eyes on the baby. Jonathan lifted her chin until her eyes had to meet his.

"You were coming back to me?" he asked softly.

"I had nowhere else to go!"

"So you were not really coming to me of your own free choice. Still you feel you are a captive." The hopelessness in Jonathan's voice tore at her heart, but she still wasn't sure of him.

"Why did you send me away?" She asked it in a whisper so low that he almost didn't hear.

"I thought you had betrayed me. I thought you were giving military secrets to Rezon, so I planted some false information for you to pass on to your brother and waited to see if he took the bait. When he did, I assumed you were a spy and that you had only been pretending to accept your life with me. I was furious. I felt very foolish, and I sent you away. I didn't learn until later that Joab was the one who had sent Rezon the message in order to implicate you."

"I would never have betrayed you, Jonathan. I love you. You are my husband." Ailea laid the baby in the thick grass beneath the tree and stood before Jonathan as she said this, clasping her hands in supplication.

Jonathan placed his fingers on her lips to silence her. "You have no need to plead or explain, my love. I know now that your heart is loyal, that I did a very foolish thing in sending you away. The Rab tried to tell me, but I was too thickheaded to listen. Can you forgive me, little warrior? I promise I will never doubt you again."

Ailea needed no more invitation. She threw her arms around her husband's neck. Jonathan clung to her and promised to never let her go.

~ ~ ~

Shageh stood upon the teaching rock, the entire population of Ziph before him. He held aloft his grandson who was finally peacefully sucking on a piece of linen soaked in honey. His protest at his circumcision had been so vigorous that the ceremony had to halt until he was pacified.

"Blessed be the Lord our God, who has sanctified us by His precepts and given us circumcision." Shageh's deep voice carried across the Judean hills.

Jonathan stepped forward and took his son, continuing where

the Rab left off. "Who has sanctified us by His precepts and has granted us to introduce our child into the covenant of Abraham our father. He shall be called 'Micah,' for who, indeed, is like our God?"

"Amen."

"Amen."

"Amen."

The benediction was repeated throughout the crowd.

The women were all gathered separately, standing behind the men, and one of them called out a blessing on the honored mother.

"Blessed are you, Ailea, wife of Jonathan, for the Lord has made you a mother in Israel. May your son be a light in the land."

Ailea thought her heart might burst with joy as she heard these words and looked up to see that her husband had joined her, his son sleeping securely in his arms. She linked her arm in his, and they led the happy procession back to their home for the feast that would celebrate the birth of their son.